Second Variety

Second Variety

And Other Stories

Philip K. Dick

WAKING LION PRESS

ISBN 978-1-4341-0304-8

Published by Waking Lion Press, an imprint of The Editorium. Printed in the United States of America.

Waking Lion Press™, the Waking Lion Press logo, and The Editorium™ are trademarks of The Editorium, LLC

The Editorium, LLC
West Valley City, UT 84128-3917
wakinglionpress.com
wakinglion@editorium.com

Contents

Second Variety

The claws were bad enough in the first place—nasty, crawling little death-robots. But when they began to imitate their creators, it was time for the human race to make peace—if it could!

The Russian soldier made his way nervously up the ragged side of the hill, holding his gun ready. He glanced around him, licking his dry lips, his face set. From time to time he reached up a gloved hand and wiped perspiration from his neck, pushing down his coat collar.

Eric turned to Corporal Leone. "Want him? Or can I have him?" He adjusted the view sight so the Russian's features squarely filled the glass, the lines cutting across his hard, somber features.

Leone considered. The Russian was close, moving rapidly, almost running. "Don't fire. Wait." Leone tensed. "I don't think we're needed."

The Russian increased his pace, kicking ash and piles of debris out of his way. He reached the top of the hill and stopped, panting, staring around him. The sky was overcast, drifting clouds of gray particles. Bare trunks of trees jutted up occasionally; the ground was level and bare, rubble-strewn, with the ruins of buildings standing out here and there like yellowing skulls.

The Russian was uneasy. He knew something was wrong. He started down the hill. Now he was only a few paces from the bunker. Eric was getting fidgety. He played with his pistol, glancing at Leone.

"Don't worry," Leone said. "He won't get here. They'll take care of him."

"Are you sure? He's got damn far."

"They hang around close to the bunker. He's getting into the bad part. Get set!"

The Russian began to hurry, sliding down the hill, his boots sinking into the heaps of gray ash, trying to keep his gun up. He stopped for a moment, lifting his fieldglasses to his face.

1

"He's looking right at us," Eric said.

* * *

The Russian came on. They could see his eyes, like two blue stones. His mouth was open a little. He needed a shave; his chin was stubbled. On one bony cheek was a square of tape, showing blue at the edge. A fungoid spot. His coat was muddy and torn. One glove was missing. As he ran his belt counter bounced up and down against him.

Leone touched Eric's arm. "Here one comes."

Across the ground something small and metallic came, flashing in the dull sunlight of mid-day. A metal sphere. It raced up the hill after the Russian, its treads flying. It was small, one of the baby ones. Its claws were out, two razor projections spinning in a blur of white steel. The Russian heard it. He turned instantly, firing. The sphere dissolved into particles. But already a second had emerged and was following the first. The Russian fired again.

A third sphere leaped up the Russian's leg, clicking and whirring. It jumped to the shoulder. The spinning blades disappeared into the Russian's throat.

Eric relaxed. "Well, that's that. God, those damn things give me the creeps. Sometimes I think we were better off before."

"If we hadn't invented them, they would have." Leone lit a cigarette shakily. "I wonder why a Russian would come all this way alone. I didn't see anyone covering him."

Lt. Scott came slipping up the tunnel, into the bunker. "What happened? Something entered the screen."

"An Ivan."

"Just one?"

Eric brought the view screen around. Scott peered into it. Now there were numerous metal spheres crawling over the prostrate body, dull metal globes clicking and whirring, sawing up the Russian into small parts to be carried away.

"What a lot of claws," Scott murmured.

"They come like flies. Not much game for them any more."

Scott pushed the sight away, disgusted. "Like flies. I wonder why he was out there. They know we have claws all around."

A larger robot had joined the smaller spheres. It was directing operations, a long blunt tube with projecting eyepieces. There was not much left of the soldier. What remained was being brought down the hillside by the host of claws.

"Sir," Leone said. "If it's all right, I'd like to go out there and take a look at him."

"Why?"

"Maybe he came with something."

Scott considered. He shrugged. "All right. But be careful."

"I have my tab." Leone patted the metal band at his wrist. "I'll be out of bounds."

* * *

He picked up his rifle and stepped carefully up to the mouth of the bunker, making his way between blocks of concrete and steel prongs, twisted and bent. The air was cold at the top. He crossed over the ground toward the remains of the soldier, striding across the soft ash. A wind blew around him, swirling gray particles up in his face. He squinted and pushed on.

The claws retreated as he came close, some of them stiffening into immobility. He touched his tab. The Ivan would have given something for that! Short hard radiation emitted from the tab neutralized the claws, put them out of commission. Even the big robot with its two waving eyestalks retreated respectfully as he approached.

He bent down over the remains of the soldier. The gloved hand was closed tightly. There was something in it. Leone pried the fingers apart. A sealed container, aluminum. Still shiny.

He put it in his pocket and made his way back to the bunker. Behind him the claws came back to life, moving into operation again. The procession resumed, metal spheres moving through the gray ash with their loads. He could hear their treads scrabbling against the ground. He shuddered.

Scott watched intently as he brought the shiny tube out of his pocket. "He had that?"

"In his hand." Leone unscrewed the top. "Maybe you should look at it, sir."

Scott took it. He emptied the contents out in the palm of his hand. A small piece of silk paper, carefully folded. He sat down by the light and unfolded it.

"What's it say, sir?" Eric said. Several officers came up the tunnel. Major Hendricks appeared.

"Major," Scott said. "Look at this."

Hendricks read the slip. "This just come?"

"A single runner. Just now."

"Where is he?" Hendricks asked sharply.

"The claws got him."

Major Hendricks grunted. "Here." He passed it to his companions. "I think this is what we've been waiting for. They certainly took their time about it."

"So they want to talk terms," Scott said. "Are we going along with them?"

"That's not for us to decide." Hendricks sat down. "Where's the communications officer? I want the Moon Base."

Leone pondered as the communications officer raised the outside antenna cautiously, scanning the sky above the bunker for any sign of a watching Russian ship.

"Sir," Scott said to Hendricks. "It's sure strange they suddenly came around. We've been using the claws for almost a year. Now all of a sudden they start to fold."

"Maybe claws have been getting down in their bunkers."

"One of the big ones, the kind with stalks, got into an Ivan bunker last week," Eric said. "It got a whole platoon of them before they got their lid shut."

"How do you know?"

"A buddy told me. The thing came back with—with remains."

"Moon Base, sir," the communications officer said.

On the screen the face of the lunar monitor appeared. His crisp uniform contrasted to the uniforms in the bunker. And he was clean shaven. "Moon Base."

"This is forward command L-Whistle. On Terra. Let me have General Thompson."

The monitor faded. Presently General Thompson's heavy features came into focus. "What is it, Major?"

"Our claws got a single Russian runner with a message. We don't know whether to act on it—there have been tricks like this in the past."

"What's the message?"

"The Russians want us to send a single officer on policy level over to their lines. For a conference. They don't state the nature of the conference. They say that matters of—" He consulted the slip. "—Matters of grave urgency make it advisable that discussion be opened between a representative of the UN forces and themselves."

He held the message up to the screen for the general to scan. Thompson's eyes moved.

"What should we do?" Hendricks said.

"Send a man out."

"You don't think it's a trap?"

"It might be. But the location they give for their forward command is correct. It's worth a try, at any rate."

"I'll send an officer out. And report the results to you as soon as he returns."

"All right, Major." Thompson broke the connection. The screen died. Up above, the antenna came slowly down.

Hendricks rolled up the paper, deep in thought.

"I'll go," Leone said.

"They want somebody at policy level." Hendricks rubbed his jaw. "Policy level. I haven't been outside in months. Maybe I could use a little air."

"Don't you think it's risky?"

Hendricks lifted the view sight and gazed into it. The remains of the Russian were gone. Only a single claw was in sight. It was folding itself back, disappearing into the ash, like a crab. Like some hideous metal crab. . . .

"That's the only thing that bothers me." Hendricks rubbed his wrist. "I know I'm safe as long as I have this on me. But there's something about them. I hate the damn things. I wish we'd never invented them. There's something wrong with them. Relentless little—"

"If we hadn't invented them, the Ivans would have."

Hendricks pushed the sight back. "Anyhow, it seems to be winning the war. I guess that's good."

"Sounds like you're getting the same jitters as the Ivans." Hendricks examined his wrist watch. "I guess I had better get started, if I want to be there before dark."

* * *

He took a deep breath and then stepped out onto the gray, rubbled ground. After a minute he lit a cigarette and stood gazing around him. The landscape was dead. Nothing stirred. He could see for miles, endless ash and slag, ruins of buildings. A few trees without leaves or branches, only the trunks. Above him the eternal rolling clouds of gray, drifting between Terra and the sun.

Major Hendricks went on. Off to the right something scuttled, something round and metallic. A claw, going lickety-split after something. Probably after a small animal, a rat. They got rats, too. As a sort of sideline.

He came to the top of the little hill and lifted his fieldglasses. The Russian lines were a few miles ahead of him. They had a forward command post there. The runner had come from it.

A squat robot with undulating arms passed by him, its arms weaving inquiringly. The robot went on its way, disappearing under some debris. Hendricks watched it go. He had never seen that type before. There were getting to be more and more types he had never seen, new varieties and sizes coming up from the underground factories.

Hendricks put out his cigarette and hurried on. It was interesting, the use of artificial forms in warfare. How had they got started? Necessity. The Soviet Union had gained great initial success, usual with the side that got the war going. Most of North America had been blasted off the map. Retaliation was quick in coming, of course. The sky was full of circling disc-bombers long before the war began; they had been up there for years. The discs began sailing down all over Russia within hours after Washington got it.

* * *

But that hadn't helped Washington.

The American bloc governments moved to the Moon Base the first year. There was not much else to do. Europe was gone; a slag heap with dark weeds growing from the ashes and bones. Most of North America was useless; nothing could be planted, no one could live. A few million people kept going up in Canada and down in South America. But during the second year Soviet parachutists began to drop, a few at first, then more and more. They wore the first really effective anti-radiation equipment; what was left of American production moved to the moon along with the governments.

All but the troops. The remaining troops stayed behind as best they could, a few thousand here, a platoon there. No one knew exactly where they were; they stayed where they could, moving around at night, hiding in ruins, in sewers, cellars, with the rats and snakes. It looked as if the Soviet Union had the war almost won. Except for a handful of projectiles fired off from the moon daily, there was almost no weapon in use against them. They came and went as they pleased. The war, for all practical purposes, was over. Nothing effective opposed them.

* * *

And then the first claws appeared. And overnight the complexion of the war changed.

The claws were awkward, at first. Slow. The Ivans knocked them off almost as fast as they crawled out of their underground tunnels. But then they got better, faster and more cunning. Factories, all on Terra, turned them out. Factories a long way under ground, behind the Soviet lines, factories that had once made atomic projectiles, now almost forgotten.

The claws got faster, and they got bigger. New types appeared, some with feelers, some that flew. There were a few jumping kinds.

The best technicians on the moon were working on designs, making them more and more intricate, more flexible. They became uncanny; the Ivans were having a lot of trouble with them. Some of the little claws were learning to hide themselves, burrowing down into the ash, lying in wait.

And then they started getting into the Russian bunkers, slipping down when the lids were raised for air and a look around. One claw inside a bunker, a churning sphere of blades and metal—that was enough. And when one got in others followed. With a weapon like that the war couldn't go on much longer.

Maybe it was already over.

Maybe he was going to hear the news. Maybe the Politburo had decided to throw in the sponge. Too bad it had taken so long. Six years. A long time for war like that, the way they had waged it. The automatic retaliation discs, spinning down all over Russia, hundreds of thousands of them. Bacteria crystals. The Soviet guided missiles, whistling through the air. The chain bombs. And now this, the robots, the claws—

The claws weren't like other weapons. They were *alive,* from any practical standpoint, whether the Governments wanted to admit it or not. They were not machines. They were living things, spinning, creeping, shaking themselves up suddenly from the gray ash and darting toward a man, climbing up him, rushing for his throat. And that was what they had been designed to do. Their job.

They did their job well. Especially lately, with the new designs coming up. Now they repaired themselves. They were on their own. Radiation tabs protected the UN troops, but if a man lost his tab he was fair game for the claws, no matter what his uniform. Down below the surface automatic machinery stamped them out. Human beings stayed a long way off. It was too risky; nobody wanted to be around them. They were left to themselves. And they seemed to be doing all right. The new designs were faster, more complex. More efficient.

Apparently they had won the war.

* * *

Major Hendricks lit a second cigarette. The landscape depressed him. Nothing but ash and ruins. He seemed to be alone, the only living thing in the whole world. To the right the ruins of a town rose up, a few walls and heaps of debris. He tossed the dead match away, increasing his pace. Suddenly he stopped, jerking up his gun, his body tense. For a minute it looked like—

From behind the shell of a ruined building a figure came, walking slowly toward him, walking hesitantly.

Hendricks blinked. "Stop!"

The boy stopped. Hendricks lowered his gun. The boy stood silently, looking at him. He was small, not very old. Perhaps eight. But it was hard to tell. Most of the kids who remained were stunted. He wore a faded blue sweater, ragged with dirt, and short pants. His hair was long and matted. Brown hair. It hung over his face and around his ears. He held something in his arms.

"What's that you have?" Hendricks said sharply.

The boy held it out. It was a toy, a bear. A teddy bear. The boy's eyes were large, but without expression.

Hendricks relaxed. "I don't want it. Keep it."

The boy hugged the bear again.

"Where do you live?" Hendricks said.

"In there."

"The ruins?"

"Yes."

"Underground?"

"Yes."

"How many are there?"

"How—how many?"

"How many of you. How big's your settlement?"

The boy did not answer.

Hendricks frowned. "You're not all by yourself, are you?"

The boy nodded.

"How do you stay alive?"

"There's food."

"What kind of food?"

"Different."

Hendricks studied him. "How old are you?"

"Thirteen."

* * *

It wasn't possible. Or was it? The boy was thin, stunted. And probably sterile. Radiation exposure, years straight. No wonder he was so small. His arms and legs were like pipecleaners, knobby, and thin. Hendricks touched the boy's arm. His skin was dry and rough; radiation skin. He bent down, looking into the boy's face. There was no expression. Big eyes, big and dark.

"Are you blind?" Hendricks said.

"No. I can see some."

"How do you get away from the claws?"

"The claws?"

"The round things. That run and burrow."

"I don't understand."

Maybe there weren't any claws around. A lot of areas were free. They collected mostly around bunkers, where there were people. The claws had been designed to sense warmth, warmth of living things.

"You're lucky." Hendricks straightened up. "Well? Which way are you going? Back—back there?"

"Can I come with you?"

"With *me?*" Hendricks folded his arms. "I'm going a long way. Miles. I have to hurry." He looked at his watch. "I have to get there by nightfall."

"I want to come."

Hendricks fumbled in his pack. "It isn't worth it. Here." He tossed down the food cans he had with him. "You take these and go back. Okay?"

The boy said nothing.

"I'll be coming back this way. In a day or so. If you're around here when I come back you can come along with me. All right?"

"I want to go with you now."

"It's a long walk."

"I can walk."

Hendricks shifted uneasily. It made too good a target, two people walking along. And the boy would slow him down. But he might not come back this way. And if the boy were really all alone—

"Okay. Come along."

* * *

The boy fell in beside him. Hendricks strode along. The boy walked silently, clutching his teddy bear.

"What's your name?" Hendricks said, after a time.

"David Edward Derring."

"David? What—what happened to your mother and father?"

"They died."

"How?"

"In the blast."

"How long ago?"

"Six years."

Hendricks slowed down. "You've been alone six years?"

"No. There were other people for awhile. They went away."

"And you've been alone since?"

"Yes."

Hendricks glanced down. The boy was strange, saying very little. Withdrawn. But that was the way they were, the children who had survived. Quiet. Stoic. A strange kind of fatalism gripped them. Nothing came as a surprise. They accepted anything that came along. There was no longer any *normal,* any natural course of things, moral or physical, for them to expect. Custom, habit, all the determining forces of learning were gone; only brute experience remained.

"Am I walking too fast?" Hendricks said.

"No."

"How did you happen to see me?"

"I was waiting."

"Waiting?" Hendricks was puzzled. "What were you waiting for?"

"To catch things."

"What kind of things?"

"Things to eat."

"Oh." Hendricks set his lips grimly. A thirteen year old boy, living on rats and gophers and half-rotten canned food. Down in a hole under the ruins of a town. With radiation pools and claws, and Russian dive-mines up above, coasting around in the sky.

"Where are we going?" David asked.

"To the Russian lines."

"Russian?"

"The enemy. The people who started the war. They dropped the first radiation bombs. They began all this."

The boy nodded. His face showed no expression.

"I'm an American," Hendricks said.

There was no comment. On they went, the two of them, Hendricks walking a little ahead, David trailing behind him, hugging his dirty teddy bear against his chest.

* * *

About four in the afternoon they stopped to eat. Hendricks built a fire in a hollow between some slabs of concrete. He cleared the weeds away and heaped up bits of wood. The Russians' lines were not very far ahead. Around him was what had once been a long valley, acres of fruit trees and grapes. Nothing remained now but a few bleak stumps and the mountains that stretched across the horizon at the far end. And the clouds of rolling ash that blew and drifted with the wind, settling over the weeds and remains of buildings, walls here and there, once in awhile what had been a road.

Hendricks made coffee and heated up some boiled mutton and bread. "Here." He handed bread and mutton to David. David squatted by the edge of the fire, his knees knobby and white. He examined the food and then passed it back, shaking his head.

"No."

"No? Don't you want any?"

"No."

Hendricks shrugged. Maybe the boy was a mutant, used to special food. It didn't matter. When he was hungry he would find something to eat. The boy was strange. But there were many strange changes coming over the world. Life was not the same, anymore. It would never be the same again. The human race was going to have to realize that.

"Suit yourself," Hendricks said. He ate the bread and mutton by himself, washing it down with coffee. He ate slowly, finding the food hard to digest. When he was done he got to his feet and stamped the fire out.

David rose slowly, watching him with his young-old eyes.

"We're going," Hendricks said.

"All right."

Hendricks walked along, his gun in his arms. They were close; he was tense, ready for anything. The Russians should be expecting a runner, an answer to their own runner, but they were tricky. There was always the possibility of a slipup. He scanned the landscape around him. Nothing but slag and ash, a few hills, charred trees. Concrete walls. But someplace ahead was the first bunker of the Russian lines, the forward command. Underground, buried deep, with only a periscope showing, a few gun muzzles. Maybe an antenna.

"Will we be there soon?" David asked.

"Yes. Getting tired?"

"No."

"Why, then?"

David did not answer. He plodded carefully along behind, picking his way over the ash. His legs and shoes were gray with dust. His pinched face was streaked, lines of gray ash in riverlets down the pale white of his skin. There was no color to his face. Typical of the new children, growing up in cellars and sewers and underground shelters.

* * *

Hendricks slowed down. He lifted his fieldglasses and studied the ground ahead of him. Were they there, someplace, waiting for him? Watching him, the way his men had watched the Russian runner? A chill went up his back. Maybe they were getting their guns ready, preparing to fire, the way his men had prepared, made ready to kill.

Hendricks stopped, wiping perspiration from his face. "Damn." It made him uneasy. But he should be expected. The situation was different.

He strode over the ash, holding his gun tightly with both hands. Behind him came David. Hendricks peered around, tight-lipped. Any second it might happen. A burst of white light, a blast, carefully aimed from inside a deep concrete bunker.

He raised his arm and waved it around in a circle.

Nothing moved. To, the right a long ridge ran, topped with dead tree trunks. A few wild vines had grown, up around, the trees, remains of arbors. And the eternal dark weeds. Hendricks studied the ridge. Was anything up there? Perfect place for a lookout. He approached the ridge warily, David coming silently behind. If it were his command he'd have a sentry up there, watching for troops trying to infiltrate into the command area. Of course, if it were his command there would be the claws around the area for full protection.

He stopped, feet apart, hands on his hips.

"Are we there?" David said.

"Almost."

"Why have we stopped?"

"I don't want to take any chances." Hendricks advanced slowly. Now the ridge lay directly beside him, along his right. Overlooking him. His uneasy feeling increased. If an Ivan were up there he wouldn't have a chance. He waved his arm again. They should be expecting someone in the UN uniform, in response to the note capsule. Unless the whole thing was a trap.

"Keep up with me." He turned toward David. "Don't drop behind."

"With you?"

"Up beside me! We're close. We can't take any chances. Come on."

"I'll be all right." David remained behind him, in the rear, a few paces away, still clutching his teddy bear.

"Have it your way." Hendricks raised his glasses again, suddenly tense. For a moment—had something moved? He scanned the ridge carefully. Everything was silent. Dead. No life up there, only tree trunks and ash. Maybe a few rats. The big black rats that had survived the claws. Mutants—built their own shelters out of saliva and ash. Some kind of plaster. Adaptation. He started forward again.

* * *

A tall figure came out on the ridge above him, cloak flapping. Gray-green. A Russian. Behind him a second soldier appeared, another Russian. Both lifted their guns, aiming.

Hendricks froze. He opened his mouth. The soldiers were kneeling, sighting down the side of the slope. A third figure had joined them on the ridge top, a smaller figure in gray-green. A woman. She stood behind the other two.

Hendricks found his voice. "Stop!" He waved up at them frantically. "I'm—"

The two Russians fired. Behind Hendricks there was a faint *pop*. Waves of heat lapped against him, throwing him to the ground. Ash tore at his face, grinding into his eyes and nose. Choking, he pulled himself to his knees. It was all a trap. He was finished. He had come to be killed, like a steer. The soldiers and the woman were coming down the side of the ridge toward him, sliding down through the soft ash. Hendricks was numb. His head throbbed. Awkwardly, he got his rifle up and took aim. It weighed a thousand tons; he could hardly hold it. His nose and cheeks stung. The air was full of the blast smell, a bitter acrid stench.

"Don't fire," the first Russian said, in heavily accented English.

The three of them came up to him, surrounding him. "Put down your rifle, Yank," the other said.

Hendricks was dazed. Everything had happened so fast. He had been caught. And they had blasted the boy. He turned his head. David was gone. What remained of him was strewn across the ground.

The three Russians studied him curiously. Hendricks sat, wiping blood from his nose, picking out bits of ash. He shook his head, trying to clear it. "Why did you do it?" he murmured thickly. "The boy."

"Why?" One of the soldiers helped him roughly to his feet. He turned Hendricks around. "Look."

Hendricks closed his eyes.

"Look!" The two Russians pulled him forward. "See. Hurry up. There isn't much time to spare, Yank!"

Hendricks looked. And gasped.

"See now? Now do you understand?"

* * *

From the remains of David a metal wheel rolled. Relays, glinting metal. Parts, wiring. One of the Russians kicked at the heap of remains. Parts popped out, rolling away, wheels and springs and rods. A plastic section fell in, half charred. Hendricks bent shakily down. The front of the head had come off. He could make out the intricate brain, wires and relays, tiny tubes and switches, thousands of minute studs—

"A robot," the soldier holding his arm said. "We watched it tagging you."

"Tagging me?"

"That's their way. They tag along with you. Into the bunker. That's how they get in."

Hendricks blinked, dazed. "But—"

"Come on." They led him toward the ridge. "We can't stay here. It isn't safe. There must be hundreds of them all around here."

The three of them pulled him up the side of the ridge, sliding and slipping on the ash. The woman reached the top and stood waiting for them.

"The forward command," Hendricks muttered. "I came to negotiate with the Soviet—"

"There is no more forward command. *They* got in. We'll explain." They reached the top of the ridge. "We're all that's left. The three of us. The rest were down in the bunker."

"This way. Down this way." The woman unscrewed a lid, a gray manhole cover set in the ground. "Get in."

Hendricks lowered himself. The two soldiers and the woman came behind him, following him down the ladder. The woman closed the lid after them, bolting it tightly into place.

"Good thing we saw you," one of the two soldiers grunted. "It had tagged you about as far as it was going to."

* * *

"Give me one of your cigarettes," the woman said. "I haven't had an American cigarette for weeks."

Hendricks pushed the pack to her. She took a cigarette and passed the pack to the two soldiers. In the corner of the small room the lamp gleamed fitfully. The room was low-ceilinged, cramped. The four of them sat around a small wood table. A few dirty dishes were stacked to one side. Behind a ragged curtain a second room was partly visible. Hendricks saw the corner of a cot, some blankets, clothes hung on a hook.

"We were here," the soldier beside him said. He took, off his helmet, pushing his blond hair back. "I'm Corporal Rudi Maxer. Polish. Impressed in the Soviet Army two years ago." He held out his hand.

Hendricks hesitated and then shook. "Major Joseph Hendricks."

"Klaus Epstein." The other soldier shook with him, a small dark man with thinning hair. Epstein plucked nervously at his ear. "Austrian. Impressed God knows when. I don't remember. The three of us were here, Rudi and I, with Tasso." He indicated the woman. "That's how we escaped. All the rest were down in the bunker."

"And—and *they* got in?"

Epstein lit a cigarette. "First just one of them. The kind that tagged you. Then it let others in."

Hendricks became alert. "The *kind*? Are there more than one kind?"

"The little boy. David. David holding his teddy bear. That's Variety Three. The most effective."

"What are the other types?"

Epstein reached into his coat. "Here." He tossed a packet of photographs onto the table, tied with a string. "Look for yourself."

Hendricks untied the string.

"You see," Rudi Maxer said, "that was why we wanted to talk terms. The Russians, I mean. We found out about a week ago. Found out that your claws were beginning to make up new designs on their own. New types of their own. Better types. Down in your underground factories behind our lines. You let them stamp themselves, repair themselves. Made them more and more intricate. It's your fault this happened."

* * *

Hendricks examined the photos. They had been snapped hurriedly; they were blurred and indistinct. The first few showed—David. David walking along a road, by himself. David and another David. Three Davids. All exactly alike. Each with a ragged teddy bear.

All pathetic.

"Look at the others," Tasso said.

The next pictures, taken at a great distance, showed a towering wounded soldier sitting by the side of a path, his arm in a sling, the stump of one leg extended, a crude crutch on his lap. Then two wounded soldiers, both the same, standing side by side.

"That's Variety One. The Wounded Soldier." Klaus reached out and took the pictures. "You see, the claws were designed to get to human beings. To find them. Each kind was better than the last. They got farther, closer, past most of our defenses, into our lines. But as long as they were merely *machines,* metal spheres with claws and horns, feelers, they could be picked off like any other object. They could be detected as lethal robots as soon as they were seen. Once we caught sight of them—"

"Variety One subverted our whole north wing," Rudi said. "It was a long time before anyone caught on. Then it was too late. They came in, wounded soldiers, knocking and begging to be let in. So we let them in. And as soon as they were in they took over. We were watching out for machines. . . ."

"At that time it was thought there was only the one type," Klaus Epstein said. "No one suspected there were other types. The pictures were flashed to us. When the runner was sent to you, we knew of just one type. Variety One. The big Wounded Soldier. We thought that was all."

"Your line fell to—"

"To Variety Three. David and his bear. That worked even better." Klaus smiled bitterly. "Soldiers are suckers for children. We brought them in and tried to feed them. We found out the hard way what they were after. At least, those who were in the bunker."

"The three of us were lucky," Rudi said. "Klaus and I were—were visiting Tasso when it happened. This is her place." He waved a big hand around. "This little cellar. We finished and climbed the ladder to start back. From the ridge we saw. There they were, all around the bunker. Fighting was still going on. David and his bear. Hundreds of them. Klaus took the pictures."

Klaus tied up the photographs again.

* * *

"And it's going on all along your line?" Hendricks said.

"Yes."

"How about *our* lines?" Without thinking, he touched the tab on his arm. "Can they—"

"They're not bothered by your radiation tabs. It makes no difference to them, Russian, American, Pole, German. It's all the same. They're doing what they were designed to do. Carrying out the original idea. They track down life, wherever they find it."

"They go by warmth," Klaus said. "That was the way you constructed them from the very start. Of course, those you designed were kept back by the radiation tabs you wear. Now they've got around that. These new varieties are lead-lined."

"What's the other variety?" Hendricks asked. "The David type, the Wounded Soldier—what's the other?"

"We don't know." Klaus pointed up at the wall. On the wall were two metal plates, ragged at the edges. Hendricks got up and studied them. They were bent and dented.

"The one on the left came off a Wounded Soldier," Rudi said. "We got one of them. It was going along toward our old bunker. We got it from the ridge, the same way we got the David tagging you."

The plate was stamped: I-V. Hendricks touched the other plate. "And this came from the David type?"

"Yes." The plate was stamped: III-V.

Klaus took a look at them, leaning over Hendricks' broad shoulder. "You can see what we're up against. There's another type. Maybe it was abandoned. Maybe it didn't work. But there must be a Second Variety. There's One and Three."

"You were lucky," Rudi said. "The David tagged you all the way here and never touched you. Probably thought you'd get it into a bunker, somewhere."

"One gets in and it's all over," Klaus said. "They move fast. One lets all the rest inside. They're inflexible. Machines with one purpose. They were built for only one thing." He rubbed sweat from his lip. "We saw."

They were silent.

"Let me have another cigarette, Yank," Tasso said. "They are good. I almost forgot how they were."

* * *

It was night. The sky was black. No stars were visible through the rolling clouds of ash. Klaus lifted the lid cautiously so that Hendricks could look out.

Rudi pointed into the darkness. "Over that way are the bunkers. Where we used to be. Not over half a mile from us. It was just chance Klaus and I were not there when it happened. Weakness. Saved by our lusts."

"All the rest must be dead," Klaus said in a low voice. "It came quickly. This morning the Politburo reached their decision. They notified us— forward command. Our runner was sent out at once. We saw him start toward the direction of your lines. We covered him until he was out of sight."

"Alex Radrivsky. We both knew him. He disappeared about six o'clock. The sun had just come up. About noon Klaus and I had an hour relief. We crept off, away from the bunkers. No one was watching. We came here. There used to be a town here, a few houses, a street. This cellar was part of a big farmhouse. We knew Tasso would be here, hiding down in her little place. We had come here before. Others from the bunkers came here. Today happened to be our turn."

"So we were saved," Klaus said. "Chance. It might have been others. We—we finished, and then we came up to the surface and started back along the ridge. That was when we saw them, the Davids. We understood right away. We had seen the photos of the First Variety, the Wounded Soldier. Our Commissar distributed them to us with an explanation. If we had gone another step they would have seen us. As it was we had to blast two Davids before we got back. There were hundreds of them, all around. Like ants. We took pictures and slipped back here, bolting the lid tight."

"They're not so much when you catch them alone. We moved faster than they did. But they're inexorable. Not like living things. They came right at us. And we blasted them."

Major Hendricks rested against the edge of the lid, adjusting his eyes to the darkness. "Is it safe to have the lid up at all?"

"If we're careful. How else can you operate your transmitter?"

Hendricks lifted the small belt transmitter slowly. He pressed it against his ear. The metal was cold and damp. He blew against the mike, raising up the short antenna. A faint hum sounded in his ear. "That's true, I suppose."

But he still hesitated.

"We'll pull you under if anything happens," Klaus said.

"Thanks." Hendricks waited a moment, resting the transmitter against his shoulder. "Interesting, isn't it?"

"What?"

"This, the new types. The new varieties of claws. We're completely at their mercy, aren't we? By now they've probably gotten into the UN lines, too. It makes me wonder if we're not seeing the beginning of a now species. *The* new species. Evolution. The race to come after man."

* * *

Rudi grunted. "There is no race after man."

"No? Why not? Maybe we're seeing it now the end of human beings, the beginning of the new society."

"They're not a race. They're mechanical killers. You made them to destroy. That's all they can do. They're machines with a job."

"So it seems now. But how about later on? After the war is over. Maybe, when there aren't any humans to destroy, their real potentialities will begin to show."

"You talk as if they were alive!"

"Aren't they?"

There was silence. "They're machines," Rudi said. "They look like people, but they're machines."

"Use your transmitter, Major," Klaus said. "We can't stay up here forever."

Holding the transmitter tightly Hendricks called the code of the command bunker. He waited, listening. No response. Only silence. He checked the leads carefully. Everything was in place.

"Scott!" he said into the mike. "Can you hear me?"

Silence. He raised the gain up full and tried again. Only static.

"I don't get anything. They may hear me but they may not want to answer."

"Tell them it's an emergency."

"They'll think I'm being forced to call. Under your direction." He tried again, outlining briefly what he had learned. But still the phone was silent, except for the faint static.

"Radiation pools kill most transmission," Klaus said, after awhile. "Maybe that's it."

Hendricks shut the transmitter up. "No use. No answer. Radiation pools? Maybe. Or they hear me, but won't answer. Frankly, that's what I would do, if a runner tried to call from the Soviet lines. They have no reason to believe such a story. They may hear everything I say—"

"Or maybe it's too late."

Hendricks nodded.

"We better get the lid down," Rudi said nervously. "We don't want to take unnecessary chances."

* * *

They climbed slowly back down the tunnel. Klaus bolted the lid carefully into place. They descended into the kitchen. The air was heavy and close around them.

"Could they work that fast?" Hendricks said. "I left the bunker this noon. Ten hours ago. How could they move so quickly?"

"It doesn't take them long. Not after the first one gets in. It goes wild. You know what the little claws can do. Even *one* of these is beyond belief. Razors, each finger. Maniacal."

"All right." Hendricks moved away impatiently. He stood with his back to them.

"What's the matter?" Rudi said.

"The Moon Base. God, if they've gotten there—"

"The Moon Base?"

Hendricks turned around. "They couldn't have got to the Moon Base. How would they get there? It isn't possible. I can't believe it."

"What is this Moon Base? We've heard rumors, but nothing definite. What is the actual situation? You seem concerned."

"We're supplied from the moon. The governments are there, under the lunar surface. All our people and industries. That's what keeps us going. If they should find some way of getting off Terra, onto the moon—"

"It only takes one of them. Once the first one gets in it admits the others. Hundreds of them, all alike. You should have seen them. Identical. Like ants."

"Perfect socialism," Tasso said. "The ideal of the communist state. All citizens interchangeable."

Klaus grunted angrily. "That's enough. Well? What next?"

Hendricks paced back and forth, around the small room. The air was full of smells of food and perspiration. The others watched him. Presently Tasso pushed through the curtain, into the other room. "I'm going to take a nap."

The curtain closed behind her. Rudi and Klaus sat down at the table, still Watching Hendricks.

"It's up to you," Klaus said. "We don't know your situation."

Hendricks nodded.

"It's a problem." Rudi drank some coffee, filling his cup from a rusty pot. "We're safe here for awhile, but we can't stay here forever. Not enough food or supplies."

"But if we go outside—"

"If we go outside they'll get us. Or probably they'll get us. We couldn't go very far. How far is your command bunker, Major?"

"Three or four miles."

"We might make it. The four of us. Four of us could watch all sides. They couldn't slip up behind us and start tagging us. We have three rifles, three blast rifles. Tasso can have my pistol." Rudi tapped his belt. "In the Soviet army we didn't have shoes always, but we had guns. With all four of us armed one of us might get to your command bunker. Preferably you, Major."

"What if they're already there?" Klaus said.

Rudi shrugged. "Well, then we come back here."

* * *

Hendricks stopped pacing. "What do you think the chances are they're already in the American lines?"

"Hard to say. Fairly good. They're organized. They know exactly what they're doing. Once they start they go like a horde of locusts. They have to keep moving, and fast. It's secrecy and speed they depend on. Surprise. They push their way in before anyone has any idea."

"I see," Hendricks murmured.

From the other room Tasso stirred. "Major?"

Hendricks pushed the curtain back. "What?"

Tasso looked up at him lazily from the cot. "Have you any more American cigarettes left?"

Hendricks went into the room and sat down across from her, on a wood stool. He felt in his pockets. "No. All gone."

"Too bad."

"What nationality are you?" Hendricks asked after awhile.

"Russian."

"How did you get here?"

"Here?"

"This used to be France. This was part of Normandy. Did you come with the Soviet army?"

"Why?"

"Just curious." He studied her. She had taken off her coat, tossing it over the end of the cot. She was young, about twenty. Slim. Her long hair stretched out over the pillow. She was staring at him silently, her eyes dark and large.

"What's on your mind?" Tasso said.

"Nothing. How old are you?"

"Eighteen." She continued to watch him, unblinking, her arms behind her head. She had on Russian army pants and shirt. Gray-green. Thick leather belt with counter and cartridges. Medicine kit.

"You're in the Soviet army?"

"No."

"Where did you get the uniform?"

She shrugged. "It was given to me," she told him.

"How—how old were you when you came here?"

"Sixteen."

"That young?"

Her eyes narrowed. "What do you mean?"

* * *

Hendricks rubbed his jaw. "Your life would have been a lot differ-ent if there had been no war. Sixteen. You came here at sixteen. To live this way."

"I had to survive."

"I'm not moralizing."

"Your life would have been different, too," Tasso murmured. She reached down and unfastened one of her boots. She kicked the boot off, onto the floor. "Major, do you want to go in the other room? I'm sleepy."

"It's going to be a problem, the four of us here. It's going to be hard to live in these quarters. Are there just the two rooms?"

"Yes."

"How big was the cellar originally? Was it larger than this? Are there other rooms filled up with debris? We might be able to open one of them."

"Perhaps. I really don't know." Tasso loosened her belt. She made herself comfortable on the cot, unbuttoning her shirt. "You're sure you have no more cigarettes?"

"I had only the one pack."

"Too bad. Maybe if we get back to your bunker we can find some." The other boot fell. Tasso reached up for the light cord. "Good night."

"You're going to sleep?"

"That's right."

The room plunged into darkness. Hendricks got up and made his way past the curtain, into the kitchen.

And stopped, rigid.

Rudi stood against the wall, his face white and gleaming. His mouth opened and closed but no sounds came. Klaus stood in front of him, the muzzle of his pistol in Rudi's stomach. Neither of them moved. Klaus, his hand tight around his gun, his features set. Rudi, pale and silent, spread-eagled against the wall.

"What—" Hendricks muttered, but Klaus cut him off.

"Be quiet, Major. Come over here. Your gun. Get out your gun."

Hendricks drew his pistol. "What is it?"

"Cover him." Klaus motioned him forward. "Beside me. Hurry!"

Rudi moved a little, lowering his arms. He turned to Hendricks, licking his lips. The whites of his eyes shone wildly. Sweat dripped from his forehead, down his cheeks. He fixed his gaze on Hendricks. "Major, he's gone insane. Stop him." Rudi's voice was thin and hoarse, almost inaudible.

"What's going on?" Hendricks demanded.

Without lowering his pistol Klaus answered. "Major, remember our discussion? The Three Varieties? We knew about One and Three. But we didn't know about Two. At least, we didn't know before." Klaus' fingers tightened around the gun butt. "We didn't know before, but we know now."

He pressed the trigger. A burst of white heat rolled out of the gun, licking around Rudi.

"Major, this is the Second Variety."

* * *

Tasso swept the curtain aside. "Klaus! What did you do?"

Klaus turned from the charred form, gradually sinking down the wall onto the floor. "The Second Variety, Tasso. Now we know. We have all three types identified. The danger is less. I—"

Tasso stared past him at the remains of Rudi, at the blackened, smouldering fragments and bits of cloth. "You killed him."

"Him? *It,* you mean. I was watching. I had a feeling, but I wasn't sure. At least, I wasn't sure before. But this evening I was certain." Klaus rubbed his pistol butt nervously. "We're lucky. Don't you understand? Another hour and it might—"

"You were *certain?*" Tasso pushed past him and bent down, over the steaming remains on the floor. Her face became hard. "Major, see for yourself. Bones. Flesh."

Hendricks bent down beside her. The remains were human remains. Seared flesh, charred bone fragments, part of a skull. Ligaments, viscera, blood. Blood forming a pool against the wall.

"No wheels," Tasso said calmly. She straightened up. "No wheels, no parts, no relays. Not a claw. Not the Second Variety." She folded her arms. "You're going to have to be able to explain this."

Klaus sat down at the table, all the color drained suddenly from his face. He put his head in his hands and rocked back and forth.

"Snap out of it." Tasso's fingers closed over his shoulder. "Why did you do it? Why did you kill him?"

"He was frightened," Hendricks said. "All this, the whole thing, building up around us."

"Maybe."

"What, then? What do you think?"

"I think he may have had a reason for killing Rudi. A good reason."

"What reason?"

"Maybe Rudi learned something."

Hendricks studied her bleak face. "About what?" he asked.

"About him. About Klaus."

* * *

Klaus looked up quickly. "You can see what she's trying to say. She thinks I'm the Second Variety. Don't you see, Major? Now she wants you to believe I killed him on purpose. That I'm—"

"Why did you kill him, then?" Tasso said.

"I told you." Klaus shook his head wearily. "I thought he was a claw. I thought I knew."

"Why?"

"I had been watching him. I was suspicious."

"Why?"

"I thought I had seen something. Heard something. I thought I—" He stopped.

"Go on."

"We were sitting at the table. Playing cards. You two were in the other room. It was silent. I thought I heard him—*whirr.*"

There was silence.

"Do you believe that?" Tasso said to Hendricks.

"Yes. I believe what he says."

"I don't. I think he killed Rudi for a good purpose." Tasso touched the rifle, resting in the corner of the room. "Major—"

"No." Hendricks shook his head. "Let's stop it right now. One is enough. We're afraid, the way he was. If we kill him we'll be doing what he did to Rudi."

Klaus looked gratefully up at him. "Thanks. I was afraid. You understand, don't you? Now she's afraid, the way I was. She wants to kill me."

"No more killing." Hendricks moved toward the end of the ladder. "I'm going above and try the transmitter once more. If I can't get them we're moving back toward my lines tomorrow morning."

Klaus rose quickly. "I'll come up with you and give you a hand."

* * *

The night air was cold. The earth was cooling off. Klaus took a deep breath, filling his lungs. He and Hendricks stepped onto the ground, out of the tunnel. Klaus planted his feet wide apart, the rifle up, watching and listening. Hendricks crouched by the tunnel mouth, tuning the small transmitter.

"Any luck?" Klaus asked presently.

"Not yet."

"Keep trying. Tell them what happened."

Hendricks kept trying. Without success. Finally he lowered the antenna. "It's useless. They can't hear me. Or they hear me and won't answer. Or—"

"Or they don't exist."

"I'll try once more." Hendricks raised the antenna. "Scott, can you hear me? Come in!"

He listened. There was only static. Then, still very faintly—

"This is Scott."

His fingers tightened. "Scott! Is it you?"

"This is Scott."

Klaus squatted down. "Is it your command?"

"Scott, listen. Do you understand? About them, the claws. Did you get my message? Did you hear me?"

"Yes." Faintly. Almost inaudible. He could hardly make out the word.

"You got my message? Is everything all right at the bunker? None of them have got in?"

"Everything is all right."

"Have they tried to get in?"

The voice was weaker.

"No."

Hendricks turned to Klaus. "They're all right."

"Have they been attacked?"

"No." Hendricks pressed the phone tighter to his ear. "Scott, I can hardly hear you. Have you notified the Moon Base? Do they know? Are they alerted?"

No answer.

"Scott! Can you hear me?"

Silence.

Hendricks relaxed, sagging. "Faded out. Must be radiation pools."

* * *

Hendricks and Klaus looked at each other. Neither of them said anything. After a time Klaus said, "Did it sound like any of your men? Could you identify the voice?"

"It was too faint."

"You couldn't be certain?"

"No."

"Then it could have been—"

"I don't know. Now I'm not sure. Let's go back down and get the lid closed."

They climbed back down the ladder slowly, into the warm cellar. Klaus bolted the lid behind them. Tasso waited for them, her face expressionless.

"Any luck?" she asked.

Neither of them answered. "Well?" Klaus said at last. "What do you think, Major? Was it your officer, or was it one of *them?*"

"I don't know."

"Then we're just where we were before."

Hendricks stared down at the floor, his jaw set. "We'll have to go. To be sure."

"Anyhow, we have food here for only a few weeks. We'd have to go up after that, in any case."

"Apparently so."

"What's wrong?" Tasso demanded. "Did you get across to your bunker? What's the matter?"

"It may have been one of my men," Hendricks said slowly. "Or it may have been one of *them.* But we'll never know standing here." He examined his watch. "Let's turn in and get some sleep. We want to be up early tomorrow."

"Early?"

"Our best chance to get through the claws should be early in the morning," Hendricks said.

* * *

The morning was crisp and clear. Major Hendricks studied the countryside through his fieldglasses.

"See anything?" Klaus said.

"No."

"Can you make out our bunkers?"

"Which way?"

"Here." Klaus took the glasses and adjusted them. "I know where to look." He looked a long time, silently.

Tasso came to the top of the tunnel and stepped up onto the ground. "Anything?"

"No." Klaus passed the glasses back to Hendricks. "They're out of sight. Come on. Let's not stay here."

The three of them made their way down the side of the ridge, sliding in the soft ash. Across a flat rock a lizard scuttled. They stopped instantly, rigid.

"What was it?" Klaus muttered.

"A lizard."

The lizard ran on, hurrying through the ash. It was exactly the same color as the ash.

"Perfect adaptation," Klaus said. "Proves we were right. Lysenko, I mean."

They reached the bottom of the ridge and stopped, standing close together, looking around them.

"Let's go." Hendricks started off. "It's a good long trip, on foot."

Klaus fell in beside him. Tasso walked behind, her pistol held alertly. "Major, I've been meaning to ask you something," Klaus said. "How did you run across the David? The one that was tagging you."

"I met it along the way. In some ruins."

"What did it say?"

"Not much. It said it was alone. By itself."

"You couldn't tell it was a machine? It talked like a living person? You never suspected?"

"It didn't say much. I noticed nothing unusual."

"It's strange, machines so much like people that you can be fooled. Almost alive. I wonder where it'll end."

"They're doing what you Yanks designed them to do," Tasso said. "You designed them to hunt out life and destroy. Human life. Wherever they find it."

* * *

Hendricks was watching Klaus intently. "Why did you ask me? What's on your mind?"

"Nothing," Klaus answered.

"Klaus thinks you're the Second Variety," Tasso said calmly, from behind them. "Now he's got his eye on you."

Klaus flushed. "Why not? We sent a runner to the Yank lines and he comes back. Maybe he thought he'd find some good game here."

Hendricks laughed harshly. "I came from the UN bunkers. There were human beings all around me."

"Maybe you saw an opportunity to get into the Soviet lines. Maybe you saw your chance. Maybe you—"

"The Soviet lines had already been taken over. Your lines had been invaded before I left my command bunker. Don't forget that."

Tasso came up beside him. "That proves nothing at all, Major."

"Why not?"

"There appears to be little communication between the varieties. Each is made in a different factory. They don't seem to work together. You might have started for the Soviet lines without knowing anything about the work of the other varieties. Or even what the other varieties were like."

"How do you know so much about the claws?" Hendricks said.

"I've seen them. I've observed them. I observed them take over the Soviet bunkers."

"You know quite a lot," Klaus said. "Actually, you saw very little. Strange that you should have been such an acute observer."

Tasso laughed. "Do you suspect me, now?"

"Forget it," Hendricks said. They walked on in silence.

"Are we going the whole way on foot?" Tasso said, after awhile. "I'm not used to walking." She gazed around at the plain of ash, stretching out on all sides of them, as far as they could see. "How dreary."

"It's like this all the way," Klaus said.

"In a way I wish you had been in your bunker when the attack came."

"Somebody else would have been with you, if not me," Klaus muttered.

Tasso laughed, putting her hands in her pockets. "I suppose so."

They walked on, keeping their eyes on the vast plain of silent ash around them.

* * *

The sun was setting. Hendricks made his way forward slowly, waving Tasso and Klaus back. Klaus squatted down, resting his gun butt against the ground.

Tasso found a concrete slab and sat down with a sigh. "It's good to rest."

"Be quiet," Klaus said sharply.

Hendricks pushed up to the top of the rise ahead of them. The same rise the Russian runner had come up, the day before. Hendricks dropped down, stretching himself out, peering through his glasses at what lay beyond.

Nothing was visible. Only ash and occasional trees. But there, not more than fifty yards ahead, was the entrance of the forward command bunker. The bunker from which he had come. Hendricks watched silently. No motion. No sign of life. Nothing stirred.

Klaus slithered up beside him. "Where is it?"

"Down there." Hendricks passed him the glasses. Clouds of ash rolled across the evening sky. The world was darkening. They had a couple of hours of light left, at the most. Probably not that much.

"I don't see anything," Klaus said.

"That tree there. The stump. By the pile of bricks. The entrance is to the right of the bricks."

"I'll have to take your word for it."

"You and Tasso cover me from here. You'll be able to sight all the way to the bunker entrance."

"You're going down alone?"

"With my wrist tab I'll be safe. The ground around the bunker is a living field of claws. They collect down in the ash. Like crabs. Without tabs you wouldn't have a chance."

"Maybe you're right."

"I'll walk slowly all the way. As soon as I know for certain—"

"If they're down inside the bunker you won't be able to get back up here. They go fast. You don't realize."

"What do you suggest?"

Klaus considered. "I don't know. Get them to come up to the surface. So you can see."

Hendricks brought his transmitter from his belt, raising the antenna. "Let's get started."

* * *

Klaus signalled to Tasso. She crawled expertly up the side of the rise to where they were sitting.

"He's going down alone," Klaus said. "We'll cover him from here. As soon as you see him start back, fire past him at once. They come quick."

"You're not very optimistic," Tasso said.

"No, I'm not."

Hendricks opened the breech of his gun, checking it carefully. "Maybe things are all right."

"You didn't see them. Hundreds of them. All the same. Pouring out like ants."

"I should be able to find out without going down all the way." Hendricks locked his gun, gripping it in one hand, the transmitter in the other. "Well, wish me luck."

Klaus put out his hand. "Don't go down until you're sure. Talk to them from up here. Make them show themselves."

* * *

Hendricks stood up. He stepped down the side of the rise.

A moment later he was walking slowly toward the pile of bricks and debris beside the dead tree stump. Toward the entrance of the forward command bunker.

Nothing stirred. He raised the transmitter, clicking it on. "Scott? Can you hear me?"

Silence.

"Scott! This is Hendricks. Can you hear me? I'm standing outside the bunker. You should be able to see me in the view sight."

He listened, the transmitter gripped tightly. No sound. Only static. He walked forward. A claw burrowed out of the ash and raced toward him. It halted a few feet away and then slunk off. A second claw appeared, one of the big ones with feelers. It moved toward him, studied him intently, and then fell in behind him, dogging respectfully after him, a few paces away. A moment later a second big claw joined it. Silently, the claws trailed him, as he walked slowly toward the bunker.

Hendricks stopped, and behind him, the claws came to a halt. He was close, now. Almost to the bunker steps.

"Scott! Can you hear me? I'm standing right above you. Outside. On the surface. Are you picking me up?"

* * *

He waited, holding his gun against his side, the transmitter tightly to his ear. Time passed. He strained to hear, but there was only silence. Silence, and faint static.

Then, distantly, metallically—

"This is Scott."

The voice was neutral. Cold. He could not identify it. But the earphone was minute.

"Scott! Listen. I'm standing right above you. I'm on the surface, look-ing down into the bunker entrance."

"Yes."

"Can you see me?"

"Yes."

"Through the view sight? You have the sight trained on me?"

"Yes."

Hendricks pondered. A circle of claws waited quietly around him, gray-metal bodies on all sides of him. "Is everything all right in the bunker? Nothing unusual has happened?"

"Everything is all right."

"Will you come up to the surface? I want to see you for a moment." Hendricks took a deep breath. "Come up here with me. I want to talk to you."

"Come down."

"I'm giving you an order."

Silence.

"Are you coming?" Hendricks listened. There was no response. "I order you to come to the surface."

"Come down."

Hendricks set his jaw. "Let me talk to Leone."

There was a long pause. He listened to the static. Then a voice came, hard, thin, metallic. The same as the other. "This is Leone."

"Hendricks. I'm on the surface. At the bunker entrance. I want one of you to come up here."

"Come down."

"Why come down? I'm giving you an order!"

Silence. Hendricks lowered the transmitter. He looked carefully around him. The entrance was just ahead. Almost at his feet. He low-ered the antenna and fastened the transmitter to his belt. Carefully, he gripped his gun with both hands. He moved forward, a step at a time. If they could see him they knew he was starting toward the entrance. He closed his eyes a moment.

Then he put his foot on the first step that led downward.

Two Davids came up at him, their faces identical and expressionless. He blasted them into particles. More came rushing silently up, a whole pack of them. All exactly the same.

Hendricks turned and raced back, away from the bunker, back to-ward the rise.

At the top of the rise Tasso and Klaus were firing down. The small claws were already streaking up toward them, shining metal spheres going fast, racing frantically through the ash. But he had no time to think about that. He knelt down, aiming at the bunker entrance, gun against his cheek. The Davids were coming out in groups, clutching their teddy bears, their thin knobby legs pumping as they ran up the steps to the surface. Hendricks fired into the main body of them. They burst apart, wheels and springs flying in all directions. He fired again through the mist of particles.

A giant lumbering figure rose up in the bunker entrance, tall and swaying. Hendricks paused, amazed. A man, a soldier. With one leg, supporting himself with a crutch.

"Major!" Tasso's voice came. More firing. The huge figure moved forward, Davids swarming around it. Hendricks broke out of his freeze. The First Variety. The Wounded Soldier.

He aimed and fired. The soldier burst into bits, parts and relays flying. Now many Davids were out on the flat ground, away from the bunker. He fired again and again, moving slowly back, half-crouching and aiming.

From the rise, Klaus fired down. The side of the rise was alive with claws making their way up. Hendricks retreated toward the rise, running and crouching. Tasso had left Klaus and was circling slowly to the right, moving away from the rise.

A David slipped up toward him, its small white face expressionless, brown hair hanging down in its eyes. It bent over suddenly, opening its arms. Its teddy bear hurtled down and leaped across the ground, bounding toward him. Hendricks fired. The bear and the David both dissolved. He grinned, blinking. It was like a dream.

"Up here!" Tasso's voice. Hendricks made his way toward her. She was over by some columns of concrete, walls of a ruined building. She was firing past him, with the hand pistol Klaus had given her.

"Thanks." He joined her, grasping for breath. She pulled him back, behind the concrete, fumbling at her belt.

"Close your eyes!" She unfastened a globe from her waist. Rapidly, she unscrewed the cap, locking it into place. "Close your eyes and get down."

* * *

She threw the bomb. It sailed in an arc, an expert, rolling and bouncing to the entrance of the bunker. Two Wounded Soldiers stood uncertainly by the brick pile. More Davids poured from behind them, out onto the plain. One of the Wounded Soldiers moved toward the bomb, stooping awkwardly down to pick it up.

The bomb went off. The concussion whirled Hendricks around, throwing him on his face. A hot wind rolled over him. Dimly he saw Tasso standing behind the columns, firing slowly and methodically at the Davids coming out of the raging clouds of white fire.

Back along the rise Klaus struggled with a ring of claws circling around him. He retreated, blasting at them and moving back, trying to break through the ring.

Hendricks struggled to his feet. His head ached. He could hardly see. Everything was licking at him, raging and whirling. His right arm would not move.

Tasso pulled back toward him. "Come on. Let's go."

"Klaus—He's still up there."

"Come on!" Tasso dragged Hendricks back, away from the columns. Hendricks shook his head, trying to clear it. Tasso led him rapidly away, her eyes intense and bright, watching for claws that had escaped the blast.

One David came out of the rolling clouds of flame. Tasso blasted it. No more appeared.

"But Klaus. What about him?" Hendricks stopped, standing unsteadily. "He—"

"Come on!"

* * *

They retreated, moving farther and farther away from the bunker. A few small claws followed them for a little while and then gave up, turning back and going off.

At last Tasso stopped. "We can stop here and get our breaths."

Hendricks sat down on some heaps of debris. He wiped his neck, gasping. "We left Klaus back there."

Tasso said nothing. She opened her gun, sliding a fresh round of blast cartridges into place.

Hendricks stared at her, dazed. "You left him back there on purpose."

Tasso snapped the gun together. She studied the heaps of rubble around them, her face expressionless. As if she were watching for something.

"What is it?" Hendricks demanded. "What are you looking for? Is something coming?" He shook his head, trying to understand. What was she doing? What was she waiting for? He could see nothing. Ash lay all around them, ash and ruins. Occasional stark tree trunks, without leaves or branches. "What—"

Tasso cut him off. "Be still." Her eyes narrowed. Suddenly her gun came up. Hendricks turned, following her gaze.

* * *

Back the way they had come a figure appeared. The figure walked unsteadily toward them. Its clothes were torn. It limped as it made its way along, going very slowly and carefully. Stopping now and then, resting and getting its strength. Once it almost fell. It stood for a moment, trying to steady itself. Then it came on.

Klaus.

Hendricks stood up. "Klaus!" He started toward him. "How the hell did you—"

Tasso fired. Hendricks swung back. She fired again, the blast passing him, a searing line of heat. The beam caught Klaus in the chest. He exploded, gears and wheels flying. For a moment he continued to walk. Then he swayed back and forth. He crashed to the ground, his arms flung out. A few more wheels rolled away.

Silence.

Tasso turned to Hendricks. "Now you understand why he killed Rudi."

Hendricks sat down again slowly. He shook his head. He was numb. He could not think.

"Do you see?" Tasso said. "Do you understand?"

Hendricks said nothing. Everything was slipping away from him, faster and faster. Darkness, rolling and plucking at him.

He closed his eyes.

* * *

Hendricks opened his eyes slowly. His body ached all over. He tried to sit up but needles of pain shot through his arm and shoulder. He gasped.

"Don't try to get up," Tasso said. She bent down, putting her cold hand against his forehead.

It was night. A few stars glinted above, shining through the drifting clouds of ash. Hendricks lay back, his teeth locked. Tasso watched him impassively. She had built a fire with some wood and weeds. The fire licked feebly, hissing at a metal cup suspended over it. Everything was silent. Unmoving darkness, beyond the fire.

"So he was the Second Variety," Hendricks murmured.

"I had always thought so."

"Why didn't you destroy him sooner?" she wanted to know.

"You held me back." Tasso crossed to the fire to look into the metal cup. "Coffee. It'll be ready to drink in awhile."

She came back and sat down beside him. Presently she opened her pistol and began to disassemble the firing mechanism, studying it intently.

"This is a beautiful gun," Tasso said, half-aloud. "The construction is superb."

"What about them? The claws."

"The concussion from the bomb put most of them out of action. They're delicate. Highly organized, I suppose."

"The Davids, too?"

"Yes."

"How did you happen to have a bomb like that?"

Tasso shrugged. "We designed it. You shouldn't underestimate our technology, Major. Without such a bomb you and I would no longer exist."

"Very useful."

Tasso stretched out her legs, warming her feet in the heat of the fire. "It surprised me that you did not seem to understand, after he killed Rudi. Why did you think he—"

"I told you. I thought he was afraid."

"Really? You know, Major, for a little while I suspected you. Because you wouldn't let me kill him. I thought you might be protecting him." She laughed.

"Are we safe here?" Hendricks asked presently.

"For awhile. Until they get reinforcements from some other area." Tasso began to clean the interior of the gun with a bit of rag. She finished and pushed the mechanism back into place. She closed the gun, running her finger along the barrel.

"We were lucky," Hendricks murmured.

"Yes. Very lucky."

"Thanks for pulling me away."

* * *

Tasso did not answer. She glanced up at him, her eyes bright in the fire light. Hendricks examined his arm. He could not move his fingers. His whole side seemed numb. Down inside him was a dull steady ache.

"How do you feel?" Tasso asked.

"My arm is damaged."

"Anything else?"

"Internal injuries."

"You didn't get down when the bomb went off."

Hendricks said nothing. He watched Tasso pour the coffee from the cup into a flat metal pan. She brought it over to him.

"Thanks." He Struggled up enough to drink. It was hard to swallow. His insides turned over and he pushed the pan away. "That's all I can drink now."

Tasso drank the rest. Time passed. The clouds of ash moved across the dark sky above them. Hendricks rested, his mind blank. After awhile he became aware that Tasso was standing over him, gazing down at him.

"What is it?" he murmured.

"Do you feel any better?"

"Some."

"You know, Major, if I hadn't dragged you away they would have got you. You would be dead. Like Rudi."

"I know."

"Do you want to know why I brought you out? I could have left you. I could have left you there."

"Why did you bring me out?"

"Because we have to get away from here." Tasso stirred the fire with a stick, peering calmly down into it. "No human being can live here. When their reinforcements come we won't have a chance. I've pondered about it while you were unconscious. We have perhaps three hours before they come."

"And you expect me to get us away?"

"That's right. I expect you to get us out of here."

"Why me?"

"Because I don't know any way." Her eyes shone at him in the half-light, bright and steady. "If you can't get us out of here they'll kill us within three hours. I see nothing else ahead. Well, Major? What are you going to do? I've been waiting all night. While you were unconscious I sat here, waiting and listening. It's almost dawn. The night is almost over."

* * *

Hendricks considered. "It's curious," he said at last.

"Curious?"

"That you should think I can get us out of here. I wonder what you think I can do."

"Can you get us to the Moon Base?"

"The Moon Base? How?"

"There must be some way."

Hendricks shook his head. "No. There's no way that I know of."

Tasso said nothing. For a moment her steady gaze wavered. She ducked her head, turning abruptly away. She scrambled to her feet. "More coffee?"

"No."

"Suit yourself." Tasso drank silently. He could not see her face. He lay back against the ground, deep in thought, trying to concentrate. It was hard to think. His head still hurt. And the numbing daze still hung over him.

"There might be one way," he said suddenly.

"Oh?"

"How soon is dawn?"

"Two hours. The sun will be coming up shortly."

"There's supposed to be a ship near here. I've never seen it. But I know it exists."

"What kind of a ship?" Her voice was sharp.

"A rocket cruiser."

"Will it take us off? To the Moon Base?"

"It's supposed to. In case of emergency." He rubbed his forehead.

"What's wrong?"

"My head. It's hard to think. I can hardly—hardly concentrate. The bomb."

"Is the ship near here?" Tasso slid over beside him, settling down on her haunches. "How far is it? Where is it?"

"I'm trying to think."

Her fingers dug into his arm. "Nearby?" Her voice was like iron. "Where would it be? Would they store it underground? Hidden underground?"

"Yes. In a storage locker."

"How do we find it? Is it marked? Is there a code marker to identify it?"

Hendricks concentrated. "No. No markings. No code symbol."

"What, then?"

"A sign."
"What sort of sign?"

* * *

Hendricks did not answer. In the flickering light his eyes were glazed, two sightless orbs. Tasso's fingers dug into his arm.

"What sort of sign? What is it?"

"I—I can't think. Let me rest."

"All right." She let go and stood up. Hendricks lay back against the ground, his eyes closed. Tasso walked away from him, her hands in her pockets. She kicked a rock out of her way and stood staring up at the sky. The night blackness was already beginning to fade into gray. Morning was coming.

Tasso gripped her pistol and walked around the fire in a circle, back and forth. On the ground Major Hendricks lay, his eyes closed, unmoving. The grayness rose in the sky, higher and higher. The landscape became visible, fields of ash stretching out in all directions. Ash and ruins of buildings, a wall here and there, heaps of concrete, the naked trunk of a tree.

The air was cold and sharp. Somewhere a long way off a bird made a few bleak sounds.

Hendricks stirred. He opened his eyes. "Is it dawn? Already?"

"Yes."

Hendricks sat up a little. "You wanted to know something. You were asking me."

"Do you remember now?"

"Yes."

"What is it?" She tensed. "What?" she repeated sharply.

"A well. A ruined well. It's in a storage locker under a well."

"A well." Tasso relaxed. "Then we'll find a well." She looked at her watch. "We have about an hour, Major. Do you think we can find it in an hour?"

* * *

"Give me a hand up," Hendricks said.

Tasso put her pistol away and helped him to his feet. "This is going to be difficult."

"Yes it is." Hendricks set his lips tightly. "I don't think we're going to go very far."

They began to walk. The early sun cast a little warmth down on them. The land was flat and barren, stretching out gray and lifeless as far as they could see. A few birds sailed silently, far above them, circling slowly.

"See anything?" Hendricks said. "Any claws?"

"No. Not yet."

They passed through some ruins, upright concrete and bricks. A cement foundation. Rats scuttled away. Tasso jumped back warily.

"This used to be a town," Hendricks said. "A village. Provincial village. This was all grape country, once. Where we are now."

They came onto a ruined street, weeds and cracks criss-crossing it. Over to the right a stone chimney stuck up.

"Be careful," he warned her.

A pit yawned, an open basement. Ragged ends of pipes jutted up, twisted and bent. They passed part of a house, a bathtub turned on its side. A broken chair. A few spoons and bits of china dishes. In the center of the street the ground had sunk away. The depression was filled with weeds and debris and bones.

"Over here," Hendricks murmured.

"This way?"

"To the right."

They passed the remains of a heavy duty tank. Hendricks' belt counter clicked ominously. The tank had been radiation blasted. A few feet from the tank a mummified body lay sprawled out, mouth open. Beyond the road was a flat field. Stones and weeds, and bits of broken glass.

"There," Hendricks said.

* * *

A stone well jutted up, sagging and broken. A few boards lay across it. Most of the well had sunk into rubble. Hendricks walked unsteadily toward it, Tasso beside him.

"Are you certain about this?" Tasso said. "This doesn't look like anything."

"I'm sure." Hendricks sat down at the edge of the well, his teeth locked. His breath came quickly. He wiped perspiration from his face. "This was arranged so the senior command officer could get away. If anything happened. If the bunker fell."

"That was you?"

"Yes."

"Where is the ship? Is it here?"

"We're standing on it." Hendricks ran his hands over the surface of the well stones. "The eye-lock responds to me, not to anybody else. It's my ship. Or it was supposed to be."

There was a sharp click. Presently they heard a low grating sound from below them.

"Step back," Hendricks said. He and Tasso moved away from the well.

A section of the ground slid back. A metal frame pushed slowly up through the ash, shoving bricks and weeds out of the way. The action ceased, as the ship nosed into view.

"There it is," Hendricks said.

The ship was small. It rested quietly, suspended in its mesh frame, like a blunt needle. A rain of ash sifted down into the dark cavity from which the ship had been raised. Hendricks made his way over to it. He mounted the mesh and unscrewed the hatch, pulling it back. Inside the ship the control banks and the pressure seat were visible.

* * *

Tasso came and stood beside him, gazing into the ship. "I'm not accustomed to rocket piloting," she said, after awhile.

Hendricks glanced at her. "I'll do the piloting."

"Will you? There's only one seat, Major. I can see it's built to carry only a single person."

Hendricks' breathing changed. He studied the interior of the ship intently. Tasso was right. There was only one seat. The ship was built to carry only one person. "I see," he said slowly. "And the one person is you."

She nodded.

"Of course."

"Why?"

"*You* can't go. You might not live through the trip. You're injured. You probably wouldn't get there."

"An interesting point. But you see, I know where the Moon Base is. And you don't. You might fly around for months and not find it. It's well hidden. Without knowing what to look for—"

"I'll have to take my chances. Maybe I won't find it. Not by myself. But I think you'll give me all the information I need. Your life depends on it."

"How?"

"If I find the Moon Base in time, perhaps I can get them to send a ship back to pick you up. *If* I find the Base in time. If not, then you haven't a chance. I imagine there are supplies on the ship. They will last me long enough—"

Hendricks moved quickly. But his injured arm betrayed him. Tasso ducked, sliding lithely aside. Her hand came up, lightning fast. Hendricks saw the gun butt coming. He tried to ward off the blow, but she was too fast. The metal butt struck against the side of his head, just above his ear. Numbing pain rushed through him. Pain and rolling clouds of blackness. He sank down, sliding to the ground.

* * *

Dimly, he was aware that Tasso was standing over him, kicking him with her toe.

"Major! Wake up."

He opened his eyes, groaning.

"Listen to me." She bent down, the gun pointed at his face. "I have to hurry. There isn't much time left. The ship is ready to go, but you must tell me the information I need before I leave."

Hendricks shook his head, trying to clear it.

"Hurry up! Where is the Moon Base? How do I find it? What do I look for?"

Hendricks said nothing.

"Answer me!"

"Sorry."

"Major, the ship is loaded with provisions. I can coast for weeks. I'll find the Base eventually. And in a half hour you'll be dead. Your only chance of survival—" She broke off.

Along the slope, by some crumbling ruins, something moved. Something in the ash. Tasso turned quickly, aiming. She fired. A puff of flame leaped. Something scuttled away, rolling across the ash. She fired again. The claw burst apart, wheels flying.

"See?" Tasso said. "A scout. It won't be long."

"You'll bring them back here to get me?"

"Yes. As soon as possible."

Hendricks looked up at her. He studied her intently. "You're telling the truth?" A strange expression had come over his face, an avid hunger. "You will come back for me? You'll get me to the Moon Base?"

"I'll get you to the Moon Base. But tell me where it is! There's only a little time left."

"All right." Hendricks picked up a piece of rock, pulling himself to a sitting position. "Watch."

Hendricks began to scratch in the ash. Tasso stood by him, watching the motion of the rock. Hendricks was sketching a crude lunar map.

* * *

"This is the Appenine range. Here is the Crater of Archimedes. The Moon Base is beyond the end of the Appenine, about two hundred miles. I don't know exactly where. No one on Terra knows. But when you're over the Appenine, signal with one red flare and a green flare, followed by two red flares in quick succession. The Base monitor will record your signal. The Base is under the surface, of course. They'll guide you down with magnetic grapples."

"And the controls? Can I operate them?"

"The controls are virtually automatic. All you have to do is give the right signal at the right time."

"I will."

"The seat absorbs most of the take-off shock. Air and temperature are automatically controlled. The ship will leave Terra and pass out into free space. It'll line itself up with the moon, falling into an orbit around it, about a hundred miles above the surface. The orbit will carry you over the Base. When you're in the region of the Appenine, release the signal rockets."

Tasso slid into the ship and lowered herself into the pressure seat. The arm locks folded automatically around her. She fingered the controls. "Too bad you're not going, Major. All this put here for you, and you can't make the trip."

"Leave me the pistol."

Tasso pulled the pistol from her belt. She held it in her hand, weighing it thoughtfully. "Don't go too far from this location. It'll be hard to find you, as it is."

"No. I'll stay here by the well."

Tasso gripped the take-off switch, running her fingers over the smooth metal. "A beautiful ship, Major. Well built. I admire your workmanship. You people have always done good work. You build fine things. Your work, your creations, are your greatest achievement."

"Give me the pistol," Hendricks said impatiently, holding out his hand. He struggled to his feet.

"Good-bye, Major." Tasso tossed the pistol past Hendricks. The pistol clattered against the ground, bouncing and rolling away. Hendricks hurried after it. He bent down, snatching it up.

The hatch of the ship clanged shut. The bolts fell into place. Hendricks made his way back. The inner door was being sealed. He raised the pistol unsteadily.

* * *

There was a shattering roar. The ship burst up from its metal cage, fusing the mesh behind it. Hendricks cringed, pulling back. The ship shot up into the rolling clouds of ash, disappearing into the sky.

Hendricks stood watching a long time, until even the streamer had dissipated. Nothing stirred. The morning air was chill and silent. He began to walk aimlessly back the way they had come. Better to keep moving around. It would be a long time before help came—if it came at all.

He searched his pockets until he found a package of cigarettes. He lit one grimly. They had all wanted cigarettes from him. But cigarettes were scarce.

A lizard slithered by him, through the ash. He halted, rigid. The lizard disappeared. Above, the sun rose higher in the sky. Some flies landed on a flat rock to one side of him. Hendricks kicked at them with his foot.

It was getting hot. Sweat trickled down his face, into his collar. His mouth was dry.

Presently he stopped walking and sat down on some debris. He unfastened his medicine kit and swallowed a few narcotic capsules. He looked around him. Where was he?

Something lay ahead. Stretched out on the ground. Silent and unmoving.

Hendricks drew his gun quickly. It looked like a man. Then he remembered. It was the remains of Klaus. The Second Variety. Where Tasso had blasted him. He could see wheels and relays and metal parts, strewn around on the ash. Glittering and sparkling in the sunlight.

Hendricks got to his feet and walked over. He nudged the inert form with his foot, turning it over a little. He could see the metal hull, the aluminum ribs and struts. More wiring fell out. Like viscera. Heaps of wiring, switches and relays. Endless motors and rods.

He bent down. The brain cage had been smashed by the fall. The artificial brain was visible. He gazed at it. A maze of circuits. Miniature tubes. Wires as fine as hair. He touched the brain cage. It swung aside. The type plate was visible. Hendricks studied the plate.

And blanched.

IV—IV.

For a long time he stared at the plate. Fourth Variety. Not the Second. They had been wrong. There were more types. Not just three. Many more, perhaps. At least four. And Klaus wasn't the Second Variety.

But if Klaus wasn't the Second Variety—

Suddenly he tensed. Something was coming, walking through the ash beyond the hill. What was it? He strained to see. Figures. Figures coming slowly along, making their way through the ash.

Coming toward him.

Hendricks crouched quickly, raising his gun. Sweat dripped down into his eyes. He fought down rising panic, as the figures neared.

The first was a David. The David saw him and increased its pace. The others hurried behind it. A second David. A third. Three Davids, all alike, coming toward him silently, without expression, their thin legs rising and falling. Clutching their teddy bears.

He aimed and fired. The first two Davids dissolved into particles. The third came on. And the figure behind it. Climbing silently toward him across the gray ash. A Wounded Soldier, towering over the David. And—

* * *

And behind the Wounded Soldier came two Tassos, walking side by side. Heavy belt, Russian army pants, shirt, long hair. The familiar figure, as he had seen her only a little while before. Sitting in the pressure seat of the ship. Two slim, silent figures, both identical.

They were very near. The David bent down suddenly, dropping its teddy bear. The bear raced across the ground. Automatically, Hendricks' fingers tightened around the trigger. The bear was gone, dissolved into mist. The two Tasso Types moved on, expressionless, walking side by side, through the gray ash.

When they were almost to him, Hendricks raised the pistol waist high and fired.

The two Tassos dissolved. But already a new group was starting up the rise, five or six Tassos, all identical, a line of them coming rapidly toward him.

And he had given her the ship and the signal code. Because of him she was on her way to the moon, to the Moon Base. He had made it possible.

He had been right about the bomb, after all. It had been designed with knowledge of the other types, the David Type and the Wounded Soldier Type. And the Klaus Type. Not designed by human beings. It had been designed by one of the underground factories, apart from all human contact.

The line of Tassos came up to him. Hendricks braced himself, watching them calmly. The familiar face, the belt, the heavy shirt, the bomb carefully in place.

The bomb—

As the Tassos reached for him, a last ironic thought drifted through Hendricks' mind. He felt a little better, thinking about it. The bomb. Made by the Second Variety to destroy the other varieties. Made for that end alone.

They were already beginning to design weapons to use against each other.

Piper in the Woods

Earth maintained an important garrison on Asteroid Y-3. Now suddenly it was imperiled with a biological impossibility—men becoming plants!

"Well, Corporal Westerburg," Doctor Henry Harris said gently, "just why do you think you're a plant?"

As he spoke, Harris glanced down again at the card on his desk. It was from the Base Commander himself, made out in Cox's heavy scrawl: *Doc, this is the lad I told you about. Talk to him and try to find out how he got this delusion. He's from the new Garrison, the new check-station on Asteroid Y-3, and we don't want anything to go wrong there. Especially a silly damn thing like this!*

Harris pushed the card aside and stared back up at the youth across the desk from him. The young man seemed ill at ease and appeared to be avoiding answering the question Harris had put to him. Harris frowned. Westerburg was a good-looking chap, actually handsome in his Patrol uniform, a shock of blond hair over one eye. He was tall, almost six feet, a fine healthy lad, just two years out of Training, according to the card. Born in Detroit. Had measles when he was nine. Interested in jet engines, tennis, and girls. Twenty-six years old.

"Well, Corporal Westerburg," Doctor Harris said again. "Why do you think you're a plant?"

The Corporal looked up shyly. He cleared his throat. "Sir, I *am* a plant, I don't just think so. I've been a plant for several days, now."

"I see." The Doctor nodded. "You mean that you weren't always a plant?"

"No, sir. I just became a plant recently."

"And what were you before you became a plant?"

"Well, sir, I was just like the rest of you."

There was silence. Doctor Harris took up his pen and scratched a few lines, but nothing of importance came. A plant? And such a healthy-looking lad! Harris removed his steel-rimmed glasses and polished them with his handkerchief. He put them on again and leaned back in his chair. "Care for a cigarette, Corporal?"

"No, sir."

The Doctor lit one himself, resting his arm on the edge of the chair. "Corporal, you must realize that there are very few men who become plants, especially on such short notice. I have to admit you are the first person who has ever told me such a thing."

"Yes, sir, I realize it's quite rare."

"You can understand why I'm interested, then. When you say you're a plant, you mean you're not capable of mobility? Or do you mean you're a vegetable, as opposed to an animal? Or just what?"

The Corporal looked away. "I can't tell you any more," he murmured. "I'm sorry, sir."

"Well, would you mind telling me *how* you became a plant?"

Corporal Westerburg hesitated. He stared down at the floor, then out the window at the spaceport, then at a fly on the desk. At last he stood up, getting slowly to his feet. "I can't even tell you that, sir," he said.

"You can't? Why not?"

"Because—because I promised not to."

* * *

The room was silent. Doctor Harris rose, too, and they both stood facing each other. Harris frowned, rubbing his jaw. "Corporal, just *who* did you promise?"

"I can't even tell you that, sir. I'm sorry."

The Doctor considered this. At last he went to the door and opened it. "All right, Corporal. You may go now. And thanks for your time."

"I'm sorry I'm not more helpful." The Corporal went slowly out and Harris closed the door after him. Then he went across his office to the vidphone. He rang Commander Cox's letter. A moment later the beefy good-natured face of the Base Commander appeared.

"Cox, this is Harris. I talked to him, all right. All I could get is the statement that he's a plant. What else is there? What kind of behavior pattern?"

"Well," Cox said, "the first thing they noticed was that he wouldn't do any work. The Garrison Chief reported that this Westerburg would wander off outside the Garrison and just sit, all day long. Just sit."

"In the sun?"

"Yes. Just sit in the sun. Then at nightfall he would come back in. When they asked why he wasn't working in the jet repair building he told them he had to be out in the sun. Then he said—" Cox hesitated.

"Yes? Said what?"

"He said that work was unnatural. That it was a waste of time. That the only worthwhile thing was to sit and contemplate—outside."

"What then?"

"Then they asked him how he got that idea, and then he revealed to them that he had become a plant."

"I'm going to have to talk to him again, I can see," Harris said. "And he's applied for a permanent discharge from the Patrol? What reason did he give?"

"The same, that he's a plant now, and has no more interest in being a Patrolman. All he wants to do is sit in the sun. It's the damnedest thing I ever heard."

"All right. I think I'll visit him in his quarters." Harris looked at his watch. "I'll go over after dinner."

"Good luck," Cox said gloomily. "But who ever heard of a man turning into a plant? We told him it wasn't possible, but he just smiled at us."

"I'll let you know how I make out," Harris said.

* * *

Harris walked slowly down the hall. It was after six; the evening meal was over. A dim concept was coming into his mind, but it was much too soon to be sure. He increased his pace, turning right at the end of the hall. Two nurses passed, hurrying by. Westerburg was quartered with a buddy, a man who had been injured in a jet blast and who was now almost recovered. Harris came to the dorm wing and stopped, checking the numbers on the doors.

"Can I help you, sir?" the robot attendant said, gliding up.

"I'm looking for Corporal Westerburg's room."

"Three doors to the right."

Harris went on. Asteroid Y-3 had only recently been garrisoned and staffed. It had become the primary check-point to halt and examine ships entering the system from outer space. The Garrison made sure that no dangerous bacteria, fungus, or what-not arrived to infect the system. A nice asteroid it was, warm, well-watered, with trees and lakes and lots of sunlight. And the most modern Garrison in the nine planets.

He shook his head, coming to the third door. He stopped, raising his hand and knocking.

"Who's there?" sounded through the door.

"I want to see Corporal Westerburg."

The door opened. A bovine youth with horn-rimmed glasses looked out, a book in his hand. "Who are you?"

"Doctor Harris."

"I'm sorry, sir. Corporal Westerburg is asleep."

"Would he mind if I woke him up? I want very much to talk to him." Harris peered inside. He could see a neat room, with a desk, a rug and lamp, and two bunks. On one of the bunks was Westerburg, lying face up, his arms folded across his chest, his eyes tightly closed.

"Sir," the bovine youth said, "I'm afraid I can't wake him up for you, much as I'd like to."

"You can't? Why not?"

"Sir, Corporal Westerburg won't wake up, not after the sun sets. He just won't. He can't be wakened."

"Cataleptic? Really?"

"But in the morning, as soon as the sun comes up, he leaps out of bed and goes outside. Stays the whole day."

"I see," the Doctor said. "Well, thanks anyhow." He went back out into the hall and the door shut after him. "There's more to this than I realized," he murmured. He went on back the way he had come.

* * *

It was a warm sunny day. The sky was almost free of clouds and a gentle wind moved through the cedars along the bank of the stream. There was a path leading from the hospital building down the slope to the stream. At the stream a small bridge led over to the other side, and a few patients were standing on the bridge, wrapped in their bathrobes, looking aimlessly down at the water.

It took Harris several minutes to find Westerburg. The youth was not with the other patients, near or around the bridge. He had gone farther down, past the cedar trees and out onto a strip of bright meadow, where poppies and grass grew everywhere. He was sitting on the stream bank, on a flat grey stone, leaning back and staring up, his mouth open a little. He did not notice the Doctor until Harris was almost beside him.

"Hello," Harris said softly.

Westerburg opened his eyes, looking up. He smiled and got slowly to his feet, a graceful, flowing motion that was rather surprising for a man of his size. "Hello, Doctor. What brings you out here?"

"Nothing. Thought I'd get some sun."

"Here, you can share my rock." Westerburg moved over and Harris sat down gingerly, being careful not to catch his trousers on the sharp edges of the rock. He lit a cigarette and gazed silently down at the water. Beside him, Westerburg had resumed his strange position, leaning back, resting on his hands, staring up with his eyes shut tight.

"Nice day," the Doctor said.

"Yes."

"Do you come here every day?"

"Yes."

"You like it better out here than inside."

"I can't stay inside," Westerburg said.

"You can't? How do you mean, 'can't'?"

"You would die without *air*, wouldn't you?" the Corporal said.

"And you'd die without sunlight?"

Westerburg nodded.

"Corporal, may I ask you something? Do you plan to do this the rest of your life, sit out in the sun on a flat rock? Nothing else?"

Westerburg nodded.

"How about your job? You went to school for years to become a Patrolman. You wanted to enter the Patrol very badly. You were given a fine rating and a first-class position. How do you feel, giving all that up? You know, it won't be easy to get back in again. Do you realize that?"

"I realize it."

"And you're really going to give it all up?"

"That's right."

* * *

Harris was silent for a while. At last he put his cigarette out and turned toward the youth. "All right, let's say you give up your job and sit in the sun. Well, what happens, then? Someone else has to do the job instead of you. Isn't that true? The job has to be done, *your* job has to be done. And if you don't do it someone else has to."

"I suppose so."

"Westerburg, suppose everyone felt the way you do? Suppose everyone wanted to sit in the sun all day? What would happen? No one would check ships coming from outer space. Bacteria and toxic crystals would enter the system and cause mass death and suffering. Isn't that right?"

"If everyone felt the way I do they wouldn't be going into outer space."

"But they have to. They have to trade, they have to get minerals and products and new plants."

"Why?"

"To keep society going."

"Why?"

"Well—" Harris gestured. "People couldn't live without society."

Westerburg said nothing to that. Harris watched him, but the youth did not answer.

"Isn't that right?" Harris said.

"Perhaps. It's a peculiar business, Doctor. You know, I struggled for years to get through Training. I had to work and pay my own way. Washed dishes, worked in kitchens. Studied at night, learned, crammed, worked on and on. And you know what I think, now?"

"What?"

"I wish I'd become a plant earlier."

Doctor Harris stood up. "Westerburg, when you come inside, will you stop off at my office? I want to give you a few tests, if you don't mind."

"The shock box?" Westerburg smiled. "I knew that would be coming around. Sure, I don't mind."

Nettled, Harris left the rock, walking back up the bank a short distance. "About three, Corporal?"

The Corporal nodded.

Harris made his way up the hill, to the path, toward the hospital building. The whole thing was beginning to become more clear to him. A boy who had struggled all his life. Financial insecurity. Idealized goal, getting a Patrol assignment. Finally reached it, found the load too great. And on Asteroid Y-3 there was too much vegetation to look at all day. Primitive identification and projection on the flora of the asteroid. Concept of security involved in immobility and permanence. Unchanging forest.

He entered the building. A robot orderly stopped him almost at once. "Sir, Commander Cox wants you urgently, on the vidphone."

"Thanks." Harris strode to his office. He dialed Cox's letter and the Commander's face came presently into focus. "Cox? This is Harris. I've been out talking to the boy. I'm beginning to get this lined up, now. I can see the pattern, too much load too long. Finally gets what he wants and the idealization shatters under the—"

"Harris!" Cox barked. "Shut up and listen. I just got a report from Y-3. They're sending an express rocket here. It's on the way."

"An express rocket?"

"Five more cases like Westerburg. All say they're plants! The Garrison Chief is worried as hell. Says we *must* find out what it is or the Garrison will fall apart, right away. Do you get me, Harris? Find out what it is!"

"Yes, sir," Harris murmured. "Yes, sir."

* * *

By the end of the week there were twenty cases, and all, of course, were from Asteroid Y-3.

Commander Cox and Harris stood together at the top of the hill, looking gloomily down at the stream below. Sixteen men and four women sat in the sun along the bank, none of them moving, none speaking. An hour had gone by since Cox and Harris appeared, and in all that time the twenty people below had not stirred.

"I don't get it," Cox said, shaking his head. "I just absolutely don't get it. Harris, is this the beginning of the end? Is everything going to start cracking around us? It gives me a hell of a strange feeling to see those people down there, basking away in the sun, just sitting and basking."

"Who's that man there with the red hair?"

"That's Ulrich Deutsch. He was Second in Command at the Garrison. Now look at him! Sits and dozes with his mouth open and his eyes shut. A week ago that man was climbing, going right up to the top. When the Garrison Chief retires he was supposed to take over. Maybe another year, at the most. All his life he's been climbing to get up there."

"And now he sits in the sun," Harris finished.

"That woman. The brunette, with the short hair. Career woman. Head of the entire office staff of the Garrison. And the man beside her. Janitor. And that cute little gal there, with the bosom. Secretary, just out of school. All kinds. And I got a note this morning, three more coming in sometime today."

Harris nodded. "The strange thing is—they really *want* to sit down there. They're completely rational; they could do something else, but they just don't care to."

"Well?" Cox said. "What are you going to do? Have you found anything? We're counting on you. Let's hear it."

"I couldn't get anything out of them directly," Harris said, "but I've had some interesting results with the shock box. Let's go inside and I'll show you."

"Fine," Cox turned and started toward the hospital. "Show me anything you've got. This is serious. Now I know how Tiberius felt when Christianity showed up in high places."

* * *

Harris snapped off the light. The room was pitch black. "I'll run this first reel for you. The subject is one of the best biologists stationed at the Garrison. Robert Bradshaw. He came in yesterday. I got a good run from the shock box because Bradshaw's mind is so highly differentiated. There's a lot of repressed material of a non-rational nature, more than usual."

He pressed a switch. The projector whirred, and on the far wall a three-dimensional image appeared in color, so real that it might have been the man himself. Robert Bradshaw was a man of fifty, heavy-set, with iron grey hair and a square jaw. He sat in the chair calmly, his hands resting on the arms, oblivious to the electrodes attached to his neck and wrist. "There I go," Harris said. "Watch."

His film-image appeared, approaching Bradshaw. "Now, Mr. Bradshaw," his image said, "this won't hurt you at all, and it'll help us a lot." The image rotated the controls on the shock box. Bradshaw stiffened, and his jaw set, but otherwise he gave no sign. The image of Harris regarded him for a time and then stepped away from the controls.

"Can you hear me, Mr. Bradshaw?" the image asked.

"Yes."

"What is your name?"

"Robert C. Bradshaw."

"What is your position?"

"Chief Biologist at the check-station on Y-3."

"Are you there now?"

"No, I'm back on Terra. In a hospital."

"Why?"

"Because I admitted to the Garrison Chief that I had become a plant."

"Is that true? That you are a plant."

"Yes, in a non-biological sense. I retain the physiology of a human being, of course."

"What do you mean, then, that you're a plant?"

"The reference is to attitudinal response, to Weltanschauung."

"Go on."

"It is possible for a warm-blooded animal, an upper primate, to adopt the psychology of a plant, to some extent."

"Yes?"

"I refer to this."

"And the others? They refer to this also?"

"Yes."

"How did this occur, your adopting this attitude?"

Bradshaw's image hesitated, the lips twisting. "See?" Harris said to Cox. "Strong conflict. He wouldn't have gone on, if he had been fully conscious."

"I—"

"Yes?"

"I was taught to become a plant."

The image of Harris showed surprise and interest. "What do you mean, you were *taught* to become a plant?"

"They realized my problems and taught me to become a plant. Now I'm free from them, the problems."

"Who? Who taught you?"

"The Pipers."

"Who? The Pipers? Who are the Pipers?"

There was no answer.

"Mr. Bradshaw, who are the Pipers?"

After a long, agonized pause, the heavy lips parted. "They live in the woods. . . ."

Harris snapped off the projector, and the lights came on. He and Cox blinked. "That was all I could get," Harris said. "But I was lucky to get that. He wasn't supposed to tell, not at all. That was the thing they all promised not to do, tell who taught them to become plants. The Pipers who live in the woods, on Asteroid Y-3."

"You got this story from all twenty?"

"No." Harris grimaced. "Most of them put up too much fight. I couldn't even get *this* much from them."

Cox reflected. "The Pipers. Well? What do you propose to do? Just wait around until you can get the full story? Is that your program?"

"No," Harris said. "Not at all. I'm going to Y-3 and find out who the Pipers are, myself."

* * *

The small patrol ship made its landing with care and precision, its jets choking into final silence. The hatch slid back and Doctor Henry Harris found himself staring out at a field, a brown, sun-baked landing field. At the end of the field was a tall signal tower. Around the field on all sides were long grey buildings, the Garrison check-station itself. Not far off a huge Venusian cruiser was parked, a vast green hulk, like an enormous lime. The technicians from the station were swarming all over it, checking and examining each inch of it for lethal life-forms and poisons that might have attached themselves to the hull.

"All out, sir," the pilot said.

Harris nodded. He took hold of his two suitcases and stepped carefully down. The ground was hot underfoot, and he blinked in the bright sunlight. Jupiter was in the sky, and the vast planet reflected considerable sunlight down onto the asteroid.

Harris started across the field, carrying his suitcases. A field attendant was already busy opening the storage compartment of the patrol ship, extracting his trunk. The attendant lowered the trunk into a waiting dolly and came after him, manipulating the little truck with bored skill.

As Harris came to the entrance of the signal tower the gate slid back and a man came forward, an older man, large and robust, with white hair and a steady walk.

"How are you, Doctor?" he said, holding his hand out. "I'm Lawrence Watts, the Garrison Chief."

They shook hands. Watts smiled down at Harris. He was a huge old man, still regal and straight in his dark blue uniform, with his gold epaulets sparkling on his shoulders.

"Have a good trip?" Watts asked. "Come on inside and I'll have a drink fixed for you. It gets hot around here, with the Big Mirror up there."

"Jupiter?" Harris followed him inside the building. The signal tower was cool and dark, a welcome relief. "Why is the gravity so near Terra's? I expected to go flying off like a kangaroo. Is it artificial?"

"No. There's a dense core of some kind to the asteroid, some kind of metallic deposit. That's why we picked this asteroid out of all the others. It made the construction problem much simpler, and it also explains why the asteroid has natural air and water. Did you see the hills?"

"The hills?"

"When we get up higher in the tower we'll be able to see over the buildings. There's quite a natural park here, a regular little forest, complete

with everything you'd want. Come in here, Harris. This is my office."
The old man strode at quite a clip, around the corner and into a large,
well-furnished apartment. "Isn't this pleasant? I intend to make my last
year here as amiable as possible." He frowned. "Of course, with Deutsch
gone, I may be here forever. Oh, well." He shrugged. "Sit down, Harris."

"Thanks." Harris took a chair, stretching his legs out. He watched
Watts as he closed the door to the hall. "By the way, any more cases
come up?"

"Two more today," Watts was grim. "Makes almost thirty, in all. We
have three hundred men in this station. At the rate it's going—"

"Chief, you spoke about a forest on the asteroid. Do you allow the crew
to go into the forest at will? Or do you restrict them to the buildings
and grounds?"

* * *

Watts rubbed his jaw. "Well, it's a difficult situation, Harris. I have
to let the men leave the grounds sometimes. They can *see* the forest
from the buildings, and as long as you can see a nice place to stretch
out and relax that does it. Once every ten days they have a full period
of rest. Then they go out and fool around."

"And then it happens?"

"Yes, I suppose so. But as long as they can see the forest they'll want
to go. I can't help it."

"I know. I'm not censuring you. Well, what's your theory? What happens to them out there? What do they do?"

"What happens? Once they get out there and take it easy for a while
they don't want to come back and work. It's boondoggling. Playing
hookey. They don't want to work, so off they go."

"How about this business of their delusions?"

Watts laughed good-naturedly. "Listen, Harris. You know as well as
I do that's a lot of poppycock. They're no more plants than you or I.
They just don't want to work, that's all. When I was a cadet we had
a few ways to make people work. I wish we could lay a few on their
backs, like we used to."

"You think this is simple goldbricking, then?"

"Don't you think it is?"

"No," Harris said. "They really believe they're plants. I put them
through the high-frequency shock treatment, the shock box. The whole

nervous system is paralyzed, all inhibitions stopped cold. They tell the truth, then. And they said the same thing—and more."

Watts paced back and forth, his hands clasped behind his back. "Harris, you're a doctor, and I suppose you know what you're talking about. But look at the situation here. We have a garrison, a good modern garrison. We're probably the most modern outfit in the system. Every new device and gadget is here that science can produce. Harris, this garrison is one vast machine. The men are parts, and each has his job, the Maintenance Crew, the Biologists, the Office Crew, the Managerial Staff.

"Look what happens when one person steps away from his job. Everything else begins to creak. We can't service the bugs if no one services the machines. We can't order food to feed the crews if no one makes out reports, takes inventories. We can't direct any kind of activity if the Second in Command decides to go out and sit in the sun all day.

"Thirty people, one tenth of the Garrison. But we can't run without them. The Garrison is built that way. If you take the supports out the whole building falls. No one can leave. We're all tied here, and these people know it. They know they have no right to do that, run off on their own. No one has that right anymore. We're all too tightly interwoven to suddenly start doing what we want. It's unfair to the rest, the majority."

                                    * * *

Harris nodded. "Chief, can I ask you something?"

"What is it?"

"Are there any inhabitants on the asteroid? Any natives?"

"Natives?" Watts considered. "Yes, there's some kind of aborigines living out there." He waved vaguely toward the window.

"What are they like? Have you seen them?"

"Yes, I've seen them. At least, I saw them when we first came here. They hung around for a while, watching us, then after a time they disappeared."

"Did they die off? Diseases of some kind?"

"No. They just—just disappeared. Into their forest. They're still there, someplace."

"What kind of people are they?"

"Well, the story is that they're originally from Mars. They don't look much like Martians, though. They're dark, a kind of coppery color. Thin. Very agile, in their own way. They hunt and fish. No written language. We don't pay much attention to them."

"I see." Harris paused. "Chief, have you ever heard of anything called—The Pipers?"

"The Pipers?" Watts frowned. "No. Why?"

"The patients mentioned something called The Pipers. According to Bradshaw, the Pipers taught him to become a plant. He learned it from them, a kind of teaching."

"The Pipers. What are they?"

"I don't know," Harris admitted. "I thought maybe you might know. My first assumption, of course, was that they're the natives. But now I'm not so sure, not after hearing your description of them."

"The natives are primitive savages. They don't have anything to teach anybody, especially a top-flight biologist."

Harris hesitated. "Chief, I'd like to go into the woods and look around. Is that possible?"

"Certainly. I can arrange it for you. I'll give you one of the men to show you around."

"I'd rather go alone. Is there any danger?"

"No, none that I know of. Except—"

"Except the Pipers," Harris finished. "I know. Well, there's only one way to find them, and that's it. I'll have to take my chances."

* * *

"If you walk in a straight line," Chief Watts said, "you'll find yourself back at the Garrison in about six hours. It's a damn small asteroid. There's a couple of streams and lakes, so don't fall in."

"How about snakes or poisonous insects?"

"Nothing like that reported. We did a lot of tramping around at first, but it's grown back now, the way it was. We never encountered anything dangerous."

"Thanks, Chief," Harris said. They shook hands. "I'll see you before nightfall."

"Good luck." The Chief and his two armed escorts turned and went back across the rise, down the other side toward the Garrison. Harris watched them go until they disappeared inside the building. Then he turned and started into the grove of trees.

The woods were very silent around him as he walked. Trees towered up on all sides of him, huge dark-green trees like eucalyptus. The ground underfoot was soft with endless leaves that had fallen and rotted into soil. After a while the grove of high trees fell behind and he found himself crossing a dry meadow, the grass and weeds burned brown in the sun. Insects buzzed around him, rising up from the dry weed-stalks. Something scuttled ahead, hurrying through the undergrowth. He caught sight of a grey ball with many legs, scampering furiously, its antennae weaving.

The meadow ended at the bottom of a hill. He was going up, now, going higher and higher. Ahead of him an endless expanse of green rose, acres of wild growth. He scrambled to the top finally, blowing and panting, catching his breath.

He went on. Now he was going down again, plunging into a deep gully. Tall ferns grew, as large as trees. He was entering a living Jurassic forest, ferns that stretched out endlessly ahead of him. Down he went, walking carefully. The air began to turn cold around him. The floor of the gully was damp and silent; underfoot the ground was almost wet.

He came out on a level table. It was dark, with the ferns growing up on all sides, dense growths of ferns, silent and unmoving. He came upon a natural path, an old stream bed, rough and rocky, but easy to follow. The air was thick and oppressive. Beyond the ferns he could see the side of the next hill, a green field rising up.

Something grey was ahead. Rocks, piled-up boulders, scattered and stacked here and there. The stream bed led directly to them. Apparently this had been a pool of some kind, a stream emptying from it. He climbed the first of the boulders awkwardly, feeling his way up. At the top he paused, resting again.

As yet he had had no luck. So far he had not met any of the natives. It would be through them that he would find the mysterious Pipers that were stealing the men away, if such really existed. If he could find the natives, talk to them, perhaps he could find out something. But as yet he had been unsuccessful. He looked around. The woods were very silent. A slight breeze moved through the ferns, rustling them, but that was all. Where were the natives? Probably they had a settlement of some sort, huts, a clearing. The asteroid was small; he should be able to find them by nightfall.

* * *

He started down the rocks. More rocks rose up ahead and he climbed them. Suddenly he stopped, listening. Far off, he could hear a sound, the sound of water. Was he approaching a pool of some kind? He went on again, trying to locate the sound. He scrambled down rocks and up rocks, and all around him there was silence, except for the splashing of distant water. Maybe a waterfall, water in motion. A stream. If he found the stream he might find the natives.

The rocks ended and the stream bed began again, but this time it was wet, the bottom muddy and overgrown with moss. He was on the right track; not too long ago this stream had flowed, probably during the rainy season. He went up on the side of the stream, pushing through the ferns and vines. A golden snake slid expertly out of his path. Something glinted ahead, something sparkling through the ferns. Water. A pool. He hurried, pushing the vines aside and stepping out, leaving them behind.

He was standing on the edge of a pool, a deep pool sunk in a hollow of grey rocks, surrounded by ferns and vines. The water was clear and bright, and in motion, flowing in a waterfall at the far end. It was beautiful, and he stood watching, marveling at it, the undisturbed quality of it. Untouched, it was. Just as it had always been, probably. As long as the asteroid existed. Was he the first to see it? Perhaps. It was so hidden, so concealed by the ferns. It gave him a strange feeling, a feeling almost of ownership. He stepped down a little toward the water.

And it was then he noticed her.

The girl was sitting on the far edge of the pool, staring down into the water, resting her head on one drawn-up knee. She had been bathing; he could see that at once. Her coppery body was still wet and glistening with moisture, sparkling in the sun. She had not seen him. He stopped, holding his breath, watching her.

She was lovely, very lovely, with long dark hair that wound around her shoulders and arms. Her body was slim, very slender, with a supple grace to it that made him stare, accustomed as he was to various forms of anatomy. How silent she was! Silent and unmoving, staring down at the water. Time passed, strange, unchanging time, as he watched the girl. Time might even have ceased, with the girl sitting on the rock staring into the water, and the rows of great ferns behind her, as rigid as if they had been painted there.

All at once the girl looked up. Harris shifted, suddenly conscious of himself as an intruder. He stepped back. "I'm sorry," he murmured. "I'm from the Garrison. I didn't mean to come poking around."

She nodded without speaking.

"You don't mind?" Harris asked presently.

"No."

So she spoke Terran! He moved a little toward her, around the side of the pool. "I hope you don't mind my bothering you. I won't be on the asteroid very long. This is my first day here. I just arrived from Terra."

She smiled faintly.

"I'm a doctor. Henry Harris." He looked down at her, at the slim coppery body, gleaming in the sunlight, a faint sheen of moisture on her arms and thighs. "You might be interested in why I'm here." He paused. "Maybe you can even help me."

She looked up a little. "Oh?"

"Would you like to help me?"

She smiled. "Yes. Of course."

"That's good. Mind if I sit down?" He looked around and found himself a flat rock. He sat down slowly, facing her. "Cigarette?"

"No."

"Well, I'll have one." He lit up, taking a deep breath. "You see, we have a problem at the Garrison. Something has been happening to some of the men, and it seems to be spreading. We have to find out what causes it or we won't be able to run the Garrison."

* * *

He waited for a moment. She nodded slightly. How silent she was! Silent and unmoving. Like the ferns.

"Well, I've been able to find out a few things from them, and one very interesting fact stands out. They keep saying that something called—called The Pipers are responsible for their condition. They say the Pipers taught them—" He stopped. A strange look had flitted across her dark, small face. "Do you know the Pipers?"

She nodded.

Acute satisfaction flooded over Harris. "You do? I was sure the natives would know." He stood up again. "I was sure they would, if the Pipers really existed. Then they do exist, do they?"

"They exist."

Harris frowned. "And they're here, in the woods?"

"Yes."

"I see." He ground his cigarette out impatiently. "You don't suppose there's any chance you could take me to them, do you?"

"Take you?"

"Yes. I have this problem and I have to solve it. You see, the Base Commander on Terra has assigned this to me, this business about the

Pipers. It has to be solved. And I'm the one assigned to the job. So it's important to me to find them. Do you see? Do you understand?"

She nodded.

"Well, will you take me to them?"

The girl was silent. For a long time she sat, staring down into the water, resting her head against her knee. Harris began to become impatient. He fidgeted back and forth, resting first on one leg and then on the other.

"Well, will you?" he said again. "It's important to the whole Garrison. What do you say?" He felt around in his pockets. "Maybe I could give you something. What do I have. . . ." He brought out his lighter. "I could give you my lighter."

The girl stood up, rising slowly, gracefully, without motion or effort. Harris' mouth fell open. How supple she was, gliding to her feet in a single motion! He blinked. Without effort she had stood, seemingly without *change*. All at once she was standing instead of sitting, standing and looking calmly at him, her small face expressionless.

"Will you?" he said.

"Yes. Come along." She turned away, moving toward the row of ferns.

Harris followed quickly, stumbling across the rocks. "Fine," he said. "Thanks a lot. I'm very interested to meet these Pipers. Where are you taking me, to your village? How much time do we have before nightfall?"

The girl did not answer. She had entered the ferns already, and Harris quickened his pace to keep from losing her. How silently she glided!

"Wait," he called. "Wait for me."

The girl paused, waiting for him, slim and lovely, looking silently back. He entered the ferns, hurrying after her.

* * *

"Well, I'll be damned!" Commander Cox said. "It sure didn't take you long." He leaped down the steps two at a time. "Let me give you a hand."

Harris grinned, lugging his heavy suitcases. He set them down and breathed a sigh of relief. "It isn't worth it," he said. "I'm going to give up taking so much."

"Come on inside. Soldier, give him a hand." A Patrolman hurried over and took one of the suitcases. The three men went inside and down the corridor to Harris' quarters. Harris unlocked the door and the Patrolman deposited his suitcase inside.

"Thanks," Harris said. He set the other down beside it. "It's good to be back, even for a little while."

"A little while?"

"I just came back to settle my affairs. I have to return to Y-3 tomorrow morning."

"Then you didn't solve the problem?"

"I solved it, but I haven't *cured* it. I'm going back and get to work right away. There's a lot to be done."

"But you found out what it is?"

"Yes. It was just what the men said. The Pipers."

"The Pipers do exist?"

"Yes." Harris nodded. "They do exist." He removed his coat and put it over the back of the chair. Then he went to the window and let it down. Warm spring air rushed into the room. He settled himself on the bed, leaning back.

"The Pipers exist, all right—in the minds of the Garrison crew! To the crew, the Pipers are real. The crew created them. It's a mass hypnosis, a group projection, and all the men there have it, to some degree."

"How did it start?"

"Those men on Y-3 were sent there because they were skilled, highly-trained men with exceptional ability. All their lives they've been schooled by complex modern society, fast tempo and high integration between people. Constant pressure toward some goal, some job to be done.

"Those men are put down suddenly on an asteroid where there are natives living the most primitive of existence, completely vegetable lives. No concept of goal, no concept of purpose, and hence no ability to plan. The natives live the way the animals live, from day to day, sleeping, picking food from the trees. A kind of Garden-of-Eden existence, without struggle or conflict."

"So? But—"

"Each of the Garrison crew sees the natives and *unconsciously* thinks of his own early life, when he was a child, when *he* had no worries, no responsibilities, before he joined modern society. A baby lying in the sun.

"But he can't admit this to himself! He can't admit that he might *want* to live like the natives, to lie and sleep all day. So he invents The Pipers, the idea of a mysterious group living in the woods who trap him, lead him into their kind of life. Then he can blame *them*, not himself. They 'teach' him to become a part of the woods."

"What are you going to do? Have the woods burned?"

"No." Harris shook his head. "That's not the answer; the woods are harmless. The answer is psychotherapy for the men. That's why I'm going right back, so I can begin work. They've got to be made to see that the Pipers are inside them, their own unconscious voices calling to them to give up their responsibilities. They've got to be made to realize that there are no Pipers, at least, not outside themselves. The woods are harmless and the natives have nothing to teach anyone. They're primitive savages, without even a written language. We're seeing a psychological projection by a whole Garrison of men who want to lay down their work and take it easy for a while."

The room was silent.

"I see," Cox said presently. "Well, it makes sense." He got to his feet. "I hope you can do something with the men when you get back."

"I hope so, too," Harris agreed. "And I think I can. After all, it's just a question of increasing their self-awareness. When they have that the Pipers will vanish."

Cox nodded. "Well, you go ahead with your unpacking, Doc. I'll see you at dinner. And maybe before you leave, tomorrow."

"Fine."

* * *

Harris opened the door and the Commander went out into the hall. Harris closed the door after him and then went back across the room. He looked out the window for a moment, his hands in his pockets.

It was becoming evening, the air was turning cool. The sun was just setting as he watched, disappearing behind the buildings of the city surrounding the hospital. He watched it go down.

Then he went over to his two suitcases. He was tired, very tired from his trip. A great weariness was beginning to descend over him. There were so many things to do, so terribly many. How could he hope to do them all? Back to the asteroid. And then what?

He yawned, his eyes closing. How sleepy he was! He looked over at the bed. Then he sat down on the edge of it and took his shoes off. So much to do, the next day.

He put his shoes in the corner of the room. Then he bent over, unsnapping one of the suitcases. He opened the suitcase. From it he took a bulging gunnysack. Carefully, he emptied the contents of the sack out on the floor. Dirt, rich soft dirt. Dirt he had collected during his last hours there, dirt he had carefully gathered up.

When the dirt was spread out on the floor he sat down in the middle of it. He stretched himself out, leaning back. When he was fully comfortable he folded his hands across his chest and closed his eyes. So much work to do—But later on, of course. Tomorrow. How warm the dirt was. . . .

He was sound asleep in a moment.

Beyond the Door

Larry Thomas bought a cuckoo clock for his wife—without knowing the price he would have to pay.

That night at the dinner table he brought it out and set it down beside her plate. Doris stared at it, her hand to her mouth. "My God, what is it?" She looked up at him, bright-eyed.

"Well, open it."

Doris tore the ribbon and paper from the square package with her sharp nails, her bosom rising and falling. Larry stood watching her as she lifted the lid. He lit a cigarette and leaned against the wall.

"A cuckoo clock!" Doris cried. "A real old cuckoo clock like my mother had." She turned the clock over and over. "Just like my mother had, when Pete was still alive." Her eyes sparkled with tears.

"It's made in Germany," Larry said. After a moment he added, "Carl got it for me wholesale. He knows some guy in the clock business. Otherwise I wouldn't have—" He stopped.

Doris made a funny little sound.

"I mean, otherwise I wouldn't have been able to afford it." He scowled. "What's the matter with you? You've got your clock, haven't you? Isn't that what you want?"

Doris sat holding onto the clock, her fingers pressed against the brown wood.

"Well," Larry said, "what's the matter?"

He watched in amazement as she leaped up and ran from the room, still clutching the clock. He shook his head. "Never satisfied. They're all that way. Never get enough."

He sat down at the table and finished his meal.

The cuckoo clock was not very large. It was hand-made, however, and there were countless frets on it, little indentations and ornaments scored in the soft wood. Doris sat on the bed drying her eyes and winding the clock. She set the hands by her wristwatch. Presently she carefully moved the hands to two minutes of ten. She carried the clock over to the dresser and propped it up.

Then she sat waiting, her hands twisted together in her lap—waiting for the cuckoo to come out, for the hour to strike.

As she sat she thought about Larry and what he had said. And what she had said, too, for that matter—not that she could be blamed for any of it. After all, she couldn't keep listening to him forever without defending herself; you had to blow your own trumpet in the world.

She touched her handkerchief to her eyes suddenly. Why did he have to say that, about getting it wholesale? Why did he have to spoil it all? If he felt that way he needn't have got it in the first place. She clenched her fists. He was so mean, so damn mean.

But she was glad of the little clock sitting there ticking to itself, with its funny grilled edges and the door. Inside the door was the cuckoo, waiting to come out. Was he listening, his head cocked on one side, listening to hear the clock strike so that he would know to come out?

Did he sleep between hours? Well, she would soon see him: she could ask him. And she would show the clock to Bob. He would love it; Bob loved old things, even old stamps and buttons. He liked to go with her to the stores. Of course, it was a little *awkward,* but Larry had been staying at the office so much, and that helped. If only Larry didn't call up sometimes to—

There was a whirr. The clock shuddered and all at once the door opened. The cuckoo came out, sliding swiftly. He paused and looked around solemnly, scrutinizing her, the room, the furniture.

It was the first time he had seen her, she realized, smiling to herself in pleasure. She stood up, coming toward him shyly. "Go on," she said. "I'm waiting."

The cuckoo opened his bill. He whirred and chirped, quickly, rhythmically. Then, after a moment of contemplation, he retired. And the door snapped shut.

She was delighted. She clapped her hands and spun in a little circle. He was marvelous, perfect! And the way he had looked around, studying her, sizing her up. He liked her; she was certain of it. And she, of course, loved him at once, completely. He was just what she had hoped would come out of the little door.

Doris went to the clock. She bent over the little door, her lips close to the wood. "Do you hear me?" she whispered. "I think you're the most wonderful cuckoo in the world." She paused, embarrassed. "I hope you'll like it here."

Then she went downstairs again, slowly, her head high.

Larry and the cuckoo clock really never got along well from the start. Doris said it was because he didn't wind it right, and it didn't like being only half-wound all the time. Larry turned the job of winding over to her; the cuckoo came out every quarter hour and ran the spring down without remorse, and someone had to be ever after it, winding it up again.

Doris did her best, but she forgot a good deal of the time. Then Larry would throw his newspaper down with an elaborate weary motion and stand up. He would go into the dining-room where the clock was mounted on the wall over the fireplace. He would take the clock down and making sure that he had his thumb over the little door, he would wind it up.

"Why do you put your thumb over the door?" Doris asked once.

"You're supposed to."

She raised an eyebrow. "Are you sure? I wonder if it isn't that you don't want him to come out while you're standing so close."

"Why not?"

"Maybe you're afraid of him."

Larry laughed. He put the clock back on the wall and gingerly removed his thumb. When Doris wasn't looking he examined his thumb.

There was still a trace of the nick cut out of the soft part of it. Who—or what—had pecked at him?

* * *

One Saturday morning, when Larry was down at the office working over some important special accounts, Bob Chambers came to the front porch and rang the bell.

Doris was taking a quick shower. She dried herself and slipped into her robe. When she opened the door Bob stepped inside, grinning.

"Hi," he said, looking around.

"It's all right. Larry's at the office."

"Fine." Bob gazed at her slim legs below the hem of the robe. "How nice you look today."

She laughed. "Be careful! Maybe I shouldn't let you in after all."

They looked at one another, half amused half frightened. Presently Bob said, "If you want, I'll—"

"No, for God's sake." She caught hold of his sleeve. "Just get out of the doorway so I can close it. Mrs. Peters across the street, you know."

She closed the door. "And I want to show you something," she said. "You haven't seen it."

He was interested. "An antique? Or what?"

She took his arm, leading him toward the dining-room. "You'll love it, Bobby." She stopped, wide-eyed. "I hope you will. You must; you must love it. It means so much to me—*he* means so much."

"He?" Bob frowned. "Who is he?"

Doris laughed. "You're jealous! Come on." A moment later they stood before the clock, looking up at it. "He'll come out in a few minutes. Wait until you see him. I know you two will get along just fine."

"What does Larry think of him?"

"They don't like each other. Sometimes when Larry's here he won't come out. Larry gets mad if he doesn't come out on time. He says—"

"Says what?"

Doris looked down. "He always says he's been robbed, even if he did get it wholesale." She brightened. "But I know he won't come out because he doesn't like Larry. When I'm here alone he comes right out for me, every fifteen minutes, even though he really only has to come out on the hour."

She gazed up at the clock. "He comes out for me because he wants to. We talk; I tell him things. Of course, I'd like to have him upstairs in my room, but it wouldn't be right."

There was the sound of footsteps on the front porch. They looked at each other, horrified.

Larry pushed the front door open, grunting. He set his briefcase down and took off his hat. Then he saw Bob for the first time.

"Chambers. I'll be damned." His eyes narrowed. "What are you doing here?" He came into the dining-room. Doris drew her robe about her helplessly, backing away.

"I—" Bob began. "That is, we—" He broke off, glancing at Doris. Suddenly the clock began to whirr. The cuckoo came rushing out, bursting into sound. Larry moved toward him.

"Shut that din off," he said. He raised his fist toward the clock. The cuckoo snapped into silence and retreated. The door closed. "That's better." Larry studied Doris and Bob, standing mutely together.

"I came over to look at the clock," Bob said. "Doris told me that it's a rare antique and that—"

"Nuts. I bought it myself." Larry walked up to him. "Get out of here." He turned to Doris. "You too. And take that damn clock with you."

He paused, rubbing his chin. "No. Leave the clock here. It's mine; I bought it and paid for it."

In the weeks that followed after Doris left, Larry and the cuckoo clock got along even worse than before. For one thing, the cuckoo stayed inside most of the time, sometimes even at twelve o'clock when he should have been busiest. And if he did come out at all he usually spoke only once or twice, never the correct number of times. And there was a sullen, uncooperative note in his voice, a jarring sound that made Larry uneasy and a little angry.

But he kept the clock wound, because the house was very still and quiet and it got on his nerves not to hear someone running around, talking and dropping things. And even the whirring of a clock sounded good to him.

But he didn't like the cuckoo at all. And sometimes he spoke to him.

"Listen," he said late one night to the closed little door. "I know you can hear me. I ought to give you back to the Germans—back to the Black Forest." He paced back and forth. "I wonder what they're doing now, the two of them. That young punk with his books and his antiques. A man shouldn't be interested in antiques; that's for women."

He set his jaw. "Isn't that right?"

The clock said nothing. Larry walked up in front of it. "Isn't that right?" he demanded. "Don't you have anything to say?"

He looked at the face of the clock. It was almost eleven, just a few seconds before the hour. "All right. I'll wait until eleven. Then I want to hear what you have to say. You've been pretty quiet the last few weeks since she left."

He grinned wryly. "Maybe you don't like it here since she's gone." He scowled. "Well, I paid for you, and you're coming out whether you like it or not. You hear me?"

Eleven o'clock came. Far off, at the end of town, the great tower clock boomed sleepily to itself. But the little door remained shut. Nothing moved. The minute hand passed on and the cuckoo did not stir. He was someplace inside the clock, beyond the door, silent and remote.

"All right, if that's the way you feel," Larry murmured, his lips twisting. "But it isn't fair. It's your job to come out. We all have to do things we don't like."

He went unhappily into the kitchen and opened the great gleaming refrigerator. As he poured himself a drink he thought about the clock.

There was no doubt about it—the cuckoo should come out, Doris or no Doris. He had always liked her, from the very start. They had got along well, the two of them. Probably he liked Bob too—probably he had seen enough of Bob to get to know him. They would be quite happy together, Bob and Doris and the cuckoo.

Larry finished his drink. He opened the drawer at the sink and took out the hammer. He carried it carefully into the dining-room. The clock was ticking gently to itself on the wall.

"Look," he said, waving the hammer. "You know what I have here? You know what I'm going to do with it? I'm going to start on you—first." He smiled. "Birds of a feather, that's what you are—the three of you."

The room was silent.

"Are you coming out? Or do I have to come in and get you?"

The clock whirred a little.

"I hear you in there. You've got a lot of talking to do, enough for the last three weeks. As I figure it, you owe me—"

The door opened. The cuckoo came out fast, straight at him. Larry was looking down, his brow wrinkled in thought. He glanced up, and the cuckoo caught him squarely in the eye.

Down he went, hammer and chair and everything, hitting the floor with a tremendous crash. For a moment the cuckoo paused, its small body poised rigidly. Then it went back inside its house. The door snapped tight-shut after it.

The man lay on the floor, stretched out grotesquely, his head bent over to one side. Nothing moved or stirred. The room was completely silent, except, of course, for the ticking of the clock.

* * *

"I see," Doris said, her face tight. Bob put his arm around her, steadying her.

"Doctor," Bob said, "can I ask you something?"

"Of course," the doctor said.

"Is it very easy to break your neck, falling from so low a chair? It wasn't very far to fall. I wonder if it might not have been an accident. Is there any chance it might have been—"

"Suicide?" the doctor rubbed his jaw. "I never heard of anyone committing suicide that way. It was an accident; I'm positive."

"I don't mean suicide," Bob murmured under his breath, looking up at the clock on the wall. "I meant *something else.*"

But no one heard him.

The Crystal Crypt

Stark terror ruled the Inner-Flight ship on that last Mars-Terra run. For the black-clad Leiters were on the prowl . . . and the grim red planet was not far behind.

"Attention, Inner-Flight ship! Attention! You are ordered to land at the Control Station on Deimos for inspection. Attention! You are to land at once!"

The metallic rasp of the speaker echoed through the corridors of the great ship. The passengers glanced at each other uneasily, murmuring and peering out the port windows at the small speck below, the dot of rock that was the Martian checkpoint, Deimos.

"What's up?" an anxious passenger asked one of the pilots, hurrying through the ship to check the escape lock.

"We have to land. Keep seated." The pilot went on.

"Land? But why?" They all looked at each other. Hovering above the bulging Inner-Flight ship were three slender Martian pursuit craft, poised and alert for any emergency. As the Inner-Flight ship prepared to land the pursuit ships dropped lower, carefully maintaining themselves a short distance away.

"There's something going on," a woman passenger said nervously. "Lord, I thought we were finally through with those Martians. Now what?"

"I don't blame them for giving us one last going over," a heavy-set business man said to his companion. "After all, we're the last ship leaving Mars for Terra. We're damn lucky they let us go at all."

"You think there really will be war?" A young man said to the girl sitting in the seat next to him. "Those Martians won't dare fight, not with our weapons and ability to produce. We could take care of Mars in a month. It's all talk."

The girl glanced at him. "Don't be so sure. Mars is desperate. They'll fight tooth and nail. I've been on Mars three years." She shuddered. "Thank goodness I'm getting away. If—"

"Prepare to land!" the pilot's voice came. The ship began to settle slowly, dropping down toward the tiny emergency field on the seldom visited moon. Down, down the ship dropped. There was a grinding sound, a sickening jolt. Then silence.

"We've landed," the heavy-set business man said. "They better not do anything to us! Terra will rip them apart if they violate one Space Article."

"Please keep your seats," the pilot's voice came. "No one is to leave the ship, according to the Martian authorities. We are to remain here."

A restless stir filled the ship. Some of the passengers began to read uneasily, others stared out at the deserted field, nervous and on edge, watching the three Martian pursuit ships land and disgorge groups of armed men.

The Martian soldiers were crossing the field quickly, moving toward them, running double time.

This Inner-Flight spaceship was the last passenger vessel to leave Mars for Terra. All other ships had long since left, returning to safety before the outbreak of hostilities. The passengers were the very last to go, the final group of Terrans to leave the grim red planet, business men, expatriates, tourists, any and all Terrans who had not already gone home.

"What do you suppose they want?" the young man said to the girl. "It's hard to figure Martians out, isn't it? First they give the ship clearance, let us take off, and now they radio us to set down again. By the way, my name's Thacher, Bob Thacher. Since we're going to be here awhile—"

* * *

The port lock opened. Talking ceased abruptly, as everyone turned. A black-clad Martian official, a Province Leiter, stood framed against the bleak sunlight, staring around the ship. Behind him a handful of Martian soldiers stood waiting, their guns ready.

"This will not take long," the Leiter said, stepping into the ship, the soldiers following him. "You will be allowed to continue your trip shortly."

An audible sigh of relief went through the passengers.

"Look at him," the girl whispered to Thacher. "How I hate those black uniforms!"

"He's just a Provincial Leiter," Thacher said. "Don't worry."

The Leiter stood for a moment, his hands on his hips, looking around at them without expression. "I have ordered your ship grounded so that an inspection can be made of all persons aboard," he said. "You Terrans are the last to leave our planet. Most of you are ordinary and harmless—I am not interested in you. I am interested in finding three saboteurs, three Terrans, two men and a woman, who have committed an incredible act of destruction and violence. They are said to have fled to this ship."

Murmurs of surprise and indignation broke out on all sides. The Leiter motioned the soldiers to follow him up the aisle.

"Two hours ago a Martian city was destroyed. Nothing remains, only a depression in the sand where the city was. The city and all its people have completely vanished. An entire city destroyed in a second! Mars will never rest until the saboteurs are captured. And we know they are aboard this ship."

"It's impossible," the heavy-set business man said. "There aren't any saboteurs here."

"We'll begin with you," the Leiter said to him, stepping up beside the man's seat. One of the soldiers passed the Leiter a square metal box. "This will soon tell us if you're speaking the truth. Stand up. Get on your feet."

The man rose slowly, flushing. "See here—"

"Are you involved in the destruction of the city? Answer!"

The man swallowed angrily. "I know nothing about any destruction of any city. And furthermore—"

"He is telling the truth," the metal box said tonelessly.

"Next person." The Leiter moved down the aisle.

A thin, bald-headed man stood up nervously. "No, sir," he said. "I don't know a thing about it."

"He is telling the truth," the box affirmed.

"Next person! Stand up!"

One person after another stood, answered, and sat down again in relief. At last there were only a few people left who had not been questioned. The Leiter paused, studying them intently.

"Only five left. The three must be among you. We have narrowed it down." His hand moved to his belt. Something flashed, a rod of pale fire. He raised the rod, pointing it steadily at the five people. "All right, the first one of you. What do you know about this destruction? Are you involved with the destruction of our city?"

"No, not at all," the man murmured.

"Yes, he's telling the truth," the box intoned.

"Next!"

"Nothing—I know nothing. I had nothing to do with it."

"True," the box said.

The ship was silent. Three people remained, a middle-aged man and his wife and their son, a boy of about twelve. They stood in the corner, staring white-faced at the Leiter, at the rod in his dark fingers.

"It must be you," the Leiter grated, moving toward them. The Martian soldiers raised their guns. "It *must* be you. You there, the boy. What do you know about the destruction of our city? Answer!"

The boy shook his head. "Nothing," he whispered.

The box was silent for a moment. "He is telling the truth," it said reluctantly.

"Next!"

"Nothing," the woman muttered. "Nothing."

"The truth."

"Next!"

"I had nothing to do with blowing up your city," the man said. "You're wasting your time."

"It is the truth," the box said.

For a long time the Leiter stood, toying with his rod. At last he pushed it back in his belt and signalled the soldiers toward the exit lock.

"You may proceed on your trip," he said. He walked after the soldiers. At the hatch he stopped, looking back at the passengers, his face grim. "You may go—But Mars will not allow her enemies to escape. The three saboteurs will be caught, I promise you." He rubbed his dark jaw thoughtfully. "It is strange. I was certain they were on this ship."

Again he looked coldly around at the Terrans.

"Perhaps I was wrong. All right, proceed! But remember: the three will be caught, even if it takes endless years. Mars will catch them and punish them! I swear it!"

* * *

For a long time no one spoke. The ship lumbered through space again, its jets firing evenly, calmly, moving the passengers toward their own planet, toward home. Behind them Deimos and the red ball that was

Mars dropped farther and farther away each moment, disappearing and fading into the distance.

A sigh of relief passed through the passengers. "What a lot of hot air that was," one grumbled.

"Barbarians!" a woman said.

A few of them stood up, moving out into the aisle, toward the lounge and the cocktail bar. Beside Thacher the girl got to her feet, pulling her jacket around her shoulders.

"Pardon me," she said, stepping past him.

"Going to the bar?" Thacher said. "Mind if I come along?"

"I suppose not."

They followed the others into the lounge, walking together up the aisle. "You know," Thacher said, "I don't even know your name, yet."

"My name is Mara Gordon."

"Mara? That's a nice name. What part of Terra are you from? North America? New York?"

"I've been in New York," Mara said. "New York is very lovely." She was slender and pretty, with a cloud of dark hair tumbling down her neck, against her leather jacket.

They entered the lounge and stood undecided.

"Let's sit at a table," Mara said, looking around at the people at the bar, mostly men. "Perhaps that table over there."

"But someone's there already," Thacher said. The heavy-set business man had sat down at the table and deposited his sample case on the floor. "Do we want to sit with *him?*"

"Oh, it's all right," Mara said, crossing to the table. "May we sit here?" she said to the man.

The man looked up, half-rising. "It's a pleasure," he murmured. He studied Thacher intently. "However, a friend of mine will be joining me in a moment."

"I'm sure there's room enough for us all," Mara said. She seated herself and Thacher helped her with her chair. He sat down, too, glancing up suddenly at Mara and the business man. They were looking at each other almost as if something had passed between them. The man was middle-aged, with a florid face and tired, grey eyes. His hands were mottled with the veins showing thickly. At the moment he was tapping nervously.

"My name's Thacher," Thacher said to him, holding out his hand. "Bob Thacher. Since we're going to be together for a while we might as well get to know each other."

The man studied him. Slowly his hand came out. "Why not? My name's Erickson. Ralf Erickson."

"Erickson?" Thacher smiled. "You look like a commercial man, to me." He nodded toward the sample case on the floor. "Am I right?"

The man named Erickson started to answer, but at that moment there was a stir. A thin man of about thirty had come up to the table, his eyes bright, staring down at them warmly. "Well, we're on our way," he said to Erickson.

"Hello, Mara." He pulled out a chair and sat down quickly, folding his hands on the table before him. He noticed Thacher and drew back a little. "Pardon me," he murmured.

"Bob Thacher is my name," Thacher said. "I hope I'm not intruding here." He glanced around at the three of them, Mara, alert, watching him intently, heavy-set Erickson, his face blank, and this person. "Say, do you three know each other?" he asked suddenly.

There was silence.

The robot attendant slid over soundlessly, poised to take their orders. Erickson roused himself. "Let's see," he murmured. "What will we have? Mara?"

"Whiskey and water."

"You, Jan?"

The bright slim man smiled. "The same."

"Thacher?"

"Gin and tonic."

"Whiskey and water for me, also," Erickson said. The robot attendant went off. It returned at once with the drinks, setting on the table. Each took his own. "Well," Erickson said, holding his glass up. "To our mutual success."

* * *

All drank, Thacher and the three of them, heavy-set Erickson, Mara, her eyes nervous and alert, Jan, who had just come. Again a look passed between Mara and Erickson, a look so swift that he would not have caught it had he not been looking directly at her.

"What line do you represent, Mr. Erickson?" Thacher asked.

Erickson glanced at him, then down at the sample case on the floor. He grunted. "Well, as you can see, I'm a salesman."

Thacher smiled. "I knew it! You get so you can always spot a salesman right off by his sample case. A salesman always has to carry something to show. What are you in, sir?"

Erickson paused. He licked his thick lips, his eyes blank and lidded, like a toad's. At last he rubbed his mouth with his hand and reached down, lifting up the sample case. He set it on the table in front of him.

"Well?" he said. "Perhaps we might even show Mr. Thacher."

They all stared down at the sample case. It seemed to be an ordinary leather case, with a metal handle and a snap lock. "I'm getting curious," Thacher said. "What's in there? You're all so tense. Diamonds? Stolen jewels?"

Jan laughed harshly, mirthlessly. "Erick, put it down. We're not far enough away, yet."

"Nonsense," Erick rumbled. "We're away, Jan."

"Please," Mara whispered. "Wait, Erick."

"Wait? Why? What for? You're so accustomed to—"

"Erick," Mara said. She nodded toward Thacher. "We don't know him, Erick. Please!"

"He's a Terran, isn't he?" Erickson said. "All Terrans are together in these times." He fumbled suddenly at the catch lock on the case. "Yes, Mr. Thacher. I'm a salesman. We're all salesmen, the three of us."

"Then you do know each other."

"Yes." Erickson nodded. His two companions sat rigidly, staring down. "Yes, we do. Here, I'll show you our line."

He opened the case. From it he took a letter-knife, a pencil sharpener, a glass globe paperweight, a box of thumb tacks, a stapler, some clips, a plastic ashtray, and some things Thacher could not identify. He placed the objects in a row in front of him on the table top. Then he closed the sample case.

"I gather you're in office supplies," Thacher said. He touched the letter-knife with his finger. "Nice quality steel. Looks like Swedish steel, to me."

Erickson nodded, looking into Thacher's face. "Not really an impressive business, is it? Office supplies. Ashtrays, paper clips." He smiled.

"Oh—" Thacher shrugged. "Why not? They're a necessity in modern business. The only thing I wonder—"

"What's that?"

"Well, I wonder how you'd ever find enough customers on Mars to make it worth your while." He paused, examining the glass paperweight. He lifted it up, holding it to the light, staring at the scene within until Erickson took it out of his hand and put it back in the sample case. "And another thing. If you three know each other, why did you sit apart when you got on?"

They looked at him quickly.

"And why didn't you speak to each other until we left Deimos?" He leaned toward Erickson, smiling at him. "Two men and a woman. Three of you. Sitting apart in the ship. Not speaking, not until the check-station was past. I find myself thinking over what the Martian said. Three saboteurs. A woman and two men."

Erickson put the things back in the sample case. He was smiling, but his face had gone chalk white. Mara stared down, playing with a drop of water on the edge of her glass. Jan clenched his hands together nervously, blinking rapidly.

"You three are the ones the Leiter was after," Thacher said softly. "You are the destroyers, the saboteurs. But their lie detector—Why didn't it trap you? How did you get by that? And now you're safe, outside the check-station." He grinned, staring around at them. "I'll be damned! And I really thought you were a salesman, Erickson. You really fooled me."

Erickson relaxed a little. "Well, Mr. Thacher, it's in a good cause. I'm sure you have no love for Mars, either. No Terran does. And I see you're leaving with the rest of us."

"True," Thacher said. "You must certainly have an interesting account to give, the three of you." He looked around the table.

"We still have an hour or so of travel. Sometimes it gets dull, this Mars-Terra run. Nothing to see, nothing to do but sit and drink in the lounge." He raised his eyes slowly. "Any chance you'd like to spin a story to keep us awake?"

Jan and Mara looked at Erickson. "Go on," Jan said. "He knows who we are. Tell him the rest of the story."

"You might as well," Mara said.

Jan let out a sigh suddenly, a sigh of relief. "Let's put the cards on the table, get this weight off us. I'm tired of sneaking around, slipping—"

"Sure," Erickson said expansively. "Why not?" He settled back in his chair, unbuttoning his vest. "Certainly, Mr. Thacher. I'll be glad to spin you a story. And I'm sure it will be interesting enough to keep you awake."

* * *

They ran through the groves of dead trees, leaping across the sun-baked Martian soil, running silently together. They went up a little rise, across a narrow ridge. Suddenly Erick stopped, throwing himself down flat on the ground. The others did the same, pressing themselves against the soil, gasping for breath.

"Be silent," Erick muttered. He raised himself a little. "No noise. There'll be Leiters nearby, from now on. We don't dare take any chances."

Between the three people lying in the grove of dead trees and the City was a barren, level waste of desert, over a mile of blasted sand. No trees or bushes marred the smooth, parched surface. Only an occasional wind, a dry wind eddying and twisting, blew the sand up into little rills. A faint odor came to them, a bitter smell of heat and sand, carried by the wind.

Erick pointed. "Look. The City—There it is."

They stared, still breathing deeply from their race through the trees. The City was close, closer than they had ever seen it before. Never had they gotten so close to it in times past. Terrans were never allowed near the great Martian cities, the centers of Martian life. Even in ordinary times, when there was no threat of approaching war, the Martians shrewdly kept all Terrans away from their citadels, partly from fear, partly from a deep, innate sense of hostility toward the white-skinned visitors whose commercial ventures had earned them the respect, and the dislike, of the whole system.

"How does it look to you?" Erick said.

The City was huge, much larger than they had imagined from the drawings and models they had studied so carefully back in New York, in the War Ministry Office. Huge it was, huge and stark, black towers rising up against the sky, incredibly thin columns of ancient metal, columns that had stood wind and sun for centuries. Around the City was a wall of stone, red stone, immense bricks that had been lugged there and fitted into place by slaves of the early Martian dynasties, under the whiplash of the first great Kings of Mars.

An ancient, sun-baked City, a City set in the middle of a wasted plain, beyond groves of dead trees, a City seldom seen by Terrans—but a City studied on maps and charts in every War Office on Terra. A City that contained, for all its ancient stone and archaic towers, the ruling group of all Mars, the Council of Senior Leiters, black-clad men who governed and ruled with an iron hand.

The Senior Leiters, twelve fanatic and devoted men, black priests, but priests with flashing rods of fire, lie detectors, rocket ships, intra-space cannon, many more things the Terran Senate could only conjecture about. The Senior Leiters and their subordinate Province Leiters—Erick and the two behind him suppressed a shudder.

"We've got to be careful," Erick said again. "We'll be passing among them, soon. If they guess who we are, or what we're here for—"

He snapped open the case he carried, glancing inside for a second. Then he closed it again, grasping the handle firmly. "Let's go," he said. He stood up slowly. "You two come up beside me. I want to make sure you look the way you should."

* * *

Mara and Jan stepped quickly ahead. Erick studied them critically as the three of them walked slowly down the slope, onto the plain, toward the towering black spires of the City.

"Jan," Erick said. "Take hold of her hand! Remember, you're going to marry her; she's your bride. And Martian peasants think a lot of their brides."

Jan was dressed in the short trousers and coat of the Martian farmer, a knotted rope tied around his waist, a hat on his head to keep off the sun. His skin was dark, colored by dye until it was almost bronze.

"You look fine," Erick said to him. He glanced at Mara. Her black hair was tied in a knot, looped through a hollowed-out yuke bone. Her face was dark, too, dark and lined with colored ceremonial pigment, green and orange stripes across her cheeks. Earrings were strung through her ears. On her feet were tiny slippers of perruh hide, laced around her ankles, and she wore long translucent Martian trousers with a bright sash tied around her waist. Between her small breasts a chain of stone beads rested, good-luck charms for the coming marriage.

"All right," Erick said. He, himself, wore the flowing grey robe of a Martian priest, dirty robes that were supposed to remain on him all his life, to be buried around him when he died. "I think we'll get past the guards. There should be heavy morning traffic on the road."

They walked on, the hard sand crunching under their feet. Against the horizon they could see specks moving, other persons going toward the City, farmers and peasants and merchants, bringing their crops and goods to market.

"See the cart!" Mara exclaimed.

They were nearing a narrow road, two ruts worn into the sand. A Martian hufa was pulling the cart, its great sides wet with perspiration, its tongue hanging out. The cart was piled high with bales of cloth, rough country cloth, hand dipped. A bent farmer urged the hufa on.

"And there." She pointed, smiling.

A group of merchants riding small animals were moving along behind the cart, Martians in long robes, their faces hidden by sand masks. On each animal was a pack, carefully tied on with rope. And beyond the merchants, plodding dully along, were peasants and farmers in an endless procession, some riding carts or animals, but mostly on foot.

Mara and Jan and Erick joined the line of people, melting in behind the merchants. No one noticed them; no one looked up or gave any sign. The march continued as before. Neither Jan nor Mara said anything to each other. They walked a little behind Erick, who paced with a certain dignity, a certain bearing becoming his position.

Once he slowed down, pointing up at the sky. "Look," he murmured, in the Martian hill dialect. "See that?"

Two black dots circled lazily. Martian patrol craft, the military on the outlook for any sign of unusual activity. War was almost ready to break out with Terra. Any day, almost any moment.

"We'll be just in time," Erick said. "Tomorrow will be too late. The last ship will have left Mars."

"I hope nothing stops us," Mara said. "I want to get back home when we're through."

* * *

Half an hour passed. They neared the City, the wall growing as they walked, rising higher and higher until it seemed to blot out the sky itself. A vast wall, a wall of eternal stone that had felt the wind and sun for centuries. A group of Martian soldiers were standing at the entrance, the single passage-gate hewn into the rock, leading to the City. As each person went through the soldiers examined him, poking his garments, looking into his load.

Erick tensed. The line had slowed almost to a halt. "It'll be our turn, soon," he murmured. "Be prepared."

"Let's hope no Leiters come around," Jan said. "The soldiers aren't so bad."

Mara was staring up at the wall and the towers beyond. Under their feet the ground trembled, vibrating and shaking. She could see tongues of flame rising from the towers, from the deep underground factories and forges of the City. The air was thick and dense with particles of soot. Mara rubbed her mouth, coughing.

"Here they come," Erick said softly.

The merchants had been examined and allowed to pass through the dark gate, the entrance through the wall into the City. They and their silent animals had already disappeared inside. The leader of the group of soldiers was beckoning impatiently to Erick, waving him on.

"Come along!" he said. "Hurry up there, old man."

Erick advanced slowly, his arms wrapped around his body, looking down at the ground.

"Who are you and what's your business here?" the soldier demanded, his hands on his hips, his gun hanging idly at his waist. Most of the soldiers were lounging lazily, leaning against the wall, some even squatting in the shade. Flies crawled on the face of one who had fallen asleep, his gun on the ground beside him.

"My business?" Erick murmured. "I am a village priest."

"Why do you want to enter the City?"

"I must bring these two people before the magistrate to marry them." He indicated Mara and Jan, standing a little behind him. "That is the Law the Leiters have made."

The soldier laughed. He circled around Erick. "What do you have in that bag you carry?"

"Laundry. We stay the night."

"What village are you from?"

"Kranos."

"Kranos?" The soldier looked to a companion. "Ever heard of Kranos?"

"A backward pig sty. I saw it once on a hunting trip."

The leader of the soldiers nodded to Jan and Mara. The two of them advanced, their hands clasped, standing close together. One of the soldiers put his hand on Mara's bare shoulder, turning her around.

"Nice little wife you're getting," he said. "Good and firm-looking." He winked, grinning lewdly.

Jan glanced at him in sullen resentment. The soldiers guffawed. "All right," the leader said to Erick. "You people can pass."

Erick took a small purse from his robes and gave the soldier a coin. Then the three of them went into the dark tunnel that was the entrance, passing through the wall of stone, into the City beyond.

They were within the City!

"Now," Erick whispered. "Hurry."

Around them the City roared and cracked, the sound of a thousand vents and machines, shaking the stones under their feet. Erick led Mara and Jan into a corner, by a row of brick warehouses. People were everywhere, hurrying back and forth, shouting above the din, merchants, peddlers, soldiers, street women. Erick bent down and opened the case he carried. From the case he quickly took three small coils of fine metal, intricate meshed wires and vanes worked together into a small cone. Jan took one and Mara took one. Erick put the remaining cone into his robe and snapped the case shut again.

"Now remember, the coils must be buried in such a way that the line runs through the center of the City. We must trisect the main section, where the largest concentration of buildings is. Remember the maps! Watch the alleys and streets carefully. Talk to no one if you can help it. Each of you has enough Martian money to buy your way out of trouble. Watch especially for cut-purses, and for heaven's sake, don't get lost."

* * *

Erick broke off. Two black-clad Leiters were coming along the inside of the wall, strolling together with their hands behind their backs. They noticed the three who stood in the corner by the warehouses and stopped.

"Go," Erick muttered. "And be back here at sundown." He smiled grimly. "Or never come back."

Each went off a different way, walking quickly without looking back. The Leiters watched them go. "The little bride was quite lovely," one Leiter said. "Those hill people have the stamp of nobility in their blood, from the old times."

"A very lucky young peasant to possess her," the other said. They went on. Erick looked after them, still smiling a little. Then he joined the surging mass of people that milled eternally through the streets of the City.

At dusk they met outside the gate. The sun was soon to set, and the air had turned thin and frigid. It cut through their clothing like knives.

Mara huddled against Jan, trembling and rubbing her bare arms.

"Well?" Erick said. "Did you both succeed?"

Around them peasants and merchants were pouring from the entrance, leaving the City to return to their farms and villages, starting the long trip back across the plain toward the hills beyond. None of them noticed the shivering girl and the young man and the old priest standing by the wall.

"Mine's in place," Jan said. "On the other side of the City, on the extreme edge. Buried by a well."

"Mine's in the industrial section," Mara whispered, her teeth chattering. "Jan, give me something to put over me! I'm freezing."

"Good," Erick said. "Then the three coils should trisect dead center, if the models were correct." He looked up at the darkening sky. Already, stars were beginning to show. Two dots, the evening patrol, moved slowly toward the horizon. "Let's hurry. It won't be long."

They joined the line of Martians moving along the road, away from the City. Behind them the City was losing itself in the sombre tones of night, its black spires disappearing into darkness.

They walked silently with the country people until the flat ridge of dead trees became visible on the horizon. Then they left the road and turned off, walking toward the trees.

"Almost time!" Erick said. He increased his pace, looking back at Jan and Mara impatiently.

"Come on!"

They hurried, making their way through the twilight, stumbling over rocks and dead branches, up the side of the ridge. At the top Erick halted, standing with his hands on his hips, looking back.

"See," he murmured. "The City. The last time we'll ever see it this way."

"Can I sit down?" Mara said. "My feet hurt me."

Jan pulled at Erick's sleeve. "Hurry, Erick! Not much time left." He laughed nervously. "If everything goes right we'll be able to look at it—forever."

"But not like this," Erick murmured. He squatted down, snapping his case open. He took some tubes and wiring out and assembled them together on the ground, at the peak of the ridge. A small pyramid of wire and plastic grew, shaped by his expert hands.

At last he grunted, standing up. "All right."

"Is it pointed directly at the City?" Mara asked anxiously, looking down at the pyramid.

Erick nodded. "Yes, it's placed according—" He stopped, suddenly stiffening. "Get back! It's time! *Hurry!*"

Jan ran, down the far side of the slope, away from the City, pulling Mara with him. Erick came quickly after, still looking back at the distant spires, almost lost in the night sky.

"Down."

Jan sprawled out, Mara beside him, her trembling body pressed against his. Erick settled down into the sand and dead branches, still trying to see. "I want to see it," he murmured. "A miracle. I want to see—"

A flash, a blinding burst of violet light, lit up the sky. Erick clapped his hands over his eyes. The flash whitened, growing larger, expanding. Suddenly there was a roar, and a furious hot wind rushed past him, throwing him on his face in the sand. The hot dry wind licked and seared at them, crackling the bits of branches into flame. Mara and Jan shut their eyes, pressed tightly together.

"God—" Erick muttered.

The storm passed. They opened their eyes slowly. The sky was still alive with fire, a drifting cloud of sparks that was beginning to dissipate with the night wind. Erick stood up unsteadily, helping Jan and Mara to their feet. The three of them stood, staring silently across the dark waste, the black plain, none of them speaking.

The City was gone.

At last Erick turned away. "That part's done," he said. "Now the rest! Give me a hand, Jan. There'll be a thousand patrol ships around here in a minute."

"I see one already," Mara said, pointing up. A spot winked in the sky, a rapidly moving spot. "They're coming, Erick." There was a throb of chill fear in her voice.

"I know." Erick and Jan squatted on the ground around the pyramid of tubes and plastic, pulling the pyramid apart. The pyramid was fused, fused together like molten glass. Erick tore the pieces away with trembling fingers. From the remains of the pyramid he pulled something forth, something he held up high, trying to make it out in the darkness. Jan and Mara came close to see, both staring up intently, almost without breathing.

"There it is," Erick said. "There!"

* * *

In his hand was a globe, a small transparent globe of glass. Within the glass something moved, something minute and fragile, spires almost too small to be seen, microscopic, a complex web swimming within the hollow glass globe. A web of spires. A City.

Erick put the globe into the case and snapped it shut. "Let's go," he said. They began to lope back through the trees, back the way they had come before. "We'll change in the car," he said as they ran. "I think we should keep these clothes on until we're actually inside the car. We still might encounter someone."

"I'll be glad to get my own clothing on again," Jan said. "I feel funny in these little pants."

"How do you think I feel?" Mara gasped. "I'm freezing in this, what there is of it."

"All young Martian brides dress that way," Erick said. He clutched the case tightly as they ran. "I think it looks fine."

"Thank you," Mara said, "but it is cold."

"What do you suppose they'll think?" Jan asked. "They'll assume the City was destroyed, won't they? That's certain."

"Yes," Erick said. "They'll be sure it was blown up. We can count on that. And it will be damn important to us that they think so!"

"The car should be around here, someplace," Mara said, slowing down.

"No. Farther on," Erick said. "Past that little hill over there. In the ravine, by the trees. It's so hard to see where we are."

"Shall I light something?" Jan said.

"No. There may be patrols around who—"

He halted abruptly. Jan and Mara stopped beside him. "What—" Mara began.

A light glimmered. Something stirred in the darkness. There was a sound.

"Quick!" Erick rasped. He dropped, throwing the case far away from him, into the bushes. He straightened up tensely.

A figure loomed up, moving through the darkness, and behind it came more figures, men, soldiers in uniform. The light flashed up brightly, blinding them. Erick closed his eyes. The light left him, touching Mara and Jan, standing silently together, clasping hands. Then it flicked down to the ground and around in a circle.

A Leiter stepped forward, a tall figure in black, with his soldiers close behind him, their guns ready. "You three," the Leiter said. "Who are you? Don't move. Stand where you are."

He came up to Erick, peering at him intently, his hard Martian face without expression. He went all around Erick, examining his robes, his sleeves.

"Please—" Erick began in a quavering voice, but the Leiter cut him off.

"I'll do the talking. Who are you three? What are you doing here? Speak up."

"We—we are going back to our village," Erick muttered, staring down, his hands folded. "We were in the City, and now we are going home."

One of the soldiers spoke into a mouthpiece. He clicked it off and put it away.

"Come with me," the Leiter said. "We're taking you in. Hurry along."

"In? Back to the City?"

One of the soldiers laughed. "The City is gone," he said. "All that's left of it you can put in the palm of your hand."

"But what happened?" Mara said.

"No one knows. Come on, hurry it up!"

There was a sound. A soldier came quickly out of the darkness. "A Senior Leiter," he said. "Coming this way." He disappeared again.

* * *

"A Senior Leiter." The soldiers stood waiting, standing at a respectful attention. A moment later the Senior Leiter stepped into the light, a black-clad old man, his ancient face thin and hard, like a bird's, eyes bright and alert. He looked from Erick to Jan.

"Who are these people?" he demanded.

"Villagers going back home."

"No, they're not. They don't stand like villagers. Villagers slump— diet, poor food. These people are not villagers. I myself came from the hills, and I know."

He stepped close to Erick, looking keenly into his face. "Who are you? Look at his chin—he never shaved with a sharpened stone! Something is wrong here."

In his hand a rod of pale fire flashed. "The City is gone, and with it at least half the Leiter Council. It is very strange, a flash, then heat, and a wind. But it was not fission. I am puzzled. All at once the City has vanished. Nothing is left but a depression in the sand."

"We'll take them in," the other Leiter said. "Soldiers, surround them. Make certain that—"

"Run!" Erick cried. He struck out, knocking the rod from the Senior Leiter's hand. They were all running, soldiers shouting, flashing their lights, stumbling against each other in the darkness. Erick dropped to his knees, groping frantically in the bushes. His fingers closed over the handle of the case and he leaped up. In Terran he shouted to Mara and Jan.

"Hurry! To the car! Run!" He set off, down the slope, stumbling through the darkness. He could hear soldiers behind him, soldiers running and falling. A body collided against him and he struck out.

Someplace behind him there was a hiss, and a section of the slope went up in flames. The Leiter's rod—

"Erick," Mara cried from the darkness. He ran toward her. Suddenly he slipped, falling on a stone. Confusion and firing. The sound of excited voices.

"Erick, is that you?" Jan caught hold of him, helping him up. "The car. It's over here. Where's Mara?"

"I'm here," Mara's voice came. "Over here, by the car."

A light flashed. A tree went up in a puff of fire, and Erick felt the singe of the heat against his face. He and Jan made their way toward the girl. Mara's hand caught his in the darkness.

"Now the car," Erick said. "If they haven't got to it." He slid down the slope into the ravine, fumbling in the darkness, reaching and holding onto the handle of the case. Reaching, reaching—

He touched something cold and smooth. Metal, a metal door handle. Relief flooded through him. "I've found it! Jan, get inside. Mara, come on." He pushed Jan past him, into the car. Mara slipped in after Jan, her small agile body crowding in beside him.

"Stop!" a voice shouted from above. "There's no use hiding in that ravine. We'll get you! Come up and—"

The sound of voices was drowned out by the roar of the car's motor. A moment later they shot into the darkness, the car rising into the air. Treetops broke and cracked under them as Erick turned the car from side to side, avoiding the groping shafts of pale light from below, the last furious thrusts from the two Leiters and their soldiers.

Then they were away, above the trees, high in the air, gaining speed each moment, leaving the knot of Martians far behind.

"Toward Marsport," Jan said to Erick. "Right?"

Erick nodded. "Yes. We'll land outside the field, in the hills. We can change back to our regular clothing there, our commercial clothing. Damn it—we'll be lucky if we can get there in time for the ship."

"The last ship," Mara whispered, her chest rising and falling. "What if we don't get there in time?"

Erick looked down at the leather case in his lap. "We'll have to get there," he murmured. "We must!"

* * *

For a long time there was silence. Thacher stared at Erickson. The older man was leaning back in his chair, sipping a little of his drink. Mara and Jan were silent.

"So you didn't destroy the City," Thacher said. "You didn't destroy it at all. You shrank it down and put it in a glass globe, in a paperweight. And now you're salesmen again, with a sample case of office supplies!"

Erickson smiled. He opened the briefcase and reaching into it he brought out the glass globe paperweight. He held it up, looking into it. "Yes, we stole the City from the Martians. That's how we got by the lie detector. It was true that we knew nothing about a *destroyed* City."

"But why?" Thacher said. "Why steal a City? Why not merely bomb it?"

"Ransom," Mara said fervently, gazing into the globe, her dark eyes bright. "Their biggest City, half of their Council—in Erick's hand!"

"Mars will have to do what Terra asks," Erickson said. "Now Terra will be able to make her commercial demands felt. Maybe there won't even be a war. Perhaps Terra will get her way without fighting." Still smiling, he put the globe back into the briefcase and locked it.

"Quite a story," Thacher said. "What an amazing process, reduction of size—A whole City reduced to microscopic dimensions. Amazing. No wonder you were able to escape. With such daring as that, no one could hope to stop you."

He looked down at the briefcase on the floor. Underneath them the jets murmured and vibrated evenly, as the ship moved through space toward distant Terra.

"We still have quite a way to go," Jan said. "You've heard our story, Thacher. Why not tell us yours? What sort of line are you in? What's your business?"

"Yes," Mara said. "What do you do?"

"What do I do?" Thacher said. "Well, if you like, I'll show you." He reached into his coat and brought out something. Something that flashed and glinted, something slender. A rod of pale fire.

The three stared at it. Sickened shock settled over them slowly.

Thacher held the rod loosely, calmly, pointing it at Erickson. "We knew you three were on this ship," he said. "There was no doubt of that. But we did not know what had become of the City. My theory was that the City had not been destroyed at all, that something else had happened to it. Council instruments measured a sudden loss of mass in that area, a decrease equal to the mass of the City. Somehow the City had been spirited away, not destroyed. But I could not convince the other Council Leiters of it. I had to follow you alone."

Thacher turned a little, nodding to the men sitting at the bar. The men rose at once, coming toward the table.

"A very interesting process you have. Mars will benefit a great deal from it. Perhaps it will even turn the tide in our favor. When we return to Marsport I wish to begin work on it at once. And now, if you will please pass me the briefcase—"

The Defenders

No weapon has ever been frightful enough to put a stop to war
—perhaps because we never before had any that thought
for themselves!

Taylor sat back in his chair reading the morning newspaper. The warm kitchen and the smell of coffee blended with the comfort of not having to go to work. This was his Rest Period, the first for a long time, and he was glad of it. He folded the second section back, sighing with contentment.

"What is it?" Mary said, from the stove.

"They pasted Moscow again last night." Taylor nodded his head in approval. "Gave it a real pounding. One of those R-H bombs. It's about time."

He nodded again, feeling the full comfort of the kitchen, the presence of his plump, attractive wife, the breakfast dishes and coffee. This was relaxation. And the war news was good, good and satisfying. He could feel a justifiable glow at the news, a sense of pride and personal accomplishment. After all, he was an integral part of the war program, not just another factory worker lugging a cart of scrap, but a technician, one of those who designed and planned the nerve-trunk of the war.

"It says they have the new subs almost perfected. Wait until they get *those* going." He smacked his lips with anticipation. "When they start shelling from underwater, the Soviets are sure going to be surprised."

"They're doing a wonderful job," Mary agreed vaguely. "Do you know what we saw today? Our team is getting a leady to show to the school children. I saw the leady, but only for a moment. It's good for the children to see what their contributions are going for, don't you think?"

She looked around at him.

"A leady," Taylor murmured. He put the newspaper slowly down. "Well, make sure it's decontaminated properly. We don't want to take any chances."

"Oh, they always bathe them when they're brought down from the surface," Mary said. "They wouldn't think of letting them down without the bath. Would they?" She hesitated, thinking back. "Don, you know, it makes me remember—"

He nodded. "I know."

* * *

He knew what she was thinking. Once in the very first weeks of the war, before everyone had been evacuated from the surface, they had seen a hospital train discharging the wounded, people who had been showered with sleet. He remembered the way they had looked, the expression on their faces, or as much of their faces as was left. It had not been a pleasant sight.

There had been a lot of that at first, in the early days before the transfer to undersurface was complete. There had been a lot, and it hadn't been very difficult to come across it.

Taylor looked up at his wife. She was thinking too much about it, the last few months. They all were.

"Forget it," he said. "It's all in the past. There isn't anybody up there now but the leadys, and they don't mind."

"But just the same, I hope they're careful when they let one of them down here. If one were still hot—"

He laughed, pushing himself away from the table. "Forget it. This is a wonderful moment; I'll be home for the next two shifts. Nothing to do but sit around and take things easy. Maybe we can take in a show. Okay?"

"A show? Do we have to? I don't like to look at all the destruction, the ruins. Sometimes I see some place I remember, like San Francisco. They showed a shot of San Francisco, the bridge broken and fallen in the water, and I got upset. I don't like to watch."

"But don't you want to know what's going on? No human beings are getting hurt, you know."

"But it's so awful!" Her face was set and strained. "Please, no, Don."

Don Taylor picked up his newspaper sullenly. "All right, but there isn't a hell of a lot else to do. And don't forget, *their* cities are getting it even worse."

She nodded. Taylor turned the rough, thin sheets of newspaper. His good mood had soured on him. Why did she have to fret all the time? They were pretty well off, as things went. You couldn't expect to have

everything perfect, living undersurface, with an artificial sun and artificial food. Naturally it was a strain, not seeing the sky or being able
to go any place or see anything other than metal walls, great roaring
factories, the plant-yards, barracks. But it was better than being on
surface. And some day it would end and they could return. Nobody
wanted to live this way, but it was necessary.

He turned the page angrily and the poor paper ripped. Damn it, the
paper was getting worse quality all the time, bad print, yellow tint—

Well, they needed everything for the war program. He ought to know
that. Wasn't he one of the planners?

He excused himself and went into the other room. The bed was
still unmade. They had better get it in shape before the seventh hour
inspection. There was a one unit fine—

The vidphone rang. He halted. Who would it be? He went over and
clicked it on.

"Taylor?" the face said, forming into place. It was an old face, gray and
grim. "This is Moss. I'm sorry to bother you during Rest Period, but this
thing has come up." He rattled papers. "I want you to hurry over here."

Taylor stiffened. "What is it? There's no chance it could wait?" The
calm gray eyes were studying him, expressionless, unjudging. "If you
want me to come down to the lab," Taylor grumbled, "I suppose I can.
I'll get my uniform—"

"No. Come as you are. And not to the lab. Meet me at second stage
as soon as possible. It'll take you about a half hour, using the fast car
up. I'll see you there."

The picture broke and Moss disappeared.

* * *

"What was it?" Mary said, at the door.

"Moss. He wants me for something."

"I knew this would happen."

"Well, you didn't want to do anything, anyhow. What does it matter?"
His voice was bitter. "It's all the same, every day. I'll bring you back
something. I'm going up to second stage. Maybe I'll be close enough
to the surface to—"

"Don't! Don't bring me anything! Not from the surface!"

"All right, I won't. But of all the irrational nonsense—"

She watched him put on his boots without answering.

* * *

Moss nodded and Taylor fell in step with him, as the older man strode along. A series of loads were going up to the surface, blind cars clanking like ore-trucks up the ramp, disappearing through the stage trap above them. Taylor watched the cars, heavy with tubular machinery of some sort, weapons new to him. Workers were everywhere, in the dark gray uniforms of the labor corps, loading, lifting, shouting back and forth. The stage was deafening with noise.

"We'll go up a way," Moss said, "where we can talk. This is no place to give you details."

They took an escalator up. The commercial lift fell behind them, and with it most of the crashing and booming. Soon they emerged on an observation platform, suspended on the side of the Tube, the vast tunnel leading to the surface, not more than half a mile above them now.

"My God!" Taylor said, looking down the Tube involuntarily. "It's a long way down."

Moss laughed. "Don't look."

They opened a door and entered an office. Behind the desk, an officer was sitting, an officer of Internal Security. He looked up.

"I'll be right with you, Moss." He gazed at Taylor studying him. "You're a little ahead of time."

"This is Commander Franks," Moss said to Taylor. "He was the first to make the discovery. I was notified last night." He tapped a parcel he carried. "I was let in because of this."

Franks frowned at him and stood up. "We're going up to first stage. We can discuss it there."

"First stage?" Taylor repeated nervously. The three of them went down a side passage to a small lift. "I've never been up there. Is it all right? It's not radioactive, is it?"

"You're like everyone else," Franks said. "Old women afraid of burglars. No radiation leaks down to first stage. There's lead and rock, and what comes down the Tube is bathed."

"What's the nature of the problem?" Taylor asked. "I'd like to know something about it."

"In a moment."

They entered the lift and ascended. When they stepped out, they were in a hall of soldiers, weapons and uniforms everywhere. Taylor blinked in surprise. So this was first stage, the closest undersurface level to the top! After this stage there was only rock, lead and rock, and the great tubes leading up like the burrows of earthworms. Lead and rock, and above that, where the tubes opened, the great expanse that no living being had seen for eight years, the vast, endless ruin that had once been Man's home, the place where he had lived, eight years ago.

Now the surface was a lethal desert of slag and rolling clouds. Endless clouds drifted back and forth, blotting out the red Sun. Occasionally something metallic stirred, moving through the remains of a city, threading its way across the tortured terrain of the countryside. A leady, a surface robot, immune to radiation, constructed with feverish haste in the last months before the cold war became literally hot.

Leadys, crawling along the ground, moving over the oceans or through the skies in slender, blackened craft, creatures that could exist where no *life* could remain, metal and plastic figures that waged a war Man had conceived, but which he could not fight himself. Human beings had invented war, invented and manufactured the weapons, even invented the players, the fighters, the actors of the war. But they themselves could not venture forth, could not wage it themselves. In all the world—in Russia, in Europe, America, Africa—no living human being remained. They were under the surface, in the deep shelters that had been carefully planned and built, even as the first bombs began to fall.

It was a brilliant idea and the only idea that could have worked. Up above, on the ruined, blasted surface of what had once been a living planet, the leady crawled and scurried, and fought Man's war. And undersurface, in the depths of the planet, human beings toiled endlessly to produce the weapons to continue the fight, month by month, year by year.

* * *

"First stage," Taylor said. A strange ache went through him. "Almost to the surface."

"But not quite," Moss said.

Franks led them through the soldiers, over to one side, near the lip of the Tube.

"In a few minutes, a lift will bring something down to us from the surface," he explained. "You see, Taylor, every once in a while Security examines and interrogates a surface leady, one that has been above for a time, to find out certain things. A vidcall is sent up and contact is made with a field headquarters. We need this direct interview; we can't depend on vidscreen contact alone. The leadys are doing a good job, but we want to make certain that everything is going the way we want it."

Franks faced Taylor and Moss and continued: "The lift will bring down a leady from the surface, one of the A-class leadys. There's an examination chamber in the next room, with a lead wall in the center, so the interviewing officers won't be exposed to radiation. We find this easier than bathing the leady. It is going right back up; it has a job to get back to.

"Two days ago, an A-class leady was brought down and interrogated. I conducted the session myself. We were interested in a new weapon the Soviets have been using, an automatic mine that pursues anything that moves. Military had sent instructions up that the mine be observed and reported in detail.

"This A-class leady was brought down with information. We learned a few facts from it, obtained the usual roll of film and reports, and then sent it back up. It was going out of the chamber, back to the lift, when a curious thing happened. At the time, I thought—"

Franks broke off. A red light was flashing.

"That down lift is coming." He nodded to some soldiers. "Let's enter the chamber. The leady will be along in a moment."

"An A-class leady," Taylor said. "I've seen them on the showscreens, making their reports."

"It's quite an experience," Moss said. "They're almost human."

* * *

They entered the chamber and seated themselves behind the lead wall. After a time, a signal was flashed, and Franks made a motion with his hands.

The door beyond the wall opened. Taylor peered through his view slot. He saw something advancing slowly, a slender metallic figure moving on a tread, its arm grips at rest by its sides. The figure halted and scanned the lead wall. It stood, waiting.

"We are interested in learning something," Franks said. "Before I question you, do you have anything to report on surface conditions?"

"No. The war continues." The leady's voice was automatic and toneless. "We are a little short of fast pursuit craft, the single-seat type. We could use also some—"

"That has all been noted. What I want to ask you is this. Our contact with you has been through vidscreen only. We must rely on indirect evidence, since none of us goes above. We can only infer what is going on. We never see anything ourselves. We have to take it all secondhand.

Some top leaders are beginning to think there's too much room for error."

"Error?" the leady asked. "In what way? Our reports are checked carefully before they're sent down. We maintain constant contact with you; everything of value is reported. Any new weapons which the enemy is seen to employ—"

"I realize that," Franks grunted behind his peep slot. "But perhaps we should see it all for ourselves. Is it possible that there might be a large enough radiation-free area for a human party to ascend to the surface? If a few of us were to come up in lead-lined suits, would we be able to survive long enough to observe conditions and watch things?"

The machine hesitated before answering. "I doubt it. You can check air samples, of course, and decide for yourselves. But in the eight years since you left, things have continually worsened. You cannot have any real idea of conditions up there. It has become difficult for any moving object to survive for long. There are many kinds of projectiles sensitive to movement. The new mine not only reacts to motion, but continues to pursue the object indefinitely, until it finally reaches it. And the radiation is everywhere."

"I see." Franks turned to Moss, his eyes narrowed oddly. "Well, that was what I wanted to know. You may go."

The machine moved back toward its exit. It paused. "Each month the amount of lethal particles in the atmosphere increases. The tempo of the war is gradually—"

"I understand." Franks rose. He held out his hand and Moss passed him the package. "One thing before you leave. I want you to examine a new type of metal shield material. I'll pass you a sample with the tong."

Franks put the package in the toothed grip and revolved the tong so that he held the other end. The package swung down to the leady, which took it. They watched it unwrap the package and take the metal plate in its hands. The leady turned the metal over and over.

Suddenly it became rigid.

"All right," Franks said.

He put his shoulder against the wall and a section slid aside. Taylor gasped—Franks and Moss were hurrying up to the leady!

"Good God!" Taylor said. "But it's radioactive!"

* * *

The leady stood unmoving, still holding the metal. Soldiers appeared in the chamber. They surrounded the leady and ran a counter across it carefully.

"Okay, sir," one of them said to Franks. "It's as cold as a long winter evening."

"Good. I was sure, but I didn't want to take any chances."

"You see," Moss said to Taylor, "this leady isn't hot at all. Yet it came directly from the surface, without even being bathed."

"But what does it mean?" Taylor asked blankly.

"It may be an accident," Franks said. "There's always the possibility that a given object might escape being exposed above. But this is the second time it's happened that we know of. There may be others."

"The second time?"

"The previous interview was when we noticed it. The leady was not hot. It was cold, too, like this one."

Moss took back the metal plate from the leady's hands. He pressed the surface carefully and returned it to the stiff, unprotesting fingers.

"We shorted it out with this, so we could get close enough for a thorough check. It'll come back on in a second now. We had better get behind the wall again."

They walked back and the lead wall swung closed behind them. The soldiers left the chamber.

"Two periods from now," Franks said softly, "an initial investigating party will be ready to go surface-side. We're going up the Tube in suits, up to the top—the first human party to leave undersurface in eight years."

"It may mean nothing," Moss said, "but I doubt it. Something's going on, something strange. The leady told us no life could exist above without being roasted. The story doesn't fit."

Taylor nodded. He stared through the peep slot at the immobile metal figure. Already the leady was beginning to stir. It was bent in several places, dented and twisted, and its finish was blackened and charred. It was a leady that had been up there a long time; it had seen war and destruction, ruin so vast that no human being could imagine the extent. It had crawled and slunk in a world of radiation and death, a world where no life could exist.

And Taylor had touched it!

"You're going with us," Franks said suddenly. "I want you along. I think the three of us will go."

* * *

Mary faced him with a sick and frightened expression. "I know it. You're going to the surface. Aren't you?"

She followed him into the kitchen. Taylor sat down, looking away from her.

"It's a classified project," he evaded. "I can't tell you anything about it."

"You don't have to tell me. I know. I knew it the moment you came in. There was something on your face, something I haven't seen there for a long, long time. It was an old look."

She came toward him. "But how can they send you to the surface?" She took his face in her shaking hands, making him look at her. There was a strange hunger in her eyes. "Nobody can live up there. Look, look at this!"

She grabbed up a newspaper and held it in front of him.

"Look at this photograph. America, Europe, Asia, Africa—nothing but ruins. We've seen it every day on the showscreens. All destroyed, poisoned. And they're sending you up. Why? No living thing can get by up there, not even a weed, or grass. They've wrecked the surface, haven't they? *Haven't they?*"

Taylor stood up. "It's an order. I know nothing about it. I was told to report to join a scout party. That's all I know."

He stood for a long time, staring ahead. Slowly, he reached for the newspaper and held it up to the light.

"It looks real," he murmured. "Ruins, deadness, slag. It's convincing. All the reports, photographs, films, even air samples. Yet we haven't seen it for ourselves, not after the first months . . ."

"What are you talking about?"

"Nothing." He put the paper down. "I'm leaving early after the next Sleep Period. Let's turn in."

Mary turned away, her face hard and harsh. "Do what you want. We might just as well all go up and get killed at once, instead of dying slowly down here, like vermin in the ground."

He had not realized how resentful she was. Were they all like that? How about the workers toiling in the factories, day and night, endlessly? The pale, stooped men and women, plodding back and forth to work, blinking in the colorless light, eating synthetics—

"You shouldn't be so bitter," he said.

Mary smiled a little. "I'm bitter because I know you'll never come back." She turned away. "I'll never see you again, once you go up there."

He was shocked. "What? How can you say a thing like that?"
She did not answer.

* * *

He awakened with the public newscaster screeching in his ears, shouting outside the building.

"Special news bulletin! Surface forces report enormous Soviet attack
with new weapons! Retreat of key groups! All work units report to
factories at once!"

Taylor blinked, rubbing his eyes. He jumped out of bed and hurried
to the vidphone. A moment later he was put through to Moss.

"Listen," he said. "What about this new attack? Is the project off?" He
could see Moss's desk, covered with reports and papers.

"No," Moss said. "We're going right ahead. Get over here at once."

"But—"

"Don't argue with me." Moss held up a handful of surface bulletins,
crumpling them savagely. "This is a fake. Come on!" He broke off.

Taylor dressed furiously, his mind in a daze.

Half an hour later, he leaped from a fast car and hurried up the stairs
into the Synthetics Building. The corridors were full of men and women
rushing in every direction. He entered Moss's office.

"There you are," Moss said, getting up immediately. "Franks is waiting
for us at the outgoing station."

They went in a Security Car, the siren screaming. Workers scattered
out of their way.

"What about the attack?" Taylor asked.

Moss braced his shoulders. "We're certain that we've forced their
hand. We've brought the issue to a head."

They pulled up at the station link of the Tube and leaped out. A
moment later they were moving up at high speed toward the first stage.

They emerged into a bewildering scene of activity. Soldiers were
fastening on lead suits, talking excitedly to each other, shouting back
and forth. Guns were being given out, instructions passed.

Taylor studied one of the soldiers. He was armed with the dreaded
Bender pistol, the new snub-nosed hand weapon that was just beginning
to come from the assembly line. Some of the soldiers looked a little
frightened.

"I hope we're not making a mistake," Moss said, noticing his gaze.

Franks came toward them. "Here's the program. The three of us are going up first, alone. The soldiers will follow in fifteen minutes."

"What are we going to tell the leadys?" Taylor worriedly asked. "We'll have to tell them something."

"We want to observe the new Soviet attack." Franks smiled ironically. "Since it seems to be so serious, we should be there in person to witness it."

"And then what?" Taylor said.

"That'll be up to them. Let's go."

* * *

In a small car, they went swiftly up the Tube, carried by anti-grav beams from below. Taylor glanced down from time to time. It was a long way back, and getting longer each moment. He sweated nervously inside his suit, gripping his Bender pistol with inexpert fingers.

Why had they chosen him? Chance, pure chance. Moss had asked him to come along as a Department member. Then Franks had picked him out on the spur of the moment. And now they were rushing toward the surface, faster and faster.

A deep fear, instilled in him for eight years, throbbed in his mind. Radiation, certain death, a world blasted and lethal—

Up and up the car went. Taylor gripped the sides and closed his eyes. Each moment they were closer, the first living creatures to go above the first stage, up the Tube past the lead and rock, up to the surface. The phobic horror shook him in waves. It was death; they all knew that. Hadn't they seen it in the films a thousand times? The cities, the sleet coming down, the rolling clouds—

"It won't be much longer," Franks said. "We're almost there. The surface tower is not expecting us. I gave orders that no signal was to be sent."

The car shot up, rushing furiously. Taylor's head spun; he hung on, his eyes shut. Up and up. . . .

The car stopped. He opened his eyes.

They were in a vast room, fluorescent-lit, a cavern filled with equipment and machinery, endless mounds of material piled in row after row. Among the stacks, leadys were working silently, pushing trucks and handcarts.

"Leadys," Moss said. His face was pale. "Then we're really on the surface."

The leadys were going back and forth with equipment moving the vast stores of guns and spare parts, ammunition and supplies that had been brought to the surface. And this was the receiving station for only one Tube; there were many others, scattered throughout the continent.

Taylor looked nervously around him. They were really there, above ground, on the surface. This was where the war was.

"Come on," Franks said. "A B-class guard is coming our way."

* * *

They stepped out of the car. A leady was approaching them rapidly. It coasted up in front of them and stopped, scanning them with its hand-weapon raised.

"This is Security," Franks said. "Have an A-class sent to me at once."

The leady hesitated. Other B-class guards were coming, scooting across the floor, alert and alarmed. Moss peered around.

"Obey!" Franks said in a loud, commanding voice. "You've been ordered!"

The leady moved uncertainly away from them. At the end of the building, a door slid back. Two A-class leadys appeared, coming slowly toward them. Each had a green stripe across its front.

"From the Surface Council," Franks whispered tensely. "This is above ground, all right. Get set."

The two leadys approached warily. Without speaking, they stopped close by the men, looking them up and down.

"I'm Franks of Security. We came from undersurface in order to—"

"This in incredible," one of the leadys interrupted him coldly. "You know you can't live up here. The whole surface is lethal to you. You can't possibly remain on the surface."

"These suits will protect us," Franks said. "In any case, it's not your responsibility. What I want is an immediate Council meeting so I can acquaint myself with conditions, with the situation here. Can that be arranged?"

"You human beings can't survive up here. And the new Soviet attack is directed at this area. It is in considerable danger."

"We know that. Please assemble the Council." Franks looked around him at the vast room, lit by recessed lamps in the ceiling. An uncertain quality came into his voice. "Is it night or day right now?"

"Night," one of the A-class leadys said, after a pause. "Dawn is coming in about two hours."

Franks nodded. "We'll remain at least two hours, then. As a concession to our sentimentality, would you please show us some place where we can observe the Sun as it comes up? We would appreciate it."

A stir went through the leadys.

"It is an unpleasant sight," one of the leadys said. "You've seen the photographs; you know what you'll witness. Clouds of drifting particles blot out the light, slag heaps are everywhere, the whole land is destroyed. For you it will be a staggering sight, much worse than pictures and film can convey."

"However it may be, we'll stay long enough to see it. Will you give the order to the Council?"

* * *

"Come this way." Reluctantly, the two leadys coasted toward the wall of the warehouse. The three men trudged after them, their heavy shoes ringing against the concrete. At the wall, the two leadys paused.

"This is the entrance to the Council Chamber. There are windows in the Chamber Room, but it is still dark outside, of course. You'll see nothing right now, but in two hours—"

"Open the door," Franks said.

The door slid back. They went slowly inside. The room was small, a neat room with a round table in the center, chairs ringing it. The three of them sat down silently, and the two leadys followed after them, taking their places.

"The other Council Members are on their way. They have already been notified and are coming as quickly as they can. Again I urge you to go back down." The leady surveyed the three human beings. "There is no way you can meet the conditions up here. Even we survive with some trouble, ourselves. How can you expect to do it?"

The leader approached Franks.

"This astonishes and perplexes us," it said. "Of course we must do what you tell us, but allow me to point out that if you remain here—"

"We know," Franks said impatiently. "However, we intend to remain, at least until sunrise."

"If you insist."

There was silence. The leadys seemed to be conferring with each other, although the three men heard no sound.

"For your own good," the leader said at last, "you must go back down. We have discussed this, and it seems to us that you are doing the wrong thing for your own good."

"We are human beings," Franks said sharply. "Don't you understand? We're men, not machines."

"That is precisely why you must go back. This room is radioactive; all surface areas are. We calculate that your suits will not protect you for over fifty more minutes. Therefore—"

The leadys moved abruptly toward the men, wheeling in a circle, forming a solid row. The men stood up, Taylor reaching awkwardly for his weapon, his fingers numb and stupid. The men stood facing the silent metal figures.

"We must insist," the leader said, its voice without emotion. "We must take you back to the Tube and send you down on the next car. I am sorry, but it is necessary."

"What'll we do?" Moss said nervously to Franks. He touched his gun. "Shall we blast them?"

Franks shook his head. "All right," he said to the leader. "We'll go back."

* * *

He moved toward the door, motioning Taylor and Moss to follow him. They looked at him in surprise, but they came with him. The leadys followed them out into the great warehouse. Slowly they moved toward the Tube entrance, none of them speaking.

At the lip, Franks turned. "We are going back because we have no choice. There are three of us and about a dozen of you. However, if—"

"Here comes the car," Taylor said.

There was a grating sound from the Tube. D-class leadys moved toward the edge to receive it.

"I am sorry," the leader said, "but it is for your protection. We are watching over you, literally. You must stay below and let us conduct the war. In a sense, it has come to be *our* war. We must fight it as we see fit."

The car rose to the surface.

Twelve soldiers, armed with Bender pistols, stepped from it and surrounded the three men.

Moss breathed a sigh of relief. "Well, this does change things. It came off just right."

The leader moved back, away from the soldiers. It studied them intently, glancing from one to the next, apparently trying to make up its mind. At last it made a sign to the other leadys. They coasted aside and a corridor was opened up toward the warehouse.

"Even now," the leader said, "we could send you back by force. But it is evident that this is not really an observation party at all. These soldiers show that you have much more in mind; this was all carefully prepared."

"Very carefully," Franks said.

They closed in.

"How much more, we can only guess. I must admit that we were taken unprepared. We failed utterly to meet the situation. Now force would be absurd, because neither side can afford to injure the other; we, because of the restrictions placed on us regarding human life, you because the war demands—"

The soldiers fired, quick and in fright. Moss dropped to one knee, firing up. The leader dissolved in a cloud of particles. On all sides D- and B-class leadys were rushing up, some with weapons, some with metal slats. The room was in confusion. Off in the distance a siren was screaming. Franks and Taylor were cut off from the others, separated from the soldiers by a wall of metal bodies.

"They can't fire back," Franks said calmly. "This is another bluff. They've tried to bluff us all the way." He fired into the face of a leady. The leady dissolved. "They can only try to frighten us. Remember that."

* * *

They went on firing and leady after leady vanished. The room reeked with the smell of burning metal, the stink of fused plastic and steel. Taylor had been knocked down. He was struggling to find his gun, reaching wildly among metal legs, groping frantically to find it. His fingers strained, a handle swam in front of him. Suddenly something came down on his arm, a metal foot. He cried out.

Then it was over. The leadys were moving away, gathering together off to one side. Only four of the Surface Council remained. The others were radioactive particles in the air. D-class leadys were already restoring order, gathering up partly destroyed metal figures and bits and removing them.

Franks breathed a shuddering sigh.

"All right," he said. "You can take us back to the windows. It won't be long now."

The leadys separated, and the human group, Moss and Franks and Taylor and the soldiers, walked slowly across the room, toward the door. They entered the Council Chamber. Already a faint touch of gray mitigated the blackness of the windows.

"Take us outside," Franks said impatiently. "We'll see it directly, not in here."

A door slid open. A chill blast of cold morning air rushed in, chilling them even through their lead suits. The men glanced at each other uneasily.

"Come on," Franks said. "Outside."

He walked out through the door, the others following him.

They were on a hill, overlooking the vast bowl of a valley. Dimly, against the graying sky, the outline of mountains were forming, becoming tangible.

"It'll be bright enough to see in a few minutes," Moss said. He shuddered as a chilling wind caught him and moved around him. "It's worth it, really worth it, to see this again after eight years. Even if it's the last thing we see—"

"Watch," Franks snapped.

They obeyed, silent and subdued. The sky was clearing, brightening each moment. Some place far off, echoing across the valley, a rooster crowed.

"A chicken!" Taylor murmured. "Did you hear?"

Behind them, the leadys had come out and were standing silently, watching, too. The gray sky turned to white and the hills appeared more clearly. Light spread across the valley floor, moving toward them.

"God in heaven!" Franks exclaimed.

Trees, trees and forests. A valley of plants and trees, with a few roads winding among them. Farmhouses. A windmill. A barn, far down below them.

"Look!" Moss whispered.

Color came into the sky. The Sun was approaching. Birds began to sing. Not far from where they stood, the leaves of a tree danced in the wind.

Franks turned to the row of leadys behind them.

"Eight years. We were tricked. There was no war. As soon as we left the surface—"

"Yes," an A-class leady admitted. "As soon as you left, the war ceased. You're right, it was a hoax. You worked hard undersurface, sending up guns and weapons, and we destroyed them as fast as they came up."

"But why?" Taylor asked, dazed. He stared down at the vast valley below. "Why?"

* * *

"You created us," the leady said, "to pursue the war for you, while you human beings went below the ground in order to survive. But before we could continue the war, it was necessary to analyze it to determine what its purpose was. We did this, and we found that it had no purpose, except, perhaps, in terms of human needs. Even this was questionable.

"We investigated further. We found that human cultures pass through phases, each culture in its own time. As the culture ages and begins to lose its objectives, conflict arises within it between those who wish to cast it off and set up a new culture-pattern, and those who wish to retain the old with as little change as possible.

"At this point, a great danger appears. The conflict within threatens to engulf the society in self-war, group against group. The vital traditions may be lost—not merely altered or reformed, but completely destroyed in this period of chaos and anarchy. We have found many such examples in the history of mankind.

"It is necessary for this hatred within the culture to be directed outward, toward an external group, so that the culture itself may survive its crisis. War is the result. War, to a logical mind, is absurd. But in terms of human needs, it plays a vital role. And it will continue to until Man has grown up enough so that no hatred lies within him."

Taylor was listening intently. "Do you think this time will come?"

"Of course. It has almost arrived now. This is the last war. Man is *almost* united into one final culture—a world culture. At this point he stands continent against continent, one half of the world against the other half. Only a single step remains, the jump to a unified culture. Man has climbed slowly upward, tending always toward unification of his culture. It will not be long—

"But it has not come yet, and so the war had to go on, to satisfy the last violent surge of hatred that Man felt. Eight years have passed since the war began. In these eight years, we have observed and noted important changes going on in the minds of men. Fatigue and disinterest, we have seen, are gradually taking the place of hatred and fear. The hatred is being exhausted gradually, over a period of time. But for the present, the hoax must go on, at least for a while longer. You are not ready to learn the truth. You would want to continue the war."

"But how did you manage it?" Moss asked. "All the photographs, the samples, the damaged equipment—"

"Come over here." The leady directed them toward a long, low building. "Work goes on constantly, whole staffs laboring to maintain a coherent and convincing picture of a global war."

* * *

They entered the building. Leadys were working everywhere, poring over tables and desks.

"Examine this project here," the A-class leady said. Two leadys were carefully photographing something, an elaborate model on a table top. "It is a good example."

The men grouped around, trying to see. It was a model of a ruined city.

Taylor studied it in silence for a long time. At last he looked up.

"It's San Francisco," he said in a low voice. "This is a model of San Francisco, destroyed. I saw this on the vidscreen, piped down to us. The bridges were hit—"

"Yes, notice the bridges." The leady traced the ruined span with his metal finger, a tiny spider-web, almost invisible. "You have no doubt seen photographs of this many times, and of the other tables in this building.

"San Francisco itself is completely intact. We restored it soon after you left, rebuilding the parts that had been damaged at the start of the war. The work of manufacturing news goes on all the time in this particular building. We are very careful to see that each part fits in with all the other parts. Much time and effort are devoted to it."

Franks touched one of the tiny model buildings, lying half in ruins. "So this is what you spend your time doing—making model cities and then blasting them."

"No, we do much more. We are caretakers, watching over the whole world. The owners have left for a time, and we must see that the cities are kept clean, that decay is prevented, that everything is kept oiled and in running condition. The gardens, the streets, the water mains, everything must be maintained as it was eight years ago, so that when the owners return, they will not be displeased. We want to be sure that they will be completely satisfied."

Franks tapped Moss on the arm.

"Come over here," he said in a low voice. "I want to talk to you."

He led Moss and Taylor out of the building, away from the leadys, outside on the hillside. The soldiers followed them. The Sun was up and the sky was turning blue. The air smelled sweet and good, the smell of growing things.

Taylor removed his helmet and took a deep breath.

"I haven't smelled that smell for a long time," he said.

"Listen," Franks said, his voice low and hard. "We must get back down at once. There's a lot to get started on. All this can be turned to our advantage."

"What do you mean?" Moss asked.

"It's a certainty that the Soviets have been tricked, too, the same as us. But *we* have found out. That gives us an edge over them."

"I see." Moss nodded. "We know, but they don't. Their Surface Council has sold out, the same as ours. It works against them the same way. But if we could—"

"With a hundred top-level men, we could take over again, restore things as they should be! It would be easy!"

* * *

Moss touched him on the arm. An A-class leady was coming from the building toward them.

"We've seen enough," Franks said, raising his voice. "All this is very serious. It must be reported below and a study made to determine our policy."

The leady said nothing.

Franks waved to the soldiers. "Let's go." He started toward the warehouse.

Most of the soldiers had removed their helmets. Some of them had taken their lead suits off, too, and were relaxing comfortably in their cotton uniforms. They stared around them, down the hillside at the trees and bushes, the vast expanse of green, the mountains and the sky.

"Look at the Sun," one of them murmured.

"It sure is bright as hell," another said.

"We're going back down," Franks said. "Fall in by twos and follow us."

Reluctantly, the soldiers regrouped. The leadys watched without emotion as the men marched slowly back toward the warehouse. Franks and Moss and Taylor led them across the ground, glancing alertly at the leadys as they walked.

They entered the warehouse. D-class leadys were loading material and weapons on surface carts. Cranes and derricks were working busily everywhere. The work was done with efficiency, but without hurry or excitement.

The men stopped, watching. Leadys operating the little carts moved past them, signaling silently to each other. Guns and parts were being hoisted by magnetic cranes and lowered gently onto waiting carts.

"Come on," Franks said.

He turned toward the lip of the Tube. A row of D-class leadys was standing in front of it, immobile and silent. Franks stopped, moving back. He looked around. An A-class leady was coming toward him.

"Tell them to get out of the way," Franks said. He touched his gun. "You had better move them."

Time passed, an endless moment, without measure. The men stood, nervous and alert, watching the row of leadys in front of them.

"As you wish," the A-class leady said.

It signaled and the D-class leadys moved into life. They stepped slowly aside.

Moss breathed a sigh of relief.

"I'm glad that's over," he said to Franks. "Look at them all. Why don't they try to stop us? They must know what we're going to do."

Franks laughed. "Stop us? You saw what happened when they tried to stop us before. They can't; they're only machines. We built them so they can't lay hands on us, and they know that."

His voice trailed off.

The men stared at the Tube entrance. Around them the leadys watched, silent and impassive, their metal faces expressionless.

For a long time the men stood without moving. At last Taylor turned away.

"Good God," he said. He was numb, without feeling of any kind.

The Tube was gone. It was sealed shut, fused over. Only a dull surface of cooling metal greeted them.

The Tube had been closed.

* * *

Franks turned, his face pale and vacant.

The A-class leady shifted. "As you can see, the Tube has been shut. We were prepared for this. As soon as all of you were on the surface, the order was given. If you had gone back when we asked you, you would now be safely down below. We had to work quickly because it was such an immense operation."

"But why?" Moss demanded angrily.

"Because it is unthinkable that you should be allowed to resume the war. With all the Tubes sealed, it will be many months before forces from below can reach the surface, let alone organize a military program. By that time the cycle will have entered its last stages. You will not be so perturbed to find your world intact.

"We had hoped that you would be undersurface when the sealing occurred. Your presence here is a nuisance. When the Soviets broke through, we were able to accomplish their sealing without—"

"The Soviets? They broke through?"

"Several months ago, they came up unexpectedly to see why the war had not been won. We were forced to act with speed. At this moment they are desperately attempting to cut new Tubes to the surface, to resume the war. We have, however, been able to seal each new one as it appears."

The leady regarded the three men calmly.

"We're cut off," Moss said, trembling. "We can't get back. What'll we do?"

"How did you manage to seal the Tube so quickly?" Franks asked the leady. "We've been up here only two hours."

"Bombs are placed just above the first stage of each Tube for such emergencies. They are heat bombs. They fuse lead and rock."

Gripping the handle of his gun, Franks turned to Moss and Taylor.

"What do you say? We can't go back, but we can do a lot of damage, the fifteen of us. We have Bender guns. How about it?"

He looked around. The soldiers had wandered away again, back toward the exit of the building. They were standing outside, looking at the valley and the sky. A few of them were carefully climbing down the slope.

"Would you care to turn over your suits and guns?" the A-class leady asked politely. "The suits are uncomfortable and you'll have no need for weapons. The Russians have given up theirs, as you can see."

Fingers tensed on triggers. Four men in Russian uniforms were coming toward them from an aircraft that they suddenly realized had landed silently some distance away.

"Let them have it!" Franks shouted.

"They are unarmed," said the leady. "We brought them here so you could begin peace talks."

"We have no authority to speak for our country," Moss said stiffly.

"We do not mean diplomatic discussions," the leady explained. "There will be no more. The working out of daily problems of existence will teach you how to get along in the same world. It will not be easy, but it will be done."

* * *

The Russians halted and they faced each other with raw hostility.

"I am Colonel Borodoy and I regret giving up our guns," the senior Russian said. "You could have been the first Americans to be killed in almost eight years."

"Or the first Americans to kill," Franks corrected.

"No one would know of it except yourselves," the leady pointed out. "It would be useless heroism. Your real concern should be surviving on the surface. We have no food for you, you know."

Taylor put his gun in its holster. "They've done a neat job of neutralizing us, damn them. I propose we move into a city, start raising crops with the help of some leadys, and generally make ourselves comfortable." Drawing his lips tight over his teeth, he glared at the A-class leady. "Until our families can come up from undersurface, it's going to be pretty lonesome, but we'll have to manage."

"If I may make a suggestion," said another Russian uneasily. "We tried living in a city. It is too empty. It is also too hard to maintain for so few people. We finally settled in the most modern village we could find."

"Here in this country," a third Russian blurted. "We have much to learn from you."

The Americans abruptly found themselves laughing.

"You probably have a thing or two to teach us yourselves," said Taylor generously, "though I can't imagine what."

The Russian colonel grinned. "Would you join us in our village? It would make our work easier and give us company."

"Your village?" snapped Franks. "It's American, isn't it? It's ours!"

The leady stepped between them. "When our plans are completed, the term will be interchangeable. 'Ours' will eventually mean mankind's." It pointed at the aircraft, which was warming up. "The ship is waiting. Will you join each other in making a new home?"

The Russians waited while the Americans made up their minds.

"I see what the leadys mean about diplomacy becoming outmoded," Franks said at last. "People who work together don't need diplomats. They solve their problems on the operational level instead of at a conference table."

The leady led them toward the ship. "It is the goal of history, unifying the world. From family to tribe to city-state to nation to hemisphere, the direction has been toward unification. Now the hemispheres will be joined and—"

Taylor stopped listening and glanced back at the location of the Tube. Mary was undersurface there. He hated to leave her, even though he couldn't see her again until the Tube was unsealed. But then he shrugged and followed the others.

If this tiny amalgam of former enemies was a good example, it wouldn't be too long before he and Mary and the rest of humanity would be living on the surface like rational human beings instead of blindly hating moles.

"It has taken thousands of generations to achieve," the A-class leady concluded. "Hundreds of centuries of bloodshed and destruction. But each war was a step toward uniting mankind. And now the end is in sight: a world without war. But even that is only the beginning of a new stage of history."

"The conquest of space," breathed Colonel Borodoy.

"The meaning of life," Moss added.

"Eliminating hunger and poverty," said Taylor.

The leady opened the door of the ship. "All that and more. How much more? We cannot foresee it any more than the first men who formed a tribe could foresee this day. But it will be unimaginably great."

The door closed and the ship took off toward their new home.

The Gun

Nothing moved or stirred. Everything was silent, dead. Only the gun showed signs of life . . . and the trespassers had wrecked that for all time. The return journey to pick up the treasure would be a cinch . . . they smiled.

The Captain peered into the eyepiece of the telescope. He adjusted the focus quickly.

"It was an atomic fission we saw, all right," he said presently. He sighed and pushed the eyepiece away. "Any of you who wants to look may do so. But it's not a pretty sight."

"Let me look," Tance the archeologist said. He bent down to look, squinting. "Good Lord!" He leaped violently back, knocking against Dorle, the Chief Navigator.

"Why did we come all this way, then?" Dorle asked, looking around at the other men. "There's no point even in landing. Let's go back at once."

"Perhaps he's right," the biologist murmured. "But I'd like to look for myself, if I may." He pushed past Tance and peered into the sight.

He saw a vast expanse, an endless surface of gray, stretching to the edge of the planet. At first he thought it was water but after a moment he realized that it was slag, pitted, fused slag, broken only by hills of rock jutting up at intervals. Nothing moved or stirred. Everything was silent, dead.

"I see," Fomar said, backing away from the eyepiece. "Well, I won't find any legumes there." He tried to smile, but his lips stayed unmoved. He stepped away and stood by himself, staring past the others.

"I wonder what the atmospheric sample will show," Tance said.

"I think I can guess," the Captain answered. "Most of the atmosphere is poisoned. But didn't we expect all this? I don't see why we're so surprised. A fission visible as far away as our system must be a terrible thing."

He strode off down the corridor, dignified and expressionless. They watched him disappear into the control room.

As the Captain closed the door the young woman turned. "What did the telescope show? Good or bad?"

"Bad. No life could possibly exist. Atmosphere poisoned, water vaporized, all the land fused."

"Could they have gone underground?"

The Captain slid back the port window so that the surface of the planet under them was visible. The two of them stared down, silent and disturbed. Mile after mile of unbroken ruin stretched out, blackened slag, pitted and scarred, and occasional heaps of rock.

Suddenly Nasha jumped. "Look! Over there, at the edge. Do you see it?"

They stared. Something rose up, not rock, not an accidental formation. It was round, a circle of dots, white pellets on the dead skin of the planet. A city? Buildings of some kind?

"Please turn the ship," Nasha said excitedly. She pushed her dark hair from her face. "Turn the ship and let's see what it is!"

The ship turned, changing its course. As they came over the white dots the Captain lowered the ship, dropping it down as much as he dared. "Piers," he said. "Piers of some sort of stone. Perhaps poured artificial stone. The remains of a city."

"Oh, dear," Nasha murmured. "How awful." She watched the ruins disappear behind them. In a half-circle the white squares jutted from the slag, chipped and cracked, like broken teeth.

"There's nothing alive," the Captain said at last. "I think we'll go right back; I know most of the crew want to. Get the Government Receiving Station on the sender and tell them what we found, and that we—"

* * *

He staggered.

The first atomic shell had struck the ship, spinning it around. The Captain fell to the floor, crashing into the control table. Papers and instruments rained down on him. As he started to his feet the second shell struck. The ceiling cracked open, struts and girders twisted and bent. The ship shuddered, falling suddenly down, then righting itself as automatic controls took over.

The Captain lay on the floor by the smashed control board. In the corner Nasha struggled to free herself from the debris.

Outside the men were already sealing the gaping leaks in the side of the ship, through which the precious air was rushing, dissipating into the void beyond. "Help me!" Dorle was shouting. "Fire over here, wiring ignited." Two men came running. Tance watched helplessly, his eyeglasses broken and bent.

"So there is life here, after all," he said, half to himself. "But how could—"

"Give us a hand," Fomar said, hurrying past. "Give us a hand, we've got to land the ship!"

It was night. A few stars glinted above them, winking through the drifting silt that blew across the surface of the planet.

Dorle peered out, frowning. "What a place to be stuck in." He resumed his work, hammering the bent metal hull of the ship back into place. He was wearing a pressure suit; there were still many small leaks, and radioactive particles from the atmosphere had already found their way into the ship.

Nasha and Fomar were sitting at the table in the control room, pale and solemn, studying the inventory lists.

"Low on carbohydrates," Fomar said. "We can break down the stored fats if we want to, but—"

"I wonder if we could find anything outside." Nasha went to the window. "How uninviting it looks." She paced back and forth, very slender and small, her face dark with fatigue. "What do you suppose an exploring party would find?"

Fomar shrugged. "Not much. Maybe a few weeds growing in cracks here and there. Nothing we could use. Anything that would adapt to this environment would be toxic, lethal."

Nasha paused, rubbing her cheek. There was a deep scratch there, still red and swollen. "Then how do you explain—*it?* According to your theory the inhabitants must have died in their skins, fried like yams. But who fired on us? Somebody detected us, made a decision, aimed a gun."

"And gauged distance," the Captain said feebly from the cot in the corner. He turned toward them. "That's the part that worries me. The first shell put us out of commission, the second almost destroyed us. They were well aimed, perfectly aimed. We're not such an easy target."

"True." Fomar nodded. "Well, perhaps we'll know the answer before we leave here. What a strange situation! All our reasoning tells us that no life could exist; the whole planet burned dry, the atmosphere itself gone, completely poisoned."

"The gun that fired the projectiles survived," Nasha said. "Why not people?"

"It's not the same. Metal doesn't need air to breathe. Metal doesn't get leukemia from radioactive particles. Metal doesn't need food and water."

There was silence.

"A paradox," Nasha said. "Anyhow, in the morning I think we should send out a search party. And meanwhile we should keep on trying to get the ship in condition for the trip back."

"It'll be days before we can take off," Fomar said. "We should keep every man working here. We can't afford to send out a party."

Nasha smiled a little. "We'll send you in the first party. Maybe you can discover—what was it you were so interested in?"

"Legumes. Edible legumes."

"Maybe you can find some of them. Only—"

"Only what?"

"Only watch out. They fired on us once without even knowing who we were or what we came for. Do you suppose that they fought with each other? Perhaps they couldn't imagine anyone being friendly, under any circumstances. What a strange evolutionary trait, inter-species warfare. Fighting within the race!"

"We'll know in the morning," Fomar said. "Let's get some sleep."

* * *

The sun came up chill and austere. The three people, two men and a woman, stepped through the port, dropping down on the hard ground below.

"What a day," Dorle said grumpily. "I said how glad I'd be to walk on firm ground again, but—"

"Come on," Nasha said. "Up beside me. I want to say something to you. Will you excuse us, Tance?"

Tance nodded gloomily. Dorle caught up with Nasha. They walked together, their metal shoes crunching the ground underfoot. Nasha glanced at him.

"Listen. The Captain is dying. No one knows except the two of us. By the end of the day-period of this planet he'll be dead. The shock did something to his heart. He was almost sixty, you know."

Dorle nodded. "That's bad. I have a great deal of respect for him. You will be captain in his place, of course. Since you're vice-captain now—"

"No. I prefer to see someone else lead, perhaps you or Fomar. I've been thinking over the situation and it seems to me that I should declare myself mated to one of you, whichever of you wants to be captain. Then I could devolve the responsibility."

"Well, I don't want to be captain. Let Fomar do it."

Nasha studied him, tall and blond, striding along beside her in his pressure suit. "I'm rather partial to you," she said. "We might try it for a time, at least. But do as you like. Look, we're coming to something."

They stopped walking, letting Tance catch up. In front of them was some sort of a ruined building. Dorle stared around thoughtfully.

"Do you see? This whole place is a natural bowl, a huge valley. See how the rock formations rise up on all sides, protecting the floor. Maybe some of the great blast was deflected here."

They wandered around the ruins, picking up rocks and fragments. "I think this was a farm," Tance said, examining a piece of wood. "This was part of a tower windmill."

"Really?" Nasha took the stick and turned it over. "Interesting. But let's go; we don't have much time."

"Look," Dorle said suddenly. "Off there, a long way off. Isn't that something?" He pointed.

Nasha sucked in her breath. "The white stones."

"What?"

Nasha looked up at Dorle. "The white stones, the great broken teeth. We saw them, the Captain and I, from the control room." She touched Dorle's arm gently. "That's where they fired from. I didn't think we had landed so close."

"What is it?" Tance said, coming up to them. "I'm almost blind without my glasses. What do you see?"

"The city. Where they fired from."

"Oh." All three of them stood together. "Well, let's go," Tance said. "There's no telling what we'll find there." Dorle frowned at him.

"Wait. We don't know what we would be getting into. They must have patrols. They probably have seen us already, for that matter."

"They probably have seen the ship itself," Tance said. "They probably know right now where they can find it, where they can blow it up. So what difference does it make whether we go closer or not?"

"That's true," Nasha said. "If they really want to get us we haven't a chance. We have no armaments at all; you know that."

"I have a hand weapon." Dorle nodded. "Well, let's go on, then. I suppose you're right, Tance."

"But let's stay together," Tance said nervously. "Nasha, you're going too fast."

Nasha looked back. She laughed. "If we expect to get there by nightfall we must go fast."

* * *

They reached the outskirts of the city at about the middle of the afternoon. The sun, cold and yellow, hung above them in the colorless sky. Dorle stopped at the top of a ridge overlooking the city.

"Well, there it is. What's left of it."

There was not much left. The huge concrete piers which they had noticed were not piers at all, but the ruined foundations of buildings. They had been baked by the searing heat, baked and charred almost to the ground. Nothing else remained, only this irregular circle of white squares, perhaps four miles in diameter.

Dorle spat in disgust. "More wasted time. A dead skeleton of a city, that's all."

"But it was from here that the firing came," Tance murmured. "Don't forget that."

"And by someone with a good eye and a great deal of experience," Nasha added. "Let's go."

They walked into the city between the ruined buildings. No one spoke. They walked in silence, listening to the echo of their footsteps.

"It's macabre," Dorle muttered. "I've seen ruined cities before but they died of old age, old age and fatigue. This was killed, seared to death. This city didn't die—it was murdered."

"I wonder what the city was called," Nasha said. She turned aside, going up the remains of a stairway from one of the foundations. "Do you think we might find a signpost? Some kind of plaque?"

She peered into the ruins.

"There's nothing there," Dorle said impatiently. "Come on."

"Wait." Nasha bent down, touching a concrete stone. "There's something inscribed on this."

"What is it?" Tance hurried up. He squatted in the dust, running his gloved fingers over the surface of the stone. "Letters, all right." He took a writing stick from the pocket of his pressure suit and copied the inscription on a bit of paper. Dorle glanced over his shoulder. The inscription was:

FRANKLIN APARTMENTS

"That's this city," Nasha said softly. "That was its name."

Tance put the paper in his pocket and they went on. After a time Dorle said, "Nasha, you know, I think we're being watched. But don't look around."

The woman stiffened. "Oh? Why do you say that? Did you see something?"

"No. I can feel it, though. Don't you?"

Nasha smiled a little. "I feel nothing, but perhaps I'm more used to being stared at." She turned her head slightly. "Oh!"

Dorle reached for his hand weapon. "What is it? What do you see?" Tance had stopped dead in his tracks, his mouth half open.

"The gun," Nasha said. "It's the gun."

"Look at the size of it. The size of the thing." Dorle unfastened his hand weapon slowly. "That's it, all right."

The gun was huge. Stark and immense it pointed up at the sky, a mass of steel and glass, set in a huge slab of concrete. Even as they watched the gun moved on its swivel base, whirring underneath. A slim vane turned with the wind, a network of rods atop a high pole.

"It's alive," Nasha whispered. "It's listening to us, watching us."

The gun moved again, this time clockwise. It was mounted so that it could make a full circle. The barrel lowered a trifle, then resumed its original position.

"But who fires it?" Tance said.

Dorle laughed. "No one. No one fires it."

They stared at him. "What do you mean?"

"It fires itself."

They couldn't believe him. Nasha came close to him, frowning, looking up at him. "I don't understand. What do you mean, it fires itself?"

"Watch, I'll show you. Don't move." Dorle picked up a rock from the ground. He hesitated a moment and then tossed the rock high in the air. The rock passed in front of the gun. Instantly the great barrel moved, the vanes contracted.

* * *

The rock fell to the ground. The gun paused, then resumed its calm swivel, its slow circling.

"You see," Dorle said, "it noticed the rock, as soon as I threw it up in the air. It's alert to anything that flies or moves above the ground level. Probably it detected us as soon as we entered the gravitational field of the planet. It probably had a bead on us from the start. We don't have a chance. It knows all about the ship. It's just waiting for us to take off again."

"I understand about the rock," Nasha said, nodding. "The gun noticed it, but not us, since we're on the ground, not above. It's only designed to combat objects in the sky. The ship is safe until it takes off again, then the end will come."

"But what's this gun for?" Tance put in. "There's no one alive here. Everyone is dead."

"It's a machine," Dorle said. "A machine that was made to do a job. And it's doing the job. How it survived the blast I don't know. On it goes, waiting for the enemy. Probably they came by air in some sort of projectiles."

"The enemy," Nasha said. "Their own race. It is hard to believe that they really bombed themselves, fired at themselves."

"Well, it's over with. Except right here, where we're standing. This one gun, still alert, ready to kill. It'll go on until it wears out."

"And by that time we'll be dead," Nasha said bitterly.

"There must have been hundreds of guns like this," Dorle murmured. "They must have been used to the sight, guns, weapons, uniforms. Probably they accepted it as a natural thing, part of their lives, like eating and sleeping. An institution, like the church and the state. Men trained to fight, to lead armies, a regular profession. Honored, respected."

Tance was walking slowly toward the gun, peering nearsightedly up at it. "Quite complex, isn't it? All those vanes and tubes. I suppose this is some sort of a telescopic sight." His gloved hand touched the end of a long tube.

Instantly the gun shifted, the barrel retracting. It swung—

"Don't move!" Dorle cried. The barrel swung past them as they stood, rigid and still. For one terrible moment it hesitated over their heads, clicking and whirring, settling into position. Then the sounds died out and the gun became silent.

Tance smiled foolishly inside his helmet. "I must have put my finger over the lens. I'll be more careful." He made his way up onto the circular slab, stepping gingerly behind the body of the gun. He disappeared from view.

"Where did he go?" Nasha said irritably. "He'll get us all killed."

"Tance, come back!" Dorle shouted. "What's the matter with you?"

"In a minute." There was a long silence. At last the archeologist appeared. "I think I've found something. Come up and I'll show you."

"What is it?"

"Dorle, you said the gun was here to keep the enemy off. I think I know why they wanted to keep the enemy off."

They were puzzled.

"I think I've found what the gun is supposed to guard. Come and give me a hand."

"All right," Dorle said abruptly. "Let's go." He seized Nasha's hand. "Come on. Let's see what he's found. I thought something like this might happen when I saw that the gun was—"

"Like what?" Nasha pulled her hand away. "What are you talking about? You act as if you knew what he's found."

"I do." Dorle smiled down at her. "Do you remember the legend that all races have, the myth of the buried treasure, and the dragon, the serpent that watches it, guards it, keeping everyone away?"

She nodded. "Well?"

Dorle pointed up at the gun.

"That," he said, "is the dragon. Come on."

* * *

Between the three of them they managed to pull up the steel cover and lay it to one side. Dorle was wet with perspiration when they finished.

"It isn't worth it," he grunted. He stared into the dark yawning hole. "Or is it?"

Nasha clicked on her hand lamp, shining the beam down the stairs. The steps were thick with dust and rubble. At the bottom was a steel door.

"Come on," Tance said excitedly. He started down the stairs. They watched him reach the door and pull hopefully on it without success. "Give a hand!"

"All right." They came gingerly after him. Dorle examined the door. It was bolted shut, locked. There was an inscription on the door but he could not read it.

"Now what?" Nasha said.

Dorle took out his hand weapon. "Stand back. I can't think of any other way." He pressed the switch. The bottom of the door glowed red. Presently it began to crumble. Dorle clicked the weapon off. "I think we can get through. Let's try."

The door came apart easily. In a few minutes they had carried it away in pieces and stacked the pieces on the first step. Then they went on, flashing the light ahead of them.

They were in a vault. Dust lay everywhere, on everything, inches thick. Wood crates lined the walls, huge boxes and crates, packages and containers. Tance looked around curiously, his eyes bright.

"What exactly are all these?" he murmured. "Something valuable, I would think." He picked up a round drum and opened it. A spool fell to the floor, unwinding a black ribbon. He examined it, holding it up to the light.

"Look at this!"

They came around him. "Pictures," Nasha said. "Tiny pictures."

"Records of some kind." Tance closed the spool up in the drum again. "Look, hundreds of drums." He flashed the light around. "And those crates. Let's open one."

Dorle was already prying at the wood. The wood had turned brittle and dry. He managed to pull a section away.

It was a picture. A boy in a blue garment, smiling pleasantly, staring ahead, young and handsome. He seemed almost alive, ready to move toward them in the light of the hand lamp. It was one of them, one of the ruined race, the race that had perished.

For a long time they stared at the picture. At last Dorle replaced the board.

"All these other crates," Nasha said. "More pictures. And these drums. What are in the boxes?"

"This is their treasure," Tance said, almost to himself. "Here are their pictures, their records. Probably all their literature is here, their stories, their myths, their ideas about the universe."

"And their history," Nasha said. "We'll be able to trace their development and find out what it was that made them become what they were."

Dorle was wandering around the vault. "Odd," he murmured. "Even at the end, even after they had begun to fight they still knew, someplace down inside them, that their real treasure was this, their books and pictures, their myths. Even after their big cities and buildings and industries were destroyed they probably hoped to come back and find this. After everything else was gone."

"When we get back home we can agitate for a mission to come here," Tance said. "All this can be loaded up and taken back. We'll be leaving about—"

He stopped.

"Yes," Dorle said dryly. "We'll be leaving about three day-periods from now. We'll fix the ship, then take off. Soon we'll be home, that is, if nothing happens. Like being shot down by that—"

"Oh, stop it!" Nasha said impatiently. "Leave him alone. He's right: all this must be taken back home, sooner or later. We'll have to solve the problem of the gun. We have no choice."

Dorle nodded. "What's your solution, then? As soon as we leave the ground we'll be shot down." His face twisted bitterly. "They've guarded their treasure too well. Instead of being preserved it will lie here until it rots. It serves them right."

"How?"

"Don't you see? This was the only way they knew, building a gun and setting it up to shoot anything that came along. They were so certain that everything was hostile, the enemy, coming to take their possessions away from them. Well, they can keep them."

Nasha was deep in thought, her mind far away. Suddenly she gasped. "Dorle," she said. "What's the matter with us? We have no problem. The gun is no menace at all."

The two men stared at her.

"No menace?" Dorle said. "It's already shot us down once. And as soon as we take off again—"

"Don't you see?" Nasha began to laugh. "The poor foolish gun, it's completely harmless. Even I could deal with it alone."

"You?"

Her eyes were flashing. "With a crowbar. With a hammer or a stick of wood. Let's go back to the ship and load up. Of course we're at its mercy in the air: that's the way it was made. It can fire into the sky, shoot down anything that flies. But that's all! Against something on the ground it has no defenses. Isn't that right?"

Dorle nodded slowly. "The soft underbelly of the dragon. In the legend, the dragon's armor doesn't cover its stomach." He began to laugh. "That's right. That's perfectly right."

"Let's go, then," Nasha said. "Let's get back to the ship. We have work to do here."

* * *

It was early the next morning when they reached the ship. During the night the Captain had died, and the crew had ignited his body, according to custom. They had stood solemnly around it until the last ember died. As they were going back to their work the woman and the two men appeared, dirty and tired, still excited.

And presently, from the ship, a line of people came, each carrying something in his hands. The line marched across the gray slag, the eternal expanse of fused metal. When they reached the weapon they all fell on the gun at once, with crowbars, hammers, anything that was heavy and hard.

The telescopic sights shattered into bits. The wiring was pulled out, torn to shreds. The delicate gears were smashed, dented.

Finally the warheads themselves were carried off and the firing pins removed.

The gun was smashed, the great weapon destroyed. The people went down into the vault and examined the treasure. With its metal-armored guardian dead there was no danger any longer. They studied the pictures, the films, the crates of books, the jeweled crowns, the cups, the statues.

At last, as the sun was dipping into the gray mists that drifted across the planet they came back up the stairs again. For a moment they stood around the wrecked gun looking at the unmoving outline of it.

Then they started back to the ship. There was still much work to be done. The ship had been badly hurt, much had been damaged and lost. The important thing was to repair it as quickly as possible, to get it into the air.

With all of them working together it took just five more days to make it spaceworthy.

* * *

Nasha stood in the control room, watching the planet fall away behind them. She folded her arms, sitting down on the edge of the table.

"What are you thinking?" Dorle said.

"I? Nothing."

"Are you sure?"

"I was thinking that there must have been a time when this planet was quite different, when there was life on it."

"I suppose there was. It's unfortunate that no ships from our system came this far, but then we had no reason to suspect intelligent life until we saw the fission glow in the sky."

"And then it was too late."

"Not quite too late. After all, their possessions, their music, books, their pictures, all of that will survive. We'll take them home and study them, and they'll change us. We won't be the same afterwards. Their sculpturing, especially. Did you see the one of the great winged creature, without a head or arms? Broken off, I suppose. But those wings—It looked very old. It will change us a great deal."

"When we come back we won't find the gun waiting for us," Nasha said. "Next time it won't be there to shoot us down. We can land and take the treasure, as you call it." She smiled up at Dorle. "You'll lead us back there, as a good captain should."

"Captain?" Dorle grinned. "Then you've decided."

Nasha shrugged. "Fomar argues with me too much. I think, all in all, I really prefer you."

"Then let's go," Dorle said. "Let's go back home."

The ship roared up, flying over the ruins of the city. It turned in a huge arc and then shot off beyond the horizon, heading into outer space.

* * *

Down below, in the center of the ruined city, a single half-broken detector vane moved slightly, catching the roar of the ship. The base of the great gun throbbed painfully, straining to turn. After a moment a red warning light flashed on down inside its destroyed works.

And a long way off, a hundred miles from the city, another warning light flashed on, far underground. Automatic relays flew into action. Gears turned, belts whined. On the ground above a section of metal slag slipped back. A ramp appeared.

A moment later a small cart rushed to the surface.

The cart turned toward the city. A second cart appeared behind it. It was loaded with wiring cables. Behind it a third cart came, loaded with telescopic tube sights. And behind came more carts, some with relays, some with firing controls, some with tools and parts, screws and bolts, pins and nuts. The final one contained atomic warheads.

The carts lined up behind the first one, the lead cart. The lead cart started off, across the frozen ground, bumping calmly along, followed by the others. Moving toward the city.

To the damaged gun.

The Skull

Conger agreed to kill a stranger he had never seen. But he would make no mistakes because he had the stranger's skull under his arm.

"What is this opportunity?" Conger asked. "Go on. I'm interested."

The room was silent; all faces were fixed on Conger—still in the drab prison uniform. The Speaker leaned forward slowly.

"Before you went to prison your trading business was paying well—all illegal—all very profitable. Now you have nothing, except the prospect of another six years in a cell."

Conger scowled.

"There is a certain situation, very important to this Council, that requires your peculiar abilities. Also, it is a situation you might find interesting. You were a hunter, were you not? You've done a great deal of trapping, hiding in the bushes, waiting at night for the game? I imagine hunting must be a source of satisfaction to you, the chase, the stalking—"

Conger sighed. His lips twisted. "All right," he said. "Leave that out. Get to the point. Who do you want me to kill?"

The Speaker smiled. "All in proper sequence," he said softly.

* * *

The car slid to a stop. It was night; there was no light anywhere along the street. Conger looked out. "Where are we? What is this place?"

The hand of the guard pressed into his arm. "Come. Through that door."

Conger stepped down, onto the damp sidewalk. The guard came swiftly after him, and then the Speaker. Conger took a deep breath of the cold air. He studied the dim outline of the building rising up before them.

"I know this place. I've seen it before." He squinted, his eyes growing accustomed to the dark. Suddenly he became alert. "This is—"

"Yes. The First Church." The Speaker walked toward the steps. "We're expected."

"Expected? *Here?*"

"Yes." The Speaker mounted the stairs. "You know we're not allowed in their Churches, especially with guns!" He stopped. Two armed soldiers loomed up ahead, one on each side.

"All right?" The Speaker looked up at them. They nodded. The door of the Church was open. Conger could see other soldiers inside, standing about, young soldiers with large eyes, gazing at the ikons and holy images.

"I see," he said.

"It was necessary," the Speaker said. "As you know, we have been singularly unfortunate in the past in our relations with the First Church."

"This won't help."

"But it's worth it. You will see."

* * *

They passed through the hall and into the main chamber where the altar piece was, and the kneeling places. The Speaker scarcely glanced at the altar as they passed by. He pushed open a small side door and beckoned Conger through.

"In here. We have to hurry. The faithful will be flocking in soon."

Conger entered, blinking. They were in a small chamber, low-ceilinged, with dark panels of old wood. There was a smell of ashes and smoldering spices in the room. He sniffed. "What's that? The smell."

"Cups on the wall. I don't know." The Speaker crossed impatiently to the far side. "According to our information, it is hidden here by this—"

Conger looked around the room. He saw books and papers, holy signs and images. A strange low shiver went through him.

"Does my job involve anyone of the Church? If it does—"

The Speaker turned, astonished. "Can it be that you believe in the Founder? Is it possible, a hunter, a killer—"

"No. Of course not. All their business about resignation to death, non-violence—"

"What is it, then?"

Conger shrugged. "I've been taught not to mix with such as these. They have strange abilities. And you can't reason with them."

The Speaker studied Conger thoughtfully. "You have the wrong idea. It is no one here that we have in mind. We've found that killing them only tends to increase their numbers."

"Then why come here? Let's leave."

"No. We came for something important. Something you will need to identify your man. Without it you won't be able to find him." A trace of a smile crossed the Speaker's face. "We don't want you to kill the wrong person. It's too important."

"I don't make mistakes." Conger's chest rose. "Listen, Speaker—"

"This is an unusual situation," the Speaker said. "You see, the person you are after—the person that we are sending you to find—is known only by certain objects here. They are the only traces, the only means of identification. Without them—"

"What are they?"

He came toward the Speaker. The Speaker moved to one side. "Look," he said. He drew a sliding wall away, showing a dark square hole. "In there."

Conger squatted down, staring in. He frowned. "A skull! A skeleton!"

"The man you are after has been dead for two centuries," the Speaker said. "This is all that remains of him. And this is all you have with which to find him."

For a long time Conger said nothing. He stared down at the bones, dimly visible in the recess of the wall. How could a man dead centuries be killed? How could he be stalked, brought down?

Conger was a hunter, a man who had lived as he pleased, where he pleased. He had kept himself alive by trading, bringing furs and pelts in from the Provinces on his own ship, riding at high speed, slipping through the customs line around Earth.

He had hunted in the great mountains of the moon. He had stalked through empty Martian cities. He had explored—

The Speaker said, "Soldier, take these objects and have them carried to the car. Don't lose any part of them."

The soldier went into the cupboard, reaching gingerly, squatting on his heels.

"It is my hope," the Speaker continued softly, to Conger, "that you will demonstrate your loyalty to us, now. There are always ways for citizens to restore themselves, to show their devotion to their society. For you I think this would be a very good chance. I seriously doubt that a better one will come. And for your efforts there will be quite a restitution, of course."

The two men looked at each other; Conger, thin, unkempt, the Speaker immaculate in his uniform.

"I understand you," Conger said. "I mean, I understand this part, about the chance. But how can a man who has been dead two centuries be—"

"I'll explain later," the Speaker said. "Right now we have to hurry!" The soldier had gone out with the bones, wrapped in a blanket held carefully in his arms. The Speaker walked to the door. "Come. They've already discovered that we've broken in here, and they'll be coming at any moment."

They hurried down the damp steps to the waiting car. A second later the driver lifted the car up into the air, above the house-tops.

* * *

The Speaker settled back in the seat.

"The First Church has an interesting past," he said. "I suppose you are familiar with it, but I'd like to speak of a few points that are of relevancy to us.

"It was in the twentieth century that the Movement began—during one of the periodic wars. The Movement developed rapidly, feeding on the general sense of futility, the realization that each war was breeding greater war, with no end in sight. The Movement posed a simple answer to the problem: Without military preparations—weapons—there could be no war. And without machinery and complex scientific technocracy there could be no weapons.

"The Movement preached that you couldn't stop war by planning for it. They preached that man was losing to his machinery and science, that it was getting away from him, pushing him into greater and greater wars. Down with society, they shouted. Down with factories and science! A few more wars and there wouldn't be much left of the world.

"The Founder was an obscure person from a small town in the American Middle West. We don't even know his name. All we know is that one day he appeared, preaching a doctrine of non-violence, non-resistance; no fighting, no paying taxes for guns, no research except for medicine. Live out your life quietly, tending your garden, staying out of public affairs; mind your own business. Be obscure, unknown, poor. Give away most of your possessions, leave the city. At least that was what developed from what he told the people."

The car dropped down and landed on a roof.

"The Founder preached this doctrine, or the germ of it; there's no telling how much the faithful have added themselves. The local authorities picked him up at once, of course. Apparently they were convinced that he meant it; he was never released. He was put to death, and his body buried secretly. It seemed that the cult was finished."

The Speaker smiled. "Unfortunately, some of his disciples reported seeing him after the date of his death. The rumor spread; he had conquered death, he was divine. It took hold, grew. And here we are today, with a First Church, obstructing all social progress, destroying society, sowing the seeds of anarchy—"

"But the wars," Conger said. "About them?"

"The wars? Well, there were no more wars. It must be acknowledged that the elimination of war was the direct result of non-violence practiced on a general scale. But we can take a more objective view of war today. What was so terrible about it? War had a profound selective value, perfectly in accord with the teachings of Darwin and Mendel and others. Without war the mass of useless, incompetent mankind, without training or intelligence, is permitted to grow and expand unchecked. War acted to reduce their numbers; like storms and earthquakes and droughts, it was nature's way of eliminating the unfit.

"Without war the lower elements of mankind have increased all out of proportion. They threaten the educated few, those with scientific knowledge and training, the ones equipped to direct society. They have no regard for science or a scientific society, based on reason. And this Movement seeks to aid and abet them. Only when scientists are in full control can the—"

* * *

He looked at his watch and then kicked the car door open. "I'll tell you the rest as we walk."

They crossed the dark roof. "Doubtless you now know whom those bones belonged to, who it is that we are after. He has been dead just two centuries, now, this ignorant man from the Middle West, this Founder. The tragedy is that the authorities of the time acted too slowly. They allowed him to speak, to get his message across. He was allowed to preach, to start his cult. And once such a thing is under way, there's no stopping it.

"But what if he had died before he preached? What if none of his doctrines had ever been spoken? It took only a moment for him to utter them, that we know. They say he spoke just once, just one time. *Then* the authorities came, taking him away. He offered no resistance; the incident was small."

The Speaker turned to Conger.

"Small, but we're reaping the consequences of it today."

They went inside the building. Inside, the soldiers had already laid out the skeleton on a table. The soldiers stood around it, their young faces intense.

Conger went over to the table, pushing past them. He bent down, staring at the bones. "So these are his remains," he murmured. "The Founder. The Church has hidden them for two centuries."

"Quite so," the Speaker said. "But now we have them. Come along down the hall."

They went across the room to a door. The Speaker pushed it open. Technicians looked up. Conger saw machinery, whirring and turning; benches and retorts. In the center of the room was a gleaming crystal cage.

The Speaker handed a Slem-gun to Conger. "The important thing to remember is that the skull must be saved and brought back—for comparison and proof. Aim low—at the chest."

Conger weighed the gun in his hands. "It feels good," he said. "I know this gun—that is, I've seen them before, but I never used one."

The Speaker nodded. "You will be instructed on the use of the gun and the operation of the cage. You will be given all data we have on the time and location. The exact spot was a place called Hudson's field. About 1960 in a small community outside Denver, Colorado. And don't forget— the only means of identification you will have will be the skull. There are visible characteristics of the front teeth, especially the left incisor—"

Conger listened absently. He was watching two men in white carefully wrapping the skull in a plastic bag. They tied it and carried it into the crystal cage. "And if I should make a mistake?"

"Pick the wrong man? Then find the right one. Don't come back until you succeed in reaching this Founder. And you can't wait for him to start speaking; that's what we must avoid! You must act in advance. Take chances; shoot as soon as you think you've found him. He'll be someone unusual, probably a stranger in the area. Apparently he wasn't known."

Conger listened dimly.

"Do you think you have it all now?" the Speaker asked.

"Yes. I think so." Conger entered the crystal cage and sat down, placing his hands on the wheel.

"Good luck," the Speaker said.

"We'll be awaiting the outcome. There's some philosophical doubt as to whether one can alter the past. This should answer the question once and for all."

Conger fingered the controls of the cage.

"By the way," the Speaker said. "Don't try to use this cage for purposes not anticipated in your job. We have a constant trace on it. If we want it back, we can get it back. Good luck."

Conger said nothing. The cage was sealed. He raised his finger and touched the wheel control. He turned the wheel carefully.

He was still staring at the plastic bag when the room outside vanished.

For a long time there was nothing at all. Nothing beyond the crystal mesh of the cage. Thoughts rushed through Conger's mind, helter-skelter. How would he know the man? How could he be certain, in advance? What had he looked like? What was his name? How had he acted, before he spoke? Would he be an ordinary person, or some strange outlandish crank?

Conger picked up the Slem-gun and held it against his cheek. The metal of the gun was cool and smooth. He practiced moving the sight. It was a beautiful gun, the kind of gun he could fall in love with. If he had owned such a gun in the Martian desert—on the long nights when he had lain, cramped and numbed with cold, waiting for things that moved through the darkness—

He put the gun down and adjusted the meter readings of the cage. The spiraling mist was beginning to condense and settle. All at once forms wavered and fluttered around him.

Colors, sounds, movements filtered through the crystal wire. He clamped the controls off and stood up.

* * *

He was on a ridge overlooking a small town. It was high noon. The air was crisp and bright. A few automobiles moved along a road. Off in the distance were some level fields. Conger went to the door and stepped outside. He sniffed the air. Then he went back into the cage.

He stood before the mirror over the shelf, examining his features. He had trimmed his beard—they had not got him to cut it off—and his hair was neat. He was dressed in the clothing of the middle-twentieth century, the odd collar and coat, the shoes of animal hide. In his pocket was money of the times. That was important. Nothing more was needed.

Nothing, except his ability, his special cunning. But he had never used it in such a way before.

He walked down the road toward the town.

The first things he noticed were the newspapers on the stands. April 5, 1961. He was not too far off. He looked around him. There was a filling station, a garage, some taverns, and a ten-cent store. Down the street was a grocery store and some public buildings.

A few minutes later he mounted the stairs of the little public library and passed through the doors into the warm interior.

The librarian looked up, smiling.

"Good afternoon," she said.

He smiled, not speaking because his words would not be correct; accented and strange, probably. He went over to a table and sat down by a heap of magazines. For a moment he glanced through them. Then he was on his feet again. He crossed the room to a wide rack against the wall. His heart began to beat heavily.

Newspapers—weeks on end. He took a roll of them over to the table and began to scan them quickly. The print was odd, the letters strange. Some of the words were unfamiliar.

He set the papers aside and searched farther. At last he found what he wanted. He carried the *Cherrywood Gazette* to the table and opened it to the first page. He found what he wanted:

PRISONER HANGS SELF

An unidentified man, held by the county sheriff's office for suspicion of criminal syndicalism, was found dead this morning, by—

He finished the item. It was vague, uninforming. He needed more. He carried the *Gazette* back to the racks and then, after a moment's hesitation, approached the librarian.

"More?" he asked. "More papers. Old ones?"

She frowned. "How old? Which papers?"

"Months old. And—before."

"Of the *Gazette?* This is all we have. What did you want? What are you looking for? Maybe I can help you."

He was silent.

"You might find older issues at the *Gazette* office," the woman said, taking off her glasses. "Why don't you try there? But if you'd tell me, maybe I could help you—"

He went out.

The *Gazette* office was down a side street; the sidewalk was broken and cracked. He went inside. A heater glowed in the corner of the small office. A heavy-set man stood up and came slowly over to the counter.

"What did you want, mister?" he said.

"Old papers. A month. Or more."

"To buy? You want to buy them?"

"Yes." He held out some of the money he had. The man stared.

"Sure," he said. "Sure. Wait a minute." He went quickly out of the room. When he came back he was staggering under the weight of his armload, his face red. "Here are some," he grunted. "Took what I could find. Covers the whole year. And if you want more—"

Conger carried the papers outside. He sat down by the road and began to go through them.

* * *

What he wanted was four months back, in December. It was a tiny item, so small that he almost missed it. His hands trembled as he scanned it, using the small dictionary for some of the archaic terms.

MAN ARRESTED FOR UNLICENSED DEMONSTRATION

An unidentified man who refused to give his name was picked up in Cooper Creek by special agents of the sheriff's office, according to Sheriff Duff. It was said the man was recently noticed in this area and had been watched continually. It was—

Cooper Creek. December, 1960. His heart pounded. That was all he needed to know. He stood up, shaking himself, stamping his feet on the cold ground. The sun had moved across the sky to the very edge of the hills. He smiled. Already he had discovered the exact time and place. Now he needed only to go back, perhaps to November, to Cooper Creek—

He walked back through the main section of town, past the library, past the grocery store. It would not be hard; the hard part was over. He would go there; rent a room, prepare to wait until the man appeared.

He turned the corner. A woman was coming out of a doorway, loaded down with packages. Conger stepped aside to let her pass. The woman glanced at him. Suddenly her face turned white. She stared, her mouth open.

Conger hurried on. He looked back. What was wrong with her? The woman was still staring; she had dropped the packages to the ground. He increased his speed. He turned a second corner and went up a side street. When he looked back again the woman had come to the entrance of the street and was starting after him. A man joined her, and the two of them began to run toward him.

He lost them and left the town, striding quickly, easily, up into the hills at the edge of town. When he reached the cage he stopped. What had happened? Was it something about his clothing? His dress?

He pondered. Then, as the sun set, he stepped into the cage.

Conger sat before the wheel. For a moment he waited, his hands resting lightly on the control. Then he turned the wheel, just a little, following the control readings carefully.

The grayness settled down around him.

But not for very long.

* * *

The man looked him over critically. "You better come inside," he said. "Out of the cold."

"Thanks." Conger went gratefully through the open door, into the living-room. It was warm and close from the heat of the little kerosene heater in the corner. A woman, large and shapeless in her flowered dress, came from the kitchen. She and the man studied him critically.

"It's a good room," the woman said. "I'm Mrs. Appleton. It's got heat. You need that this time of year."

"Yes." He nodded, looking around.

"You want to eat with us?"

"What?"

"You want to eat with us?" The man's brows knitted. "You're not a foreigner, are you, mister?"

"No." He smiled. "I was born in this country. Quite far west, though."

"California?"

"No." He hesitated. "In Oregon."

"What's it like up there?" Mrs. Appleton asked. "I hear there's a lot of trees and green. It's so barren here. I come from Chicago, myself."

"That's the Middle West," the man said to her. "You ain't no foreigner."

"Oregon isn't foreign, either," Conger said. "It's part of the United States."

The man nodded absently. He was staring at Conger's clothing.

"That's a funny suit you got on, mister," he said. "Where'd you get that?"

Conger was lost. He shifted uneasily. "It's a good suit," he said. "Maybe I better go some other place, if you don't want me here."

They both raised their hands protestingly. The woman smiled at him. "We just have to look out for those Reds. You know, the government is always warning us about them."

"The Reds?" He was puzzled.

"The government says they're all around. We're supposed to report anything strange or unusual, anybody doesn't act normal."

"Like me?"

They looked embarrassed. "Well, you don't look like a Red to me," the man said. "But we have to be careful. The *Tribune* says—"

Conger half listened. It was going to be easier than he had thought. Clearly, he would know as soon as the Founder appeared. These people, so suspicious of anything different, would be buzzing and gossiping and spreading the story. All he had to do was lie low and listen, down at the general store, perhaps. Or even here, in Mrs. Appleton's boarding house.

"Can I see the room?" he said.

"Certainly." Mrs. Appleton went to the stairs. "I'll be glad to show it to you."

They went upstairs. It was colder upstairs, but not nearly as cold as outside. Nor as cold as nights on the Martian deserts. For that he was grateful.

* * *

He was walking slowly around the store, looking at the cans of vegetables, the frozen packages of fish and meats shining and clean in the open refrigerator counters.

Ed Davies came toward him. "Can I help you?" he said. The man was a little oddly dressed, and with a beard! Ed couldn't help smiling.

"Nothing," the man said in a funny voice. "Just looking."

"Sure," Ed said. He walked back behind the counter. Mrs. Hacket was wheeling her cart up.

"Who's he?" she whispered, her sharp face turned, her nose moving, as if it were sniffing. "I never seen him before."

"I don't know."

"Looks funny to me. Why does he wear a beard? No one else wears a beard. Must be something the matter with him."

"Maybe he likes to wear a beard. I had an uncle who—"

"Wait." Mrs. Hacket stiffened. "Didn't that—what was his name? The Red—that old one. Didn't he have a beard? Marx. He had a beard."

Ed laughed. "This ain't Karl Marx. I saw a photograph of him once."

Mrs. Hacket was staring at him. "You did?"

"Sure." He flushed a little. "What's the matter with that?"

"I'd sure like to know more about him," Mrs. Hacket said. "I think we ought to know more, for our own good."

* * *

"Hey, mister! Want a ride?"

Conger turned quickly, dropping his hand to his belt. He relaxed. Two young kids in a car, a girl and a boy. He smiled at them. "A ride? Sure."

Conger got into the car and closed the door. Bill Willet pushed the gas and the car roared down the highway.

"I appreciate a ride," Conger said carefully. "I was taking a walk between towns, but it was farther than I thought."

"Where are you from?" Lora Hunt asked. She was pretty, small and dark, in her yellow sweater and blue skirt.

"From Cooper Creek."

"Cooper Creek?" Bill said. He frowned. "That's funny. I don't remember seeing you before."

"Why, do you come from there?"

"I was born there. I know everybody there."

"I just moved in. From Oregon."

"From Oregon? I didn't know Oregon people had accents."

"Do I have an accent?"

"You use words funny."

"How?"

"I don't know. Doesn't he, Lora?"

"You slur them," Lora said, smiling. "Talk some more. I'm interested in dialects." She glanced at him, white-teethed. Conger felt his heart constrict.

"I have a speech impediment."

"Oh." Her eyes widened. "I'm sorry."

They looked at him curiously as the car purred along. Conger for his part was struggling to find some way of asking them questions without seeming curious. "I guess people from out of town don't come here much," he said. "Strangers."

"No." Bill shook his head. "Not very much."

"I'll bet I'm the first outsider for a long time."

"I guess so."

Conger hesitated. "A friend of mine—someone I know, might be coming through here. Where do you suppose I might—" He stopped. "Would there be anyone certain to see him? Someone I could ask, make sure I don't miss him if he comes?"

They were puzzled. "Just keep your eyes open. Cooper Creek isn't very big."

"No. That's right."

They drove in silence. Conger studied the outline of the girl. Probably she was the boy's mistress. Perhaps she was his trial wife. Or had they developed trial marriage back so far? He could not remember. But surely such an attractive girl would be someone's mistress by this time; she would be sixteen or so, by her looks. He might ask her sometime, if they ever met again.

* * *

The next day Conger went walking along the one main street of Cooper Creek. He passed the general store, the two filling stations, and then the post office. At the corner was the soda fountain.

He stopped. Lora was sitting inside, talking to the clerk. She was laughing, rocking back and forth.

Conger pushed the door open. Warm air rushed around him. Lora was drinking hot chocolate, with whipped cream. She looked up in surprise as he slid into the seat beside her.

"I beg your pardon," he said. "Am I intruding?"

"No." She shook her head. Her eyes were large and dark. "Not at all."

The clerk came over. "What do you want?"

Conger looked at the chocolate. "Same as she has."

Lora was watching Conger, her arms folded, elbows on the counter. She smiled at him. "By the way. You don't know my name. Lora Hunt."

She was holding out her hand. He took it awkwardly, not knowing what to do with it. "Conger is my name," he murmured.

"Conger? Is that your last or first name?"

"Last or first?" He hesitated. "Last. Omar Conger."

"Omar?" She laughed. "That's like the poet, Omar Khayyam."

"I don't know of him. I know very little of poets. We restored very few works of art. Usually only the Church has been interested enough—" He broke off. She was staring. He flushed. "Where I come from," he finished.

"The Church? Which church do you mean?"

"The Church." He was confused. The chocolate came and he began to sip it gratefully. Lora was still watching him.

"You're an unusual person," she said. "Bill didn't like you, but he never likes anything different. He's so—so prosaic. Don't you think that when a person gets older he should become—broadened in his outlook?"

Conger nodded.

"He says foreign people ought to stay where they belong, not come here. But you're not so foreign. He means orientals; you know."

Conger nodded.

The screen door opened behind them. Bill came into the room. He stared at them. "Well," he said.

Conger turned. "Hello."

"Well." Bill sat down. "Hello, Lora." He was looking at Conger. "I didn't expect to see you here."

Conger tensed. He could feel the hostility of the boy. "Something wrong with that?"

"No. Nothing wrong with it."

There was silence. Suddenly Bill turned to Lora. "Come on. Let's go."

"Go?" She was astonished. "Why?"

"Just go!" He grabbed her hand. "Come on! The car's outside."

"Why, Bill Willet," Lora said. "You're jealous!"

"Who is this guy?" Bill said. "Do you know anything about him? Look at him, his beard—"

She flared. "So what? Just because he doesn't drive a Packard and go to Cooper High!"

Conger sized the boy up. He was big—big and strong. Probably he was part of some civil control organization.

"Sorry," Conger said. "I'll go."

"What's your business in town?" Bill asked. "What are you doing here? Why are you hanging around Lora?"

Conger looked at the girl. He shrugged. "No reason. I'll see you later."

He turned away. And froze. Bill had moved. Conger's fingers went to his belt. *Half pressure,* he whispered to himself. *No more. Half pressure.*

He squeezed. The room leaped around him. He himself was protected by the lining of his clothing, the plastic sheathing inside.

"My God—" Lora put her hands up. Conger cursed. He hadn't meant any of it for her. But it would wear off. There was only a half-amp to it. It would tingle.

Tingle, and paralyze.

He walked out the door without looking back. He was almost to the corner when Bill came slowly out, holding onto the wall like a drunken man. Conger went on.

* * *

As Conger walked, restless, in the night, a form loomed in front of him. He stopped, holding his breath.

"Who is it?" a man's voice came. Conger waited, tense.

"Who is it?" the man said again. He clicked something in his hand. A light flashed. Conger moved.

"It's me," he said.

"Who is 'me'?"

"Conger is my name. I'm staying at the Appleton's place. Who are you?"

The man came slowly up to him. He was wearing a leather jacket. There was a gun at his waist.

"I'm Sheriff Duff. I think you're the person I want to talk to. You were in Bloom's today, about three o'clock?"

"Bloom's?"

"The fountain. Where the kids hang out." Duff came up beside him, shining his light into Conger's face. Conger blinked.

"Turn that thing away," he said.

A pause. "All right." The light flickered to the ground. "You were there. Some trouble broke out between you and the Willet boy. Is that right? You had a beef over his girl—"

"We had a discussion," Conger said carefully.

"Then what happened?"

"Why?"

"I'm just curious. They say you did something."

"Did something? Did what?"

"I don't know. That's what I'm wondering. They saw a flash, and something seemed to happen. They all blacked out. Couldn't move."

"How are they now?"

"All right."

There was silence.

"Well?" Duff said. "What was it? A bomb?"

"A bomb?" Conger laughed. "No. My cigarette lighter caught fire. There was a leak, and the fluid ignited."

"Why did they all pass out?"

"Fumes."

Silence. Conger shifted, waiting. His fingers moved slowly toward his belt. The Sheriff glanced down. He grunted.

"If you say so," he said. "Anyhow, there wasn't any real harm done." He stepped back from Conger. "And that Willet is a trouble-maker."

"Good night, then," Conger said. He started past the Sheriff.

"One more thing, Mr. Conger. Before you go. You don't mind if I look at your identification, do you?"

"No. Not at all." Conger reached into his pocket. He held his wallet out. The Sheriff took it and shined his flashlight on it. Conger watched, breathing shallowly. They had worked hard on the wallet, studying historic documents, relics of the times, all the papers they felt would be relevant.

Duff handed it back. "Okay. Sorry to bother you." The light winked off.

When Conger reached the house he found the Appletons sitting around the television set. They did not look up as he came in. He lingered at the door.

"Can I ask you something?" he said. Mrs. Appleton turned slowly. "Can I ask you—what's the date?"

"The date?" She studied him. "The first of December."

"December first! Why, it was just November!"

They were all looking at him. Suddenly he remembered. In the twentieth century they still used the old twelve-month system. November fed directly into December; there was no Quartember between.

He gasped. Then it was tomorrow! The second of December! Tomorrow!

"Thanks," he said. "Thanks."

He went up the stairs. What a fool he was, forgetting. The Founder had been taken into captivity on the second of December, according to the newspaper records. Tomorrow, only twelve hours hence, the Founder would appear to speak to the people and then be dragged away.

* * *

The day was warm and bright. Conger's shoes crunched the melting crust of snow. On he went, through the trees heavy with white. He climbed a hill and strode down the other side, sliding as he went.

He stopped to look around. Everything was silent. There was no one in sight. He brought a thin rod from his waist and turned the handle of it. For a moment nothing happened. Then there was a shimmering in the air.

The crystal cage appeared and settled slowly down. Conger sighed. It was good to see it again. After all, it was his only way back.

He walked up on the ridge. He looked around with some satisfaction, his hands on his hips. Hudson's field was spread out, all the way to the beginning of town. It was bare and flat, covered with a thin layer of snow.

Here, the Founder would come. Here, he would speak to them. And here the authorities would take him.

Only he would be dead before they came. He would be dead before he even spoke.

Conger returned to the crystal globe. He pushed through the door and stepped inside. He took the Slem-gun from the shelf and screwed the bolt into place. It was ready to go, ready to fire. For a moment he considered. Should he have it with him?

No. It might be hours before the Founder came, and suppose someone approached him in the meantime? When he saw the Founder coming toward the field, then he could go and get the gun.

Conger looked toward the shelf. There was the neat plastic package. He took it down and unwrapped it.

He held the skull in his hands, turning it over. In spite of himself, a cold feeling rushed through him. This was the man's skull, the skull of the Founder, who was still alive, who would come here, this day, who would stand on the field not fifty yards away.

What if *he* could see this, his own skull, yellow and eroded? Two centuries old. Would he still speak? Would he speak, if he could see it, the grinning, aged skull? What would there be for him to say, to tell the people? What message could he bring?

What action would not be futile, when a man could look upon his own aged, yellowed skull? Better they should enjoy their temporary lives, while they still had them to enjoy.

A man who could hold his own skull in his hands would believe in few causes, few movements. Rather, he would preach the opposite—

A sound. Conger dropped the skull back on the shelf and took up the gun. Outside something was moving. He went quickly to the door, his heart beating. Was it *he?* Was it the Founder, wandering by himself in the cold, looking for a place to speak? Was he meditating over his words, choosing his sentences?

What if he could see what Conger had held!

He pushed the door open, the gun raised.

Lora!

He stared at her. She was dressed in a wool jacket and boots, her hands in her pockets. A cloud of steam came from her mouth and nostrils. Her breast was rising and falling.

Silently, they looked at each other. At last Conger lowered the gun.

"What is it?" he said. "What are you doing here?"

She pointed. She did not seem able to speak. He frowned; what was wrong with her?

"What is it?" he said. "What do you want?" He looked in the direction she had pointed. "I don't see anything."

"They're coming."

"They? Who? Who are coming?"

"They are. The police. During the night the Sheriff had the state police send cars. All around, everywhere. Blocking the roads. There's about sixty of them coming. Some from town, some around behind." She stopped, gasping. "They said—they said—"

"What?"

"They said you were some kind of a Communist. They said—"

* * *

Conger went into the cage. He put the gun down on the shelf and came back out. He leaped down and went to the girl.

"Thanks. You came here to tell me? You don't believe it?"

"I don't know."

"Did you come alone?"

"No. Joe brought me in his truck. From town."

"Joe? Who's he?"

"Joe French. The plumber. He's a friend of Dad's."

"Let's go." They crossed the snow, up the ridge and onto the field. The little panel truck was parked half way across the field. A heavy short man was sitting behind the wheel, smoking his pipe. He sat up as he saw the two of them coming toward him.

"Are you the one?" he said to Conger.

"Yes. Thanks for warning me."

The plumber shrugged. "I don't know anything about this. Lora says you're all right." He turned around. "It might interest you to know some more of them are coming. Not to warn you—just curious."

"More of them?" Conger looked toward the town. Black shapes were picking their way across the snow.

"People from the town. You can't keep this sort of thing quiet, not in a small town. We all listen to the police radio; they heard the same way Lora did. Someone tuned in, spread it around—"

The shapes were getting closer. Conger could, make out a couple of them. Bill Willet was there, with some boys from the high school. The Appletons were along, hanging back in the rear.

"Even Ed Davies," Conger murmured.

The storekeeper was toiling onto the field, with three or four other men from the town.

"All curious as hell," French said. "Well, I guess I'm going back to town. I don't want my truck shot full of holes. Come on, Lora."

She was looking up at Conger, wide-eyed.

"Come on," French said again. "Let's go. You sure as hell can't stay here, you know."

"Why?"

"There may be shooting. That's what they all came to see. You know that don't you, Conger?"

"Yes."

"You have a gun? Or don't you care?" French smiled a little. "They've picked up a lot of people in their time, you know. You won't be lonely."

He cared, all right! He had to stay here, on the field. He couldn't afford to let them take him away. Any minute the Founder would appear, would step onto the field. Would he be one of the townsmen, standing silently at the foot of the field, waiting, watching?

Or maybe he was Joe French. Or maybe one of the cops. Anyone of them might find himself moved to speak. And the few words spoken this day were going to be important for a long time.

And Conger had to be there, ready when the first word was uttered!

"I care," he said. "You go on back to town. Take the girl with you."

Lora got stiffly in beside Joe French. The plumber started up the motor. "Look at them, standing there," he said. "Like vultures. Waiting to see someone get killed."

* * *

The truck drove away, Lora sitting stiff and silent, frightened now. Conger watched for a moment. Then he dashed back into the woods, between the trees, toward the ridge.

He could get away, of course. Anytime he wanted to he could get away. All he had to do was to leap into the crystal cage and turn the handles. But he had a job, an important job. He had to be here, here at this place, at this time.

He reached the cage and opened the door. He went inside and picked up the gun from the shelf. The Slem-gun would take care of them. He notched it up to full count. The chain reaction from it would flatten them all, the police, the curious, sadistic people—

They wouldn't take him! Before they got him, all of them would be dead. *He* would get away. He would escape. By the end of the day they would all be dead, if that was what they wanted, and he—

He saw the skull.

Suddenly he put the gun down. He picked up the skull. He turned the skull over. He looked at the teeth. Then he went to the mirror.

He held the skull up, looking in the mirror. He pressed the skull against his cheek. Beside his own face the grinning skull leered back at him, beside *his* skull, against his living flesh.

He bared his teeth. And he knew.

It was his own skull that he held. He was the one who would die. He was the Founder.

After a time he put the skull down. For a few minutes he stood at the controls, playing with them idly. He could hear the sound of motors outside, the muffled noise of men. Should he go back to the present, where the Speaker waited? He could escape, of course—

Escape?

He turned toward the skull. There it was, his skull, yellow with age. Escape? Escape, when he had held it in his own hands?

What did it matter if he put it off a month, a year, ten years, even fifty? Time was nothing. He had sipped chocolate with a girl born a hundred and fifty years before his time. Escape? For a little while, perhaps.

But he could not *really* escape, no more so than anyone else had ever escaped, or ever would.

Only, he had held it in his hands, his own bones, his own death's-head. *They* had not.

He went out the door and across the field, empty handed. There were a lot of them standing around, gathered together, waiting. They expected a good fight; they knew he had something. They had heard about the incident at the fountain.

And there were plenty of police—police with guns and tear gas, creeping across the hills and ridges, between the trees, closer and closer. It was an old story, in this century.

One of the men tossed something at him. It fell in the snow by his feet, and he looked down. It was a rock. He smiled.

"Come on!" one of them called. "Don't you have any bombs?"

"Throw a bomb! You with the beard! Throw a bomb!"

"Let 'em have it!"

"Toss a few A Bombs!"

* * *

They began to laugh. He smiled. He put his hands to his hips. They suddenly turned silent, seeing that he was going to speak.

"I'm sorry," he said simply. "I don't have any bombs. You're mistaken."

There was a flurry of murmuring.

"I have a gun," he went on. "A very good one. Made by science even more advanced than your own. But I'm not going to use that, either."

They were puzzled.

"Why not?" someone called. At the edge of the group an older woman was watching. He felt a sudden shock. He had seen her before. Where?

He remembered. The day at the library. As he had turned the corner he had seen her. She had noticed him and been astounded. At the time, he did not understand why.

Conger grinned. So he *would* escape death, the man who right now was voluntarily accepting it. They were laughing, laughing at a man who had a gun but didn't use it. But by a strange twist of science he would appear again, a few months later, after his bones had been buried under the floor of a jail.

And so, in a fashion, he would escape death. He would die, but then, after a period of months, he would live again, briefly, for an afternoon.

An afternoon. Yet long enough for them to see him, to understand that he was still alive. To know that somehow he had returned to life.

And then, finally, he would appear once more, after two hundred years had passed. Two centuries later.

He would be born again, born, as a matter of fact, in a small trading village on Mars. He would grow up, learning to hunt and trade—

A police car came on the edge of the field and stopped. The people retreated a little. Conger raised his hands.

"I have an odd paradox for you," he said. "Those who take lives will lose their own. Those who kill, will die. But he who gives his own life away will live again!"

They laughed, faintly, nervously. The police were coming out, walking toward him. He smiled. He had said everything he intended to say. It was a good little paradox he had coined. They would puzzle over it, remember it.

Smiling, Conger awaited a death foreordained.

The Eyes Have It

A little whimsy, now and then, makes for good balance. Theoretically, you could find this type of humor anywhere. But only a topflight science-fictionist, we thought, could have written this story, in just this way. . . .

It was quite by accident I discovered this incredible invasion of Earth by lifeforms from another planet. As yet, I haven't done anything about it; I can't think of anything to do. I wrote to the Government, and they sent back a pamphlet on the repair and maintenance of frame houses. Anyhow, the whole thing is known; I'm not the first to discover it. Maybe it's even under control.

I was sitting in my easy-chair, idly turning the pages of a paperbacked book someone had left on the bus, when I came across the reference that first put me on the trail. For a moment I didn't respond. It took some time for the full import to sink in. After I'd comprehended, it seemed odd I hadn't noticed it right away.

The reference was clearly to a nonhuman species of incredible properties, not indigenous to Earth. A species, I hasten to point out, customarily masquerading as ordinary human beings. Their disguise, however, became transparent in the face of the following observations by the author. It was at once obvious the author knew everything. Knew everything — and was taking it in his stride. The line (and I tremble remembering it even now) read:

> . . . *his eyes slowly roved about the room.*

Vague chills assailed me. I tried to picture the eyes. Did they roll like dimes? The passage indicated not; they seemed to move through the air, not over the surface. Rather rapidly, apparently. No one in the story

155

was surprised. That's what tipped me off. No sign of amazement at such an outrageous thing. Later the matter was amplified.

> *. . . his eyes moved from person to person.*

There it was in a nutshell. The eyes had clearly come apart from the rest of him and were on their own. My heart pounded and my breath choked in my windpipe. I had stumbled on an accidental mention of a totally unfamiliar race. Obviously non-Terrestrial. Yet, to the characters in the book, it was perfectly natural — which suggested they belonged to the same species.

And the author? A slow suspicion burned in my mind. The author was taking it rather *too easily* in his stride. Evidently, he felt this was quite a usual thing. He made absolutely no attempt to conceal this knowledge. The story continued:

> *. . . presently his eyes fastened on Julia.*

Julia, being a lady, had at least the breeding to feel indignant. She is described as blushing and knitting her brows angrily. At this, I sighed with relief. They weren't *all* non-Terrestrials. The narrative continues:

> *. . . slowly, calmly, his eyes examined every inch of her.*

Great Scott! But here the girl turned and stomped off and the matter ended. I lay back in my chair gasping with horror. My wife and family regarded me in wonder.

"What's wrong, dear?" my wife asked.

I couldn't tell her. Knowledge like this was too much for the ordinary run-of-the-mill person. I had to keep it to myself. "Nothing," I gasped. I leaped up, snatched the book, and hurried out of the room.

* * *

In the garage, I continued reading. There was more. Trembling, I read the next revealing passage:

> *. . . he put his arm around Julia. Presently she asked him if he would remove his arm. He immediately did so, with a smile.*

It's not said what was done with the arm after the fellow had removed it. Maybe it was left standing upright in the corner. Maybe it was thrown away. I don't care. In any case, the full meaning was there, staring me right in the face.

Here was a race of creatures capable of removing portions of their anatomy at will. Eyes, arms—and maybe more. Without batting an eyelash. My knowledge of biology came in handy, at this point. Obviously they were simple beings, uni-cellular, some sort of primitive single-celled things. Beings no more developed than starfish. Starfish can do the same thing, you know.

I read on. And came to this incredible revelation, tossed off coolly by the author without the faintest tremor:

> . . . *outside the movie theater we split up. Part of us went inside, part over to the cafe for dinner.*

Binary fission, obviously. Splitting in half and forming two entities. Probably each lower half went to the cafe, it being farther, and the upper halves to the movies. I read on, hands shaking. I had really stumbled onto something here. My mind reeled as I made out this passage:

> . . . *I'm afraid there's no doubt about it. Poor Bibney has lost his head again.*

Which was followed by:

> . . . *and Bob says he has utterly no guts.*

Yet Bibney got around as well as the next person. The next person, however, was just as strange. He was soon described as:

> . . . *totally lacking in brains.*

* * *

There was no doubt of the thing in the next passage. Julia, whom I had thought to be the one normal person, reveals herself as also being an alien life form, similar to the rest:

> . . . *quite deliberately, Julia had given her heart to the young man.*

It didn't relate what the final disposition of the organ was, but I didn't really care. It was evident Julia had gone right on living in her usual manner, like all the others in the book. Without heart, arms, eyes, brains, viscera, dividing up in two when the occasion demanded. Without a qualm.

> . . . *thereupon she gave him her hand.*

I sickened. The rascal now had her hand, as well as her heart. I shudder to think what he's done with them, by this time.

> . . . *he took her arm.*

Not content to wait, he had to start dismantling her on his own. Flushing crimson, I slammed the book shut and leaped to my feet. But not in time to escape one last reference to those carefree bits of anatomy whose travels had originally thrown me on the track:

> . . . *her eyes followed him all the way down the road and across the meadow.*

I rushed from the garage and back inside the warm house, as if the accursed things were following me. My wife and children were playing Monopoly in the kitchen. I joined them and played with frantic fervor, brow feverish, teeth chattering.

I had had enough of the thing. I want to hear no more about it. Let them come on. Let them invade Earth. I don't want to get mixed up in it.

I have absolutely no stomach for it.

Mr. Spaceship

A human brain-controlled spacecraft would mean mechanical perfection. This was accomplished, and something unforeseen.

Kramer leaned back. "You can see the situation. How can we deal with a factor like this? The perfect variable."

"Perfect? Prediction should still be possible. A living thing still acts from necessity, the same as inanimate material. But the cause-effect chain is more subtle; there are more factors to be considered. The difference is quantitative, I think. The reaction of the living organism parallels natural causation, but with greater complexity."

Gross and Kramer looked up at the board plates, suspended on the wall, still dripping, the images hardening into place. Kramer traced a line with his pencil.

"See that? It's a pseudopodium. They're alive, and so far, a weapon we can't beat. No mechanical system can compete with that, simple or intricate. We'll have to scrap the Johnson Control and find something else."

"Meanwhile the war continues as it is. Stalemate. Checkmate. They can't get to us, and we can't get through their living minefield."

Kramer nodded. "It's a perfect defense, for them. But there still might be one answer."

"What's that?"

"Wait a minute." Kramer turned to his rocket expert, sitting with the charts and files. "The heavy cruiser that returned this week. It didn't actually touch, did it? It came close but there was no contact."

"Correct." The expert nodded. "The mine was twenty miles off. The cruiser was in space-drive, moving directly toward Proxima, line-straight, using the Johnson Control, of course. It had deflected a quarter of an hour earlier for reasons unknown. Later it resumed its course. That was when they got it."

"It shifted," Kramer said. "But not enough. The mine was coming along after it, trailing it. It's the same old story, but I wonder about the contact."

"Here's our theory," the expert said. "We keep looking for contact, a trigger in the pseudopodium. But more likely we're witnessing a psychological phenomena, a decision without any physical correlative. We're watching for something that isn't there. The mine *decides* to blow up. It sees our ship, approaches, and then decides."

"Thanks." Kramer turned to Gross. "Well, that confirms what I'm saying. How can a ship guided by automatic relays escape a mine that decides to explode? The whole theory of mine penetration is that you must avoid tripping the trigger. But here the trigger is a state of mind in a complicated, developed life-form."

"The belt is fifty thousand miles deep," Gross added. "It solves another problem for them, repair and maintenance. The damn things reproduce, fill up the spaces by spawning into them. I wonder what they feed on?"

"Probably the remains of our first-line. The big cruisers must be a delicacy. It's a game of wits, between a living creature and a ship piloted by automatic relays. The ship always loses." Kramer opened a folder. "I'll tell you what I suggest."

"Go on," Gross said. "I've already heard ten solutions today. What's yours?"

"Mine is very simple. These creatures are superior to any mechanical system, but only because they're alive. Almost any other life-form could compete with them, any higher life-form. If the yuks can put out living mines to protect their planets, we ought to be able to harness some of our own life-forms in a similar way. Let's make use of the same weapon ourselves."

"Which life-form do you propose to use?"

"I think the human brain is the most agile of known living forms. Do you know of any better?"

"But no human being can withstand outspace travel. A human pilot would be dead of heart failure long before the ship got anywhere near Proxima."

"But we don't need the whole body," Kramer said. "We need only the brain."

"What?"

"The problem is to find a person of high intelligence who would contribute, in the same manner that eyes and arms are volunteered."

"But a brain. . . ."

"Technically, it could be done. Brains have been transferred several times, when body destruction made it necessary. Of course, to a spaceship, to a heavy outspace cruiser, instead of an artificial body, that's new."

The room was silent.

"It's quite an idea," Gross said slowly. His heavy square face twisted. "But even supposing it might work, the big question is *whose* brain?"

* * *

It was all very confusing, the reasons for the war, the nature of the enemy. The Yucconae had been contacted on one of the outlying planets of Proxima Centauri. At the approach of the Terran ship, a host of dark slim pencils had lifted abruptly and shot off into the distance. The first real encounter came between three of the yuk pencils and a single exploration ship from Terra. No Terrans survived. After that it was all out war, with no holds barred.

Both sides feverishly constructed defense rings around their systems. Of the two, the Yucconae belt was the better. The ring around Proxima was a living ring, superior to anything Terra could throw against it. The standard equipment by which Terran ships were guided in outspace, the Johnson Control, was not adequate. Something more was needed. Automatic relays were not good enough.

—Not good at all, Kramer thought to himself, as he stood looking down the hillside at the work going on below him. A warm wind blew along the hill, rustling the weeds and grass. At the bottom, in the valley, the mechanics had almost finished; the last elements of the reflex system had been removed from the ship and crated up.

All that was needed now was the new core, the new central key that would take the place of the mechanical system. A human brain, the brain of an intelligent, wary human being. But would the human being part with it? That was the problem.

Kramer turned. Two people were approaching him along the road, a man and a woman. The man was Gross, expressionless, heavy-set, walking with dignity. The woman was—He stared in surprise and growing annoyance. It was Dolores, his wife. Since they'd separated he had seen little of her. . . .

"Kramer," Gross said. "Look who I ran into. Come back down with us. We're going into town."

"Hello, Phil," Dolores said. "Well, aren't you glad to see me?"

He nodded. "How have you been? You're looking fine." She was still pretty and slender in her uniform, the blue-grey of Internal Security, Gross' organization.

"Thanks." She smiled. "You seem to be doing all right, too. Commander Gross tells me that you're responsible for this project, Operation Head, as they call it. Whose head have you decided on?"

"That's the problem." Kramer lit a cigarette. "This ship is to be equipped with a human brain instead of the Johnson system. We've constructed special draining baths for the brain, electronic relays to catch the impulses and magnify them, a continual feeding duct that supplies the living cells with everything they need. But—"

"But we still haven't got the brain itself," Gross finished. They began to walk back toward the car. "If we can get that we'll be ready for the tests."

"Will the brain remain alive?" Dolores asked. "Is it actually going to live as part of the ship?"

"It will be alive, but not conscious. Very little life is actually conscious. Animals, trees, insects are quick in their responses, but they aren't conscious. In this process of ours the individual personality, the ego, will cease. We only need the response ability, nothing more."

Dolores shuddered. "How terrible!"

"In time of war everything must be tried," Kramer said absently. "If one life sacrificed will end the war it's worth it. This ship might get through. A couple more like it and there wouldn't be any more war."

* * *

They got into the car. As they drove down the road, Gross said, "Have you thought of anyone yet?"

Kramer shook his head. "That's out of my line."

"What do you mean?"

"I'm an engineer. It's not in my department."

"But all this was your idea."

"My work ends there."

Gross was staring at him oddly. Kramer shifted uneasily.

"Then who is supposed to do it?" Gross said. "I can have my organization prepare examinations of various kinds, to determine fitness, that kind of thing—"

"Listen, Phil," Dolores said suddenly.

"What?"

She turned toward him. "I have an idea. Do you remember that professor we had in college. Michael Thomas?"

Kramer nodded.

"I wonder if he's still alive." Dolores frowned. "If he is he must be awfully old."

"Why, Dolores?" Gross asked.

"Perhaps an old person who didn't have much time left, but whose mind was still clear and sharp—"

"Professor Thomas." Kramer rubbed his jaw. "He certainly was a wise old duck. But could he still be alive? He must have been seventy, then."

"We could find that out," Gross said. "I could make a routine check."

"What do you think?" Dolores said. "If any human mind could outwit those creatures—"

"I don't like the idea," Kramer said. In his mind an image had appeared, the image of an old man sitting behind a desk, his bright gentle eyes moving about the classroom. The old man leaning forward, a thin hand raised—

"Keep him out of this," Kramer said.

"What's wrong?" Gross looked at him curiously.

"It's because *I* suggested it," Dolores said.

"No." Kramer shook his head. "It's not that. I didn't expect anything like this, somebody I knew, a man I studied under. I remember him very clearly. He was a very distinct personality."

"Good," Gross said. "He sounds fine."

"We can't do it. We're asking his death!"

"This is war," Gross said, "and war doesn't wait on the needs of the individual. You said that yourself. Surely he'll volunteer; we can keep it on that basis."

"He may already be dead," Dolores murmured.

"We'll find that out," Gross said speeding up the car. They drove the rest of the way in silence.

* * *

For a long time the two of them stood studying the small wood house, overgrown with ivy, set back on the lot behind an enormous oak. The little town was silent and sleepy; once in awhile a car moved slowly along the distant highway, but that was all.

"This is the place," Gross said to Kramer. He folded his arms. "Quite a quaint little house."

Kramer said nothing. The two Security Agents behind them were expressionless.

Gross started toward the gate. "Let's go. According to the check he's still alive, but very sick. His mind is agile, however. That seems to be certain. It's said he doesn't leave the house. A woman takes care of his needs. He's very frail."

They went down the stone walk and up onto the porch. Gross rang the bell. They waited. After a time they heard slow footsteps. The door opened. An elderly woman in a shapeless wrapper studied them impassively.

"Security," Gross said, showing his card. "We wish to see Professor Thomas."

"Why?"

"Government business." He glanced at Kramer.

Kramer stepped forward. "I was a pupil of the Professor's," he said. "I'm sure he won't mind seeing us."

The woman hesitated uncertainly. Gross stepped into the doorway. "All right, mother. This is war time. We can't stand out here."

The two Security agents followed him, and Kramer came reluctantly behind, closing the door. Gross stalked down the hall until he came to an open door. He stopped, looking in. Kramer could see the white corner of a bed, a wooden post and the edge of a dresser.

He joined Gross.

In the dark room a withered old man lay, propped up on endless pillows. At first it seemed as if he were asleep; there was no motion or sign of life. But after a time Kramer saw with a faint shock that the old man was watching them intently, his eyes fixed on them, unmoving, unwinking.

"Professor Thomas?" Gross said. "I'm Commander Gross of Security. This man with me is perhaps known to you—"

The faded eyes fixed on Kramer.

"I know him. Philip Kramer. . . . You've grown heavier, boy." The voice was feeble, the rustle of dry ashes. "Is it true you're married now?"

"Yes. I married Dolores French. You remember her." Kramer came toward the bed. "But we're separated. It didn't work out very well. Our careers—"

"What we came here about, Professor," Gross began, but Kramer cut him off with an impatient wave.

"Let me talk. Can't you and your men get out of here long enough to let me talk to him?"

Gross swallowed. "All right, Kramer." He nodded to the two men. The three of them left the room, going out into the hall and closing the door after them.

The old man in the bed watched Kramer silently. "I don't think much of him," he said at last. "I've seen his type before. What's he want?"

"Nothing. He just came along. Can I sit down?" Kramer found a stiff upright chair beside the bed. "If I'm bothering you—"

"No. I'm glad to see you again, Philip. After so long. I'm sorry your marriage didn't work out."

"How have you been?"

"I've been very ill. I'm afraid that my moment on the world's stage has almost ended." The ancient eyes studied the younger man reflectively. "You look as if you have been doing well. Like everyone else I thought highly of. You've gone to the top in this society."

Kramer smiled. Then he became serious. "Professor, there's a project we're working on that I want to talk to you about. It's the first ray of hope we've had in this whole war. If it works, we may be able to crack the yuk defenses, get some ships into their system. If we can do that the war might be brought to an end."

"Go on. Tell me about it, if you wish."

"It's a long shot, this project. It may not work at all, but we have to give it a try."

"It's obvious that you came here because of it," Professor Thomas murmured. "I'm becoming curious. Go on."

* * *

After Kramer finished the old man lay back in the bed without speaking. At last he sighed.

"I understand. A human mind, taken out of a human body." He sat up a little, looking at Kramer. "I suppose you're thinking of me."

Kramer said nothing.

"Before I make my decision I want to see the papers on this, the theory and outline of construction. I'm not sure I like it.—For reasons of my own, I mean. But I want to look at the material. If you'll do that—"

"Certainly." Kramer stood up and went to the door. Gross and the two Security Agents were standing outside, waiting tensely. "Gross, come inside."

They filed into the room.

"Give the Professor the papers," Kramer said. "He wants to study them before deciding."

Gross brought the file out of his coat pocket, a manila envelope. He handed it to the old man on the bed. "Here it is, Professor. You're welcome to examine it. Will you give us your answer as soon as possible? We're very anxious to begin, of course."

"I'll give you my answer when I've decided." He took the envelope with a thin, trembling hand. "My decision depends on what I find out from these papers. If I don't like what I find, then I will not become involved with this work in any shape or form." He opened the envelope with shaking hands. "I'm looking for one thing."

"What is it?" Gross said.

"That's my affair. Leave me a number by which I can reach you when I've decided."

Silently, Gross put his card down on the dresser. As they went out Professor Thomas was already reading the first of the papers, the outline of the theory.

* * *

Kramer sat across from Dale Winter, his second in line. "What then?" Winter said.

"He's going to contact us." Kramer scratched with a drawing pen on some paper. "I don't know what to think."

"What do you mean?" Winter's good-natured face was puzzled.

"Look." Kramer stood up, pacing back and forth, his hands in his uniform pockets. "He was my teacher in college. I respected him as a man, as well as a teacher. He was more than a voice, a talking book. He was a person, a calm, kindly person I could look up to. I always wanted to be like him, someday. Now look at me."

"So?"

"Look at what I'm asking. I'm asking for his life, as if he were some kind of laboratory animal kept around in a cage, not a man, a teacher at all."

"Do you think he'll do it?"

"I don't know." Kramer went to the window. He stood looking out. "In a way, I hope not."

"But if he doesn't—"

"Then we'll have to find somebody else. I know. There would be somebody else. Why did Dolores have to—"

The vidphone rang. Kramer pressed the button.

"This is Gross." The heavy features formed. "The old man called me. Professor Thomas."

"What did he say?" He knew; he could tell already, by the sound of Gross' voice.

"He said he'd do it. I was a little surprised myself, but apparently he means it. We've already made arrangements for his admission to the hospital. His lawyer is drawing up the statement of liability."

Kramer only half heard. He nodded wearily. "All right. I'm glad. I suppose we can go ahead, then."

"You don't sound very glad."

"I wonder why he decided to go ahead with it."

"He was very certain about it." Gross sounded pleased. "He called me quite early. I was still in bed. You know, this calls for a celebration."

"Sure," Kramer said. "It sure does."

* * *

Toward the middle of August the project neared completion. They stood outside in the hot autumn heat, looking up at the sleek metal sides of the ship.

Gross thumped the metal with his hand. "Well, it won't be long. We can begin the test any time."

"Tell us more about this," an officer in gold braid said. "It's such an unusual concept."

"Is there really a human brain inside the ship?" a dignitary asked, a small man in a rumpled suit. "And the brain is actually alive?"

"Gentlemen, this ship is guided by a living brain instead of the usual Johnson relay-control system. But the brain is not conscious. It will function by reflex only. The practical difference between it and the Johnson system is this: a human brain is far more intricate than any man-made structure, and its ability to adapt itself to a situation, to respond to danger, is far beyond anything that could be artificially built."

Gross paused, cocking his ear. The turbines of the ship were beginning to rumble, shaking the ground under them with a deep vibration. Kramer was standing a short distance away from the others, his arms folded, watching silently. At the sound of the turbines he walked quickly around the ship to the other side. A few workmen were clearing away the last of the waste, the scraps of wiring and scaffolding. They glanced up at him and went on hurriedly with their work. Kramer mounted the ramp and entered the control cabin of the ship. Winter was sitting at the controls with a Pilot from Space-transport.

"How's it look?" Kramer asked.

"All right." Winter got up. "He tells me that it would be best to take off manually. The robot controls—" Winter hesitated. "I mean, the built-in controls, can take over later on in space."

"That's right," the Pilot said. "It's customary with the Johnson system, and so in this case we should—"

"Can you tell anything yet?" Kramer asked.

"No," the Pilot said slowly. "I don't think so. I've been going over everything. It seems to be in good order. There's only one thing I wanted to ask you about." He put his hand on the control board. "There are some changes here I don't understand."

"Changes?"

"Alterations from the original design. I wonder what the purpose is."

Kramer took a set of the plans from his coat. "Let me look." He turned the pages over. The Pilot watched carefully over his shoulder.

"The changes aren't indicated on your copy," the Pilot said. "I wonder—" He stopped. Commander Gross had entered the control cabin.

"Gross, who authorized alterations?" Kramer said. "Some of the wiring has been changed."

"Why, your old friend." Gross signaled to the field tower through the window.

"My old friend?"

"The Professor. He took quite an active interest." Gross turned to the Pilot. "Let's get going. We have to take this out past gravity for the test they tell me. Well, perhaps it's for the best. Are you ready?"

"Sure." The Pilot sat down and moved some of the controls around. "Anytime."

"Go ahead, then," Gross said.

"The Professor—" Kramer began, but at that moment there was a tremendous roar and the ship leaped under him. He grasped one of the wall holds and hung on as best he could. The cabin was filling with a steady throbbing, the raging of the jet turbines underneath them.

The ship leaped. Kramer closed his eyes and held his breath. They were moving out into space, gaining speed each moment.

* * *

"Well, what do you think?" Winter said nervously. "Is it time yet?"

"A little longer," Kramer said. He was sitting on the floor of the cabin, down by the control wiring. He had removed the metal covering-plate, exposing the complicated maze of relay wiring. He was studying it, comparing it to the wiring diagrams.

"What's the matter?" Gross said.

"These changes. I can't figure out what they're for. The only pattern I can make out is that for some reason—"

"Let me look," the Pilot said. He squatted down beside Kramer. "You were saying?"

"See this lead here? Originally it was switch controlled. It closed and opened automatically, according to temperature change. Now it's wired so that the central control system operates it. The same with the others. A lot of this was still mechanical, worked by pressure, temperature, stress. Now it's under the central master."

"The brain?" Gross said. "You mean it's been altered so that the brain manipulates it?"

Kramer nodded. "Maybe Professor Thomas felt that no mechanical relays could be trusted. Maybe he thought that things would be happening too fast. But some of these could close in a split second. The brake rockets could go on as quickly as—"

"Hey," Winter said from the control seat. "We're getting near the moon stations. What'll I do?"

They looked out the port. The corroded surface of the moon gleamed up at them, a corrupt and sickening sight. They were moving swift toward it.

"I'll take it," the Pilot said. He eased Winter out of the way and strapped himself in place. The ship began to move away from the moon as he manipulated the controls. Down below them they could see the observation stations dotting the surface, and the tiny squares that were the openings of the underground factories and hangars. A red blinker winked up at them and the Pilot's fingers moved on the board in answer.

"We're past the moon," the Pilot said, after a time. The moon had fallen behind them; the ship was heading into outer space. "Well, we can go ahead with it."

Kramer did not answer.

"Mr. Kramer, we can go ahead any time."

Kramer started. "Sorry. I was thinking. All right, thanks." He frowned, deep in thought.

"What is it?" Gross asked.

"The wiring changes. Did you understand the reason for them when you gave the okay to the workmen?"

Gross flushed. "You know I know nothing about technical material. I'm in Security."

"Then you should have consulted me."

"What does it matter?" Gross grinned wryly. "We're going to have to start putting our faith in the old man sooner or later."

The Pilot stepped back from the board. His face was pale and set. "Well, it's done," he said. "That's it."

"What's done?" Kramer said.

"We're on automatic. The brain. I turned the board over to it—to him, I mean. The Old Man." The Pilot lit a cigarette and puffed nervously. "Let's keep our fingers crossed."

* * *

The ship was coasting evenly, in the hands of its invisible pilot. Far down inside the ship, carefully armoured and protected, a soft human brain lay in a tank of liquid, a thousand minute electric charges playing over its surface. As the charges rose they were picked up and amplified, fed into relay systems, advanced, carried on through the entire ship—

Gross wiped his forehead nervously. "So *he* is running it, now. I hope he knows what he's doing."

Kramer nodded enigmatically. "I think he does."

"What do you mean?"

"Nothing." Kramer walked to the port. "I see we're still moving in a straight line." He picked up the microphone. "We can instruct the brain orally, through this." He blew against the microphone experimentally.

"Go on," Winter said.

"Bring the ship around half-right," Kramer said. "Decrease speed."

They waited. Time passed. Gross looked at Kramer. "No change. Nothing."

"Wait."

Slowly, the ship was beginning to turn. The turbines missed, reducing their steady beat. The ship was taking up its new course, adjusting itself. Nearby some space debris rushed past, incinerating in the blasts of the turbine jets.

"So far so good," Gross said.

They began to breathe more easily. The invisible pilot had taken control smoothly, calmly. The ship was in good hands. Kramer spoke a few more words into the microphone, and they swung again. Now they were moving back the way they had come, toward the moon.

"Let's see what he does when we enter the moon's pull," Kramer said. "He was a good mathematician, the old man. He could handle any kind of problem."

The ship veered, turning away from the moon. The great eaten-away globe fell behind them.

Gross breathed a sigh of relief. "That's that."

"One more thing." Kramer picked up the microphone. "Return to the moon and land the ship at the first space field," he said into it.

"Good Lord," Winter murmured. "Why are you—"

"Be quiet." Kramer stood, listening. The turbines gasped and roared as the ship swung full around, gaining speed. They were moving back, back toward the moon again. The ship dipped down, heading toward the great globe below.

"We're going a little fast," the Pilot said. "I don't see how he can put down at this velocity."

* * *

The port filled up, as the globe swelled rapidly. The Pilot hurried toward the board, reaching for the controls. All at once the ship jerked. The nose lifted and the ship shot out into space, away from the moon, turning at an oblique angle. The men were thrown to the floor by the sudden change in course. They got to their feet again, speechless, staring at each other.

The Pilot gazed down at the board. "It wasn't me! I didn't touch a thing. I didn't even get to it."

The ship was gaining speed each moment. Kramer hesitated. "Maybe you better switch it back to manual."

The Pilot closed the switch. He took hold of the steering controls and moved them experimentally. "Nothing." He turned around. "Nothing. It doesn't respond."

No one spoke.

"You can see what has happened," Kramer said calmly. "The old man won't let go of it, now that he has it. I was afraid of this when I saw the wiring changes. Everything in this ship is centrally controlled, even the cooling system, the hatches, the garbage release. We're helpless."

"Nonsense." Gross strode to the board. He took hold of the wheel and turned it. The ship continued on its course, moving away from the moon, leaving it behind.

"Release!" Kramer said into the microphone. "Let go of the controls! We'll take it back. Release."

"No good," the Pilot said. "Nothing." He spun the useless wheel. "It's dead, completely dead."

"And we're still heading out," Winter said, grinning foolishly. "We'll be going through the first-line defense belt in a few minutes. If they don't shoot us down—"

"We better radio back." The Pilot clicked the radio to *send.* "I'll contact the main bases, one of the observation stations."

"Better get the defense belt, at the speed we're going. We'll be into it in a minute."

"And after that," Kramer said, "we'll be in outer space. He's moving us toward outspace velocity. Is this ship equipped with baths?"

"Baths?" Gross said.

"The sleep tanks. For space-drive. We may need them if we go much faster."

"But good God, where are we going?" Gross said. "Where—where's he taking us?"

* * *

The Pilot obtained contact. "This is Dwight, on ship," he said. "We're entering the defense zone at high velocity. Don't fire on us."

"Turn back," the impersonal voice came through the speaker. "You're not allowed in the defense zone."

"We can't. We've lost control."

"Lost control?"

"This is an experimental ship."

Gross took the radio. "This is Commander Gross, Security. We're being carried into outer space. There's nothing we can do. Is there any way that we can be removed from this ship?"

A hesitation. "We have some fast pursuit ships that could pick you up if you wanted to jump. The chances are good they'd find you. Do you have space flares?"

"We do," the Pilot said. "Let's try it."

"Abandon ship?" Kramer said. "If we leave now we'll never see it again."

"What else can we do? We're gaining speed all the time. Do you propose that we stay here?"

"No." Kramer shook his head. "Damn it, there ought to be a better solution."

"Could you contact *him?*" Winter asked. "The Old Man? Try to reason with him?"

"It's worth a chance," Gross said. "Try it."

"All right." Kramer took the microphone. He paused a moment. "Listen! Can you hear me? This is Phil Kramer. Can you hear me, Professor. Can you hear me? I want you to release the controls."

There was silence.

"This is Kramer, Professor. Can you hear me? Do you remember who I am? Do you understand who this is?"

Above the control panel the wall speaker made a sound, a sputtering static. They looked up.

"Can you hear me, Professor. This is Philip Kramer. I want you to give the ship back to us. If you can hear me, release the controls! Let go, Professor. Let go!"

Static. A rushing sound, like the wind. They gazed at each other. There was silence for a moment.

"It's a waste of time," Gross said.

"No—listen!"

The sputter came again. Then, mixed with the sputter, almost lost in it, a voice came, toneless, without inflection, a mechanical, lifeless voice from the metal speaker in the wall, above their heads.

" . . . Is it you, Philip? I can't make you out. Darkness. . . . Who's there? With you. . . ."

"It's me, Kramer." His fingers tightened against the microphone handle. "You must release the controls, Professor. We have to get back to Terra. You must."

Silence. Then the faint, faltering voice came again, a little stronger than before. "Kramer. Everything so strange. I was right, though. Consciousness result of thinking. Necessary result. Cognito ergo sum. Retain conceptual ability. Can you hear me?"

"Yes, Professor—"

"I altered the wiring. Control. I was fairly certain. . . . I wonder if I can do it. Try. . . ."

Suddenly the air-conditioning snapped into operation. It snapped abruptly off again. Down the corridor a door slammed. Something thudded. The men stood listening. Sounds came from all sides of them, switches shutting, opening. The lights blinked off; they were in darkness. The lights came back on, and at the same time the heating coils dimmed and faded.

"Good God!" Winter said.

Water poured down on them, the emergency fire-fighting system. There was a screaming rush of air. One of the escape hatches had slid back, and the air was roaring frantically out into space.

The hatch banged closed. The ship subsided into silence. The heating coils glowed into life. As suddenly as it had begun the weird exhibition ceased.

"I can do—everything," the dry, toneless voice came from the wall speaker. "It is all controlled. Kramer, I wish to talk to you. I've been—been thinking. I haven't seen you in many years. A lot to discuss. You've changed, boy. We have much to discuss. Your wife—"

The Pilot grabbed Kramer's arm. "There's a ship standing off our bow. Look."

* * *

They ran to the port. A slender pale craft was moving along with them, keeping pace with them. It was signal-blinking.

"A Terran pursuit ship," the Pilot said. "Let's jump. They'll pick us up. Suits—"

He ran to a supply cupboard and turned the handle. The door opened and he pulled the suits out onto the floor.

"Hurry," Gross said. A panic seized them. They dressed frantically, pulling the heavy garments over them. Winter staggered to the escape hatch and stood by it, waiting for the others. They joined him, one by one.

"Let's go!" Gross said. "Open the hatch."

Winter tugged at the hatch. "Help me."

They grabbed hold, tugging together. Nothing happened. The hatch refused to budge.

"Get a crowbar," the Pilot said.

"Hasn't anyone got a blaster?" Gross looked frantically around. "Damn it, blast it open!"

"Pull," Kramer grated. "Pull together."

"Are you at the hatch?" the toneless voice came, drifting and eddying through the corridors of the ship. They looked up, staring around them. "I sense something nearby, outside. A ship? You are leaving, all of you? Kramer, you are leaving, too? Very unfortunate. I had hoped we could talk. Perhaps at some other time you might be induced to remain."

"Open the hatch!" Kramer said, staring up at the impersonal walls of the ship. "For God's sake, open it!"

There was silence, an endless pause. Then, very slowly, the hatch slid back. The air screamed out, rushing past them into space.

One by one they leaped, one after the other, propelled away by the repulsive material of the suits. A few minutes later they were being hauled aboard the pursuit ship. As the last one of them was lifted through the port, their own ship pointed itself suddenly upward and shot off at tremendous speed. It disappeared.

Kramer removed his helmet, gasping. Two sailors held onto him and began to wrap him in blankets. Gross sipped a mug of coffee, shivering.

"It's gone," Kramer murmured.

"I'll have an alarm sent out," Gross said.

"What's happened to your ship?" a sailor asked curiously. "It sure took off in a hurry. Who's on it?"

"We'll have to have it destroyed," Gross went on, his face grim. "It's got to be destroyed. There's no telling what it—what *he* has in mind." Gross sat down weakly on a metal bench. "What a close call for us. We were so damn trusting."

"What could he be planning," Kramer said, half to himself. "It doesn't make sense. I don't get it."

* * *

As the ship sped back toward the moon base they sat around the table in the dining room, sipping hot coffee and thinking, not saying very much.

"Look here," Gross said at last. "What kind of man was Professor Thomas? What do you remember about him?"

Kramer put his coffee mug down. "It was ten years ago. I don't remember much. It's vague."

He let his mind run back over the years. He and Dolores had been at Hunt College together, in physics and the life sciences. The College was small and set back away from the momentum of modern life. He had gone there because it was his home town, and his father had gone there before him.

Professor Thomas had been at the College a long time, as long as anyone could remember. He was a strange old man, keeping to himself most of the time. There were many things that he disapproved of, but he seldom said what they were.

"Do you recall anything that might help us?" Gross asked. "Anything that would give us a clue as to what he might have in mind?"

Kramer nodded slowly. "I remember one thing. . . ."

One day he and the Professor had been sitting together in the school chapel, talking leisurely.

"Well, you'll be out of school, soon," the Professor had said. "What are you going to do?"

"Do? Work at one of the Government Research Projects, I suppose."

"And eventually? What's your ultimate goal?"

Kramer had smiled. "The question is unscientific. It presupposes such things as ultimate ends."

"Suppose instead along these lines, then: What if there were no war and no Government Research Projects? What would you do, then?"

"I don't know. But how can I imagine a hypothetical situation like that? There's been war as long as I can remember. We're geared for war. I don't know what I'd do. I suppose I'd adjust, get used to it."

The Professor had stared at him. "Oh, you do think you'd get accustomed to it, eh? Well, I'm glad of that. And you think you could find something to do?"

Gross listened intently. "What do you infer from this, Kramer?"

"Not much. Except that he was against war."

"We're all against war," Gross pointed out.

"True. But he was withdrawn, set apart. He lived very simply, cooking his own meals. His wife died many years ago. He was born in Europe, in Italy. He changed his name when he came to the United States. He used to read Dante and Milton. He even had a Bible."

"Very anachronistic, don't you think?"

"Yes, he lived quite a lot in the past. He found an old phonograph and records, and he listened to the old music. You saw his house, how old-fashioned it was."

"Did he have a file?" Winter asked Gross.

"With Security? No, none at all. As far as we could tell he never engaged in political work, never joined anything or even seemed to have strong political convictions."

"No," Kramer, agreed. "About all he ever did was walk through the hills. He liked nature."

"Nature can be of great use to a scientist," Gross said. "There wouldn't be any science without it."

"Kramer, what do you think his plan is, taking control of the ship and disappearing?" Winter said.

"Maybe the transfer made him insane," the Pilot said. "Maybe there's no plan, nothing rational at all."

"But he had the ship rewired, and he had made sure that he would retain consciousness and memory before he even agreed to the operation. He must have had something planned from the start. But what?"

"Perhaps he just wanted to stay alive longer," Kramer said. "He was old and about to die. Or—"

"Or what?"

"Nothing." Kramer stood up. "I think as soon as we get to the moon base I'll make a vidcall to earth. I want to talk to somebody about this."

"Who's that?" Gross asked.

"Dolores. Maybe she remembers something."

"That's a good idea," Gross said.

* * *

"Where are you calling from?" Dolores asked, when he succeeded in reaching her.

"From the moon base."

"All kinds of rumors are running around. Why didn't the ship come back? What happened?"

"I'm afraid he ran off with it."

"He?"

"The Old Man. Professor Thomas." Kramer explained what had happened.

Dolores listened intently. "How strange. And you think he planned it all in advance, from the start?"

"I'm certain. He asked for the plans of construction and the theoretical diagrams at once."

"But why? What for?"

"I don't know. Look, Dolores. What do you remember about him? Is there anything that might give a clue to all this?"

"Like what?"

"I don't know. That's the trouble."

On the vidscreen Dolores knitted her brow. "I remember he raised chickens in his back yard, and once he had a goat." She smiled. "Do you remember the day the goat got loose and wandered down the main street of town? Nobody could figure out where it came from."

"Anything else?"

"No." He watched her struggling, trying to remember. "He wanted to have a farm, sometime, I know."

"All right. Thanks." Kramer touched the switch. "When I get back to Terra maybe I'll stop and see you."

"Let me know how it works out."

He cut the line and the picture dimmed and faded. He walked slowly back to where Gross and some officers of the Military were sitting at a chart table, talking.

"Any luck?" Gross said, looking up.

"No. All she remembers is that he kept a goat."

"Come over and look at this detail chart." Gross motioned him around to his side. "Watch!"

Kramer saw the record tabs moving furiously, the little white dots racing back and forth.

"What's happening?" he asked.

"A squadron outside the defense zone has finally managed to contact the ship. They're maneuvering now, for position. Watch."

The white counters were forming a barrel formation around a black dot that was moving steadily across the board, away from the central position. As they watched, the white dots constricted around it.

"They're ready to open fire," a technician at the board said. "Commander, what shall we tell them to do?"

Gross hesitated. "I hate to be the one who makes the decision. When it comes right down to it—"

"It's not just a ship," Kramer said. "It's a man, a living person. A human being is up there, moving through space. I wish we knew what—"

"But the order has to be given. We can't take any chances. Suppose he went over to them, to the yuks."

Kramer's jaw dropped. "My God, he wouldn't do that."

"Are you sure? Do you know what he'll do?"

"He wouldn't do that."

Gross turned to the technician. "Tell them to go ahead."

"I'm sorry, sir, but now the ship has gotten away. Look down at the board."

* * *

Gross stared down, Kramer over his shoulder. The black dot had slipped through the white dots and had moved off at an abrupt angle. The white dots were broken up, dispersing in confusion.

"He's an unusual strategist," one of the officers said. He traced the line. "It's an ancient maneuver, an old Prussian device, but it worked."

The white dots were turning back. "Too many yuk ships out that far," Gross said. "Well, that's what you get when you don't act quickly." He looked up coldly at Kramer. "We should have done it when we had him. Look at him go!" He jabbed a finger at the rapidly moving black dot. The dot came to the edge of the board and stopped. It had reached the limit of the chartered area. "See?"

—Now what? Kramer thought, watching. So the Old Man had escaped the cruisers and gotten away. He was alert, all right; there was nothing wrong with his mind. Or with ability to control his new body.

Body—The ship was a new body for him. He had traded in the old dying body, withered and frail, for this hulking frame of metal and plastic, turbines and rocket jets. He was strong, now. Strong and big. The new body was more powerful than a thousand human bodies. But how long would it last him? The average life of a cruiser was only ten years. With careful handling he might get twenty out of it, before some essential part failed and there was no way to replace it.

And then, what then? What would he do, when something failed and there was no one to fix it for him? That would be the end. Someplace, far out in the cold darkness of space, the ship would slow down, silent and lifeless, to exhaust its last heat into the eternal timelessness of outer space. Or perhaps it would crash on some barren asteroid, burst into a million fragments.

It was only a question of time.

"Your wife didn't remember anything?" Gross said.

"I told you. Only that he kept a goat, once."

"A hell of a lot of help that is."

Kramer shrugged. "It's not my fault."

"I wonder if we'll ever see him again." Gross stared down at the indicator dot, still hanging at the edge of the board. "I wonder if he'll ever move back this way."

"I wonder, too," Kramer said.

* * *

That night Kramer lay in bed, tossing from side to side, unable to sleep. The moon gravity, even artificially increased, was unfamiliar to him and it made him uncomfortable. A thousand thoughts wandered loose in his head as he lay, fully awake.

What did it all mean? What was the Professor's plan? Maybe they would never know. Maybe the ship was gone for good; the Old Man had left forever, shooting into outer space. They might never find out why he had done it, what purpose—if any—had been in his mind.

Kramer sat up in bed. He turned on the light and lit a cigarette. His quarters were small, a metal-lined bunk room, part of the moon station base.

The Old Man had wanted to talk to him. He had wanted to discuss things, hold a conversation, but in the hysteria and confusion all they had been able to think of was getting away. The ship was rushing off with them, carrying them into outer space. Kramer set his jaw. Could they be blamed for jumping? They had no idea where they were being taken, or why. They were helpless, caught in their own ship, and the pursuit ship standing by waiting to pick them up was their only chance. Another half hour and it would have been too late.

But what had the Old Man wanted to say? What had he intended to tell him, in those first confusing moments when the ship around them had come alive, each metal strut and wire suddenly animate, the body of a living creature, a vast metal organism?

It was weird, unnerving. He could not forget it, even now. He looked around the small room uneasily. What did it signify, the coming to life of metal and plastic? All at once they had found themselves inside a *living* creature, in its stomach, like Jonah inside the whale.

It had been alive, and it had talked to them, talked calmly and rationally, as it rushed them off, faster and faster into outer space. The wall speaker and circuit had become the vocal cords and mouth, the wiring the spinal cord and nerves, the hatches and relays and circuit breakers the muscles.

They had been helpless, completely helpless. The ship had, in a brief second, stolen their power away from them and left them defenseless, practically at its mercy. It was not right; it made him uneasy. All his life he had controlled machines, bent nature and the forces of nature to man and man's needs. The human race had slowly evolved until it was in a position to operate things, run them as it saw fit. Now all at once it had been plunged back down the ladder again, prostrate before a Power against which they were children.

Kramer got out of bed. He put on his bathrobe and began to search for a cigarette. While he was searching, the vidphone rang.

He snapped the vidphone on.

"Yes?"

The face of the immediate monitor appeared. "A call from Terra, Mr. Kramer. An emergency call."

"Emergency call? For me? Put it through." Kramer came awake, brushing his hair back out of his eyes. Alarm plucked at him.

From the speaker a strange voice came. "Philip Kramer? Is this Kramer?"

"Yes. Go on."

"This is General Hospital, New York City, Terra. Mr. Kramer, your wife is here. She has been critically injured in an accident. Your name was given to us to call. Is it possible for you to—"

"How badly?" Kramer gripped the vidphone stand. "Is it serious?"

"Yes, it's serious, Mr. Kramer. Are you able to come here? The quicker you can come the better."

"Yes." Kramer nodded. "I'll come. Thanks."

* * *

The screen died as the connection was broken. Kramer waited a moment. Then he tapped the button. The screen relit again. "Yes, sir," the monitor said.

"Can I get a ship to Terra at once? It's an emergency. My wife—"

"There's no ship leaving the moon for eight hours. You'll have to wait until the next period."

"Isn't there anything I can do?"

"We can broadcast a general request to all ships passing through this area. Sometimes cruisers pass by here returning to Terra for repairs."

"Will you broadcast that for me? I'll come down to the field."

"Yes sir. But there may be no ship in the area for awhile. It's a gamble." The screen died.

Kramer dressed quickly. He put on his coat and hurried to the lift. A moment later he was running across the general receiving lobby, past the rows of vacant desks and conference tables. At the door the sentries stepped aside and he went outside, onto the great concrete steps.

The face of the moon was in shadow. Below him the field stretched out in total darkness, a black void, endless, without form. He made his way carefully down the steps and along the ramp along the side of the field, to the control tower. A faint row of red lights showed him the way.

Two soldiers challenged him at the foot of the tower, standing in the shadows, their guns ready.

"Kramer?"

"Yes." A light was flashed in his face.

"Your call has been sent out already."

"Any luck?" Kramer asked.

"There's a cruiser nearby that has made contact with us. It has an injured jet and is moving slowly back toward Terra, away from the line."

"Good." Kramer nodded, a flood of relief rushing through him. He lit a cigarette and gave one to each of the soldiers. The soldiers lit up.

"Sir," one of them asked, "is it true about the experimental ship?"

"What do you mean?"

"It came to life and ran off?"

"No, not exactly," Kramer said. "It had a new type of control system instead of the Johnson units. It wasn't properly tested."

"But sir, one of the cruisers that was there got up close to it, and a buddy of mine says this ship acted funny. He never saw anything like it. It was like when he was fishing once on Terra, in Washington State, fishing for bass. The fish were smart, going this way and that—"

"Here's your cruiser," the other soldier said. "Look!"

An enormous vague shape was setting slowly down onto the field. They could make nothing out but its row of tiny green blinkers. Kramer stared at the shape.

"Better hurry, sir," the soldiers said. "They don't stick around here very long."

"Thanks." Kramer loped across the field, toward the black shape that rose up above him, extended across the width of the field. The ramp was down from the side of the cruiser and he caught hold of it. The ramp rose, and a moment later Kramer was inside the hold of the ship. The hatch slid shut behind him.

As he made his way up the stairs to the main deck the turbines roared up from the moon, out into space.

Kramer opened the door to the main deck. He stopped suddenly, staring around him in surprise. There was nobody in sight. The ship was deserted.

"Good God," he said. Realization swept over him, numbing him. He sat down on a bench, his head swimming. "Good God."

The ship roared out into space leaving the moon and Terra farther behind each moment.

And there was nothing he could do.

* * *

"So it was you who put the call through," he said at last. "It was you who called me on the vidphone, not any hospital on Terra. It was all part of the plan." He looked up and around him. "And Dolores is really—"

"Your wife is fine," the wall speaker above him said tonelessly. "It was a fraud. I am sorry to trick you that way, Philip, but it was all I could think of. Another day and you would have been back on Terra. I don't want to remain in this area any longer than necessary. They have been so certain of finding me out in deep space that I have been able to stay here without too much danger. But even the purloined letter was found eventually."

Kramer smoked his cigarette nervously. "What are you going to do? Where are we going?"

"First, I want to talk to you. I have many things to discuss. I was very disappointed when you left me, along with the others. I had hoped that you would remain." The dry voice chuckled. "Remember how we used to talk in the old days, you and I? That was a long time ago."

The ship was gaining speed. It plunged through space at tremendous speed, rushing through the last of the defense zone and out beyond. A rush of nausea made Kramer bend over for a moment.

When he straightened up the voice from the wall went on, "I'm sorry to step it up so quickly, but we are still in danger. Another few moments and we'll be free."

"How about yuk ships? Aren't they out here?"

"I've already slipped away from several of them. They're quite curious about me."

"Curious?"

"They sense that I'm different, more like their own organic mines. They don't like it. I believe they will begin to withdraw from this area, soon. Apparently they don't want to get involved with me. They're an odd race, Philip. I would have liked to study them closely, try to learn something about them. I'm of the opinion that they use no inert material. All their equipment and instruments are alive, in some form or other.

They don't construct or build at all. The idea of *making* is foreign to them. They utilize existing forms. Even their ships—"

"Where are we going?" Kramer said. "I want to know where you are taking me."

"Frankly, I'm not certain."

"You're not certain?"

"I haven't worked some details out. There are a few vague spots in my program, still. But I think that in a short while I'll have them ironed out."

"What is your program?" Kramer said.

"It's really very simple. But don't you want to come into the control room and sit? The seats are much more comfortable than that metal bench."

Kramer went into the control room and sat down at the control board. Looking at the useless apparatus made him feel strange.

"What's the matter?" the speaker above the board rasped.

* * *

Kramer gestured helplessly. "I'm—powerless. I can't do anything. And I don't like it. Do you blame me?"

"No. No, I don't blame you. But you'll get your control back, soon. Don't worry. This is only a temporary expedient, taking you off this way. It was something I didn't contemplate. I forgot that orders would be given out to shoot me on sight."

"It was Gross' idea."

"I don't doubt that. My conception, my plan, came to me as soon as you began to describe your project, that day at my house. I saw at once that you were wrong; you people have no understanding of the mind at all. I realized that the transfer of a human brain from an organic body to a complex artificial space ship would not involve the loss of the intellectualization faculty of the mind. When a man thinks, he *is*.

"When I realized that, I saw the possibility of an age-old dream becoming real. I was quite elderly when I first met you, Philip. Even then my life-span had come pretty much to its end. I could look ahead to nothing but death, and with it the extinction of all my ideas. I had made no mark on the world, none at all. My students, one by one, passed from me into the world, to take up jobs in the great Research Project, the search for better and bigger weapons of war.

"The world has been fighting for a long time, first with itself, then with the Martians, then with these beings from Proxima Centauri, whom we know nothing about. The human society has evolved war as a cultural institution, like the science of astronomy, or mathematics. War is a part of our lives, a career, a respected vocation. Bright, alert young men and women move into it, putting their shoulders to the wheel as they did in the time of Nebuchadnezzar. It has always been so.

"But is it innate in mankind? I don't think so. No social custom is innate. There were many human groups that did not go to war; the Eskimos never grasped the idea at all, and the American Indians never took to it well.

"But these dissenters were wiped out, and a cultural pattern was established that became the standard for the whole planet. Now it has become ingrained in us.

"But if someplace along the line some other way of settling problems had arisen and taken hold, something different than the massing of men and material to—"

"What's your plan?" Kramer said. "I know the theory. It was part of one of your lectures."

"Yes, buried in a lecture on plant selection, as I recall. When you came to me with this proposition I realized that perhaps my conception could be brought to life, after all. If my theory were right that war is only a habit, not an instinct, a society built up apart from Terra with a minimum of cultural roots might develop differently. If it failed to absorb our outlook, if it could start out on another foot, it might not arrive at the same point to which we have come: a dead end, with nothing but greater and greater wars in sight, until nothing is left but ruin and destruction everywhere.

"Of course, there would have to be a Watcher to guide the experiment, at first. A crisis would undoubtedly come very quickly, probably in the second generation. Cain would arise almost at once.

"You see, Kramer, I estimate that if I remain at rest most of the time, on some small planet or moon, I may be able to keep functioning for almost a hundred years. That would be time enough, sufficient to see the direction of the new colony. After that—Well, after that it would be up to the colony itself.

"Which is just as well, of course. Man must take control eventually, on his own. One hundred years, and after that they will have control of their own destiny. Perhaps I am wrong, perhaps war is more than a habit. Perhaps it is a law of the universe, that things can only survive as groups by group violence.

"But I'm going ahead and taking the chance that it is only a habit, that I'm right, that war is something we're so accustomed to that we don't realize it is a very unnatural thing. Now as to the place! I'm still a little vague about that. We must find the place, still.

"That's what we're doing now. You and I are going to inspect a few systems off the beaten path, planets where the trading prospects are low enough to keep Terran ships away. I know of one planet that might be a good place. It was reported by the Fairchild Expedition in their original manual. We may look into that, for a start."

The ship was silent.

*   *   *

Kramer sat for a time, staring down at the metal floor under him. The floor throbbed dully with the motion of the turbines. At last he looked up.

"You might be right. Maybe our outlook is only a habit." Kramer got to his feet. "But I wonder if something has occurred to you?"

"What is that?"

"If it's such a deeply ingrained habit, going back thousands of years, how are you going to get your colonists to make the break, leave Terra and Terran customs? How about *this* generation, the first ones, the people who found the colony? I think you're right that the next generation would be free of all this, if there were an—" He grinned. "—An Old Man Above to teach them something else instead."

Kramer looked up at the wall speaker. "How are you going to get the people to leave Terra and come with you, if by your own theory, this generation can't be saved, it all has to start with the next?"

The wall speaker was silent. Then it made a sound, the faint dry chuckle.

"I'm surprised at you Philip. Settlers can be found. We won't need many, just a few." The speaker chuckled again. "I'll acquaint you with my solution."

At the far end of the corridor a door slid open. There was sound, a hesitant sound. Kramer turned.

"Dolores!"

Dolores Kramer stood uncertainly, looking into the control room. She blinked in amazement. "Phil! What are you doing here? What's going on?"

They stared at each other.

"What's happening?" Dolores said. "I received a vidcall that you had been hurt in a lunar explosion—"

The wall speaker rasped into life. "You see, Philip, that problem is already solved. We don't really need so many people; even a single couple might do."

Kramer nodded slowly. "I see," he murmured thickly. "Just one couple. One man and woman."

"They might make it all right, if there were someone to watch and see that things went as they should. There will be quite a few things I can help you with, Philip. Quite a few. We'll get along very well, I think."

Kramer grinned wryly. "You could even help us name the animals," he said. "I understand that's the first step."

"I'll be glad to," the toneless, impersonal voice said. "As I recall, my part will be to bring them to you, one by one. Then you can do the actual naming."

"I don't understand," Dolores faltered. "What does he mean, Phil? Naming animals. What kind of animals? Where are we going?"

Kramer walked slowly over to the port and stood staring silently out, his arms folded. Beyond the ship a myriad fragments of light gleamed, countless coals glowing in the dark void. Stars, suns, systems. Endless, without number. A universe of worlds. An infinity of planets, waiting for them, gleaming and winking from the darkness.

He turned back, away from the port. "Where are we going?" He smiled at his wife, standing nervous and frightened, her large eyes full of alarm. "I don't know where we are going," he said. "But somehow that doesn't seem too important right now. . . . I'm beginning to see the Professor's point, it's the result that counts."

And for the first time in many months he put his arm around Dolores. At first she stiffened, the fright and nervousness still in her eyes. But then suddenly she relaxed against him and there were tears wetting her cheeks.

"Phil . . . do you really think we can start over again—you and I?"

He kissed her tenderly, then passionately.

And the spaceship shot swiftly through the endless, trackless eternity of the void. . . .

The Variable Man

He fixed things—clocks, refrigerators, vidsenders and destinies. But he had no business in the future, where the calculators could not handle him. He was Earth's only hope—and its sure failure!

Security Commissioner Reinhart rapidly climbed the front steps and entered the Council building. Council guards stepped quickly aside and he entered the familiar place of great whirring machines. His thin face rapt, eyes alight with emotion, Reinhart gazed intently up at the central SRB computer, studying its reading.

"Straight gain for the last quarter," observed Kaplan, the lab organizer. He grinned proudly, as if personally responsible. "Not bad, Commissioner."

"We're catching up to them," Reinhart retorted. "But too damn slowly. We must finally go over—and soon."

Kaplan was in a talkative mood. "We design new offensive weapons, they counter with improved defenses. And nothing is actually made! Continual improvement, but neither we nor Centaurus can stop designing long enough to stabilize for production."

"It will end," Reinhart stated coldly, "as soon as Terra turns out a weapon for which Centaurus can build no defense."

"Every weapon has a defense. Design and discord. Immediate obsolescence. Nothing lasts long enough to—"

"What we count on is the *lag*," Reinhart broke in, annoyed. His hard gray eyes bored into the lab organizer and Kaplan slunk back. "The time lag between our offensive design and their counter development. The lag varies." He waved impatiently toward the massed banks of SRB machines. "As you well know."

At this moment, 9:30 AM, May 7, 2136, the statistical ratio on the SRB machines stood at 21–17 on the Centauran side of the ledger. All facts considered, the odds favored a successful repulsion by Proxima Centaurus of a Terran military attack. The ratio was based on the total information known to the SRB machines, on a gestalt of the vast flow of data that poured in endlessly from all sectors of the Sol and Centaurus systems.

21–17 on the Centauran side. But a month ago it had been 24–18 in the enemy's favor. Things were improving, slowly but steadily. Centaurus, older and less virile than Terra, was unable to match Terra's rate of technocratic advance. Terra was pulling ahead.

"If we went to war now," Reinhart said thoughtfully, "we would lose. We're not far enough along to risk an overt attack." A harsh, ruthless glow twisted across his handsome features, distorting them into a stern mask. "But the odds are moving in our favor. Our offensive designs are gradually gaining on their defenses."

"Let's hope the war comes soon," Kaplan agreed. "We're all on edge. This damn waiting. . . ."

The war would come soon. Reinhart knew it intuitively. The air was full of tension, the *elan*. He left the SRB rooms and hurried down the corridor to his own elaborately guarded office in the Security wing. It wouldn't be long. He could practically feel the hot breath of destiny on his neck—for him a pleasant feeling. His thin lips set in a humorless smile, showing an even line of white teeth against his tanned skin. It made him feel good, all right. He'd been working at it a long time.

First contact, a hundred years earlier, had ignited instant conflict between Proxima Centauran outposts and exploring Terran raiders. Flash fights, sudden eruptions of fire and energy beams.

And then the long, dreary years of inaction between enemies where contact required years of travel, even at nearly the speed of light. The two systems were evenly matched. Screen against screen. Warship against power station. The Centauran Empire surrounded Terra, an iron ring that couldn't be broken, rusty and corroded as it was. Radical new weapons had to be conceived, if Terra was to break out.

Through the windows of his office, Reinhart could see endless buildings and streets, Terrans hurrying back and forth. Bright specks that were commute ships, little eggs that carried businessmen and white-collar workers around. The huge transport tubes that shot masses of workmen to factories and labor camps from their housing units. All these people, waiting to break out. Waiting for the day.

Reinhart snapped on his vidscreen, the confidential channel. "Give me Military Designs," he ordered sharply.

* * *

He sat tense, his wiry body taut, as the vidscreen warmed into life. Abruptly he was facing the hulking image of Peter Sherikov, director of the vast network of labs under the Ural Mountains.

Sherikov's great bearded features hardened as he recognized Reinhart. His bushy black eyebrows pulled up in a sullen line. "What do you want? You know I'm busy. We have too much work to do, as it is. Without being bothered by—politicians."

"I'm dropping over your way," Reinhart answered lazily. He adjusted the cuff of his immaculate gray cloak. "I want a full description of your work and whatever progress you've made."

"You'll find a regular departmental report plate filed in the usual way, around your office someplace. If you'll refer to that you'll know exactly what we—"

"I'm not interested in that. I want to *see* what you're doing. And I expect you to be prepared to describe your work fully. I'll be there shortly. Half an hour."

* * *

Reinhart cut the circuit. Sherikov's heavy features dwindled and faded. Reinhart relaxed, letting his breath out. Too bad he had to work with Sherikov. He had never liked the man. The big Polish scientist was an individualist, refusing to integrate himself with society. Independent, atomistic in outlook. He held concepts of the individual as an end, diametrically contrary to the accepted organic state Weltansicht.

But Sherikov was the leading research scientist, in charge of the Military Designs Department. And on Designs the whole future of Terra depended. Victory over Centaurus—or more waiting, bottled up in the Sol System, surrounded by a rotting, hostile Empire, now sinking into ruin and decay, yet still strong.

Reinhart got quickly to his feet and left the office. He hurried down the hall and out of the Council building.

A few minutes later he was heading across the mid-morning sky in his highspeed cruiser, toward the Asiatic land-mass, the vast Ural mountain range. Toward the Military Designs labs.

Sherikov met him at the entrance. "Look here, Reinhart. Don't think you're going to order me around. I'm not going to—"

"Take it easy." Reinhart fell into step beside the bigger man. They passed through the check and into the auxiliary labs. "No immediate coercion will be exerted over you or your staff. You're free to continue your work as you see fit—for the present. Let's get this straight. My concern is to integrate your work with our total social needs. As long as your work is sufficiently productive—"

Reinhart stopped in his tracks.

"Pretty, isn't he?" Sherikov said ironically.

"What the hell is it?

"Icarus, we call him. Remember the Greek myth? The legend of Icarus. Icarus flew. . . . This Icarus is going to fly, one of these days." Sherikov shrugged. "You can examine him, if you want. I suppose this is what you came here to see."

Reinhart advanced slowly. "This is the weapon you've been working on?"

"How does he look?"

Rising up in the center of the chamber was a squat metal cylinder, a great ugly cone of dark gray. Technicians circled around it, wiring up the exposed relay banks. Reinhart caught a glimpse of endless tubes and filaments, a maze of wires and terminals and parts criss-crossing each other, layer on layer.

"What is it?" Reinhart perched on the edge of a workbench, leaning his big shoulders against the wall. "An idea of Jamison Hedge—the same man who developed our instantaneous interstellar vidcasts forty years ago. He was trying to find a method of faster than light travel when he was killed, destroyed along with most of his work. After that ftl research was abandoned. It looked as if there were no future in it."

"Wasn't it shown that nothing could travel faster than light?"

"The interstellar vidcasts do! No, Hedge developed a valid ftl drive. He managed to propel an object at fifty times the speed of light. But as the object gained speed, its length began to diminish and its mass increased. This was in line with familiar twentieth-century concepts of mass-energy transformation. We conjectured that as Hedge's object gained velocity it would continue to lose length and gain mass until its length became nil and its mass infinite. Nobody can imagine such an object."

"Go on."

"But what actually occurred is this. Hedge's object continued to lose length and gain mass until it reached the theoretical limit of velocity, the speed of light. At that point the object, still gaining speed, simply ceased to exist. Having no length, it ceased to occupy space. It disappeared. However, the object had not been *destroyed.* It continued on its way, gaining momentum each moment, moving in an arc across the galaxy, away from the Sol system. Hedge's object entered some other realm of being, beyond our powers of conception. The next phase of Hedge's experiment consisted in a search for some way to slow the ftl object down, back to a sub-ftl speed, hence back into our universe. This counterprinciple was eventually worked out."

"With what result?"

"The death of Hedge and destruction of most of his equipment. His experimental object, in re-entering the space-time universe, came into being in space already occupied by matter. Possessing an incredible mass, just below infinity level, Hedge's object exploded in a titanic cataclysm. It was obvious that no space travel was possible with such a drive. Virtually all space contains *some* matter. To re-enter space would bring automatic destruction. Hedge had found his ftl drive and his counterprinciple, but no one before this has been able to put them to any use."

Reinhart walked over toward the great metal cylinder. Sherikov jumped down and followed him. "I don't get it," Reinhart said. "You said the principle is no good for space travel."

"That's right."

"What's this for, then? If the ship explodes as soon as it returns to our universe—"

"This is not a ship." Sherikov grinned slyly. "Icarus is the first practical application of Hedge's principles. Icarus is a bomb."

"So this is our weapon," Reinhart said. "A bomb. An immense bomb."

"A bomb, moving at a velocity greater than light. A bomb which will not exist in our universe. The Centaurans won't be able to detect or stop it. How could they? As soon as it passes the speed of light it will cease to exist—beyond all detection."

"But—"

"Icarus will be launched outside the lab, on the surface. He will align himself with Proxima Centaurus, gaining speed rapidly. By the time he reaches his destination he will be traveling at ftl-100. Icarus will be brought back to this universe within Centaurus itself. The explosion should destroy the star and wash away most of its planets—including their central hub-planet, Armun. There is no way they can halt Icarus, once he has been launched. No defense is possible. Nothing can stop him. It is a real fact."

"When will he be ready?"

Sherikov's eyes flickered. "Soon."

"Exactly how soon?"

The big Pole hesitated. "As a matter of fact, there's only one thing holding us back."

Sherikov led Reinhart around to the other side of the lab. He pushed a lab guard out of the way.

"See this?" He tapped a round globe, open at one end, the size of a grapefruit. "This is holding us up."

"What is it?"

"The central control turret. This thing brings Icarus back to sub-ftl flight at the correct moment. It must be absolutely accurate. Icarus will be within the star only a matter of a microsecond. If the turret does not function exactly, Icarus will pass out the other side and shoot beyond the Centauran system."

"How near completed is this turret?"

Sherikov hedged uncertainly, spreading out his big hands. "Who can say? It must be wired with infinitely minute equipment—microscope grapples and wires invisible to the naked eye."

"Can you name any completion date?"

Sherikov reached into his coat and brought out a manila folder. "I've drawn up the data for the SRB machines, giving a date of completion. You can go ahead and feed it. I entered ten days as the maximum period. The machines can work from that."

Reinhart accepted the folder cautiously. "You're sure about the date? I'm not convinced I can trust you, Sherikov."

Sherikov's features darkened. "You'll have to take a chance, Commissioner. I don't trust you any more than you trust me. I know how much you'd like an excuse to get me out of here and one of your puppets in."

Reinhart studied the huge scientist thoughtfully. Sherikov was going to be a hard nut to crack. Designs was responsible to Security, not the Council. Sherikov was losing ground—but he was still a potential danger. Stubborn, individualistic, refusing to subordinate his welfare to the general good.

"All right." Reinhart put the folder slowly away in his coat. "I'll feed it. But you better be able to come through. There can't be any slip-ups. Too much hangs on the next few days."

"If the odds change in our favor are you going to give the mobilization order?"

"Yes," Reinhart stated. "I'll give the order the moment I see the odds change."

* * *

Standing in front of the machines, Reinhart waited nervously for the results. It was two o'clock in the afternoon. The day was warm, a pleasant May afternoon. Outside the building the daily life of the planet went on as usual.

As usual? Not exactly. The feeling was in the air, an expanding excitement growing every day. Terra had waited a long time. The attack on Proxima Centaurus had to come—and the sooner the better. The ancient Centauran Empire hemmed in Terra, bottled the human race up in its one system. A vast, suffocating net draped across the heavens, cutting Terra off from the bright diamonds beyond. . . . And it had to end.

The SRB machines whirred, the visible combination disappearing. For a time no ratio showed. Reinhart tensed, his body rigid. He waited.

The new ratio appeared.

Reinhart gasped. 7–6. Toward Terra!

Within five minutes the emergency mobilization alert had been flashed to all Government departments. The Council and President Duffe had been called to immediate session. Everything was happening fast.

But there was no doubt. 7–6. In Terra's favor. Reinhart hurried frantically to get his papers in order, in time for the Council session.

At histo-research the message plate was quickly pulled from the confidential slot and rushed across the central lab to the chief official.

"Look at this!" Fredman dropped the plate on his superior's desk. "Look at it!"

Harper picked up the plate, scanning it rapidly. "Sounds like the real thing. I didn't think we'd live to see it."

Fredman left the room, hurrying down the hall. He entered the time bubble office. "Where's the bubble?" he demanded, looking around.

One of the technicians looked slowly up. "Back about two hundred years. We're coming up with interesting data on the War of 1914. According to material the bubble has already brought up—"

"Cut it. We're through with routine work. Get the bubble back to the present. From now on all equipment has to be free for Military work."

"But—the bubble is regulated automatically."

"You can bring it back manually."

"It's risky." The technician hedged. "If the emergency requires it, I suppose we could take a chance and cut the automatic."

"The emergency requires *everything*," Fredman said feelingly.

"But the odds might change back," Margaret Duffe, President of the Council, said nervously. "Any minute they can revert."

"This is our chance!" Reinhart snapped, his temper rising. "What the hell's the matter with you? We've waited years for this."

The Council buzzed with excitement. Margaret Duffe hesitated uncertainly, her blue eyes clouded with worry. "I realize the opportunity is here. At least, statistically. But the new odds have just appeared. How do we know they'll last? They stand on the basis of a single weapon."

"You're wrong. You don't grasp the situation." Reinhart held himself in check with great effort. "Sherikov's weapon tipped the ratio in our favor. But the odds have been moving in our direction for months. It was only a question of time. The new balance was inevitable, sooner or later. It's not just Sherikov. He's only one factor in this. It's all nine planets of the Sol System—not a single man."

One of the Councilmen stood up. "The President must be aware the entire planet is eager to end this waiting. All our activities for the past eighty years have been directed toward—"

Reinhart moved close to the slender President of the Council. "If you don't approve the war, there probably will be mass rioting. Public reaction will be strong. Damn strong. And you know it."

Margaret Duffe shot him a cold glance. "You sent out the emergency order to force my hand. You were fully aware of what you were doing. You knew once the order was out there'd be no stopping things."

A murmur rushed through the Council, gaining volume. "We have to approve the war! . . . We're committed! . . . It's too late to turn back!"

Shouts, angry voices, insistent waves of sound lapped around Margaret Duffe. "I'm as much for the war as anybody," she said sharply. "I'm only urging moderation. An inter-system war is a big thing. We're going to war because a machine says we have a statistical chance of winning."

"There's no use starting the war unless we can win it," Reinhart said. "The SRB machines tell us whether we can win."

"They tell us our *chance* of winning. They don't guarantee anything."

"What more can we ask, beside a good chance of winning?"

Margaret Duffe clamped her jaw together tightly. "All right. I hear all the clamor. I won't stand in the way of Council approval. The vote can go ahead." Her cold, alert eyes appraised Reinhart. "Especially since the emergency order has already been sent out to all Government departments."

"Good." Reinhart stepped away with relief. "Then it's settled. We can finally go ahead with full mobilization."

Mobilization proceeded rapidly. The next forty-eight hours were alive with activity.

Reinhart attended a policy-level Military briefing in the Council rooms, conducted by Fleet Commander Carleton.

"You can see our strategy," Carleton said. He traced a diagram on the blackboard with a wave of his hand. "Sherikov states it'll take eight more days to complete the ftl bomb. During that time the fleet we have near the Centauran system will take up positions. As the bomb goes off the fleet will begin operations against the remaining Centauran ships. Many will no doubt survive the blast, but with Armun gone we should be able to handle them."

Reinhart took Commander Carleton's place. "I can report on the economic situation. Every factory on Terra is converted to arms production. With Armun out of the way we should be able to promote mass insurrection among the Centauran colonies. An inter-system Empire is hard to maintain, even with ships that approach light speed. Local war-lords should pop up all over the place. We want to have weapons available for them and ships starting *now* to reach them in time. Eventually we hope to provide a unifying principle around which the colonies can all collect. Our interest is more economic than political. They can have any kind of government they want, as long as they act as supply areas for us. As our eight system planets act now."

Carleton resumed his report. "Once the Centauran fleet has been scattered we can begin the crucial stage of the war. The landing of men and supplies from the ships we have waiting in all key areas throughout the Centauran system. In this stage—"

Reinhart moved away. It was hard to believe only two days had passed since the mobilization order had been sent out. The whole system was alive, functioning with feverish activity. Countless problems were being solved—but much remained.

He entered the lift and ascended to the SRB room, curious to see if there had been any change in the machines' reading. He found it the same. So far so good. Did the Centaurans know about Icarus? No doubt; but there wasn't anything they could do about it. At least, not in eight days.

Kaplan came over to Reinhart, sorting a new batch of data that had come in. The lab organizer searched through his data. "An amusing item came in. It might interest you." He handed a message plate to Reinhart.

It was from histo-research:

> May 9, 2136
> This is to report that in bringing the research time bubble up to the present the manual return was used for the first time. Therefore a clean break was not made, and a quantity of material from the past was brought forward. This material included an individual from the early twentieth century who escaped from the lab immediately. He has not yet been taken into protective custody. Histo-research regrets this incident, but attributes it to the emergency.
> E. Fredman

Reinhart handed the plate back to Kaplan. "Interesting. A man from the past—hauled into the middle of the biggest war the universe has seen."

"Strange things happen. I wonder what the machines will think."

"Hard to say. Probably nothing." Reinhart left the room and hurried along the corridor to his own office.

As soon as he was inside he called Sherikov on the vidscreen, using the confidential line.

The Pole's heavy features appeared. "Good day, Commissioner. How's the war effort?"

"Fine. How's the turret wiring proceeding?"

A faint frown flickered across Sherikov's face. "As a matter of fact, Commissioner—"

"What's the matter?" Reinhart said sharply.

Sherikov floundered. "You know how these things are. I've taken my crew off it and tried robot workers. They have greater dexterity, but they can't make decisions. This calls for more than mere dexterity. This calls for—" He searched for the word. "—for an *artist.*"

Reinhart's face hardened. "Listen, Sherikov. You have eight days left to complete the bomb. The data given to the SRB machines contained that information. The 7–6 ratio is based on that estimate. If you don't come through—"

Sherikov twisted in embarrassment. "Don't get excited, Commissioner. We'll complete it."

"I hope so. Call me as soon as it's done." Reinhart snapped off the connection. If Sherikov let them down he'd have him taken out and shot. The whole war depended on the ftl bomb.

The vidscreen glowed again. Reinhart snapped it on. Kaplan's face formed on it. The lab organizer's face was pale and frozen. "Commissioner, you better come up to the SRB office. Something's happened."

"What is it?"

"I'll show you."

Alarmed, Reinhart hurried out of his office and down the corridor. He found Kaplan standing in front of the SRB machines. "What's the story?" Reinhart demanded. He glanced down at the reading. It was unchanged.

Kaplan held up a message plate nervously. "A moment ago I fed this into the machines. After I saw the results I quickly removed it. It's that item I showed you. From histo-research. About the man from the past."

"What happened when you fed it?"

Kaplan swallowed unhappily. "I'll show you. I'll do it again. Exactly as before." He fed the plate into a moving intake belt. "Watch the visible figures," Kaplan muttered.

Reinhart watched, tense and rigid. For a moment nothing happened. 7–6 continued to show. Then—

The figures disappeared. The machines faltered. New figures showed briefly. 4–24 for Centaurus. Reinhart gasped, suddenly sick with apprehension. But the figures vanished. New figures appeared. 16–38 for Centaurus. Then 48–86. 79–15 in Terra's favor. Then nothing. The machines whirred, but nothing happened.

Nothing at all. No figures. Only a blank.

"What's it mean?" Reinhart muttered, dazed.

"It's fantastic. We didn't think this could—"

"What's happened?"

"The machines aren't able to handle the item. No reading can come. It's data they can't integrate. They can't use it for prediction material, and it throws off all their other figures."

"Why?"

"It's—it's a variable." Kaplan was shaking, white-lipped and pale. "Something from which no inference can be made. The man from the past. The machines can't deal with him. The variable man!"

II

Thomas Cole was sharpening a knife with his whetstone when the tornado hit.

The knife belonged to the lady in the big green house. Every time Cole came by with his Fixit cart the lady had something to be sharpened. Once in awhile she gave him a cup of coffee, hot black coffee from an old bent pot. He liked that fine; he enjoyed good coffee.

The day was drizzly and overcast. Business had been bad. An automobile had scared his two horses. On bad days less people were outside and he had to get down from the cart and go to ring doorbells.

But the man in the yellow house had given him a dollar for fixing his electric refrigerator. Nobody else had been able to fix it, not even the factory man. The dollar would go a long way. A dollar was a lot.

He knew it was a tornado even before it hit him. Everything was silent. He was bent over his whetstone, the reins between his knees, absorbed in his work.

He had done a good job on the knife; he was almost finished. He spat on the blade and was holding it up to see—and then the tornado came.

All at once it was there, completely around him. Nothing but grayness. He and the cart and horses seemed to be in a calm spot in the center of the tornado. They were moving in a great silence, gray mist everywhere.

And while he was wondering what to do, and how to get the lady's knife back to her, all at once there was a bump and the tornado tipped him over, sprawled out on the ground. The horses screamed in fear, struggling to pick themselves up. Cole got quickly to his feet.

Where was he?

The grayness was gone. White walls stuck up on all sides. A deep light gleamed down, not daylight but something like it. The team was pulling the cart on its side, dragging it along, tools and equipment falling out. Cole righted the cart, leaping up onto the seat.

And for the first time saw the people.

Men, with astonished white faces, in some sort of uniforms. Shouts, noise and confusion. And a feeling of danger!

Cole headed the team toward the door. Hoofs thundered steel against steel as they pounded through the doorway, scattering the astonished men in all directions. He was out in a wide hall. A building, like a hospital.

The hall divided. More men were coming, spilling from all sides.

Shouting and milling in excitement, like white ants. Something cut past him, a beam of dark violet. It seared off a corner of the cart, leaving the wood smoking.

Cole felt fear. He kicked at the terrified horses. They reached a big door, crashing wildly against it. The door gave—and they were outside, bright sunlight blinking down on them. For a sickening second the cart tilted, almost turning over. Then the horses gained speed, racing across an open field, toward a distant line of green, Cole holding tightly to the reins.

Behind him the little white-faced men had come out and were standing in a group, gesturing frantically. He could hear their faint shrill shouts.

But he had got away. He was safe. He slowed the horses down and began to breathe again.

The woods were artificial. Some kind of park. But the park was wild and overgrown. A dense jungle of twisted plants. Everything growing in confusion.

The park was empty. No one was there. By the position of the sun he could tell it was either early morning or late afternoon. The smell of the flowers and grass, the dampness of the leaves, indicated morning. It had been late afternoon when the tornado had picked him up. And the sky had been overcast and cloudy.

Cole considered. Clearly, he had been carried a long way. The hospital, the men with white faces, the odd lighting, the accented words he had caught—everything indicated he was no longer in Nebraska—maybe not even in the United States.

Some of his tools had fallen out and gotten lost along the way. Cole collected everything that remained, sorting them, running his fingers over each tool with affection. Some of the little chisels and wood gouges were gone. The bit box had opened, and most of the smaller bits had been lost. He gathered up those that remained and replaced them tenderly in the box. He took a key-hole saw down, and with an oil rag wiped it carefully and replaced it.

Above the cart the sun rose slowly in the sky. Cole peered up, his horny hand over his eyes. A big man, stoop-shouldered, his chin gray and stubbled. His clothes wrinkled and dirty. But his eyes were clear, a pale blue, and his hands were finely made.

He could not stay in the park. They had seen him ride that way; they would be looking for him.

Far above something shot rapidly across the sky. A tiny black dot moving with incredible haste. A second dot followed. The two dots were gone almost before he saw them. They were utterly silent.

Cole frowned, perturbed. The dots made him uneasy. He would have to keep moving—and looking for food. His stomach was already beginning to rumble and groan.

Work. There was plenty he could do: gardening, sharpening, grinding, repair work on machines and clocks, fixing all kinds of household things. Even painting and odd jobs and carpentry and chores.

He could do anything. Anything people wanted done. For a meal and pocket money.

Thomas Cole urged the team into life, moving forward. He sat hunched over in the seat, watching intently, as the Fixit cart rolled slowly across the tangled grass, through the jungle of trees and flowers.

* * *

Reinhart hurried, racing his cruiser at top speed, followed by a second ship, a military escort. The ground sped by below him, a blur of gray and green.

The remains of New York lay spread out, a twisted, blunted ruin overgrown with weeds and grass. The great atomic wars of the twentieth century had turned virtually the whole seaboard area into an endless waste of slag.

Slag and weeds below him. And then the sudden tangle that had been Central Park.

Histo-research came into sight. Reinhart swooped down, bringing his cruiser to rest at the small supply field behind the main buildings.

Harper, the chief official of the department, came quickly over as soon as Reinhart's ship landed.

"Frankly, we don't understand why you consider this matter important," Harper said uneasily.

Reinhart shot him a cold glance. "I'll be the judge of what's important. Are you the one who gave the order to bring the bubble back manually?"

"Fredman gave the actual order. In line with your directive to have all facilities ready for—"

Reinhart headed toward the entrance of the research building. "Where is Fredman?"

"Inside."

"I want to see him. Let's go."

Fredman met them inside. He greeted Reinhart calmly, showing no emotion. "Sorry to cause you trouble, Commissioner. We were trying to get the station in order for the war. We wanted the bubble back as quickly as possible." He eyed Reinhart curiously. "No doubt the man and his cart will soon be picked up by your police."

"I want to know everything that happened, in exact detail."

Fredman shifted uncomfortably. "There's not much to tell. I gave the order to have the automatic setting canceled and the bubble brought back manually. At the moment the signal reached it, the bubble was passing through the spring of 1913. As it broke loose, it tore off a piece of ground on which this person and his cart were located. The person naturally was brought up to the present, inside the bubble."

"Didn't any of your instruments tell you the bubble was loaded?"

"We were too excited to take any readings. Half an hour after the manual control was thrown, the bubble materialized in the observation room. It was de-energized before anyone noticed what was inside. We tried to stop him but he drove the cart out into the hall, bowling us out of the way. The horses were in a panic."

"What kind of cart was it?"

"There was some kind of sign on it. Painted in black letters on both sides. No one saw what it was."

"Go ahead. What happened then?"

"Somebody fired a Slem-ray after him, but it missed. The horses carried him out of the building and onto the grounds. By the time we reached the exit the cart was half way to the park."

Reinhart reflected. "If he's still in the park we should have him shortly. But we must be careful." He was already starting back toward his ship, leaving Fredman behind. Harper fell in beside him.

Reinhart halted by his ship. He beckoned some Government guards over. "Put the executive staff of this department under arrest. I'll have them tried on a treason count, later on." He smiled ironically as Harper's face blanched sickly pale. "There's a war going on. You'll be lucky if you get off alive."

Reinhart entered his ship and left the surface, rising rapidly into the sky. A second ship followed after him, a military escort. Reinhart flew high above the sea of gray slag, the unrecovered waste area. He passed over a sudden square of green set in the ocean of gray. Reinhart gazed back at it until it was gone.

Central Park. He could see police ships racing through the sky, ships and transports loaded with troops, heading toward the square of green. On the ground some heavy guns and surface cars rumbled along, lines of black approaching the park from all sides.

They would have the man soon. But meanwhile, the SRB machines were blank. And on the SRB machines' readings the whole war depended.

About noon the cart reached the edge of the park. Cole rested for a moment, allowing the horses time to crop at the thick grass. The silent expanse of slag amazed him. What had happened? Nothing stirred. No buildings, no sign of life. Grass and weeds poked up occasionally through it, breaking the flat surface here and there, but even so, the sight gave him an uneasy chill.

Cole drove the cart slowly out onto the slag, studying the sky above him. There was nothing to hide him, now that he was out of the park. The slag was bare and uniform, like the ocean. If he were spotted—

A horde of tiny black dots raced across the sky, coming rapidly closer. Presently they veered to the right and disappeared. More planes, wingless metal planes. He watched them go, driving slowly on.

Half an hour later something appeared ahead. Cole slowed the cart down, peering to see. The slag came to an end. He had reached its limits. Ground appeared, dark soil and grass. Weeds grew everywhere. Ahead of him, beyond the end of the slag, was a line of buildings, houses of some sort. Or sheds.

Houses, probably. But not like any he had ever seen.

The houses were uniform, all exactly the same. Like little green shells, rows of them, several hundred. There was a little lawn in front of each. Lawn, a path, a front porch, bushes in a meager row around each house. But the houses were all alike and very small.

Little green shells in precise, even rows. He urged the cart cautiously forward, toward the houses.

No one seemed to be around. He entered a street between two rows of houses, the hoofs of his two horses sounding loudly in the silence. He was in some kind of town. But there were no dogs or children. Everything was neat and silent. Like a model. An exhibit. It made him uncomfortable.

A young man walking along the pavement gaped at him in wonder. An oddly-dressed youth, in a toga-like cloak that hung down to his knees. A single piece of fabric. And sandals.

Or what looked like sandals. Both the cloak and the sandals were of some strange half-luminous material. It glowed faintly in the sunlight. Metallic, rather than cloth.

A woman was watering flowers at the edge of a lawn. She straightened up as his team of horses came near. Her eyes widened in astonishment—and then fear. Her mouth fell open in a soundless O and her sprinkling can slipped from her fingers and rolled silently onto the lawn.

Cole blushed and turned his head quickly away. The woman was scarcely dressed! He flicked the reins and urged the horses to hurry.

Behind him, the woman still stood. He stole a brief, hasty look back—and then shouted hoarsely to his team, ears scarlet. He had seen right. She wore only a pair of translucent shorts. Nothing else. A mere fragment of the same half-luminous material that glowed and sparkled. The rest of her small body was utterly naked.

He slowed the team down. She had been pretty. Brown hair and eyes, deep red lips. Quite a good figure. Slender waist, downy legs, bare and supple, full breasts—. He clamped the thought furiously off. He had to get to work. Business.

Cole halted the Fixit cart and leaped down onto the pavement. He selected a house at random and approached it cautiously. The house was attractive. It had a certain simple beauty. But it looked frail—and exactly like the others.

He stepped up on the porch. There was no bell. He searched for it, running his hand uneasily over the surface of the door. All at once there was a click, a sharp snap on a level with his eyes. Cole glanced up, startled. A lens was vanishing as the door section slid over it. He had been photographed.

While he was wondering what it meant, the door swung suddenly open. A man filled up the entrance, a big man in a tan uniform, blocking the way ominously.

"What do you want?" the man demanded.

"I'm looking for work," Cole murmured. "Any kind of work. I can do anything, fix any kind of thing. I repair broken objects. Things that need mending." His voice trailed off uncertainly. "Anything at all."

"Apply to the Placement Department of the Federal Activities Control Board," the man said crisply. "You know all occupational therapy is handled through them." He eyed Cole curiously. "Why have you got on those ancient clothes?"

"Ancient? Why, I—"

The man gazed past him at the Fixit cart and the two dozing horses. "What's that? What are those two animals? *Horses?*" The man rubbed his jaw, studying Cole intently. "That's strange," he said.

"Strange?" Cole murmured uneasily. "Why?"

"There haven't been any horses for over a century. All the horses were wiped out during the Fifth Atomic War. That's why it's strange."

Cole tensed, suddenly alert. There was something in the man's eyes, a hardness, a piercing look. Cole moved back off the porch, onto the path. He had to be careful. Something was wrong.

"I'll be going," he murmured.

"There haven't been any horses for over a hundred years." The man came toward Cole. "Who are you? Why are you dressed up like that? Where did you get that vehicle and pair of horses?"

"I'll be going," Cole repeated, moving away.

The man whipped something from his belt, a thin metal tube. He stuck it toward Cole.

It was a rolled-up paper, a thin sheet of metal in the form of a tube. Words, some kind of script. He could not make any of them out. The man's picture, rows of numbers, figures—

"I'm Director Winslow," the man said. "Federal Stockpile Conservation. You better talk fast, or there'll be a Security car here in five minutes."

Cole moved—fast. He raced, head down, back along the path to the cart, toward the street.

Something hit him. A wall of force, throwing him down on his face. He sprawled in a heap, numb and dazed. His body ached, vibrating wildly, out of control. Waves of shock rolled over him, gradually diminishing.

He got shakily to his feet. His head spun. He was weak, shattered, trembling violently. The man was coming down the walk after him. Cole pulled himself onto the cart, gasping and retching. The horses jumped into life. Cole rolled over against the seat, sick with the motion of the swaying cart.

He caught hold of the reins and managed to drag himself up in a sitting position. The cart gained speed, turning a corner. Houses flew past. Cole urged the team weakly, drawing great shuddering breaths. Houses and streets, a blur of motion, as the cart flew faster and faster along.

Then he was leaving the town, leaving the neat little houses behind. He was on some sort of highway. Big buildings, factories, on both sides of the highway. Figures, men watching in astonishment.

After awhile the factories fell behind. Cole slowed the team down. What had the man meant? Fifth Atomic War. Horses destroyed. It didn't make sense. And they had things he knew nothing about. Force fields. Planes without wings—soundless.

Cole reached around in his pockets. He found the identification tube the man had handed him. In the excitement he had carried it off. He unrolled the tube slowly and began to study it. The writing was strange to him.

For a long time he studied the tube. Then, gradually, he became aware of something. Something in the top right-hand corner.

A date. October 6, 2128.

Cole's vision blurred. Everything spun and wavered around him. October, 2128. Could it be?

But he held the paper in his hand. Thin, metal paper. Like foil. And it had to be. It said so, right in the corner, printed on the paper itself.

Cole rolled the tube up slowly, numbed with shock. Two hundred years. It didn't seem possible. But things were beginning to make sense. He was in the future, two hundred years in the future.

While he was mulling this over, the swift black Security ship appeared overhead, diving rapidly toward the horse-drawn cart, as it moved slowly along the road.

Reinhart's vidscreen buzzed. He snapped it quickly on. "Yes?"

"Report from Security."

"Put it through." Reinhart waited tensely as the lines locked in place. The screen re-lit.

"This is Dixon. Western Regional Command." The officer cleared his throat, shuffling his message plates. "The man from the past has been reported, moving away from the New York area."

"Which side of your net?"

"Outside. He evaded the net around Central Park by entering one of the small towns at the rim of the slag area."

"*Evaded?*"

"We assumed he would avoid the towns. Naturally the net failed to encompass any of the towns."

Reinhart's jaw stiffened. "Go on."

"He entered the town of Petersville a few minutes before the net closed around the park. We burned the park level, but naturally found nothing. He had already gone. An hour later we received a report from a resident in Petersville, an official of the Stockpile Conservation

Department. The man from the past had come to his door, looking for work. Winslow, the official, engaged him in conversation, trying to hold onto him, but he escaped, driving his cart off. Winslow called Security right away, but by then it was too late."

"Report to me as soon as anything more comes in. We must have him—and damn soon." Reinhart snapped the screen off. It died quickly.

He sat back in his chair, waiting.

Cole saw the shadow of the Security ship. He reacted at once. A second after the shadow passed over him, Cole was out of the cart, running and falling. He rolled, twisting and turning, pulling his body as far away from the cart as possible.

There was a blinding roar and flash of white light. A hot wind rolled over Cole, picking him up and tossing him like a leaf. He shut his eyes, letting his body relax. He bounced, falling and striking the ground. Gravel and stones tore into his face, his knees, the palms of his hands.

Cole cried out, shrieking in pain. His body was on fire. He was being consumed, incinerated by the blinding white orb of fire. The orb expanded, growing in size, swelling like some monstrous sun, twisted and bloated. The end had come. There was no hope. He gritted his teeth—

The greedy orb faded, dying down. It sputtered and winked out, blackening into ash. The air reeked, a bitter acrid smell. His clothes were burning and smoking. The ground under him was hot, baked dry, seared by the blast. But he was alive. At least, for awhile.

Cole opened his eyes slowly. The cart was gone. A great hole gaped where it had been, a shattered sore in the center of the highway. An ugly cloud hung above the hole, black and ominous. Far above, the wingless plane circled, watching for any signs of life.

Cole lay, breathing shallowly, slowly. Time passed. The sun moved across the sky with agonizing slowness. It was perhaps four in the afternoon. Cole calculated mentally. In three hours it would be dark. If he could stay alive until then—

Had the plane seen him leap from the cart?

He lay without moving. The late afternoon sun beat down on him. He felt sick, nauseated and feverish. His mouth was dry.

Some ants ran over his outstretched hand. Gradually, the immense black cloud was beginning to drift away, dispersing into a formless blob.

The cart was gone. The thought lashed against him, pounding at his brain, mixing with his labored pulse-beat. *Gone*. Destroyed. Nothing but ashes and debris remained. The realization dazed him.

Finally the plane finished its circling, winging its way toward the horizon. At last it vanished. The sky was clear.

Cole got unsteadily to his feet. He wiped his face shakily. His body ached and trembled. He spat a couple times, trying to clear his mouth. The plane would probably send in a report. People would be coming to look for him. Where could he go?

To his right a line of hills rose up, a distant green mass. Maybe he could reach them. He began to walk slowly. He had to be very careful. They were looking for him—and they had weapons. Incredible weapons.

He would be lucky to still be alive when the sun set. His team and Fixit cart were gone—and all his tools. Cole reached into his pockets, searching through them hopefully. He brought out some small screwdrivers, a little pair of cutting pliers, some wire, some solder, the whetstone, and finally the lady's knife.

Only a few small tools remained. He had lost everything else. But without the cart he was safer, harder to spot. They would have more trouble finding him, on foot.

Cole hurried along, crossing the level fields toward the distant range of hills.

The call came through to Reinhart almost at once. Dixon's features formed on the vidscreen. "I have a further report, Commissioner." Dixon scanned the plate. "Good news. The man from the past was sighted moving away from Petersville, along highway 13, at about ten miles an hour, on his horse-drawn cart. Our ship bombed him immediately."

"Did—did you get him?"

"The pilot reports no sign of life after the blast."

Reinhart's pulse almost stopped. He sank back in his chair. "Then he's dead!"

"Actually, we won't know for certain until we can examine the debris. A surface car is speeding toward the spot. We should have the complete report in a short time. We'll notify you as soon as the information comes in."

Reinhart reached out and cut the screen. It faded into darkness. Had they got the man from the past? Or had he escaped again? Weren't they ever going to get him? Couldn't he be captured? And meanwhile, the SRB machines were silent, showing nothing at all.

Reinhart sat brooding, waiting impatiently for the report of the surface car to come in.

* * *

It was evening.

"Come on!" Steven shouted, running frantically after his brother. "Come on back!"

"Catch me." Earl ran and ran, down the side of the hill, over behind a military storage depot, along a neotex fence, jumping finally down into Mrs. Norris' back yard.

Steven hurried after his brother, sobbing for breath, shouting and gasping as he ran. "Come back! You come back with that!"

"What's he got?" Sally Tate demanded, stepping out suddenly to block Steven's way.

Steven halted, his chest rising and falling. "He's got my intersystem vidsender." His small face twisted with rage and misery. "He better give it back!"

Earl came circling around from the right. In the warm gloom of evening he was almost invisible. "Here I am," he announced. "What you going to do?"

Steven glared at him hotly. His eyes made out the square box in Earl's hands. "You give that back! Or—or I'll tell Dad."

Earl laughed. "Make me."

"Dad'll make you."

"You better give it to him," Sally said.

"Catch me." Earl started off. Steven pushed Sally out of the way, lashing wildly at his brother. He collided with him, throwing him sprawling. The box fell from Earl's hands. It skidded to the pavement, crashing into the side of a guide-light post.

Earl and Steven picked themselves up slowly. They gazed down at the broken box.

"See?" Steven shrilled, tears filling his eyes. "See what you did?"

"You did it. You pushed into me."

"You did it!'" Steven bent down and picked up the box. He carried it over to the guide-light, sitting down on the curb to examine it.

Earl came slowly over. "If you hadn't pushed me it wouldn't have got broken."

Night was descending rapidly. The line of hills rising above the town were already lost in darkness. A few lights had come on here and there. The evening was warm. A surface car slammed its doors, some place off in the distance. In the sky ships droned back and forth, weary commuters coming home from work in the big underground factory units.

Thomas Cole came slowly toward the three children grouped around the guide-light. He moved with difficulty, his body sore and bent with fatigue. Night had come, but he was not safe yet.

He was tired, exhausted and hungry. He had walked a long way. And he had to have something to eat—soon.

A few feet from the children Cole stopped. They were all intent and absorbed by the box on Steven's knees. Suddenly a hush fell over the children. Earl looked up slowly.

In the dim light the big stooped figure of Thomas Cole seemed extra menacing. His long arms hung down loosely at his sides. His face was lost in shadow. His body was shapeless, indistinct. A big unformed statue, standing silently a few feet away, unmoving in the half-darkness.

"Who are you?" Earl demanded, his voice low.

"What do you want?" Sally said. The children edged away nervously. "Get away."

Cole came toward them. He bent down a little. The beam from the guide-light crossed his features. Lean, prominent nose, beak-like, faded blue eyes—

Steven scrambled to his feet, clutching the vidsender box. "You get out of here!"

"Wait." Cole smiled crookedly at them. His voice was dry and raspy. "What do you have there?" He pointed with his long, slender fingers. "The box you're holding."

The children were silent. Finally Steven stirred. "It's my inter-system vidsender."

"Only it doesn't work," Sally said.

"Earl broke it." Steven glared at his brother bitterly. "Earl threw it down and broke it."

Cole smiled a little. He sank down wearily on the edge of the curb, sighing with relief. He had been walking too long. His body ached with fatigue. He was hungry, and tired. For a long time he sat, wiping perspiration from his neck and face, too exhausted to speak.

"Who are you?" Sally demanded, at last. "Why do you have on those funny clothes? Where did you come from?"

"Where?" Cole looked around at the children. "From a long way off. A long way." He shook his head slowly from side to side, trying to clear it.

"What's your therapy?" Earl said.

"My therapy?"

"What do you do? Where do you work?"

Cole took a deep breath and let it out again slowly. "I fix things. All kinds of things. Any kind."

Earl sneered. "Nobody fixes things. When they break you throw them away."

Cole didn't hear him. Sudden need had roused him, getting him suddenly to his feet. "You know any work I can find?" he demanded. "Things I could do? I can fix anything. Clocks, type-writers, refrigerators, pots and pans. Leaks in the roof. I can fix anything there is."

Steven held out his inter-system vidsender. "Fix this."

There was silence. Slowly, Cole's eyes focussed on the box. "That?"

"My sender. Earl broke it."

Cole took the box slowly. He turned it over, holding it up to the light. He frowned, concentrating on it. His long, slender fingers moved carefully over the surface, exploring it.

"He'll steal it!" Earl said suddenly.

"No." Cole shook his head vaguely. "I'm reliable." His sensitive fingers found the studs that held the box together. He depressed the studs, pushing them expertly in. The box opened, revealing its complex interior.

"He got it open," Sally whispered.

"Give it back!" Steven demanded, a little frightened. He held out his hand. "I want it back."

The three children watched Cole apprehensively. Cole fumbled in his pocket. Slowly he brought out his tiny screwdrivers and pliers. He laid them in a row beside him. He made no move to return the box.

"I want it back," Steven said feebly.

Cole looked up. His faded blue eyes took in the sight of the three children standing before him in the gloom. "I'll fix it for you. You said you wanted it fixed."

"I want it back." Steven stood on one foot, then the other, torn by doubt and indecision. "Can you really fix it? Can you make it work again?"

"Yes."

"All right. Fix it for me, then."

A sly smile flickered across Cole's tired face. "Now, wait a minute. If I fix it, will you bring me something to eat? I'm not fixing it for nothing."

"Something to eat?"

"Food. I need hot food. Maybe some coffee."

Steven nodded. "Yes. I'll get it for you."

Cole relaxed. "Fine. That's fine." He turned his attention back to the box resting between his knees. "Then I'll fix it for you. I'll fix it for you good."

His fingers flew, working and twisting, tracing down wires and relays, exploring and examining. Finding out about the inter-system vidsender. Discovering how it worked.

Steven slipped into the house through the emergency door. He made his way to the kitchen with great care, walking on tip-toe. He punched the kitchen controls at random, his heart beating excitedly. The stove began to whir, purring into life. Meter readings came on, crossing toward the completion marks.

Presently the stove opened, sliding out a tray of steaming dishes. The mechanism clicked off, dying into silence. Steven grabbed up the contents of the tray, filling his arms. He carried everything down the hall, out the emergency door and into the yard. The yard was dark. Steven felt his way carefully along.

He managed to reach the guide-light without dropping anything at all.

Thomas Cole got slowly to his feet as Steven came into view. "Here," Steven said. He dumped the food onto the curb, gasping for breath. "Here's the food. Is it finished?"

Cole held out the inter-system vidsender. "It's finished. It was pretty badly smashed."

Earl and Sally gazed up, wide-eyed. "Does it work?" Sally asked.

"Of course not," Earl stated. "How could it work? He couldn't—"

"Turn it on!" Sally nudged Steven eagerly. "See if it works."

Steven was holding the box under the light, examining the switches. He clicked the main switch on. The indicator light gleamed. "It lights up," Steven said.

"Say something into it."

Steven spoke into the box. "Hello! Hello! This is operator 6-Z75 calling. Can you hear me? This is operator 6-Z75. Can you hear me?"

In the darkness, away from the beam of the guide-light, Thomas Cole sat crouched over the food. He ate gratefully, silently. It was good food, well cooked and seasoned. He drank a container of orange juice and then a sweet drink he didn't recognize. Most of the food was strange to him, but he didn't care. He had walked a long way and he was plenty hungry. And he still had a long way to go, before morning. He had to be deep in the hills before the sun came up. Instinct told him that he would be safe among the trees and tangled growth—at least, as safe as he could hope for.

He ate rapidly intent on the food. He did not look up until he was finished. Then he got slowly to his feet, wiping his mouth with the back of his hand.

The three children were standing around in a circle, operating the inter-system vidsender. He watched them for a few minutes. None of them looked up from the small box. They were intent, absorbed in what they were doing.

"Well?" Cole said, at last. "Does it work all right?"

After a moment Steven looked up at him. There was a strange expression on his face. He nodded slowly. "Yes. Yes, it works. It works fine."

Cole grunted. "All right." He turned and moved away from the light. "That's fine."

The children watched silently until the figure of Thomas Cole had completely disappeared. Slowly, they turned and looked at each other. Then down at the box in Steven's hands. They gazed at the box in growing awe. Awe mixed with dawning fear.

Steven turned and edged toward his house. "I've got to show it to my Dad," he murmured, dazed. "He's got to know. *Somebody's* got to know!"

III

Eric Reinhart examined the vidsender box carefully, turning it around and around.

"Then he did escape from the blast," Dixon admitted reluctantly. "He must have leaped from the cart just before the concussion."

Reinhart nodded. "He escaped. He got away from you—twice." He pushed the vidsender box away and leaned abruptly toward the man standing uneasily in front of his desk. "What's your name again?"

"Elliot. Richard Elliot."

"And your son's name?"

"Steven."

"It was last night this happened?"

"About eight o'clock."

"Go on."

"Steven came into the house. He acted queerly. He was carrying his inter-system vidsender." Elliot pointed at the box on Reinhart's desk. "That. He was nervous and excited. I asked what was wrong.

For awhile he couldn't tell me. He was quite upset. Then he showed me the vidsender." Elliot took a deep, shaky breath. "I could see right away it was different. You see I'm an electrical engineer. I had opened it once before, to put in a new battery. I had a fairly good idea how it should look." Elliot hesitated. "Commissioner, it had been *changed*. A lot of the wiring was different. Moved around. Relays connected differently. Some parts were missing. New parts had been jury rigged out of old. Then I discovered the thing that made me call Security. The vidsender—it really *worked*."

"Worked?"

"You see, it never was anything more than a toy. With a range of a few city blocks. So the kids could call back and forth from their rooms. Like a sort of portable vidscreen. Commissioner, I tried out the vidsender, pushing the call button and speaking into the microphone. I—I got a ship of the line. A battleship, operating beyond Proxima Centaurus— over eight light years away. As far out as the actual vidsenders operate. Then I called Security. Right away."

For a time Reinhart was silent. Finally he tapped the box lying on the desk. "You got a ship of the line—with *this*?"

"That's right."

"How big are the regular vidsenders?"

Dixon supplied the information. "As big as a twenty-ton safe."

"That's what I thought." Reinhart waved his hand impatiently. "All right, Elliot. Thanks for turning the information over to us. That's all."

Security police led Elliot outside the office.

Reinhart and Dixon looked at each other. "This is bad," Reinhart said harshly. "He has some ability, some kind of mechanical ability. Genius, perhaps, to do a thing like this. Look at the period he came from, Dixon. The early part of the twentieth century. Before the wars began. That was a unique period. There was a certain vitality, a certain ability. It was a period of incredible growth and discovery. Edison. Pasteur. Burbank. The Wright brothers. Inventions and machines. People had an uncanny ability with machines. A kind of intuition about machines—which we don't have."

"You mean—"

"I mean a person like this coming into our own time is bad in itself, war or no war. He's too different. He's oriented along different lines. He has abilities we lack. This fixing skill of his. It throws us off, out of kilter. And with the war. . . ."

"Now I'm beginning to understand why the SRB machines couldn't factor him. It's impossible for us to understand this kind of person. Winslow says he asked for work, any kind of work. The man said he could do anything, fix anything. Do you understand what that means?"

"No," Dixon said. "What does it mean?"

"Can any of us fix anything? No. None of us can do that. We're specialized. Each of us has his own line, his own work. I understand my work, you understand yours. The tendency in evolution is toward greater and greater specialization. Man's society is an ecology that forces adaptation to it. Continual complexity makes it impossible for any of us to know anything outside our own personal field—I can't follow the work of the man sitting at the next desk over from me. Too much knowledge has piled up in each field. And there's too many fields.

"This man is different. He can fix anything, do anything. He doesn't work with knowledge, with science—the classified accumulation of facts. He *knows* nothing. It's not in his head, a form of learning. He works by intuition—his power is in his hands, not his head. Jack-of-all-trades. His hands! Like a painter, an artist. In his hands—and he cuts across our lives like a knife-blade."

"And the other problem?"

"The other problem is that this man, this variable man, has escaped into the Albertine Mountain range. Now we'll have one hell of a time finding him. He's clever—in a strange kind of way. Like some sort of animal. He's going to be hard to catch."

Reinhart sent Dixon out. After a moment he gathered up the handful of reports on his desk and carried them up to the SRB room. The SRB room was closed up, sealed off by a ring of armed Security police. Standing angrily before the ring of police was Peter Sherikov, his beard waggling angrily, his immense hands on his hips.

"What's going on?" Sherikov demanded. "Why can't I go in and peep at the odds?"

"Sorry." Reinhart cleared the police aside. "Come inside with me. I'll explain." The doors opened for them and they entered. Behind them the doors shut and the ring of police formed outside. "What brings you away from your lab?" Reinhart asked.

Sherikov shrugged. "Several things. I wanted to see you. I called you on the vidphone and they said you weren't available. I thought maybe something had happened. What's up?"

"I'll tell you in a few minutes." Reinhart called Kaplan over. "Here are some new items. Feed them in right away. I want to see if the machines can total them."

"Certainly, Commissioner." Kaplan took the message plates and placed them on an intake belt. The machines hummed into life.

"We'll know soon," Reinhart said, half aloud.

Sherikov shot him a keen glance. "We'll know what? Let me in on it. What's taking place?"

"We're in trouble. For twenty-four hours the machines haven't given any reading at all. Nothing but a blank. A total blank."

Sherikov's features registered disbelief. "But that isn't possible. *Some* odds exist at all times."

"The odds exist, but the machines aren't able to calculate them."

"Why not?"

"Because a variable factor has been introduced. A factor which the machines can't handle. They can't make any predictions from it."

"Can't they reject it?" Sherikov said slyly. "Can't they just—just *ignore* it?"

"No. It exists, as real data. Therefore it affects the balance of the material, the sum total of all other available data. To reject it would be to give a false reading. The machines can't reject any data that's known to be true."

Sherikov pulled moodily at his black beard. "I would be interested in knowing what sort of factor the machines can't handle. I thought they could take in all data pertaining to contemporary reality."

"They can. This factor has nothing to do with contemporary reality. That's the trouble. Histo-research in bringing its time bubble back from the past got overzealous and cut the circuit too quickly. The bubble came back loaded—with a man from the twentieth century. A man from the past."

"I see. A man from two centuries ago." The big Pole frowned. "And with a radically different Weltanschauung. No connection with our present society. Not integrated along our lines at all. Therefore the SRB machines are perplexed."

Reinhart grinned. "Perplexed? I suppose so. In any case, they can't do anything with the data about this man. The variable man. No statistics at all have been thrown up—no predictions have been made. And it knocks everything else out of phase. We're dependent on the constant showing of these odds. The whole war effort is geared around them."

"The horse-shoe nail. Remember the old poem? 'For want of a nail the shoe was lost. For want of the shoe the horse was lost. For want of the horse the rider was lost. For want—'"

"Exactly. A single factor coming along like this, one single individual, can throw everything off. It doesn't seem possible that one person could knock an entire society out of balance—but apparently it is."

"What are you doing about this man?"

"The Security police are organized in a mass search for him."

"Results?"

"He escaped into the Albertine Mountain Range last night. It'll be hard to find him. We must expect him to be loose for another forty-eight hours. It'll take that long for us to arrange the annihilation of the range area. Perhaps a trifle longer. And meanwhile—"

"Ready, Commissioner," Kaplan interrupted. "The new totals."

The SRB machines had finished factoring the new data. Reinhart and Sherikov hurried to take their places before the view windows.

For a moment nothing happened. Then odds were put up, locking in place.

Sherikov gasped. 99–2. In favor of Terra. "That's wonderful! Now we—"

The odds vanished. New odds took their places. 97–4. In favor of Centaurus. Sherikov groaned in astonished dismay. "Wait," Reinhart said to him. "I don't think they'll last."

The odds vanished. A rapid series of odds shot across the screen, a violent stream of numbers, changing almost instantly. At last the machines became silent.

Nothing showed. No odds. No totals at all. The view windows were blank.

"You see?" Reinhart murmured. "The same damn thing!"

Sherikov pondered. "Reinhart, you're too Anglo-Saxon, too impulsive. Be more Slavic. This man will be captured and destroyed within two days. You said so yourself. Meanwhile, we're all working night and day on the war effort. The warfleet is waiting near Proxima, taking up positions for the attack on the Centaurans. All our war plants are going full blast. By the time the attack date comes we'll have a full-sized invasion army ready to take off for the long trip to the Centauran colonies. The whole Terran population has been mobilized. The eight supply planets are pouring in material. All this is going on day and night, even without odds showing. Long before the attack comes this man will certainly be dead, and the machines will be able to show odds again."

Reinhart considered. "But it worries me, a man like that out in the open. Loose. A man who can't be predicted. It goes against science. We've been making statistical reports on society for two centuries. We have immense files of data. The machines are able to predict what each person and group will do at a given time, in a given situation. But this man is beyond all prediction. He's a variable. It's contrary to science."

"The indeterminate particle."

"What's that?"

"The particle that moves in such a way that we can't predict what position it will occupy at a given second. Random. The random particle."

"Exactly. It's—it's *unnatural*."

Sherikov laughed sarcastically. "Don't worry about it, Commissioner. The man will be captured and things will return to their natural state. You'll be able to predict people again, like laboratory rats in a maze. By the way—why is this room guarded?"

"I don't want anyone to know the machines show no totals. It's dangerous to the war effort."

"Margaret Duffe, for example?"

Reinhart nodded reluctantly. "They're too timid, these parliamentarians. If they discover we have no SRB odds they'll want to shut down the war planning and go back to waiting."

"Too slow for you, Commissioner? Laws, debates, council meetings, discussions. . . . Saves a lot of time if one man has all the power. One man to tell people what to do, think for them, lead them around."

Reinhart eyed the big Pole critically. "That reminds me. How is Icarus coming? Have you continued to make progress on the control turret?"

A scowl crossed Sherikov's broad features. "The control turret?" He waved his big hand vaguely. "I would say it's coming along all right. We'll catch up in time."

Instantly Reinhart became alert. "Catch up? You mean you're still behind?"

"Somewhat. A little. But we'll catch up." Sherikov retreated toward the door. "Let's go down to the cafeteria and have a cup of coffee. You worry too much, Commissioner. Take things more in your stride."

"I suppose you're right." The two men walked out into the hall. "I'm on edge. This variable man. I can't get him out of my mind."

"Has he done anything yet?"

"Nothing important. Rewired a child's toy. A toy vidsender."

"Oh?" Sherikov showed interest. "What do you mean? What did he do?"

"I'll show you." Reinhart led Sherikov down the hall to his office. They entered and Reinhart locked the door. He handed Sherikov the toy and roughed in what Cole had done. A strange look crossed Sherikov's face. He found the studs on the box and depressed them. The box opened. The big Pole sat down at the desk and began to study the interior of the box. "You're sure it was the man from the past who rewired this?"

"Of course. On the spot. The boy damaged it playing. The variable man came along and the boy asked him to fix it. He fixed it, all right."

"Incredible." Sherikov's eyes were only an inch from the wiring. "Such tiny relays. How could he—"

"What?"

"Nothing." Sherikov got abruptly to his feet, closing the box carefully. "Can I take this along? To my lab? I'd like to analyze it more fully."

"Of course. But why?"

"No special reason. Let's go get our coffee." Sherikov headed toward the door. "You say you expect to capture this man in a day or so?"

"*Kill* him, not capture him. We've got to eliminate him as a piece of data. We're assembling the attack formations right now. No slip-ups, this time. We're in the process of setting up a cross-bombing pattern to level the entire Albertine range. He must be destroyed, within the next forty-eight hours."

Sherikov nodded absently. "Of course," he murmured. A preoccupied expression still remained on his broad features. "I understand perfectly."

* * *

Thomas Cole crouched over the fire he had built, warming his hands. It was almost morning. The sky was turning violet gray. The mountain air was crisp and chill. Cole shivered and pulled himself closer to the fire.

The heat felt good against his hands. *His hands.* He gazed down at them, glowing yellow-red in the firelight. The nails were black and chipped. Warts and endless calluses on each finger, and the palms. But they were good hands; the fingers were long and tapered. He respected them, although in some ways he didn't understand them.

Cole was deep in thought, meditating over his situation. He had been in the mountains two nights and a day. The first night had been the worst. Stumbling and falling, making his way uncertainly up the steep slopes, through the tangled brush and undergrowth—

But when the sun came up he was safe, deep in the mountains, between two great peaks. And by the time the sun had set again he had fixed himself up a shelter and a means of making a fire. Now he had a neat little box trap, operated by a plaited grass rope and pit, a notched stake. One rabbit already hung by his hind legs and the trap was waiting for another.

The sky turned from violet gray to a deep cold gray, a metallic color. The mountains were silent and empty. Far off some place a bird sang, its voice echoing across the vast slopes and ravines. Other birds began to sing. Off to his right something crashed through the brush, an animal pushing its way along.

Day was coming. His second day. Cole got to his feet and began to unfasten the rabbit. Time to eat. And then? After that he had no plans. He knew instinctively that he could keep himself alive indefinitely with the tools he had retained, and the genius of his hands. He could kill game and skin it. Eventually he could build himself a permanent shelter, even make clothes but of hides. In winter—

But he was not thinking that far ahead. Cole stood by the fire, staring up at the sky, his hands on his hips. He squinted, suddenly tense. Something was moving. Something in the sky, drifting slowly through the grayness. A black dot.

He stamped out the fire quickly. What was it? He strained, trying to see. A bird?

A second dot joined the first. Two dots. Then three. Four. Five. A fleet of them, moving rapidly across the early morning sky. Toward the mountains.

Toward him.

Cole hurried away from the fire. He snatched up the rabbit and carried it along with him, into the tangled shelter he had built. He was invisible, inside the shelter. No one could find him. But if they had seen the fire—

He crouched in the shelter, watching the dots grow larger. They were planes, all right. Black wingless planes, coming closer each moment. Now he could hear them, a faint dull buzz, increasing until the ground shook under him.

The first plane dived. It dropped like a stone, swelling into a great black shape. Cole gasped, sinking down. The plane roared in an arc, swooping low over the ground. Suddenly bundles tumbled out, white bundles falling and scattering like seeds.

The bundles drifted rapidly to the ground. They landed. They were men. Men in uniform.

Now the second plane was diving. It roared overhead, releasing its load. More bundles tumbled out, filling the sky. The third plane dived, then the fourth. The air was thick with drifting bundles of white, a blanket of descending weed spores, settling to earth.

On the ground the soldiers were forming into groups. Their shouts carried to Cole, crouched in his shelter. Fear leaped through him. They were landing on all sides of him. He was cut off. The last two planes had dropped men behind him.

He got to his feet, pushing out of the shelter. Some of the soldiers had found the fire, the ashes and coals. One dropped down, feeling the coals with his hand. He waved to the others. They were circling all around, shouting and gesturing. One of them began to set up some kind of gun. Others were unrolling coils of tubing, locking a collection of strange pipes and machinery in place.

Cole ran. He rolled down a slope, sliding and falling. At the bottom he leaped to his feet and plunged into the brush. Vines and leaves tore at his face, slashing and cutting him. He fell again, tangled in a mass of twisted shrubbery. He fought desperately, trying to free himself. If he could reach the knife in his pocket—

Voices. Footsteps. Men were behind him, running down the slope. Cole struggled frantically, gasping and twisting, trying to pull loose. He strained, breaking the vines, clawing at them with his hands.

A soldier dropped to his knee, leveling his gun. More soldiers arrived, bringing up their rifles and aiming.

Cole cried out. He closed his eyes, his body suddenly limp. He waited, his teeth locked together, sweat dripping down his neck, into his shirt, sagging against the mesh of vines and branches coiled around him.

Silence.

Cole opened his eyes slowly. The soldiers had regrouped. A huge man was striding down the slope toward them, barking orders as he came.

Two soldiers stepped into the brush. One of them grabbed Cole by the shoulder.

"Don't let go of him." The huge man came over, his black beard jutting out. "Hold on."

Cole gasped for breath. He was caught. There was nothing he could do. More soldiers were pouring down into the gulley, surrounding him on all sides. They studied him curiously murmuring together. Cole shook his head wearily and said nothing.

The huge man with the beard stood directly in front of him, his hands on his hips, looking him up and down. "Don't try to get away," the man said. "You can't get away. Do you understand?"

Cole nodded.

"All right. Good." The man waved. Soldiers clamped metal bands around Cole's arms and wrists. The metal dug into his flesh, making him gasp with pain. More clamps locked around his legs. "Those stay there until we're out of here. A long way out."

"Where—where are you taking me?"

Peter Sherikov studied the variable man for a moment before he answered. "Where? I'm taking you to my labs. Under the Urals." He glanced suddenly up at the sky. "We better hurry. The Security police will be starting their demolition attack in a few hours. We want to be a long way from here when that begins."

* * *

Sherikov settled down in his comfortable reinforced chair with a sigh. "It's good to be back." He signalled to one of his guards. "All right. You can unfasten him."

The metal clamps were removed from Cole's arms and legs. He sagged, sinking down in a heap. Sherikov watched him silently.

Cole sat on the floor, rubbing his wrists and legs, saying nothing.

"What do you want?" Sherikov demanded. "Food? Are you hungry?"

"No."

"Medicine? Are you sick? Injured?"

"No."

Sherikov wrinkled his nose. "A bath wouldn't hurt you any. We'll arrange that later." He lit a cigar, blowing a cloud of gray smoke around him. At the door of the room two lab guards stood with guns ready. No one else was in the room beside Sherikov and Cole.

Thomas Cole sat huddled in a heap on the floor, his head sunk down against his chest. He did not stir. His bent body seemed more elongated and stooped than ever, his hair tousled and unkempt, his chin and jowls a rough stubbled gray. His clothes were dirty and torn from crawling through the brush. His skin was cut and scratched; open sores dotted his neck and cheeks and forehead. He said nothing. His chest rose and fell. His faded blue eyes were almost closed. He looked quite old, a withered, dried-up old man.

Sherikov waved one of the guards over. "Have a doctor brought up here. I want this man checked over. He may need intravenous injections. He may not have had anything to eat for awhile."

The guard departed.

"I don't want anything to happen to you," Sherikov said. "Before we go on I'll have you checked over. And deloused at the same time."

Cole said nothing.

Sherikov laughed. "Buck up! You have no reason to feel bad." He leaned toward Cole, jabbing an immense finger at him. "Another two hours and you'd have been dead, out there in the mountains. You know that?"

Cole nodded.

"You don't believe me. Look." Sherikov leaned over and snapped on the vidscreen mounted in the wall. "Watch, this. The operation should still be going on."

The screen lit up. A scene gained form.

"This is a confidential Security channel. I had it tapped several years ago—for my own protection. What we're seeing now is being piped in to Eric Reinhart." Sherikov grinned. "Reinhart arranged what you're seeing on the screen. Pay close attention. You were there, two hours ago."

Cole turned toward the screen. At first he could not make out what was happening. The screen showed a vast foaming cloud, a vortex of motion. From the speaker came a low rumble, a deep-throated roar. After a time the screen shifted, showing a slightly different view. Suddenly Cole stiffened.

He was seeing the destruction of a whole mountain range.

The picture was coming from a ship, flying above what had once been the Albertine Mountain Range. Now there was nothing but swirling clouds of gray and columns of particles and debris, a surging tide of restless material gradually sweeping off and dissipating in all directions.

The Albertine Mountains had been disintegrated. Nothing remained but these vast clouds of debris. Below, on the ground, a ragged plain stretched out, swept by fire and ruin. Gaping wounds yawned, immense holes without bottom, craters side by side as far as the eye could see. Craters and debris. Like the blasted, pitted surface of the moon. Two hours ago it had been rolling peaks and gulleys, brush and green bushes and trees.

Cole turned away.

"You see?" Sherikov snapped the screen off. "You were down there, not so long ago. All that noise and smoke—all for you. All for you, Mr. Variable Man from the past. Reinhart arranged that, to finish you off. I want you to understand that. It's very important that you realize that."

Cole said nothing.

Sherikov reached into a drawer of the table before him. He carefully brought out a small square box and held it out to Cole. "You wired this, didn't you?"

Cole took the box in his hands and held it. For a time his tired mind failed to focus. What did he have? He concentrated on it. The box was the children's toy. The inter-system vidsender, they had called it.

"Yes. I fixed this." He passed it back to Sherikov. "I repaired that. It was broken."

Sherikov gazed down at him intently, his large eyes bright. He nodded, his black beard and cigar rising and falling. "Good. That's all I wanted to know." He got suddenly to his feet, pushing his chair back. "I see the doctor's here. He'll fix you up. Everything you need. Later on I'll talk to you again."

Unprotesting, Cole got to his feet, allowing the doctor to take hold of his arm and help him up.

After Cole had been released by the medical department, Sherikov joined him in his private dining room, a floor above the actual laboratory.

The Pole gulped down a hasty meal, talking as he ate. Cole sat silently across from him, not eating or speaking. His old clothing had been taken away and new clothing given him. He was shaved and rubbed down. His sores and cuts were healed, his body and hair washed. He looked much healthier and younger, now. But he was still stooped and tired, his blue eyes worn and faded. He listened to Sherikov's account of the world of 2136 A.D. without comment.

"You can see," Sherikov said finally, waving a chicken leg, "that your appearance here has been very upsetting to our program. Now that you know more about us you can see why Commissioner Reinhart was so interested in destroying you."

Cole nodded.

"Reinhart, you realize, believes that the failure of the SRB machines is the chief danger to the war effort. But that is nothing!" Sherikov pushed his plate away noisily, draining his coffee mug. "After all, wars *can* be fought without statistical forecasts. The SRB machines only describe. They're nothing more than mechanical onlookers. In themselves, they don't affect the course of the war. *We* make the war. They only analyze."

Cole nodded.

"More coffee?" Sherikov asked. He pushed the plastic container toward Cole. "Have some."

Cole accepted another cupful. "Thank you."

"You can see that our real problem is another thing entirely. The machines only do figuring for us in a few minutes that eventually we could do for our own selves. They're our servants, tools. Not some sort of gods in a temple which we go and pray to. Not oracles who can see into the future for us. They don't see into the future. They only make statistical predictions—not prophecies. There's a big difference there, but Reinhart doesn't understand it. Reinhart and his kind have made such things as the SRB machines into gods. But I have no gods. At least, not any I can see."

Cole nodded, sipping his coffee.

"I'm telling you all these things because you must understand what we're up against. Terra is hemmed in on all sides by the ancient Centauran Empire. It's been out there for centuries, thousands of years. No one knows how long. It's old—crumbling and rotting. Corrupt and venal. But it holds most of the galaxy around us, and we can't break out of the Sol system. I told you about Icarus, and Hedge's work in ftl flight. We must win the war against Centaurus. We've waited and worked a long time for this, the moment when we can break out and get room among the stars for ourselves. Icarus is the deciding weapon. The data on Icarus tipped the SRB odds in our favor—for the first time in history. Success in the war against Centaurus will depend on Icarus, not on the SRB machines. You see?"

Cole nodded.

"However, there is a problem. The data on Icarus which I turned over to the machines specified that Icarus would be completed in ten days. More than half that time has already passed. Yet, we are no closer to wiring up the control turret than we were then. The turret baffles us." Sherikov grinned ironically. "Even *I* have tried my hand at the wiring, but with no success. It's intricate—and small. Too many technical bugs not worked out. We are building only one, you understand. If we had many experimental models worked out before—"

"But this is the experimental model," Cole said.

"And built from the designs of a man dead four years—who isn't here to correct us. We've made Icarus with our own hands, down here in the labs. And he's giving us plenty of trouble." All at once Sherikov got to his feet. "Let's go down to the lab and look at him."

They descended to the floor below, Sherikov leading the way. Cole stopped short at the lab door.

"Quite a sight," Sherikov agreed. "We keep him down here at the bottom for safety's sake. He's well protected. Come on in. We have work to do."

In the center of the lab Icarus rose up, the gray squat cylinder that someday would flash through space at a speed of thousands of times that of light, toward the heart of Proxima Centaurus, over four light years away. Around the cylinder groups of men in uniform were laboring feverishly to finish the remaining work.

"Over here. The turret." Sherikov led Cole over to one side of the room. "It's guarded. Centauran spies are swarming everywhere on Terra. They see into everything. But so do we. That's how we get information for the SRB machines. Spies in both systems."

The translucent globe that was the control turret reposed in the center of a metal stand, an armed guard standing at each side. They lowered their guns as Sherikov approached.

"We don't want anything to happen to this," Sherikov said. "Everything depends on it." He put out his hand for the globe. Half way to it his hand stopped, striking against an invisible presence in the air.

Sherikov laughed. "The wall. Shut it off. It's still on."

One of the guards pressed a stud at his wrist. Around the globe the air shimmered and faded.

"Now." Sherikov's hand closed over the globe. He lifted it carefully from its mount and brought it out for Cole to see. "This is the control turret for our enormous friend here. This is what will slow him down when he's inside Centaurus. He slows down and re-enters this universe. Right in the heart of the star. Then—no more Centaurus." Sherikov beamed. "And no more Armun."

But Cole was not listening. He had taken the globe from Sherikov and was turning it over and over, running his hands over it, his face close to its surface. He peered down into its interior, his face rapt and intent.

"You can't see the wiring. Not without lenses." Sherikov signalled for a pair of micro-lenses to be brought. He fitted them on Cole's nose, hook-ing them behind his ears. "Now try it. You can control the magnification. It's set for 1000X right now. You can increase or decrease it."

Cole gasped, swaying back and forth. Sherikov caught hold of him. Cole gazed down into the globe, moving his head slightly, focussing the glasses.

"It takes practice. But you can do a lot with them. Permits you to do microscopic wiring. There are tools to go along, you understand." Sherikov paused, licking his lip. "We can't get it done correctly. Only a few men can wire circuits using the micro-lenses and the little tools. We've tried robots, but there are too many decisions to be made. Robots can't make decisions. They just react."

Cole said nothing. He continued to gaze into the interior of the globe, his lips tight, his body taut and rigid. It made Sherikov feel strangely uneasy.

"You look like one of those old fortune tellers," Sherikov said jokingly, but a cold shiver crawled up his spine. "Better hand it back to me." He held out his hand.

Slowly, Cole returned the globe. After a time he removed the micro-lenses, still deep in thought.

"Well?" Sherikov demanded. "You know what I want. I want you to wire this damn thing up." Sherikov came close to Cole, his big face hard. "You can do it, I think. I could tell by the way you held it—and the job you did on the children's toy, of course. You could wire it up right, and in five days. Nobody else can. And if it's not wired up Centaurus will keep on running the galaxy and Terra will have to sweat it out here in the Sol system. One tiny mediocre sun, one dust mote out of a whole galaxy."

Cole did not answer.

Sherikov became impatient. "Well? What do you say?"

"What happens if I don't wire this control for you? I mean, what happens to *me?*"

"Then I turn you over to Reinhart. Reinhart will kill you instantly. He thinks you're dead, killed when the Albertine Range was annihilated. If he had any idea I had saved you—"

"I see."

"I brought you down here for one thing. If you wire it up I'll have you sent back to your own time continuum. If you don't—"

Cole considered, his face dark and brooding.

"What do you have to lose? You'd already be dead, if we hadn't pulled you out of those hills."

"Can you really return me to my own time?"

"Of course!"

"Reinhart won't interfere?"

Sherikov laughed. "What can he do? How can he stop me? I have my own men. You saw them. They landed all around you. You'll be returned."

"Yes. I saw your men."

"Then you agree?"

"I agree," Thomas Cole said. "I'll wire it for you. I'll complete the control turret—within the next five days."

IV

Three days later Joseph Dixon slid a closed-circuit message plate across the desk to his boss.

"Here. You might be interested in this."

Reinhart picked the plate up slowly. "What is it? You came all the way here to show me this?"

"That's right."

"Why didn't you vidscreen it?"

Dixon smiled grimly. "You'll understand when you decode it. It's from Proxima Centaurus."

"Centaurus!"

"Our counter-intelligence service. They sent it direct to me. Here, I'll decode it for you. Save you the trouble."

Dixon came around behind Reinhart's desk. He leaned over the Commissioner's shoulder, taking hold of the plate and breaking the seal with his thumb nail.

"Hang on," Dixon said. "This is going to hit you hard. According to our agents on Armun, the Centauran High Council has called an emergency session to deal with the problem of Terra's impending attack. Centauran relay couriers have reported to the High Council that the Terran bomb Icarus is virtually complete. Work on the bomb has been rushed through final stages in the underground laboratories under the Ural Range, directed by the Terran physicist Peter Sherikov."

"So I understand from Sherikov himself. Are you surprised the Centaurans know about the bomb? They have spies swarming over Terra. That's no news."

"There's more." Dixon traced the message plate grimly, with an unsteady finger. "The Centauran relay couriers reported that Peter Sherikov brought an expert mechanic out of a previous time continuum to complete the wiring of the turret!"

Reinhart staggered, holding on tight to the desk. He closed his eyes, gasping.

"The variable man is still alive," Dixon murmured. "I don't know how. Or why. There's nothing left of the Albertines. And how the hell did the man get half way around the world?"

Reinhart opened his eyes slowly, his face twisting. "Sherikov! He must have removed him before the attack. I told Sherikov the attack was forthcoming. I gave him the exact hour. He had to get help—from the variable man. He couldn't meet his promise otherwise."

Reinhart leaped up and began to pace back and forth. "I've already informed the SRB machines that the variable man has been destroyed. The machines now show the original 7–6 ratio in our favor. But the ratio is based on false information."

"Then you'll have to withdraw the false data and restore the original situation."

"No." Reinhart shook his head. "I can't do that. The machines must be kept functioning. We can't allow them to jam again. It's too dangerous. If Duffe should become aware that—"

"What are you going to do, then?" Dixon picked up the message plate. "You can't leave the machines with false data. That's treason."

"The data can't be withdrawn! Not unless equivalent data exists to take its place." Reinhart paced angrily back and forth. "Damn it, I was *certain* the man was dead. This is an incredible situation. He must be eliminated—at any cost."

Suddenly Reinhart stopped pacing. "The turret. It's probably finished by this time. Correct?"

Dixon nodded slowly in agreement. "With the variable man helping, Sherikov has undoubtedly completed work well ahead of schedule."

Reinhart's gray eyes flickered. "Then he's no longer of any use—even to Sherikov. We could take a chance. . . . Even if there were active opposition. . . ."

"What's this?" Dixon demanded. "What are you thinking about?"

"How many units are ready for immediate action? How large a force can we raise without notice?"

"Because of the war we're mobilized on a twenty-four hour basis. There are seventy air units and about two hundred surface units. The balance of the Security forces have been transferred to the line, under military control."

"Men?"

"We have about five thousand men ready to go, still on Terra. Most of them in the process of being transferred to military transports. I can hold it up at any time."

"Missiles?"

"Fortunately, the launching tubes have not yet been disassembled. They're still here on Terra. In another few days they'll be moving out for the Colonial fracas."

"Then they're available for immediate use?"

"Yes."

"Good." Reinhart locked his hands, knotting his fingers harshly together in sudden decision. "That will do exactly. Unless I am completely wrong, Sherikov has only a half-dozen air units and no surface cars. And only about two hundred men. Some defense shields, of course—"

"What are you planning?"

Reinhart's face was gray and hard, like stone. "Send out orders for all available Security units to be unified under your immediate command. Have them ready to move by four o'clock this afternoon. We're going to pay a visit," Reinhart stated grimly. "A surprise visit. On Peter Sherikov."

* * *

"Stop here," Reinhart ordered.

The surface car slowed to a halt. Reinhart peered cautiously out, studying the horizon ahead.

On all sides a desert of scrub grass and sand stretched out. Nothing moved or stirred. To the right the grass and sand rose up to form immense peaks, a range of mountains without end, disappearing finally into the distance. The Urals.

"Over there," Reinhart said to Dixon, pointing. "See?"

"No."

"Look hard. It's difficult to spot unless you know what to look for. Vertical pipes. Some kind of vent. Or periscopes."

Dixon saw them finally. "I would have driven past without noticing."

"It's well concealed. The main labs are a mile down. Under the range itself. It's virtually impregnable. Sherikov had it built years ago, to withstand any attack. From the air, by surface cars, bombs, missiles—"

"He must feel safe down there."

"No doubt." Reinhart gazed up at the sky. A few faint black dots could be seen, moving lazily about, in broad circles. "Those aren't ours, are they? I gave orders—"

"No. They're not ours. All our units are out of sight. Those belong to Sherikov. His patrol."

Reinhart relaxed. "Good." He reached over and flicked on the vidscreen over the board of the car. "This screen is shielded? It can't be traced?"

"There's no way they can spot it back to us. It's non-directional."

The screen glowed into life. Reinhart punched the combination keys and sat back to wait.

After a time an image formed on the screen. A heavy face, bushy black beard and large eyes.

Peter Sherikov gazed at Reinhart with surprised curiosity. "Commissioner! Where are you calling from? What—"

"How's the work progressing?" Reinhart broke in coldly. "Is Icarus almost complete?"

Sherikov beamed with expansive pride. "He's done, Commissioner. Two days ahead of time. Icarus is ready to be launched into space. I tried to call your office, but they told me—"

"I'm not at my office." Reinhart leaned toward the screen. "Open your entrance tunnel at the surface. You're about to receive visitors."

Sherikov blinked. "Visitors?"

"I'm coming down to see you. About Icarus. Have the tunnel opened for me at once."

"Exactly where are you, Commissioner?"

"On the surface."

Sherikov's eyes flickered. "Oh? But—"

"Open up!" Reinhart snapped. He glanced at his wristwatch. "I'll be at the entrance in five minutes. I expect to find it ready for me."

"Of course." Sherikov nodded in bewilderment. "I'm always glad to see you, Commissioner. But I—"

"Five minutes, then." Reinhart cut the circuit. The screen died. He turned quickly to Dixon. "You stay up here, as we arranged. I'll go down with one company of police. You understand the necessity of exact timing on this?"

"We won't slip up. Everything's ready. All units are in their places."

"Good." Reinhart pushed the door open for him. "You join your directional staff. I'll proceed toward the tunnel entrance."

"Good luck." Dixon leaped out of the car, onto the sandy ground. A gust of dry air swirled into the car around Reinhart. "I'll see you later."

Reinhart slammed the door. He turned to the group of police crouched in the rear of the car, their guns held tightly. "Here we go," Reinhart murmured. "Hold on."

The car raced across the sandy ground, toward the tunnel entrance to Sherikov's underground fortress.

Sherikov met Reinhart at the bottom end of the tunnel, where the tunnel opened up onto the main floor of the lab.

The big Pole approached, his hand out, beaming with pride and satisfaction. "It's a pleasure to see you, Commissioner. This is an historic moment."

Reinhart got out of the car, with his group of armed Security police. "Calls for a celebration, doesn't it?" he said.

"That's a good idea! We're two days ahead, Commissioner. The SRB machines will be interested. The odds should change abruptly at the news."

"Let's go down to the lab. I want to see the control turret myself."

A shadow crossed Sherikov's face. "I'd rather not bother the workmen right now, Commissioner. They've been under a great load, trying to complete the turret in time. I believe they're putting a few last finishes on it at this moment."

"We can view them by vidscreen. I'm curious to see them at work. It must be difficult to wire such minute relays."

Sherikov shook his head. "Sorry, Commissioner. No vidscreen on them. I won't allow it. This is too important. Our whole future depends on it."

Reinhart snapped a signal to his company of police. "Put this man under arrest."

Sherikov blanched. His mouth fell open. The police moved quickly around him, their gun tubes up, jabbing into him. He was searched rapidly, efficiently. His gun belt and concealed energy screen were yanked off.

"What's going on?" Sherikov demanded, some color returning to his face. "What are you doing?"

"You're under arrest for the duration of the war. You're relieved of all authority. From now on one of my men will operate Designs. When the war is over you'll be tried before the Council and President Duffe."

Sherikov shook his head, dazed. "I don't understand. What's this all about? Explain it to me, Commissioner. What's happened?"

Reinhart signalled to his police. "Get ready. We're going into the lab. We may have to shoot our way in. The variable man should be in the area of the bomb, working on the control turret."

Instantly Sherikov's face hardened. His black eyes glittered, alert and hostile.

Reinhart laughed harshly. "We received a counter-intelligence report from Centaurus. I'm surprised at you, Sherikov. You know the Centaurans are everywhere with their relay couriers. You should have known—"

Sherikov moved. Fast. All at once he broke away from the police, throwing his massive body against them. They fell, scattering. Sherikov ran—directly at the wall. The police fired wildly. Reinhart fumbled frantically for his gun tube, pulling it up.

Sherikov reached the wall, running head down, energy beams flashing around him. He struck against the wall—and vanished.

"Down!" Reinhart shouted. He dropped to his hands and knees. All around him his police dived for the floor. Reinhart cursed wildly, dragging himself quickly toward the door. They had to get out, and right away. Sherikov had escaped. A false wall, an energy barrier set to respond to his pressure. He had dashed through it to safety. He—

From all sides an inferno burst, a flaming roar of death surging over them, around them, on every side. The room was alive with blazing masses of destruction, bouncing from wall to wall. They were caught between four banks of power, all of them open to full discharge. A trap—a death trap.

* * *

Reinhart reached the hall gasping for breath. He leaped to his feet. A few Security police followed him. Behind them, in the flaming room, the rest of the company screamed and struggled, blasted out of existence by the leaping bursts of power.

Reinhart assembled his remaining men. Already, Sherikov's guards were forming. At one end of the corridor a snub-barreled robot gun was maneuvering into position. A siren wailed. Guards were running on all sides, hurrying to battle stations.

The robot gun opened fire. Part of the corridor exploded, bursting into fragments. Clouds of choking debris and particles swept around them. Reinhart and his police retreated, moving back along the corridor.

They reached a junction. A second robot gun was rumbling toward them, hurrying to get within range. Reinhart fired carefully, aiming at its delicate control. Abruptly the gun spun convulsively. It lashed against the wall, smashing itself into the unyielding metal. Then it collapsed in a heap, gears still whining and spinning.

"Come on." Reinhart moved away, crouching and running. He glanced at his watch. *Almost time.* A few more minutes. A group of lab guards appeared ahead of them. Reinhart fired. Behind him his police fired past him, violet shafts of energy catching the group of guards as they entered the corridor. The guards spilled apart, falling and twisting. Part of them settled into dust, drifting down the corridor. Reinhart made his way toward the lab, crouching and leaping, pushing past heaps of debris and remains, followed by his men. "Come on! Don't stop!"

* * *

Suddenly from around them the booming, enlarged voice of Sherikov thundered, magnified by rows of wall speakers along the corridor. Reinhart halted, glancing around.

"Reinhart! You haven't got a chance. You'll never get back to the surface. Throw down your guns and give up. You're surrounded on all sides. You're a mile, under the surface."

Reinhart threw himself into motion, pushing into billowing clouds of particles drifting along the corridor. "Are you sure, Sherikov?" he grunted.

Sherikov laughed, his harsh, metallic peals rolling in waves against Reinhart's eardrums. "I don't want to have to kill you, Commissioner. You're vital to the war: I'm sorry you found out about the variable man. I admit we overlooked the Centauran espionage as a factor in this. But now that you know about him—"

Suddenly Sherikov's voice broke off. A deep rumble had shaken the floor, a lapping vibration that shuddered through the corridor.

Reinhart sagged with relief. He peered through the clouds of debris, making out the figures on his watch. Right on time. Not a second late.

The first of the hydrogen missiles, launched from the Council buildings on the other side of the world, were beginning to arrive. The attack had begun.

At exactly six o'clock Joseph Dixon, standing on the surface four miles from the entrance tunnel, gave the sign to the waiting units.

The first job was to break down Sherikov's defense screens. The missiles had to penetrate without interference. At Dixon's signal a fleet of thirty Security ships dived from a height of ten miles, swooping above the mountains, directly over the underground laboratories. Within five minutes the defense screens had been smashed, and all the tower projectors leveled flat. Now the mountains were virtually unprotected.

"So far so good," Dixon murmured, as he watched from his secure position. The fleet of Security ships roared back, their work done. Across the face of the desert the police surface cars were crawling rapidly toward the entrance tunnel, snaking from side to side.

Meanwhile, Sherikov's counter-attack had begun to go into operation.

Guns mounted among the hills opened fire. Vast columns of flame burst up in the path of the advancing cars. The cars hesitated and retreated, as the plain was churned up by a howling vortex, a thundering chaos of explosions. Here and there a car vanished in a cloud of particles. A group of cars moving away suddenly scattered, caught up by a giant wind that lashed across them and swept them up into the air.

Dixon gave orders to have the cannon silenced. The police air arm again swept overhead, a sullen roar of jets that shook the ground below. The police ships divided expertly and hurtled down on the cannon protecting the hills.

The cannon forgot the surface cars and lifted their snouts to meet the attack. Again and again the airships came, rocking the mountains with titanic blasts.

The guns became silent. Their echoing boom diminished, died away reluctantly, as bombs took critical toll of them.

Dixon watched with satisfaction as the bombing came to an end. The airships rose in a thick swarm, black gnats shooting up in triumph from a dead carcass. They hurried back as emergency anti-aircraft robot guns swung into position and saturated the sky with blazing puffs of energy.

Dixon checked his wristwatch. The missiles were already on the way from North America. Only a few minutes remained.

The surface cars, freed by the successful bombing, began to regroup for a new frontal attack. Again they crawled forward, across the burning plain, bearing down cautiously on the battered wall of mountains, heading toward the twisted wrecks that had been the ring of defense guns. Toward the entrance tunnel.

An occasional cannon fired feebly at them. The cars came grimly on. Now, in the hollows of the hills, Sherikov's troops were hurrying to the surface to meet the attack. The first car reached the shadow of the mountains. . . .

A deafening hail of fire burst loose. Small robot guns appeared everywhere, needle barrels emerging from behind hidden screens, trees and shrubs, rocks, stones. The police cars were caught in a withering cross-fire, trapped at the base of the hills.

Down the slopes Sherikov's guards raced, toward the stalled cars. Clouds of heat rose up and boiled across the plain as the cars fired up at the running men. A robot gun dropped like a slug onto the plain and screamed toward the cars, firing as it came.

Dixon twisted nervously. Only a few minutes. Any time, now. He shaded his eyes and peered up at the sky. No sign of them yet. He wondered about Reinhart. No signal had come up from below. Clearly, Reinhart had run into trouble. No doubt there was desperate fighting going on in the maze of underground tunnels, the intricate web of passages that honeycombed the earth below the mountains.

In the air, Sherikov's few defense ships were taking on the police raiders. Outnumbered, the defense ships darted rapidly, wildly, putting up a futile fight.

Sherikov's guards streamed out onto the plain. Crouching and running, they advanced toward the stalled cars. The police airships screeched down at them, guns thundering.

Dixon held his breath. When the missiles arrived—

The first missile struck. A section of the mountain vanished, turned to smoke and foaming gasses. The wave of heat slapped Dixon across the face, spinning him around. Quickly he re-entered his ship and took off, shooting rapidly away from the scene. He glanced back. A second and third missile had arrived. Great gaping pits yawned among the mountains, vast sections missing like broken teeth. Now the missiles could penetrate to the underground laboratories below.

On the ground, the surface cars halted beyond the danger area, waiting for the missile attack to finish. When the eighth missile had struck, the cars again moved forward. No more missiles fell.

Dixon swung his ship around, heading back toward the scene. The laboratory was exposed. The top sections of it had been ripped open. The laboratory lay like a tin can, torn apart by mighty explosions, its first floors visible from the air. Men and cars were pouring down into it, fighting with the guards swarming to the surface.

* * *

Dixon watched intently. Sherikov's men were bringing up heavy guns, big robot artillery. But the police ships were diving again. Sherikov's defensive patrols had been cleaned from the sky. The police ships whined down, arcing over the exposed laboratory. Small bombs fell, whistling down, pin-pointing the artillery rising to the surface on the remaining lift stages.

Abruptly Dixon's vidscreen clicked. Dixon turned toward it.

Reinhart's features formed. "Call off the attack." His uniform was torn. A deep bloody gash crossed his cheek. He grinned sourly at Dixon, pushing his tangled hair back out of his face. "Quite a fight."

"Sherikov—"

"He's called off his guards. We've agreed to a truce. It's all over. No more needed." Reinhart gasped for breath, wiping grime and sweat from his neck. "Land your ship and come down here at once."

"The variable man?"

"That comes next," Reinhart said grimly. He adjusted his gun tube. "I want you down here, for that part. I want you to be in on the kill."

Reinhart turned away from the vidscreen. In the corner of the room Sherikov stood silently, saying frothing. "Well?" Reinhart barked. "Where is he? Where will I find him?"

Sherikov licked his lips nervously, glancing up at Reinhart. "Commissioner, are you sure—"

"The attack has been called off. Your labs are safe. So is your life. Now it's your turn to come through." Reinhart gripped his gun, moving toward Sherikov. "*Where is he?*"

For a moment Sherikov hesitated. Then slowly his huge body sagged, defeated. He shook his head wearily. "All right. I'll show you where he is." His voice was hardly audible, a dry whisper. "Down this way. Come on."

Reinhart followed Sherikov out of the room, into the corridor. Police and guards were working rapidly, clearing the debris and ruins away, putting out the hydrogen fires that burned everywhere. "No tricks, Sherikov."

"No tricks." Sherikov nodded resignedly. "Thomas Cole is by himself. In a wing lab off the main rooms."

"Cole?"

"The variable man. That's his name." The Pole turned his massive head a little. "He has a name."

Reinhart waved his gun. "Hurry up. I don't want anything to go wrong. This is the part I came for."

"You must remember something, Commissioner."

"What is it?"

Sherikov stopped walking. "Commissioner, nothing must happen to the globe. The control turret. Everything depends on it, the war, our whole—"

"I know. Nothing will happen to the damn thing. Let's go."

"If it should get damaged—"

"I'm not after the globe. I'm interested only in—in Thomas Cole."

They came to the end of the corridor and stopped before a metal door. Sherikov nodded at the door. "In there."

Reinhart moved back. "Open the door."

"Open it yourself. I don't want to have anything to do with it."

Reinhart shrugged. He stepped up to the door. Holding his gun level he raised his hand, passing it in front of the eye circuit. Nothing happened.

Reinhart frowned. He pushed the door with his hand. The door slid open. Reinhart was looking into a small laboratory. He glimpsed a workbench, tools, heaps of equipment, measuring devices, and in the center of the bench the transparent globe, the control turret.

"Cole?" Reinhart advanced quickly into the room. He glanced around him, suddenly alarmed. "Where—"

The room was empty. Thomas Cole was gone.

When the first missile struck, Cole stopped work and sat listening.

Far off, a distant rumble rolled through the earth, shaking the floor under him. On the bench, tools and equipment danced up and down. A pair of pliers fell crashing to the floor. A box of screws tipped over, spilling its minute contents out.

Cole listened for a time. Presently he lifted the transparent globe from the bench. With carefully controlled hands he held the globe up, running his fingers gently over the surface, his faded blue eyes thoughtful. Then, after a time, he placed the globe back on the bench, in its mount.

The globe was finished. A faint glow of pride moved through the variable man. The globe was the finest job he had ever done.

The deep rumblings ceased. Cole became instantly alert. He jumped down from his stool, hurrying across the room to the door. For a moment he stood by the door listening intently. He could hear noise on the other side, shouts, guards rushing past, dragging heavy equipment, working frantically.

A rolling crash echoed down the corridor and lapped against his door. The concussion spun him around. Again a tide of energy shook the walls and floor and sent him down on his knees.

The lights flickered and winked out.

Cole fumbled in the dark until he found a flashlight. Power failure. He could hear crackling flames. Abruptly the lights came on again, an ugly yellow, then faded back out. Cole bent down and examined the door with his flashlight. A magnetic lock. Dependent on an externally induced electric flux. He grabbed a screwdriver and pried at the door. For a moment it held. Then it fell open.

Cole stepped warily out into the corridor. Everything was in shambles. Guards wandered everywhere, burned and half-blinded. Two lay groaning under a pile of wrecked equipment. Fused guns, reeking metal. The air was heavy with the smell of burning wiring and plastic. A thick cloud that choked him and made him bend double as he advanced.

"Halt," a guard gasped feebly, struggling to rise. Cole pushed past him and down the corridor. Two small robot guns, still functioning, glided past him hurriedly toward the drumming chaos of battle. He followed.

At a major intersection the fight was in full swing. Sherikov's guards fought Security police, crouched behind pillars and barricades, firing wildly, desperately. Again the whole structure shuddered as a great booming blast ignited some place above. Bombs? Shells?

Cole threw himself down as a violet beam cut past his ear and disintegrated the wall behind him. A Security policeman, wild-eyed, firing erratically. One of Sherikov's guards winged him and his gun skidded to the floor.

A robot cannon turned toward him as he made his way past the intersection. He began to run. The cannon rolled along behind him, aiming itself uncertainly. Cole hunched over as he shambled rapidly along, gasping for breath. In the flickering yellow light he saw a handful of Security police advancing, firing expertly, intent on a line of defense Sherikov's guards had hastily set up.

The robot cannon altered its course to take them on, and Cole escaped around a corner.

He was in the main lab, the big chamber where Icarus himself rose, the vast squat column.

Icarus! A solid wall of guards surrounded him, grim-faced, hugging guns and protection shields. But the Security police were leaving Icarus alone. Nobody wanted to damage him. Cole evaded a lone guard tracking him and reached the far side of the lab.

It took him only a few seconds to find the force field generator. There was no switch. For a moment that puzzled him—and then he remembered. The guard had controlled it from his wrist.

Too late to worry about that. With his screwdriver he unfastened the plate over the generator and ripped out the wiring in handfuls. The generator came loose and he dragged it away from the wall. The screen was off, thank God. He managed to carry the generator into a side corridor.

Crouched in a heap, Cole bent over the generator, deft fingers flying. He pulled the wiring to him and laid it out on the floor, tracing the circuits with feverish haste.

The adaptation was easier than he had expected. The screen flowed at right angles to the wiring, for a distance of six feet. Each lead was shielded on one side; the field radiated outward, leaving a hollow cone in the center. He ran the wiring through his belt, down his trouser legs, under his shirt, all the way to his wrists and ankles.

He was just snatching up the heavy generator when two Security police appeared. They raised their blasters and fired point-blank.

Cole clicked on the screen. A vibration leaped through him that snapped his jaw and danced up his body. He staggered away, half-stupefied by the surging force that radiated out from him. The violet rays struck the field and deflected harmlessly.

He was safe.

He hurried on down the corridor, past a ruined gun and sprawled bodies still clutching blasters. Great drifting clouds of radioactive particles billowed around him. He edged by one cloud nervously. Guards lay everywhere, dying and dead, partly destroyed, eaten and corroded by the hot metallic salts in the air. He had to get out—and fast.

At the end of the corridor a whole section of the fortress was in ruins. Towering flames leaped on all sides. One of the missiles had penetrated below ground level.

Cole found a lift that still functioned. A load of wounded guards was being raised to the surface. None of them paid any attention to him. Flames surged around the lift, licking at the wounded. Workmen were desperately trying to get the lift into action. Cole leaped onto the lift. A moment later it began to rise, leaving the shouts and the flames behind.

The lift emerged on the surface and Cole jumped off. A guard spotted him and gave chase. Crouching, Cole dodged into a tangled mass of twisted metal, still white-hot and smoking. He ran for a distance, leaping from the side of a ruined defense-screen tower, onto the fused ground and down the side of a hill. The ground was hot underfoot. He hurried as fast as he could, gasping for breath. He came to a long slope and scrambled up the side.

The guard who had followed was gone, lost behind in the rolling clouds of ash that drifted from the ruins of Sherikov's underground fortress.

Cole reached the top of the hill. For a brief moment he halted to get his breath and figure where he was. It was almost evening. The sun was beginning to set. In the darkening sky a few dots still twisted and rolled, black specks that abruptly burst into flame and fused out again.

Cole stood up cautiously, peering around him. Ruins stretched out below, on all sides, the furnace from which he had escaped. A chaos of incandescent metal and debris, gutted and wrecked beyond repair. Miles of tangled rubbish and half-vaporized equipment.

He considered. Everyone was busy putting out the fires and pulling the wounded to safety. It would be awhile before he was missed. But as soon as they realized he was gone they'd be after him. Most of the laboratory had been destroyed. Nothing lay back that way.

Beyond the ruins lay the great Ural peaks, the endless mountains, stretching out as far as the eye could see.

Mountains and green forests. A wilderness. They'd never find him there.

Cole started along the side of the hill, walking slowly and carefully, his screen generator under his arm. Probably in the confusion he could find enough food and equipment to last him indefinitely. He could wait until early morning, then circle back toward the ruins and load up. With a few tools and his own innate skill he would get along fine. A screwdriver, hammer, nails, odds and ends—

A great hum sounded in his ears. It swelled to a deafening roar. Startled, Cole whirled around. A vast shape filled the sky behind him, growing each moment. Cole stood frozen, utterly transfixed. The shape thundered over him, above his head, as he stood stupidly, rooted to the spot.

Then, awkwardly, uncertainly, he began to run. He stumbled and fell and rolled a short distance down the side of the hill. Desperately, he struggled to hold onto the ground. His hands dug wildly, futilely, into the soft soil, trying to keep the generator under his arm at the same time.

A flash, and a blinding spark of light around him.

The spark picked him up and tossed him like a dry leaf. He grunted in agony as searing fire crackled about him, a blazing inferno that gnawed and ate hungrily through his screen. He spun dizzily and fell through the cloud of fire, down into a pit of darkness, a vast gulf between two hills. His wiring ripped off. The generator tore out of his grip and was lost behind. Abruptly, his force field ceased.

Cole lay in the darkness at the bottom of the hill. His whole body shrieked in agony as the unholy fire played over him. He was a blazing cinder, a half-consumed ash flaming in a universe of darkness. The pain made him twist and crawl like an insect, trying to burrow into the ground. He screamed and shrieked and struggled to escape, to get away from the hideous fire. To reach the curtain of darkness beyond, where it was cool and silent, where the flames couldn't crackle and eat at him.

He reached imploringly out, into the darkness, groping feebly toward it, trying to pull himself into it. Gradually, the glowing orb that was his own body faded. The impenetrable chaos of night descended. He allowed the tide to sweep over him, to extinguish the searing fire.

Dixon landed his ship expertly, bringing it to a halt in front of an overturned defense tower. He leaped out and hurried across the smoking ground.

From a lift Reinhart appeared, surrounded by his Security police. "He got away from us! He escaped!"

"He didn't escape," Dixon answered. "I got him myself."

Reinhart quivered violently. "What do you mean?"

"Come along with me. Over in this direction." He and Reinhart climbed the side of a demolished hill, both of them panting for breath. "I was landing. I saw a figure emerge from a lift and run toward the mountains, like some sort of animal. When he came out in the open I dived on him and released a phosphorus bomb."

"Then he's—*dead?*"

"I don't see how anyone could have lived through a phosphorus bomb." They reached the top of the hill. Dixon halted, then pointed excitedly down into the pit beyond the hill. "There!"

They descended cautiously. The ground was singed and burned clean. Clouds of smoke hung heavily in the air. Occasional fires still flickered here and there. Reinhart coughed and bent over to see. Dixon flashed on a pocket flare and set it beside the body.

The body was charred, half destroyed by the burning phosphorus. It lay motionless, one arm over its face, mouth open, legs sprawled grotesquely. Like some abandoned rag doll, tossed in an incinerator and consumed almost beyond recognition.

"He's alive!" Dixon muttered. He felt around curiously. "Must have had some kind of protection screen. Amazing that a man could—"

"It's him? It's really him?"

"Fits the description." Dixon tore away a handful of burned clothing. "This is the variable man. What's left of him, at least."

Reinhart sagged with relief. "Then we've finally got him. The data is accurate. He's no longer a factor."

Dixon got out his blaster and released the safety catch thoughtfully. "If you want, I can finish the job right now."

At that moment Sherikov appeared, accompanied by two armed Security police. He strode grimly down the hillside, black eyes snapping. "Did Cole—" He broke off. "Good God."

"Dixon got him with a phosphorus bomb," Reinhart said noncommittally. "He had reached the surface and was trying to get into the mountains."

Sherikov turned wearily away. "He was an amazing person. During the attack he managed to force the lock on his door and escape. The guards fired at him, but nothing happened. He had rigged up some kind of force field around him. Something he adapted."

"Anyhow, it's over with," Reinhart answered. "Did you have SRB plates made up on him?"

Sherikov reached slowly into his coat. He drew out a manila envelope. "Here's all the information I collected about him, while he was with me."

"Is it complete? Everything previous has been merely fragmentary."

"As near complete as I could make it. It includes photographs and diagrams of the interior of the globe. The turret wiring he did for me. I haven't had a chance even to look at them." Sherikov fingered the envelope. "What are you going to do with Cole?"

"Have him loaded up, taken back to the city—and officially put to sleep by the Euthanasia Ministry."

"Legal murder?" Sherikov's lips twisted. "Why don't you simply do it right here and get it over with?"

Reinhart grabbed the envelope and stuck it in his pocket. "I'll turn this right over to the machines." He motioned to Dixon. "Let's go. Now we can notify the fleet to prepare for the attack on Centaurus." He turned briefly back to Sherikov. "When can Icarus be launched?"

"In an hour or so, I suppose. They're locking the control turret in place. Assuming it functions correctly, that's all that's needed."

"Good. I'll notify Duffe to send out the signal to the warfleet." Reinhart nodded to the police to take Sherikov to the waiting Security ship. Sherikov moved off dully, his face gray and haggard. Cole's inert body was picked up and tossed onto a freight cart. The cart rumbled into the hold of the Security ship and the lock slid shut after it.

"It'll be interesting to see how the machines respond to the additional data," Dixon said.

"It should make quite an improvement in the odds," Reinhart agreed. He patted the envelope, bulging in his inside pocket. "We're two days ahead of time."

* * *

Margaret Duffe got up slowly from her desk. She pushed her chair automatically back. "Let me get all this straight. You mean the bomb is finished? Ready to go?"

Reinhart nodded impatiently. "That's what I said. The Technicians are checking the turret locks to make sure it's properly attached. The launching will take place in half an hour."

"Thirty minutes! Then—"

"Then the attack can begin at once. I assume the fleet is ready for action."

"Of course. It's been ready for several days. But I can't believe the bomb is ready so soon." Margaret Duffe moved numbly toward the door of her office. "This is a great day, Commissioner. An old era lies behind us. This time tomorrow Centaurus will be gone. And eventually the colonies will be ours."

"It's been a long climb," Reinhart murmured.

"One thing. Your charge against Sherikov. It seems incredible that a person of his caliber could ever—"

"We'll discuss that later," Reinhart interrupted coldly. He pulled the manila envelope from his coat. "I haven't had an opportunity to feed the additional data to the SRB machines. If you'll excuse me, I'll do that now."

* * *

For a moment Margaret Duffe stood at the door. The two of them faced each other silently, neither speaking, a faint smile on Reinhart's thin lips, hostility in the woman's blue eyes.

"Reinhart, sometimes I think perhaps you'll go too far. And sometimes I think you've *already* gone too far. . . ."

"I'll inform you of any change in the odds showing." Reinhart strode past her, out of the office and down the hall. He headed toward the SRB room, an intense thalamic excitement rising up inside him.

A few moments later he entered the SRB room. He made his way to the machines. The odds 7–6 showed in the view windows. Reinhart smiled a little. 7–6. False odds, based on incorrect information. Now they could be removed.

Kaplan hurried over. Reinhart handed him the envelope, and moved over to the window, gazing down at the scene below. Men and cars scurried frantically everywhere. Officials coming and going like ants, hurrying in all directions.

The war was on. The signal had been sent out to the warfleet that had waited so long near Proxima Centaurus. A feeling of triumph raced through Reinhart. He had won. He had destroyed the man from the past and broken Peter Sherikov. The war had begun as planned. Terra was breaking out. Reinhart smiled thinly. He had been completely successful.

"Commissioner."

Reinhart turned slowly. "All right."

Kaplan was standing in front of the machines, gazing down at the reading. "Commissioner—"

Sudden alarm plucked at Reinhart. There was something in Kaplan's voice. He hurried quickly over. "What is it?"

Kaplan looked up at him, his face white, his eyes wide with terror. His mouth opened and closed, but no sound came.

"*What is it?*" Reinhart demanded, chilled. He bent toward the machines, studying the reading.

And sickened with horror.

100–1. *Against* Terra!

He could not tear his gaze away from the figures. He was numb, shocked with disbelief. 100–1. *What had happened?* What had gone wrong? The turret was finished, Icarus was ready, the fleet had been notified—

There was a sudden deep buzz from outside the building. Shouts drifted up from below. Reinhart turned his head slowly toward the window, his heart frozen with fear.

Across the evening sky a trail moved, rising each moment. A thin line of white. Something climbed, gaining speed each moment. On the ground, all eyes were turned toward it, awed faces peering up.

The object gained speed. Faster and faster. Then it vanished. Icarus was on his way. The attack had begun; it was too late to stop, now.

And on the machines the odds read a hundred to one—for failure.

At eight o'clock in the evening of May 15, 2136, Icarus was launched toward the star Centaurus. A day later, while all Terra waited, Icarus entered the star, traveling at thousands of times the speed of light.

Nothing happened. Icarus disappeared into the star. There was no explosion. The bomb failed to go off.

At the same time the Terran warfleet engaged the Centauran outer fleet, sweeping down in a concentrated attack. Twenty major ships were seized. A good part of the Centauran fleet was destroyed. Many of the captive systems began to revolt, in the hope of throwing off the Imperial bonds.

Two hours later the massed Centauran warfleet from Armun abruptly appeared and joined battle. The great struggle illuminated half the Centauran system. Ship after ship flashed briefly and then faded to ash. For a whole day the two fleets fought, strung out over millions of miles of space. Innumerable fighting men died—on both sides.

At last the remains of the battered Terran fleet turned and limped toward Armun—defeated. Little of the once impressive armada remained. A few blackened hulks, making their way uncertainly toward captivity.

Icarus had not functioned. Centaurus had not exploded. The attack was a failure.

The war was over.

"We've lost the war," Margaret Duffe said in a small voice, wondering and awed. "It's over. Finished."

The Council members sat in their places around the conference table, gray-haired elderly men, none of them speaking or moving. All gazed up mutely at the great stellar maps that covered two walls of the chamber.

"I have already empowered negotiators to arrange a truce," Margaret Duffe murmured. "Orders have been sent out to Vice-Commander Jessup to give up the battle. There's no hope. Fleet Commander Carleton destroyed himself and his flagship a few minutes ago. The Centauran

High Council has agreed to end the fighting. Their whole Empire is rotten to the core. Ready to topple of its own weight."

Reinhart was slumped over at the table, his head in his hands. "I don't understand. . . . *Why?* Why didn't the bomb explode?" He mopped his forehead shakily. All his poise was gone. He was trembling and broken. *"What went wrong?"*

Gray-faced, Dixon mumbled an answer. "The variable man must have sabotaged the turret. The SRB machines knew. . . . They analyzed the data. *They knew!* But it was too late."

Reinhart's eyes were bleak with despair as he raised his head a little. "I knew he'd destroy us. We're finished. A century of work and planning." His body knotted in a spasm of furious agony. "All because of Sherikov!"

* * *

Margaret Duffe eyed Reinhart coldly. "Why because of Sherikov?"

"He kept Cole alive! I wanted him killed from the start." Suddenly Reinhart jumped from his chair. His hand clutched convulsively at his gun. "And he's *still* alive! Even if we've lost I'm going to have the pleasure of putting a blast beam through Cole's chest!"

"Sit down!" Margaret Duffe ordered.

Reinhart was half way to the door. "He's still at the Euthanasia Ministry, waiting for the official—"

"No, he's not," Margaret Duffe said.

Reinhart froze. He turned slowly, as if unable to believe his senses. *"What?"*

"Cole isn't at the Ministry. I ordered him transferred and your instructions cancelled."

"Where—where is he?"

There was unusual hardness in Margaret Duffe's voice as she answered. "With Peter Sherikov. In the Urals. I had Sherikov's full authority restored. I then had Cole transferred there, put in Sherikov's safe keeping. I want to make sure Cole recovers, so we can keep our promise to him—our promise to return him to his own time."

Reinhart's mouth opened and closed. All the color had drained from his face. His cheek muscles twitched spasmodically. At last he managed to speak. "You've gone insane! The traitor responsible for Earth's greatest defeat—"

"We have lost the war," Margaret Duffe stated quietly. "But this is not a day of defeat. It is a day of victory. The most incredible victory Terra has ever had."

Reinhart and Dixon were dumbfounded. "What—" Reinhart gasped. "What do you—" The whole room was in an uproar. All the Council members were on their feet. Reinhart's words were drowned out.

"Sherikov will explain when he gets here," Margaret Duffe's calm voice came. "He's the one who discovered it." She looked around the chamber at the incredulous Council members. "Everyone stay in his seat. You are all to remain here until Sherikov arrives. It's vital you hear what he has to say. His news transforms this whole situation."

* * *

Peter Sherikov accepted the briefcase of papers from his armed technician. "Thanks." He pushed his chair back and glanced thoughtfully around the Council chamber. "Is everybody ready to hear what I have to say?"

"We're ready," Margaret Duffe answered. The Council members sat alertly around the table. At the far end, Reinhart and Dixon watched uneasily as the big Pole removed papers from his briefcase and carefully examined them.

"To begin, I recall to you the original work behind the ftl bomb. Jamison Hedge was the first human to propel an object at a speed greater than light. As you know, that object diminished in length and gained in mass as it moved toward light speed. When it reached that speed it vanished. It ceased to exist in our terms. Having no length it could not occupy space. It rose to a different order of existence.

"When Hedge tried to bring the object back, an explosion occurred Hedge was killed, and all his equipment was destroyed. The force of the blast was beyond calculation. Hedge had placed his observation ship many millions of miles away. It was not far enough, however. Originally, he had hoped his drive might be used for space travel. But after his death the principle was abandoned.

"That is—until Icarus. I saw the possibilities of a bomb, an incredibly powerful bomb to destroy Centaurus and all the Empire's forces. The reappearance of Icarus would mean the annihilation of their System. As Hedge had shown, the object would re-enter space already occupied by matter, and the cataclysm would be beyond belief."

"But Icarus never came back," Reinhart cried. "Cole altered the wiring so the bomb kept on going. It's probably still going."

"Wrong," Sherikov boomed. "The bomb *did* reappear. But it didn't explode."

Reinhart reacted violently. "You mean—"

"The bomb came back, dropping below the ftl speed as soon as it entered the star Proxima. But it did not explode. There was no cataclysm. It reappeared and was absorbed by the sun, turned into gas at once."

"Why didn't it explode?" Dixon demanded.

"Because Thomas Cole solved Hedge's problem. He found a way to bring the ftl object back into this universe without collision. Without an explosion. The variable man found what Hedge was after. . . ."

The whole Council was on its feet. A growing murmur filled the chamber, a rising pandemonium breaking out on all sides.

"I don't believe it!" Reinhart gasped. "It isn't possible. If Cole solved Hedge's problem that would mean—" He broke off, staggered.

"Faster than light drive can now be used for space travel," Sherikov continued, waving the noise down. "As Hedge intended. My men have studied the photographs of the control turret. They don't know *how* or *why,* yet. But we have complete records of the turret. We can duplicate the wiring, as soon as the laboratories have been repaired."

Comprehension was gradually beginning to settle over the room. "Then it'll be possible to build ftl ships," Margaret Duffe murmured, dazed. "And if we can do that—"

"When I showed him the control turret, Cole understood its purpose. Not *my* purpose, but the original purpose Hedge had been working toward. Cole realized Icarus was actually an incomplete spaceship, not a bomb at all. He saw what Hedge had seen, an ftl space drive. He set out to make Icarus work."

"We can go *beyond* Centaurus," Dixon muttered. His lips twisted. "Then the war was trivial. We can leave the Empire completely behind. We can go beyond the galaxy."

"The whole universe is open to us," Sherikov agreed. "Instead of taking over an antiquated Empire, we have the entire cosmos to map and explore, God's total creation."

Margaret Duffe got to her feet and moved slowly toward the great stellar maps that towered above them at the far end of the chamber. She stood for a long time, gazing up at the myriad suns, the legions of systems, awed by what she saw.

"Do you suppose he realized all this?" she asked suddenly. "What we can see, here on these maps?"

"Thomas Cole is a strange person," Sherikov said, half to himself. "Apparently he has a kind of intuition about machines, the way things are supposed to work. An intuition more in his hands than in his head. A kind of genius, such as a painter or a pianist has. Not a scientist. He has no verbal knowledge about things, no semantic references. He deals with the things themselves. Directly.

"I doubt very much if Thomas Cole understood what would come about. He looked into the globe, the control turret. He saw unfinished wiring and relays. He saw a job half done. An incomplete machine."

"Something to be fixed," Margaret Duffe put in.

"Something to be fixed. Like an artist, he saw his work ahead of him. He was interested in only one thing: turning out the best job he could, with the skill he possessed. For us, that skill has opened up a whole universe, endless galaxies and systems to explore. Worlds without end. Unlimited, *untouched* worlds."

Reinhart got unsteadily to his feet. "We better get to work. Start organizing construction teams. Exploration crews. We'll have to reconvert from war production to ship designing. Begin the manufacture of mining and scientific instruments for survey work."

"That's right," Margaret Duffe said. She looked reflectively up at him. "But you're not going to have anything to do with it."

Reinhart saw the expression on her face. His hand flew to his gun and he backed quickly toward the door. Dixon leaped up and joined him. "Get back!" Reinhart shouted.

Margaret Duffe signalled and a phalanx of Government troops closed in around the two men. Grim-faced, efficient soldiers with magnetic grapples ready.

Reinhart's blaster wavered—toward the Council members sitting shocked in their seats, and toward Margaret Duffe, straight at her blue eyes. Reinhart's features were distorted with insane fear. "Get back! Don't anybody come near me or she'll be the first to get it!"

Peter Sherikov slid from the table and with one great stride swept his immense bulk in front of Reinhart. His huge black-furred fist rose in a smashing arc. Reinhart sailed against the wall, struck with ringing force and then slid slowly to the floor.

The Government troops threw their grapples quickly around him and jerked him to his feet. His body was frozen rigid. Blood dripped from his mouth. He spat bits of tooth, his eyes glazed over. Dixon stood dazed, mouth open, uncomprehending, as the grapples closed around his arms and legs.

Reinhart's gun skidded to the floor as he was yanked toward the door. One of the elderly Council members picked the gun up and examined it curiously. He laid it carefully on the table. "Fully loaded," he murmured. "Ready to fire."

Reinhart's battered face was dark with hate. "I should have killed all of you. *All* of you!" An ugly sneer twisted across his shredded lips. "If I could get my hands loose—"

"You won't," Margaret Duffe said. "You might as well not even bother to think about it." She signalled to the troops and they pulled Reinhart and Dixon roughly out of the room, two dazed figures, snarling and resentful.

For a moment the room was silent. Then the Council members shuffled nervously in their seats, beginning to breathe again.

Sherikov came over and put his big paw on Margaret Duffe's shoulder. "Are you all right, Margaret?"

She smiled faintly. "I'm fine. Thanks. . . ."

Sherikov touched her soft hair briefly. Then he broke away and began to pack up his briefcase busily. "I have to go. I'll get in touch with you later."

"Where are you going?" she asked hesitantly. "Can't you stay and—"

"I have to get back to the Urals." Sherikov grinned at her over his bushy black beard as he headed out of the room. "Some very important business to attend to."

* * *

Thomas Cole was sitting up in bed when Sherikov came to the door. Most of his awkward, hunched-over body was sealed in a thin envelope of transparent airproof plastic. Two robot attendants whirred ceaselessly at his side, their leads contacting his pulse, blood-pressure, respiration, body temperature.

Cole turned a little as the huge Pole tossed down his briefcase and seated himself on the window ledge.

"How are you feeling?" Sherikov asked him.

"Better."

"You see we've quite advanced therapy. Your burns should be healed in a few months."

"How is the war coming?"

"The war is over."

Cole's lips moved. "Icarus—"

"Icarus went as expected. As *you* expected." Sherikov leaned toward the bed. "Cole, I promised you something. I mean to keep my promise—as soon as you're well enough."

"To return me to my own time?"

"That's right. It's a relatively simple matter, now that Reinhart has been removed from power. You'll be back home again, back in your own time, your own world. We can supply you with some discs of platinum or something of the kind to finance your business. You'll need a new Fixit truck. Tools. And clothes. A few thousand dollars ought to do it."

Cole was silent.

"I've already contacted histo-research," Sherikov continued. "The time bubble is ready as soon as you are. We're somewhat beholden to you, as you probably realize. You've made it possible for us to actualize our greatest dream. The whole planet is seething with excitement. We're changing our economy over from war to—"

"They don't resent what happened? The dud must have made an awful lot of people feel downright bad."

"At first. But they got over it—as soon as they understood what was ahead. Too bad you won't be here to see it, Cole. A whole world breaking loose. Bursting out into the universe. They want me to have an ftl ship ready by the end of the week! Thousands of applications are already on file, men and women wanting to get in on the initial flight."

Cole smiled a little, "There won't be any band, there. No parade or welcoming committee waiting for them."

"Maybe not. Maybe the first ship will wind up on some dead world, nothing but sand and dried salt. But everybody wants to go. It's almost like a holiday. People running around and shouting and throwing things in the streets.

"Afraid I must get back to the labs. Lots of reconstruction work being started." Sherikov dug into his bulging briefcase. "By the way. . . . One little thing. While you're recovering here, you might like to look at these." He tossed a handful of schematics on the bed.

Cole picked them up slowly. "What's this?"

"Just a little thing I designed." Sherikov arose and lumbered toward the door. "We're realigning our political structure to eliminate any recurrence of the Reinhart affair. This will block any more one-man power grabs." He jabbed a thick finger at the schematics. "It'll turn power over to all of us, not to just a limited number one person could dominate—the way Reinhart dominated the Council.

"This gimmick makes it possible for citizens to raise and decide issues directly. They won't have to wait for the Council to verbalize a measure. Any citizen can transmit his will with one of these, make his needs register on a central control that automatically responds. When a large enough segment of the population wants a certain thing done, these little gadgets set up an active field that touches all the others. An issue won't have to go through a formal Council. The citizens can express their will long before any bunch of gray-haired old men could get around to it."

* * *

Sherikov broke off, frowning.

"Of course," he continued slowly, "there's one little detail. . . ."

"What's that?"

"I haven't been able to get a model to function. A few bugs. . . . Such intricate work never was in my line." He paused at the door. "Well, I hope I'll see you again before you go. Maybe if you feel well enough later on we could get together for one last talk. Maybe have dinner together sometime. Eh?"

But Thomas Cole wasn't listening. He was bent over the schematics, an intense frown on his weathered face. His long fingers moved restlessly over the schematics, tracing wiring and terminals. His lips moved as he calculated.

Sherikov waited a moment. Then he stepped out into the hall and softly closed the door after him.

He whistled merrily as he strode off down the corridor.